Milly Johnson is a 4ft 11″ half-Barnsley, half-Glaswegian author, BBC Radio Sheffield broadcaster, greetings-card copywriter and award-winning chef (winner of Channel 4's *Come Dine With Me* Barnsley). She likes cruising on big ships, mingling with big wrestlers and savouring big hampers full of rum truffles, carrot cake and Canadian Icewine.

She lives in Barnsley, South Yorkshire, bang opposite her mam and dad with her two hulking lads, four moggies and Teddy, her German Eurasier dog. She is a proud patron of Haworthcatrescue.org and The Core – a complementary-therapy centre for cancer sufferers, associated with St Peter's Hospice, Barnsley.

Visit www.millyjohnson.co.uk

The Birds & the Bees

Milly Johnson

**SIMON &
SCHUSTER**

London · New York · Sydney · Toronto

A CBS COMPANY

First published in Great Britain by Pocket Books, 2008
An imprint of Simon & Schuster UK Ltd
This edition published by Simon & Schuster UK Ltd, 2011
A CBS COMPANY

14

Simon & Schuster UK Ltd
1st Floor
222 Gray's Inn Road
London WC1X 8HB

www.simonandschuster.co.uk

Simon & Schuster Australia
Sydney

A CIP catalogue record for this book is available
from the British Library.

ISBN 978-1-84983-409-4

Typeset in Bembo by M Rules
Printed and bound by CPI Group (UK) Ltd, Croydon, CR0 4YY

This book is dedicated to two Flowers of Scotland who are gone now and sadly, I will never see their likes again – my darling beloved great-aunts Elizabeth 'Lizzie' Lindie and Helen 'Nelly' Cunningham.

Thank you for the love, the laughs and the Jaffa Cakes

The Birds and the Bees: As well as being the gentle way of explaining how creatures of nature 'do business with one another', *The Birds and the Bees* (Eun S'na Sheillein) is also a Scottish country dance originating from the hamlet of Bonniebride (Buinne-Bhrìghde) in the former county of Duffshire, famed locally for the large apiary and aviary that once existed there. It is an energetic reel in which couples complete a series of many cast-offs and changes of partner. It is considered extremely fortuitous to dance this at weddings, due to its connections with an ancient ritual dedicated to Creide, faery goddess of women who ruled over love magick and the search for the perfect mate.

The Sassenach's Guide to the Wonders of Gaelic, by Maggie Knockater.

Chapter 1

Making a cake for Danny's school raffle was always going to be a messy business, given Stevie's predilection for taste-testing the gloopy, raw mixture at one-minute intervals. Not to mention her impatience in waiting for the blades to stop whisking before she lifted them up, which resulted in her splattering herself and the kitchen with chocolate cream. Then, as usual, the bag of flour split and sent up a white nuclear cloud to descend over all flat surfaces. She really must get a proper flour container, she said to herself for the six-hundredth time, knowing, deep down, that she never would.

With the cake rising nicely in the oven, she was just in the process of licking out the bowl and the big spoon when the doorbell rang. However, there was no need to panic and rush to clean herself up, Stevie decided, as it could only be her friend Catherine bringing Danny home after a post-school romp with her mob and the family mongrels. So she answered the door garnished with flour and enough cocoa on her face to pass an audition for the part of main slapstick stooge in a Christmas Panto.

The trouble was that it wasn't Catherine. It was, in fact,

a big rough-looking man, approximately the size of Edinburgh Castle, with a long auburn ponytail, a wild red beard, a tribal-looking scar on his left cheek and Bluto-esque tattooed arms which he used to push gently past Stevie in order to barge straight into her front room like the proverbial bull looking for her best crockery.

'Whurrrissseee?' came a broad Scottish burr that belonged on someone with their face painted half-blue and half-white, wearing a battle kilt and swinging an axe.

'Excuse me, do you mind!' said Stevie, torn between calling the police and reaching for some wet wipes. Tough decision but the wet wipes won on embarrassment points.

'Whurrr's Finch?'

'Who the hell are you?'

'Adam MacLean, Joanna MacLean's man.'

So this was the mythical creature Stevie had heard so much about then. This loud, hard intruder standing on her sheepskin rug was *him*. She gave his big muscular frame a quick once-over. And there she was, thinking Jo had been exaggerating when describing the control-freak nutter she was married to. No wonder Matthew was so sympathetic to her at work. Well, Stevie wasn't going to be scared of him too and cower in a corner of her own home waiting for him to stick his whisky-fuelled boot in, like Jo did.

In the same second, Adam MacLean had affirmed that this woman was, in fact, the greedy, lazy, rarely sober, slob *thing* that Jo had reported her to be. That's why the kitchen behind her resembled Beirut on a bad day and why she herself looked as if she had been hit at close range by a chocolate bomb. On a binge, most likely. That's what these women who sat at home did all day – eat cakes, drink sherry and watch *Trisha*. And read all those stupid *Midnight Moon* crappy romance books that seemed to be littered around the room, he noted. No wonder Jo had been so sympathetic to the poor bloke at work, about to be married to *that*.

Stevie pulled herself up to her full height of five foot two.

'Matthew is on business in Aberdeen.'

'I think you'll find he's no',' said Adam grimly. 'He's in bloody Magalluf with ma Jo!'

'Don't be ridiculous!' said Stevie. Crikey, Matthew had said that the Scot was a possessive, unhinged psycho with the part of his head empty that should have had a brain in it, but she hadn't realized to what degree. Poor Jo.

'I thought you might say that,' said Adam, reaching in his back pocket to bring out a crumpled piece of paper, which he stuck under Stevie's nose. She pulled back, reclaiming some of her personal space, unfolded it impatiently and looked straight at a confirmation letter of bookings, hotel, flight numbers, today's date and names: *Sunshine Holidays, Hotel Flora, Magalluf, Mr Matthew Finch and Ms Joanna MacLean, 25 April for 7 days*. It had their address in the top corner: 15 Blossom Lane, Dodmoor. She would have slumped to the chair had the doorbell not rung again.

'Excuse me, it's my son,' said Stevie in a half-daze. She opened the door to find her best friend there, holding the hand of her small bespectacled boy. The half-daze expanded into a full daze as she noticed that Catherine's normally auburn hair was now bright pink, like candyfloss.

The only things that were missing were the stick, the plastic bag and a fair in the background.

I'm going mad, thought Stevie, blinking twice, but no – the hair was still pink.

Adam, seeing the guest there on the doorstep, was unsurprised. He noticed the cheap trollop hair. That she had friends who went out looking like that further confirmed his low opinion of the woman in whose house he was standing. And the boy was too old to be Finch's if they had only been together a couple of years. Boy, she sure got around, didn't she?

'Hi, what a day, I've brought Dan—' Catherine looked at her friend's pale and chocolate-splodged face then spotted the man beyond her. 'Are you all right?'

'No, not really,' said Stevie. 'Just got . . . something . . . to do.'

Catherine did a quick assessment of the situation and bobbed down to the little fair-haired boy.

'Danny, let's go for a bun and some orange juice to the café round the corner for half an hour. Mummy's just sorting something out.'

'Cool!' said Danny with a face-splitting grin. That was the cherry on the perfect-day cake for him.

Catherine then turned to Stevie. 'Go on, it's fine. I'll see you in a bit.'

'Thanks, Cath,' said Stevie, gulping back a big ball of emotion that she couldn't quite put a name to.

As Stevie came slowly back into the room, Adam said with a subdued cough, 'I'm sorry, I never thought about your wee wan being here.'

Stevie answered him with a glare loaded with loathing as she dropped to the sofa. Adam continued to tower over her like the Cairngorms as he continued, 'I found that note this morning when she'd gone. To a health farm in Wales, so she said. That explained the bikini but didnae explain why she'd taken her passporrrt.'

It was all too big to take in. Stevie hoped it was her brain playing tricks on her – early menopause or something – or that the raw eggs in the cake-mix had caused a rogue hallucination. Something which had become more of a possibility when she saw the state of Catherine's hair.

One part of her head was telling her that Matthew wouldn't *ever* do *anything* like that. He'd known how hurt she was by what had happened to her in the past and had sworn that he would never put her through pain like that. Matthew was thoughtful and considerate. Matthew was the sort of man who befriended his work colleague, Jo MacLean, a woman desperately trying to muster the courage to leave her brute of a husband because he made her so unhappy – and you couldn't fake those sorts of tears! She and Jo had been shopping together. She had even cooked Jo tea. And bought her a birthday present. Matthew wouldn't have brought her home if there had been anything going on – NO! There was no question but that she trusted both of them implicitly. Jo had become a friend in her own right now. Jo was sweet and uncomplicated, and she was lovely to Danny. She had even been allowed to see *the* dress that was hanging up in the spare room. She and Jo had talked for hours and Jo would be a wedding guest when Stevie put it on and married Matthew in exactly thirty-nine days' time.

However, the other part of her brain governed the eyes, and those were reading over and over again the brutal evidence on the paper that she was still holding limply in her trembling hands.

'You could have made this up yourself on a computer!' Stevie blurted out.

'Aye,' said Adam MacLean, clicking his fingers in an 'I am undone' way. 'Do you know, I have so much spare time I often do things like this. I really must stop it, it's becoming a dreadful habit.'

Okay, so she believed it wasn't a fake. Then again, she knew Jo and she knew Matthew and she didn't know this blaze-haired thug. Then again, Matthew had bought three pairs of shorts last week. For the honeymoon, he'd said. Then again, this was *Matthew*! Her head felt like a John McEnroe, Bjorn Borg Wimbledon final, batting arguments back and forth over a net of reason. *Advantage, deuce, advantage, deuce . . .*

A light bulb went on in Stevie's head.

'I'll ring him!'

'You think he's going tae answer, do ya?' said the big Scot with a mocking laugh. Ignoring him, Stevie picked up the house phone and rang the short-dial for Matthew's number. She waited, heard the dialling tone, and a second later a muffled version of the song, 'Goodbye-ee' started playing nearby. Stevie put the phone down, opened a drawer and retrieved the mobile tinkling out its mocking ringtone.

'Cocky bstarrr',' said Adam with a low but nasty growl.

'It's from *Oh What a Lovely War*,' explained Stevie. 'It's his favourite musical.'

Those details didn't help either of them. In fact, they made Adam want to not only smack Finch in the teeth but knock them all out as well and replant them in his skull.

'Well anyway,' Adam said, the fire of his fury now dropping to still hot but more quietly burning embers, 'I thought you had the right tae know.'

'Thanks for telling me,' said Stevie numbly, which sounded a bit odd – but what did one say in these circumstances? What was the correct protocol after being informed that one's fiancé was knocking off someone else's wife in the middle of Majorca? Especially when still in a state of denial, despite all the hard evidence. Bravely, her mind was still manically sifting through the information available, looking for the loophole that would enable her to say, '*Ah ha, you've got it all wrong*,' because it was there, she was sure of it. Matthew wouldn't, he just wouldn't do this. She *knew* him inside out. She knew that he wouldn't, *couldn't* be that cruel.

Adam stroked his red beard like a small facial pet. 'Right, I'll go then.'

'Yes, I think you should rather,' said Stevie, and almost blindly showed him out without further comment. Then she shut the door hard on him and stood behind it, fighting the urge to slither down it and become an emotional mess on the floor.

She went to the dresser where they kept their passports, hardly daring to open it in case Matthew's wasn't there. Of course it's there, don't be stupid, Stevie, she reprimanded herself, and opened the drawer with one swift, sure movement – but she couldn't find it. Yet it was always there with her own, the pages of his around hers, as if they were spooning. *Maybe he moved it. Maybe he threw it away because it was out of date. Maybe he needed to take it with him as a form of ID.* Her head tried its best to rationalize the passport's absence, but it couldn't compete with the mighty guns of the information on the booking form.

And then smoke started billowing out of the kitchen and set off the alarm, and it felt like all hell had been let loose in her head.

Danny came home to find all the downstairs windows open in the hope of clearing the acrid smell of burnt baking, and his mum covered in even more flour, frenetically stirring up an anaemic and lumpy mixture in a bowl. Stevie forced herself into jolly mode as he ran in to greet her. She grabbed him and picked him up and kissed him and asked him all the right questions: Did he have a nice time? Did he mind his manners? Did he throw the ball for Chico and Boot, like he was going to? Catherine noticed how desperately she seemed to bury her head into his hair and how tightly she cuddled him.

'Is that my cake?' asked the little boy with a much-wrinkled nose as he looked over his mum's shoulder at the still-smoking charcoal lumps in the cake-tin.

'No, of course not,' said Stevie, sniffing back the tears that his baby smell had brought rushing up her ducts. 'I'm making yours now; it's going to be very special.'

'Go upstairs, love, and get your pyjamas on,' said Catherine, sending him away with a light pat on his bottom. Then, when she was sure he was out of earshot, she said, 'So who the hell was that?'

'Adam MacLean.'

'Ada . . . As in that Jo's husband? What did he want?'

'I'll never get this cake done. I've only got one egg left.'

'Sod the cake, Stevie,' said Catherine to her friend, who looked as grey as the horrible stuff in the bowl. 'Look, go and put the kettle on and I'll tuck Danny up and read him a quick story. Then we'll talk.'

'I haven't said good night to him.'

'One night won't kill either of you. He's bushed, anyway. He's been bouncing about since he came back from school and I bet he won't even notice. I'll be back in ten minutes max,' and with that Catherine rushed upstairs, leaving Stevie feeling far more of a helpless child than her four year old currently slipping into his 'Incredibles' pyjamas and about to clean his teeth with Strawberry Sparkle toothpaste.

She had not brewed the tea by the time Catherine returned. She was still stirring the limp liquid in the bowl, her head scrabbling for a solution to the cake problem because she couldn't let Danny down. She had promised him a wonderful cake to take into class and she always kept her promises. Double always for her son.

'*I promise I'd never do anything to hurt you,*' Matthew had said. It was just a shame other people weren't as conscientious, it seemed.

'Is he okay?' asked Stevie.

'Course he is. Out like a light.'

'What happened to your hair?' said Stevie. The sight of it was claiming a huge percentage of her attention.

'Marilyn Monroe bleaching kit from abroad, don't ask.

And don't ever let our Kate use you to test out her eBay buys. Bloody student beauticians! Anyway, never mind about me, what's been going on? What did Billy Connolly want?'

'Oh, just to tell me that Jo has run off with Matthew to Magalluf.' She said it so matter-of-factly that Catherine presumed she was joking and laughed.

'Oh, right. Stupid lout! Did you say you'd ring the police? What is he on? Run off with Jo, ha. As if Matt . . .'

Her words dried up as Stevie handed her the booking confirmation and her mouth moved like a goldfish that was wondering where all the water in his bowl had gone. She read it three times and each time it seemed more ridiculous than the last.

'No! He wouldn't . . . he couldn't do that to you! Not Matthew. Where is he? Have you rung him?'

'He left his mobile at home.'

'Did you check it for text messages?'

'It's wiped clean. And there's no number for Jo in his phone book.'

'Well, have you looked for his passport?'

'It's gone,' said Stevie, crumbling a little more. It was starting to sink in that this might actually be happening to her. That Redbeard might be right.

Catherine looked at the paper again. 'Is it genuine?'

'Why would he make it up?'

'Because . . . er . . .' Catherine tried to think of something constructive to say, but all that came out was another flurry of denials. 'No way would Matthew do this to you! Not him. Not Matt!'

'It looks as if he has, Cath,' said Stevie in the sort of

voice that Catherine's youngest used when she was trying very desperately to be brave. She continued to stir until Catherine forcibly extracted the bowl from her, gently, because it looked as if Stevie badly needed something to hold onto, and gripping the spoon seemed to be the only thing keeping her from falling over.

'This isn't going to make a cake, ever,' she said. 'Not even a starving Oliver Twist would want a second helping of this. Come on, leave it. I'll get our Kate to knock one up tonight and I'll bring it over in the morning. It's the least she can do after this,' and she pointed upwards at her pink cloud of hair. Stevie gave none of her usual protests and just said a weary, 'Thank you.' Then Catherine tipped the mix down the sink. She was impressed. Stevie had actually managed to make it thinner than water.

'Danny wanted to start calling Matt Daddy,' said Stevie. 'It was a good job I told him to wait until after the wedding.'

'Look, Stevie, you need to talk to Matthew and find out what is going on. Will he ring you, to say he's arrived in wherever he's supposed to be – Inverness?'

'Aberdeen. Maybe. He hasn't been away before for any length of time so I don't know what the usual sequence of events would be,' Stevie shrugged. She didn't know if he would ring or not. She didn't know anything any more.

'Of course he'll ring,' said Catherine heartily. Every man was innocent until proven guilty. Except Mick, who should have been hung, drawn and quartered and his knackers cut off before he'd even got to trial. Although she shouldn't think ill of the dead.

'What if it's true? What do I do?' said Stevie, trying to keep the panic out of her voice. She'd panicked last time and it had made her lose her grip, sent her into such a downward spiral of emotional quicksand that she thought she was destined to drown in it. Until Matthew held out his hand and offered her the lifeline of his love.

And what about Danny? This was the only dad he'd ever known. He would lose two men in his life who had gone for the title and then bogged off before the crown was on their heads. What sort of damage would that do to his little heart? She was going through partners faster than Henry VIII, and look how *his* kids turned out. At that thought, Stevie caved into the huge pressure of tears and Catherine, her future chief bridesmaid, came over to give her a big hug, because that was easier than trying to work out what the hell to say to give any comfort.

'I don't know what you'll do, love. Let's cross that bridge when we come to it, eh? Look, pass me the phone. I'll ring Eddie and tell him I'm staying with you tonight.'

'No, I'm okay,' said Stevie, pulling away and wiping madly at her eyes. 'I need to think straight, and I can do that better on my own. I'll just cry if you're here and I really don't want to do that. I'll be fine. You go – you've got three hundred kids and a zoo to sort out.'

'Cheeky!' said Catherine, smiling softly.

'Lucky you, though,' said Stevie.

'I can't leave you,' said Catherine. 'Come home with me. You and Danny.'

'Honestly, I'd rather be alone.'

'Well, look,' said Catherine, when she was fully

convinced that Stevie really did want that and wasn't being her usual overly independent self, 'I'll go and sort out this cake for Danny and I'll be round first thing in the morning.' She pre-empted the little protest that she saw coming, 'And no, it isn't a problem, before you start. My daughter owes me big time.'

After extracting another fifty affirmations that Stevie would ring her immediately if she felt out of her depth and wanted to change her mind about coming over, Catherine went on her way back to her huge brood to tackle an urgent hair repair and an emergency baking project. Making a cake for her godson was the least she could do after breaking the vow she had made to herself: never to let another dickhead break his mother's heart.

The phone rang about ten minutes after Catherine had gone; it showed 'number withheld' on the caller display unit. Knowing instinctively who it would be, Stevie's hand came out to pick it up. Then, realizing she couldn't trust herself to act 'normal', she overrode the compulsion to speak to him, collapse into uncontrolled tears and beg him to come home. Instead, she let the answerphone handle it. It was, as she knew it would be, Matthew, her gorgeous tall fiancé with the dark brown hair and the dark brown eyes and the smile that made her heart melt like ice cream on a hotplate.

'Hi, Stevie, it's Matthew. You . . . er . . . must be in bed. Anyway, just a quick call to let you know that I've arrived safely – motorway's a nightmare! Looks very busy, lots of people. All set for a good hard week so I don't know when

I'll have the chance to speak to you again. Forgot my mobile didn't I, ha ha! Anyway, take care and hope everything's okay. Er . . . bye then.'

No *I love you*, no *Hope Danny's okay*, no *Miss you*. His voice sounded a lot further away than Aberdeen. And she was probably imagining it, but every one of the three million times she played that message back, she was sure she could hear the strains of 'Guantanamera' in the background.

Chapter 2

In Catherine's big homely Waltonesque-style kitchen in the neighbouring village of Hoodley, black-haired, black-gowned, scarlet-lipped Kate Flanagan was expertly baking a cake. In her mother's frilly apron, she looked rather like a beautiful domestic vampire.

Her father gave her a big squashy squeeze as he passed her on his way to the teapot and said, 'Eeh, you'll make someone a lovely little housewife one day!' knowing that it would greatly offend her feminist principles, and though Kate shoved him away, she was laughing a little too.

Catherine, towelled up and sitting in the front room, waiting for the auburn dye to restore her locks to their former fake glory, watched the interchange and it brought an unexpected flurry of tears to her eyes; a curious mix of happy ones that she had such a loving family and sad ones because life seemed determined always to short-change her dear friend on that score. What was it about Stevie that attracted plonkers? Stevie who was sweet and selfless and deserved so much better than the Micks and Matthews of this world, whereas she – Catherine Flanagan, outspoken, brash and loud – had been blessed with a wonderful husband, six gorgeous (when they weren't fighting) kids and a big chaotic house full of love, laughter and daft pets. How would *she* feel if a Jo MacLean took all this away from her?

'Here you are, love,' Eddie said, handing his wife a cup of tea. He looked at her worried face and knew instantly what she was thinking. 'You should have brought her and the little one back with you.'

'She wouldn't come,' said Catherine. 'I was all for frog-marching them over, but she really did want to be alone.'

'Can't believe it,' said Eddie, shaking his head. 'Matthew Finch! I'd have put my all on him not doing that to Stevie.'

'Tell me about it,' said Catherine, a quarter angry but threequarters sad and disappointed. She had grown very fond of Matthew. She had never liked Mick and been proved right on that one, but Matthew was a good bloke – decent, caring, considerate. Catherine had been instrumental in pushing Stevie and Matt together, following their initial meeting at a mutual friend's engagement party, because she knew they would be well-matched. He was handsome, kind, big-hearted, and willing to take on a little boy who wasn't his, which spoke bucketloads. Stevie would never have settled for anyone who didn't treat Danny well. She knew what a minefield the whole step-parent thing could be.

After Mick had broken her best friend's heart, five years earlier, Catherine had screened every male who came within fifty miles of her. Matthew had put a big fat tick in every box on her score-sheet of essentials.

'I'd be lying if I said a warning hadn't flagged up in my

head when Stevie told me about this Jo woman he'd got friendly with at work,' said Catherine. 'Vulnerable women are never fully aware of the power they have to make a bloke feel like a hero, but admittedly it wasn't much of a warning. After all, this was Matthew we were talking about. Reliable, faithful old Matthew!' Catherine laughed hard.

'You ever seen her, that Jo?' asked Eddie.

'Just the once,' said Catherine. 'I must admit I'd been curious when Stevie started talking about her and I was dying to see her and check her out. Then we bumped into her in town one day.'

'And?'

'She seemed nice and friendly enough. A little too nice, if you know what I mean.'

'How "too nice"?' asked Eddie, offering her a bite of his Jaffa Cake.

'Well, when she spotted Stevie she came rushing over as if she'd been a long-lost relative she hadn't seen for twenty years. It crossed my mind that it was a bit over the top, but then, given all that she had been going through and how kind Matthew and Stevie had been to her, maybe she really was *that* pleased to see her. That's what I thought at the time, anyway.'

'What's she look like?'

'Tall, slim, long dark hair, big brown eyes. Very, very pretty.' Catherine suddenly realized that she wouldn't have liked a vulnerable Jo MacLean anywhere near Eddie, had the roles been reversed. What's more, for all the gushing she had done over Stevie, Catherine hadn't noticed a lot of warmth in Jo MacLean's eyes.

'It's a flaming weird business,' said Eddie, having a long gulp of tea. 'I reckon he's having a mid-life crisis and he'll be back.'

Catherine looked over at him and smiled. Brad Pitt he wasn't, but she loved the bones of her big, eighteen-stone husband with the Worzel Gummidge hairdo. Never once had she thought he would be unfaithful to her, but after the shocker of today, she wondered if anyone really knew their partners as well as they thought they did. Her own nice cosy world felt a little rocked too.

Eddie saw that look in her eye and laughed. 'Oy, you! Don't be tarring us all with the same brush,' he warned with a twinkle in his soft, hazel eyes.

'I don't know what you mean,' said Catherine unconvincingly.

'Yes, you do, you lying little bugger.' He tweaked her nose.

'Well, I think I'll have you electronically tagged just to be on the safe side,' said Catherine, but it only sounded like half a joke.

'It's more likely you'd leave me,' said Eddie. 'I'm hardly chuffing Hugh Grant, am I?'

'I don't like chuffing Hugh Grant,' Catherine told him. 'Well, I do to watch, but I wouldn't want to snog him.'

'I wouldn't leave you, babe,' said Eddie, tilting her face up towards his and giving her a kiss on her lips that still made something deep within her tingle. He smelt of soap and Fahrenheit aftershave and home.

'Ugh, gross,' said the cake-baking Goth in the background.

'Mind your own business, Morticia,' commanded Eddie over his shoulder, before turning back to his wife. 'And you, drink your tea and try to stop worrying about things you can do nothing about.'

That was easier said than done because Catherine felt that she had let her friend down in a terrible way. It was impossible for this to have happened. NO ONE got through Catherine's hair-trigger defence system for Stevie. She would never let the woman she was closer to than her own sisters go through all that crap again. Or so she had promised herself.

'Well, all I can say is, that's men for you!' said seventeen-year-old Kate with a heavy sigh of experience. She drifted from the room like a dramatic black plume of smoke, leaving Eddie and Catherine crippled from the effort of keeping in a bout of laughter that, at that moment, was so very well-needed.

Chapter 3

When Adam left Stevie's house he got into his very nice car and took a minute to study the medium-sized detached house of his love rival. Boring, neat enough outside but nothing spectacular, how he'd always imagined Matthew Finch to be from the way Jo had described him. That was, until he'd seen a framed photo on the dresser (next to another ridiculous *Midnight Moon* book) of the frumpy (most likely bottle) blonde, lumpy girlfriend snuggling up to a clean-shaven Prince Charming type: dark hair, dark eyes, nice white-toothed smile. He presumed that must be *him*, and he was far too good-looking for *her*. Surely she must have realized that it was only a matter of time before Finch's chocolate-coloured eyes were drawn towards someone his physical equal, like his own doe-eyed Jo. *By Jings*, the very least that short, unspecial-looking untidy woman could have done was look after her house and brush her hair occasionally to keep her man interested. Anger management classes might have been a good idea too. That way, her man might not have been on red alert, looking for company and desperate for love and attention. And he might not have presented a tortured and vulnerable side to

Adam's beautiful, sensitive lady of eighteen months – Joanna.

Funny though, he hadn't expected Finch's woman to look as stunned as she had done by his revelation. By all accounts, she was a heartless cow. On second thoughts, she was probably thinking about being split up from his money. That type always did.

Adam sped off down the bypass, out of the town and towards the sprawling estate of newly built 'Paradise' properties on the edge of an ex-pit village that had recently been given an extreme makeover. There, he pulled onto the drive of the fortieth finished double-fronted detached house, a design at the top of the luxury bracket. He turned the key in the lock and then quickly deactivated the alarm that protected all their state-of-the-art entertainment equipment, although he was far more of an effective deterrent to would-be burglars than any bell would be.

She'll be back, he thought. How could she leave all this? Her dream home. He looked around at the expensive curtains and carpets, the extensive CD and DVD collection, all the creature comforts anyone could desire. All for her. *He'd get her back; whatever it took, he'd get her back. How could she leave him? She couldn't leave him, he wouldn't let her.*

He smoothed his hand over the freshly plastered wall where the dining room led out to their almost finished conservatory. Then with a huge primal roar, he pulled back his fist and drove it into the wall, leaving the deep, wide impression of his knuckles.

★

That night, Stevie didn't give way to the tears that threatened, despite a concrete blockage the size of Venus stuck in her throat. Crying meant grieving, and grieving meant she had already lost him. Crying would have sapped the energy reserves that she badly needed to draw from. This wasn't a time for emotional output; she needed her head clear in order to think. *What was it about Jo that was better than her?* She began to write a list. It went on a bit longer than she had anticipated and began to look like a seriously bad idea.

She remembered how, on all the occasions when she'd moaned about her figure not being quite what she wanted it to be, or that there seemed to be more little laughter lines appearing at her eye-corners, Matthew had kissed her far from perfect nose and said she was just fine and dandy as she was. Obviously not fine and dandy enough if he'd buggered off to Majorca with someone with a flatter stomach, longer legs, smaller conk and all the other sickening ers that she couldn't compete with. Not without major plastic surgery and a magic wand anyway.

Stevie turned to a new page in the pad. This time her head would lead on how to tackle this one, not her heart. She would work out a plan to get him back. She would let him slip back seamlessly into her life and pretend this had never happened. He would never suspect she knew of his unfaithful escapade. Whatever it took to make this happen, she would do.

Whatever.

Chapter 4

The next morning, Stevie found Danny downstairs, wearing, or rather drowning in, his dressing-gown. On the label, it said it was for four to five year olds, but omitted to add the word hippos. He was staring at the empty cake-tin he had just found on the kitchen table. His bottom lip protruded so far, it should have had a cliff warning on it.

'Mummy, where's the cake you promised me?' he asked.

'Wait and see. Breakfast first,' said Stevie, clapping her hands like Joyce Grenfell in teacher mode. Danny had his usual orange juice and Coco Pops, and then sucked up the chocolatey milk with a straw. Then he washed his face and brushed his teeth, before getting his blue and grey uniform on for school, socks first. Everything always in the same order. Danny was a creature of habit and got upset if his routines were interrupted. Apparently, that was a sign of a gifted child, the nursery teacher had told her after an infuriating morning getting Danny down the path to school after they were late and rushing, and there hadn't been enough time to let him read out aloud all the numbers of the houses they passed, like they usually did. Sign of a child that wants his bottom walloped more like, she had thought at the time.

Though, there was no getting away from it, he was certainly a bright little button, an added bonus because when he was born, Danny was so premature that there was a real chance he might have had some brain damage. Sitting in a hospital scared to go to sleep in case your child doesn't survive the night was something she wouldn't wish on any parent; they were dark, dark times.

Miraculously, her baby boy had pulled through and every year he got a birthday card from 'The Little Fighters' Club' at the Special Care Unit up at the hospital. Hard to imagine that the tiny, fragile scrap and the sturdy, clever little boy now in front of her were one and the same person.

Danny was always writing and making little books, like she used to do, although hopefully not for the same reasons. She would have liked him to follow in her footsteps and write for a living, but something a little loftier than *Midnight Moon* fiction, which was for ladies who liked to escape to a land where men were men and women sighed a lot and fainted but at least the endings were happy.

'Is my cake ready yet, Mummy?' he asked again, as Stevie straightened his tie, playing for time.

'Well er, . . . the thing is . . .'

The doorbell bing-bonged, a sound that translated as a hallelujah chorus in Stevie's head as she opened the door to Catherine, newly restored to her usual auburn, wearing her best and widest smile and wooden-acting worse than an extra in *Crossroads*.

'Hi, Stevie, here's the cake you baked last night. I'm sorry, I walked off with it instead of the empty tin, that I was borrowing off of you. Ha, ha, how silly of me.'

Stevie mouthed, 'I will love you forever,' to her friend and Danny's eyes rounded to dinner-plates as the four-layer cake covered with crushed Maltesers, Buttons, Crunchie bits and melted down Mars Bar icing made its fanfare entrance into the Honeywell/Finch kitchen.

'Wow!' said Danny, which, along with 'cool', was his favourite buzzword of the moment.

'Go get your shoes on,' said Stevie, spurring him on with, 'The sooner you do so, the sooner you'll get to show off your cake at school,' which sent him flying down to the cabinet in the hallway as if his slipper was caught on Schumacher's tow bar.

'Thank you, thank you, thank you,' said Stevie, enfolding Catherine in a big hug.

'Don't thank me, thank Kate. She did the cake, and after she'd put my hair right, I shoved all the bits on.' Catherine sniffed. 'Wasn't that long a job,' she added, fobbing off the fuss.

Catherine had six children, a husband, four cats, a ferret, a Chihuahua called Chico and some huge mad-looking cross-breed called Boot that looked as if it ate prop forwards for snacks. She had her hands full, but she still had found the time to get Stevie out of a hole.

'I owe you both big time for this, Cath.'

'Don't be silly. So, did you sleep? How are you feeling? And did he ring?'

'A little,' said Stevie, 'crap and yes.'

'What did he say?'

'I let the answerphone pick it up. He said he was in Aberdeen.'

'Did you 1471 it?'

'Withheld.'

'Sod it. So what's your gut feeling?' Catherine cringed in advance. It didn't look good from where she was standing.

'He's in Majorca, I reckon.'

'Holy shit! You're a lot calmer than I would be,' said Catherine, who would have been chewing on Eddie's cooked liver with some chips and a nice Chianti by now, if the same thing had happened to her.

'Yes, but I've got a plan,' said Stevie, snapping off the conversation as Danny made a fully-shod appearance.

They both walked the proud little boy to school; he was champing at the bit to show off the Empress of all chocolate cakes to his friends and teacher. Lockelands was a nice little school, only a ten-minute, and very pleasant, tree-heavy walk away from Stevie and Matthew's house in Blossom Lane. Well, it was Matthew's house really. Stevie had sold her little terraced house, situated a few streets away, just after Christmas and moved in with him on New Year's Day. She had been so excited then, thinking how the next Christmas on she would be Mrs Finch and Danny would have a dad. What a year it was going to be! Well, at least she had got that last bit right, but alas, not in the way she had intended.

The two sides of Blossom Lane were very different, like a new world and an old world meeting in a Dr Who-like time warp. On one side were eight clones of early 1980s box-like dwellings with a short path at the front and small square gardens at the back; on the other side was a row of four early-1800s large detached cottages, all individual, very chocolate-box pretty. Ivy and honeysuckle rampaged over the stone and gave a delicious noseful of heady scent to passers-by in late summer. They had long gardens at the back all the way down to a little ribbon of stream and the railway line, and high crumbly walls overgrown with foliage secured each cottage's privacy from its neighbours. The far end cottage, opposite to Matthew's house, had been to let for a couple of months now. It was the largest of the four with a substantial old-stone garage tucked into its side. There had been no takers. It appeared character cottages went hand in hand with phenomenal 'you-must-be-joking' rents.

'So fill me in on the plan then,' said Catherine, who never failed to peer into the empty cottage window in the hope of seeing some new detail she had missed. It was her dream home: gnarled beams, big kitchen fireplace, exposed stonework. When all the children had grown up and left, she wanted a cottage just like this for her and Eddie to receive their grandchildren. She sighed at its gorgeousness.

'Time for a coffee?'

'Quick one. Eddie's sorted the kids out this morning, he'll be on his third nervous breakdown by now.' They both knew that was a joke. There was only one creature more laid-back than Eddie and that was Boot, the dog. Eddie had found him as a puppy on a landfill site. His head was stuck in a tatty Wellington boot and Eddie's initial thought, after extricating him, was that he was as ugly as an old boot, hence the name. He had been roughly the size of Chico the Chihuahua when Eddie brought him home. Now he could have dragged a gypsy caravan single-handed with a shire horse asleep in the back, yet he would let a baby take a bone from his mouth. He played the part of a family guard dog, though, and a cat burglar wouldn't have staked his chances – but you only had to look into his soft gentle eyes to know he didn't have the capacity to hurt anything. Everyone loved Boot, Danny especially, and the dog loved him back, as he did all kids.

Stevie made Catherine wait for the details until the kettle had boiled. Catherine humoured her strange hopefulness, despite having a heavy feeling about it all, but any positive plan that kept her friend from going down the path she had gone down last time had to be supported.

'Right!' said Stevie, stirring in the milk. 'Here's what I'm going to do.'

'Go on then,' said Catherine, sitting comfortably.

'I've got six days left until Matthew comes back. So at lunchtime tomorrow I'm having my hair done.'

'Right,' Catherine nodded. 'Good girl. Make yourself feel better.'

'Then I'm going to join the gym to get some weight off.' Stevie beamed at Catherine waiting for her approval.

'Well, that's great,' said her friend, trying her best to smile encouragingly. 'But . . .'

'But what?' Stevie's smile slipped a little.

Catherine sighed. With the best will in the world, Stevie wasn't going to get down to a size zero and look like a Supermodel in six days. Even if she did, that wasn't going to bring Matthew back to her. There were darker forces at work here, forces for which a hair-do fairy was no match.

Then again, it wouldn't do Stevie any harm to go to a gym and see some nice fit males with bulging biceps and trim bums. Surely that was better than sitting in and thinking about what those cheating scumbags were doing. She hoped their duplicity would catch up with them; after all, a sneaky week away on holiday was not the best way to cement a new relationship, if that's what it was and not a one-off fling. Matthew had a conscience, and Jo *surely* would be thinking of what the mad Scot would do if he found out. That was bound to get in the way of the enjoyment of their sun and sangria, and any other 's's' they were participating in with abandon.

Catherine smiled. 'But nothing. In fact, I'll come with you for the first session if you like, for moral support. They're always giving out free day passes, aren't they, these gyms, trying to get you to join up? You can blag me one.'

'Oh Catherine, that would be fab,' said Stevie, her smile lit up with gratitude.

'Which gym?'

'Well, Matthew goes to the Gym Village one, so maybe I'd be better going to the other – Well Life.'

'Ooh, posh and expensive – go and do it immediately. Ring up and find out how you join before I go home.' Catherine slid the cordless phone over the table.

So, Stevie started the three-point plan that would totally absorb her over the next six days and get her man back for her.

1) have great new-image hairdo
2) join gym and start to get thinner
3) practise pretending to have suspected nothing about his affair

Easy.

Chapter 5

Listening to the gently shushing waves, savouring the scent of sun oil that smelt of coconuts, and lying next to a long, leggy woman with a Supermodel-type body nearly covered by a white bikini with a sexy little rhinestone clasp between the twin swells of her small but perfect breasts, Matthew waited for the guilt to kick in. A stray thought visited plump, ordinary little Stevie at home. She would be sitting at her computer, writing love stories for the lonely and rejected, blissfully unaware that she was about to join them in exactly five days' time. It made him feel guilty only for not feeling guilty.

He really had not meant for this to happen at all. He had been content enough with Stevie and sliding himself gradually into the role of dad for Danny, until he had found Jo MacLean, one of the new designers, crying by his black Punto in the company car park the day after Valentine's Day. He had only seen her a couple of times before but, Jo MacLean, with her big brown eyes and her long, dark hair and her even longer legs, was someone once spotted, never forgotten. They had spoken once, after a meeting in late January. A few of them had hung around the buffet table drinking the last of the coffee. He'd found himself puffing up in front of her, trying to impress, implying *things*. Then a fortnight later, there he was, offering her his handkerchief in the cold and the rain and asking if she wanted a coffee in the little café around the corner from work. There she had spilled out her life to him – a relative stranger – so desperate was she for consolation. She had told him how she had recently moved into a new house with the husband she so needed to get away from but didn't know how to because he watched her every move. She poured out stories of horrific verbal and physical abuse and Matthew had sat and patiently listened. Who could have predicted what she would be doing to the rest of his body, so soon after he'd offered up his shoulder?

Despite being flattered by her attention, at first, he really had only genuinely wanted to help her escape Adam MacLean before the big Scot went too far one day and killed her. He had told Stevie all about her at the beginning, when it had been innocent, and, horrified that someone could be treated so badly, that she had offered herself as a friend to Jo too. Stevie just couldn't bear to see anyone being unhappy, especially when she was so happy herself, planning her wedding to the man of her dreams.

It hadn't felt right to keep bringing Jo into his home when he knew he was falling in love with her, but Matt couldn't help himself – he just had to see her whenever he could. Then, when Jo admitted she felt the same about him, he had almost exploded with Pools-winning pleasure. Jo and Stevie got on so well, which made it both harder and easier, but either way messier. The longer it went on, the more hurt people were going to get, but he couldn't give Jo up – it was not an option. Jo was a drug and he was hooked.

They hot-footed it to the sun to plan how he would finally leave Stevie and little Danny, and orchestrate how Jo could escape the Incredible McHulk. Matthew would have to make sure that he watched his back there. There was no telling what MacLean would do to Matthew, if he had no reservations about hitting a woman as fragile as Jo.

Propping himself up to look at the vision on the sun-bed next to his, Matthew knew it was all going to be worth it though. He couldn't feel any guilt because there was no room for it in his heart, which was just too full of desire for this gorgeous being. She was *perfect* – well, except for the scar on the top of her leg where Adam's kicking boot went in once. He had always hit her where the bruises didn't show, she said, although she looked pretty undamaged now, and in fantastic shape. And all the sex with that fantastic shape had almost succeeded in blowing his head clean off his shoulders. Sex that was long and languorous in bed, like this week. Sex that was fast and furious as it had had to be back home, like the time in the back of Stevie's car, which he'd felt a bit bad about, but it still hadn't stopped him. Obviously, Stevie hadn't been there to witness it; he had merely borrowed the car to take Jo home the night when she had come up to see the wedding dress. It had been quick, steamy, and very erotic. Sex that was dangerous and exciting, like when they did it up against a wall of an unfinished house on Jo's estate, her long slim legs around his back, pulling him further and deeper into her. She had been very noisy but he wouldn't have cared if the whole British Army and the Pope had come around the corner at that moment; it would just have given it all an extra edge and he would have carried on even more enthusiastically. As he came, he remembered that Stevie would be washing up the pans and dishes in which she had just cooked them all supper. He realized then how much his feelings for Stevie paled in the face of this beautiful, long-limbed, washboard-stomached woman who needed his love and protection so much. She made him feel like he'd never felt before: a giant, a hero, a prince, Robin Hood crossed with Shrek – after the latter had taken the magic potion, obviously.

At first it crossed Matt's mind that Jo was so desperate to get away from Adam that she might be using him as a stepping stone, until she had suggested the two of them fly away abroad in order to plan the final logistics of partner-leaving, wedding-cancelling and moving in together. Then she had gone down on him in a staff toilet to seal her intentions. By the time his breathing had got back to normal, he had booked the flights and the five-star hotel on his already overloaded Visa card.

Now he was here and it was heaven. He kicked away a stray spore of remorse, imagining Stevie, ironing his shirts and looking forward to him coming home. She would be worrying about him driving all the way from Aberdeen and not having a clue that he was 1,500 miles in the other direction sponging up the Spanish sun, blood running like sangria through his veins making him permanently half-drunk with lust.

Stevie would be okay, he had convinced himself of that. Well, heartbreak didn't kill you, did it, and she had come through far worse. She would have to move out (thank God the house was still solely in his name!) so that Jo could move in. Little Danny would forget him soon enough. It wasn't as if he had got used to calling him 'Daddy' or anything, and kids adjusted. He tried not to let the thoughts in about Danny's Euro-Disney trip because that really would make him feel bad. Especially as the savings for it were financing his Majorcan expenses. He would put the money back in the account, obviously. He wasn't a thief.

If asked, he would say he got the tan in the leisure facilities at the Aberdeen hotel, while Jo would say she had been under the sun-bed at the Welsh health farm. At least Stevie would never know he'd jetted off with another woman to the sun. That detail really would be too cruel.

Chapter 6

Lindsay flicked at Stevie's long, honey-coloured hair and together they studied the difference it made to her reflection. First she pulled it back, then she swooped it forwards until she looked like Cousin Itt from the Addams Family.

'Know what? I think you should have it all lopped off. To here,' said Lindsay, making a chopping motion on her client's shoulders.

Stevie's eyes registered horror. 'A bob?' She wasn't convinced.

'Not quite,' said Lindsay, shaking her head vehemently. 'I don't think that would suit your face shape. You could end up looking like a child of royal first cousins. Something funkier, I think. Nice and choppy and really easy to do yourself at home.'

Stevie gulped. She was just about to change her mind and ask for a trim when she heard Catherine's voice in her head nagging her: '*What's the point of booking in with the top stylist at Anthony Fawkes and then not taking her advice?*'

'And a few really pale highlights running through it as well,' Lindsay went on. 'I think it will make you look a hell of a lot younger.'

Younger.

There. She had spoken the magic word. At thirty-six, Stevie was five years older than Jo, who had just recently had her thirty-first birthday. Stevie had bought her the (size ten) bikini they had both spotted on display in a shop window and wowed at. It was glistening white with a glittery rhinestone clasp at the front. Wouldn't that be ironic if Jo had it on now – modelling it for Matthew on a Balearic beach whilst she was oiled up to buggery with Piz Buin. Stevie smacked that thought away before she showed herself up by crying in public, supplanting it with one of Matthew's delighted face when he saw her new image.

'Okay, let's do it,' said Stevie, taking a deep breath as the scissors went in for the kill.

Two hours later and she was staring at herself in the mirror, from varied angles, admiring the shorter, chopped style, brighter in colour at the front and the sides and infinitely lighter in weight. She was astounded how much thinner her face seemed. If only it could have done the same to her bum.

'I'm stunned!' said Stevie, who was. Whatever the damage on her Switch card was, it would be worth it. It cost a lot, but she didn't care. The plan had started to work. Now there was just the rest of her body to sort out.

Adam smoothed the plaster over the wall with the trowel. Apart from the colour, there was no evidence that his temper had given way and that he'd cannoned a fury-loaded fist into the wall. He knew that losing it was not the way forward, not this time. He had tried that one with Diane – and where had that got him? Shouting and screaming and breaking things and being totally out of control had done nothing but drive her right out of his life. And scare the neighbours. And lose his cat for him.

He thought back to that fateful day. The scene of devastation was burned onto his brain like a top quality colour photograph: Diane screaming and running out towards her car with a hastily packed suitcase and Humbug the striped tabby in his basket whilst Adam stood there holding a roaring chainsaw. The neighbours' curtains had twitched, but no one dared to ring the police. Diane had given him that look he had seen in his mum's eyes too many times when his da' came in from the pub. Some folks turned jolly with spirit, not big Andy MacLean. The whisky went straight into his fists, and then the fists went straight into his mammy and his sisters and little Adam. *Blood will out –* that's what they said, wasn't it?

Adam MacLean knew what he looked like with his archetypal boxer's nose, scarred cheek, powerful build and a voice that could vibrate owls out of trees. He also knew exactly how Jo would suppose him to behave if she left him for another man. And, likewise, what old Matty Boy (who was probably enjoying the last days for quite a while when he could maintain total control over his bowels) would expect from him. So, as he did the plastering repair, Adam MacLean had been thinking it all calmly and methodically through. And now he had a plan.

Chapter 7

Kitted out in her new tracksuit bottoms, trainers, snazzy Adidas top and a very strong bra that totally flattened her generously proportioned chest so that she didn't give black eyes to either herself or people on adjacent treadmills, Stevie presented herself at the gym for her induction hour with Hilary. She was horrified to find that Hilary was in fact a bloke. Not just an ordinary bloke either but a young, fit, tall, love-god bloke with a killer smile and a backside that could crack open Brazil nuts. Then again, she of all people should have known that a name didn't always guarantee the sex. *Midnight Moon* had asked her to use a pseudonym, as 'Stevie' suggested she might be male, and *Midnight Moon* readers were very specific that only women writers were able to tap into their feminine needs. Their pen-names needed to conjure up softness and romance and sweetness, which is why her fellow writers Paul Slack and Alec Sleaford became Paula Sheer and Alexis Tracey, and why she herself was published under Beatrice Pollen, her darling late granny's name. It was from Granny Bea that Stevie inherited her creative talents, her warm, considerate heart and her big, sky-blue eyes.

As if monitoring her whilst she went on the workout machines to ascertain what she could, or rather couldn't, manage wasn't embarrassing enough, Hilary weighed her in the office, took her height, blood pressure and worked out her body mass index, which basically classified her as a crate of lard. To be fair, the gorgeous Hilary didn't seem all that horrified by the way she puffed after doing three sit-ups or turned aubergine on the StairMaster. At least the weighing scales didn't flash up 'one fat bird at a time please'.

She paid a huge cheque over for a year's subscription, because that way Stevie knew she was fully committing herself to her cause, plus she was seduced by the offers of a free month and a special 'mystery' gift pack. Catherine was sitting in Reception when Hilary officially welcomed Stevie to the club, alas not with a big tonguey snog, but with a complimentary water container, a gym bag, an introductory booklet of money-off vouchers for the sun-bed, various massages and treatments, and a free seven-day pass for a friend of her choice, who at that moment was eagerly waiting for it, clad in some pretty impressive pink and grey gear. Stevie wolf-whistled as she approached her.

'It's our Kate's,' explained Catherine.

'Must be nice, to be able to fit into your seventeen-year-old daughter's clothes,' said Stevie.

'It is, until you see me naked and discover that most of my body is made up of stretchmarks,' exaggerated Catherine who, considering the major brood she'd had, had managed to stay remarkably slim, give or take a little rounded tum that she was always moaning about. 'By the way, Steve, the hair is fab.'

'It looked better when I'd had it done this morning, before I had fourteen litres of sweat dampening it down.'

'Makes you look a hell of a lot younger. No bull.'

'Really?'

'Really.'

Stevie beamed. First stage of 'getting Matthew back' was mission accomplished, then.

The two gym-bunnies had a go on a few machines. Catherine was surprisingly fit. Then again, she was forever running up and down stairs and gardens after the kids, plus she took the dogs out walking and she went to a yoga class every Thursday evening. She liked yoga and did a lot of fifteen-minute stretches during the day and evening, which helped her relax in a way that smashing plates against the wall and tearing her hair out wouldn't. She knew that for definite because she'd tried those too. Then they went off for a coffee in the very luxurious café after a slow walk past the spinning class to check out some very nice male bottoms.

Stevie's stomach suddenly made a noise like a mortally wounded hound as they waited in the queue.

'Have you eaten?' said Catherine.

'Not really,' Stevie said.

'What's that supposed to mean? You either have or you haven't.'

'Er . . . no, then.'

'You won't lose weight by not eating.'

'Try telling that to people on hunger strike.'

'You know what I mean,' said Catherine, who was suddenly concerned. She had been waiting for Stevie to start cracking up. Her friend was far too composed for it to last. Not eating sounded suspiciously like the start of it. Again.

'I'm not deliberately not eating,' said Stevie. 'I just haven't felt hungry.'

'Right, well, you're having something now. You go and get those seats over there and I'll be with you in a minute.'

It was no good protesting with Catherine. It was never any good protesting with Catherine. Eddie had tried that one quite a few times and had been beaten back into a perpetual state of 'give in', so Stevie retired to the small metal table by the window as instructed. She did feel a bit shaky, all that exercise and hairdo-ing with nothing in her stomach but cappuccinos and half a slice of unbuttered toast – well, since Madman MacLean came around smashing up her life anyway.

Catherine brought over big frothy coffees in pseudo-soup bowls, two flat toasted panini sandwiches, the length of Stevie's leg, filled with ham and Brie, and two enormous chocolate-covered slabs that smelt suspiciously of peanut butter.

'Do they sell this sort of stuff here?' said Stevie open-mouthed. She had been expecting two lettuce leaves and a spring onion on something brown and inedible.

'Course they do, it's not Stalag 17. Some people just come in for lunch, not to exercise.' Catherine stuck the sandwich in her mouth and pulled it out quickly. 'Ow, ow, ow – watch it, that cheese is molten.' Then her face froze and she gave Stevie a sharp nudge. 'Braveheart alert at three o'clock,' she said through one side of her barely moving mouth, like ventriloquist Roger De Courcey with Nookie Bear.

'What?'

Stevie twisted around to see the unmistakable figure of *him*, resplendent in black tracksuit bottoms and a black T-shirt, with his luxuriant red hair flowing behind him. He looked like a muscular Duracell battery.

'Oh bloody hell, he's seen me,' said Stevie, as the big man's eyes locked onto hers and he started to come over. In slow motion – like the Terminator.

'Want a minute to yourselves?' said Catherine. 'You are in this together, after all.'

'Don't you dare leave me with that . . . that caber tosser without an armed escort!' said Stevie.

'Don't be daft, Steve. He's not going to do anything to you here – the place is packed. Anyway, I really do need the loo and he looks as if he wants to talk to you.' Catherine got up, just as Adam MacLean reached the table and nodded her a stiff hello as they crossed paths.

'I didnae know you were a member of ma gym,' he said, looking down at Stevie.

His gym? Crikey, he was possessive!

'Well, I am,' said Stevie, taking a diversionary sip of coffee, which burnt her lip, and then she accidentally bit it as well in an unfortunate reflex action.

'Can I sit down forrr a wee minute, please?' he said. Civilized for him, thought Stevie, who glared at him but didn't say no, which he obviously took to mean yes, because he dropped his big-honed body into the chair that Catherine had vacated.

'Have you hearrrd anything?' he asked, his eyes compulsively drawn to her swelling split lip.

'No,' Stevie lied. 'Have you?'

'No. Jo left her mobile behind too, funnily enough. Probably so I couldn't ring her. The number she left for the health farm doesn't exist, of course. No doubt she'll tell me she wrote it down wrang.'

'Oh.' Stevie felt a little guilty about fibbing then after he had been so candid, but she didn't want to give him any details that might trigger him to go off and kill Matthew. She had one dead lover, she didn't want another, she thought with black amusement. It was, however, a thought that quickly soured in her head and made her feel slightly sick.

'I have a plan to stop aw this nonsense,' he said.

'So have I,' said Stevie stiffly. She suspected her plan of hair-dos and gentle body toning might be slightly different from his, which would involve hi-jacking a plane and forcing Matthew to jump out of it above the bit of sea with the most sharks in it.

'You see, ba ma way of thinkin', it's aw to dae with basic psychology . . .'

Stevie cut him off with a mirthless little laugh. *Like he would know!* The only thing he knew about heads was that they were meant to propel forwards at great speed into someone else's nose. Most likely someone he was married to, too.

'Please don't take this wrongly, *Mr* MacLean but I'll handle this in my own fashion,' she said bravely. Her lip throbbed and she was fighting back some annoying tears, and she didn't know if they were down to bodily pain or his frustrating, hateful presence and all he stood for.

Adam pulled out a card from his tracksuit pocket and slammed it on the table, which made both her and the plates jump.

'Sorry, I'm a wee bit heavy-handed.'

You can say that again, she thought.

'Here's ma card. If you change yer mind and want to hear whit I have to say, then gi' me a ring. We could smash this thing up before it gets too big and get back tae being happy.'

She didn't like the way he said 'smash' with such relish, or maybe it was just his accent. Either way, she wouldn't have fancied his chances in a lullaby-singing competition.

'That is, if you seriously want tae get yerrr man back.' He looked accusingly at the feast on the table. Not exactly food for a seriously devoted body sculptor, he thought. Then he was off, just as Catherine made her perfectly timed return.

'So?' she said, and then jumped back. 'Shit – your lip! He didn't hit you after all, did he?'

'Like he'd dare,' said Stevie, but knowing he'd dare quite easily. 'No, I burnt my lip on the coffee.'

'And?'

'Then I bit it and it hurt.'

'No, you clumsy tart, I meant "and" as in "and what did he want"?'

'Oh, he says he has a plan to break up Matthew and Jo,' Stevie said unenthusiastically.

'What was it then?' Catherine leant eagerly forward.

'Haven't a clue,' shrugged Stevie. 'I said I wasn't interested in hearing it.'

'Why not? You could at least have listened to what he had to say! You do have something in common here, after all.'

Stevie shuddered at the thought of having anything in common with *him*.

'I think I could guess at a push what *he'd* suggest,' she said. 'Something to do with sawn-offs and hitmen.'

'Ooh look,' said Catherine, picking up his card. 'He's the General Manager here.'

'I hope you're flaming joking. I've just signed up for a whole year!' said Stevie, snatching back the card to see it there in black and white, and red and a touch of navy blue – *Adam MacLean, General Manager of Well Life Super-gym, Dodmoor, Barnsley*, and the scribble of his mobile number. The information knocked Stevie for six because he looked more like the head of 'Thugs International' than something sensible, respectable and managerial.

A picture came into her head of him pushing past her and coming into the house. If she hadn't opened the door, she would still have been in blissful ignorance. Jo and Matthew might have just had a quick fling and that could have been the end of it. Maybe that's all it was: a last-minute explosion of freedom before he finally settled down and got married. It happened. Stevie was thirty-six; she wasn't the naïve baby she'd been nearly five years ago when she had found out about Mick, even if Mick and Matthew were very different animals. Mick wouldn't have felt the slightest bit of guilt, but she knew Matthew would be crip-pled with it and most likely pacing the Spanish hotel foyer vowing never to do anything like that again. But then *he* had to go and tell her just because *he* found out about it and got upset and wanted to upset everyone else too. No, she'd heard what McBigmouth had to say once; she wouldn't make that mistake again.

'He can go and stuff a live haggis up his backside,' said Stevie decisively. Then she bit down and burnt the other side of her mouth on the panini.

Chapter 8

Paris smiled that special smile of hers as Brandon took her into his arms.

'I love you so much,' she said, her red lips parting slowly to alert him to the fact that she was ready for his kiss.
Brandon let her fall heavily to the ground.

'I'm sorry, love, but I'm mad crazy bonkers over another woman. She's got everything you haven't, so no one can blame me really. So this is the big El Dumpo, I'm afraid. Well, have a nice life, pet.' And with that he expertly mounted his Spanish black stallion and, bearing a rose between his teeth, stuck his boot spurs into the side of his horse, who whinnied and galloped him away to his new love La Joanna, which in Spanish means 'crafty two-faced cow'.

Stevie sighed, pushed back her chair and looked at the words that plopped out of her printer on the page. Yet another sheet to join the ream of bad writing destined for the recycling bin in the garage.

'Yeah, this is really going to pay the bills, pratting around like this,' she said to herself. She had a block as big as Everest in her writer's flow. In fact, she might as well log off for ever, then get a job in a factory sprinkling cheese on pizzas.

It was not often that writing felt like hard work, but today it did. Not that she usually wrote at the weekend, but seeing as she hadn't touched her keyboard since last Monday, she thought she might take advantage of the hour whilst Danny played *Harry Potter* on his GameCube. He was busy zapping toadstools to get Bertie Botts beans to buy some spells at Hogwarts, and he seemed quite content, although Stevie felt guilty that she wasn't doing anything more exciting herself to entertain him.

She always tried to do something special at the weekends – take him for a walk to the park, or do some gardening together, or play board games. It was a kickback, she supposed, from her own childhood. She would get piles of games for Christmas and birthdays, but find there was no one to play them with. Her mum was always too busy to sit down and shake a dice, and even though their tiny home was like a new pin, Edna Honeywell was continuously scrubbing or Brasso-ing the ornaments. Later, Stevie suspected that was probably just an excuse to avoid getting roped into playing *Frustration* or *Ker Plunk* and, much as she herself liked a nicely kept home, she vowed never to make such a god of the housework that she was too busy to play with her own children. Her dad worked long hours and so when he did get home, he could barely manage a 'hello', never mind a game of *Cluedo*. He needed to save his energies for the rabid arguments that Stevie listened to as she lay trembling in her bed.

So one day, Stevie simply stopped asking her parents to

play and turned to herself for entertainment, drawing and scribbling, reading and writing, constructing little books and stories of love and happy families that became longer and more structured and crafted. She never showed them to anyone, they were her own private treasures. Her diaries were highly detailed too. In them, she found an overflow pipe for her frustrations and ambitions and crazily mixed-up emotions. Especially when her father ran off with the woman with a really thick neck a few doors away, and her mother, in vengeance, took a slimy lover whose eyes were too close together and who stared too long at Stevie's budding breasts for her comfort. It had been a difficult time and stained her teenage years with some memories she would rather forget. She had burnt the diaries in the end; they had been useful to write but far too painful to read.

It had been a relief to get away to university to study English, made possible because it was in the old days when students of moderate-earning parents got grants and they only had to stump up the minimum payment, which her dad did out of guilt because it was easier to give presents and money than time. That was why she always wanted to give a child what she had never had – a parent's interest and attention. Preferably two parents, although that chance seemed forever to be slipping past her.

Today, though, she did not want to play with Danny and that made her feel mean, although she had accepted a long time ago that she wasn't Supermum. She just wanted to go to the gym and hurt herself with big weights, then come home and soothe the aches in a hot bath, wrap herself in her fluffy towelling robe and fold onto the sofa to sleep until Tuesday, the day that Matthew came home.

It was an incredibly soggy day. The air was damp and the Yorkshire earth was dealing with the aftermath of heavy showers through the night.

'I'm bored,' said Danny, quitting Harry.

'Me too,' said Stevie. Paris and Brandon would have to wait. If only she could write her own destiny as easily as she could theirs. Then again, maybe that wasn't wise, with the self-destructive mood she was in at the moment. She would only have had herself trampled by Brandon's horse just to get some relief from the pain gnawing away inside her.

Well, she couldn't curl up and do nothing, that was for sure. Cooping a bored child up in the house with a bored adult was like mixing petrol and struck matches.

'Danny, get your wellies on and your big coat,' she said impulsively.

'Cool. Where are we going?'

'Bluebelling,' said Stevie.

There was a lovely wood at Pogley Top that she had once discovered with Mick when they had driven aimlessly out to christen her new (well to her, anyway) car. The ground had been far too muddy to explore in his best shoes and her heels, which was a shame as Mick was all for having his wicked way with her, right there on the thick carpet of scented bluebells. It was on that day he proposed.

Matthew had taken her there too one warm spring day when they had first started courting. He had made up a basket that was full of the most delicious food, only for most of it to get wasted when they spent all afternoon snogging on the gingham tablecloth under the trees, feeding each other the odd Twiglet to keep up the strength in their lip muscles.

Danny sat in the front of the car on his booster seat, trying to read the road signs and asking what they meant.

'Why's that say "n"?'

'It's not an n, love, it's an upside down u. It means No U-turns – you can't turn round there.'

'What's that one mean, Mummy?'

'Hump-back bridge,' said Stevie, checking for oncoming traffic and then taking the bump at a speed not conducive to good car maintenance. Her son gave a thrilled little scream, the way she used to on the trip to the grand annual Church picnic at Higher Hoppleton Park. Every Sunday, Stevie was shunted off to St John's, whilst Edna gave the house a good bottoming. It was one of her better moves though, for Sunday School gave Stevie most, if not all, of the lovely warm moments she would carry with her into adulthood, the picnics being top of her list. The kindly old men of the church would ferry everyone from the holy meeting-place to the park, overtaking each other en route, much to the delighted shrieks of the 300 kids piled up on the back seats well before the days of rear seat car belts. Then, young and old, little old ladies in hats and the Reverend alike had played rounders, football, picked bluebells, eaten egg and cress sandwiches, and butterfly buns. Aw, those picnics had been so wonderful. She loved May bluebells for the fond memories they evoked. They seemed to feature in all her happiest memories.

There were nicer woods than Pogley Top, but none felt

quite as magical. Maybe it was because the trees all conspired overhead to give it a dark, mysterious feel. Maybe it was because it was sheltered on all sides and the air seemed extra still there. She had come here so many times when things turned bad with Mick, hoping to rewind time to that perfect day.

'Come on, mate,' said Stevie, holding the car door open for her son and then helping him out. His little wellies were sucked down straight away into the squelchy mud and together they went for a drunken, giggly walk in between the trees. That musty, pungent smell never failed to take her back to happier times. If ever there were fairies, she was sure they resided in these silent bluebell woods, where their fragile wings would never be blown off-course. As if to add credence to her imaginings, there was an Enid Blyton fairy ring at her feet that her trendy pink welly narrowly missed.

They picked a way through the flowers, collecting armfuls, although Danny dropped three for every two he picked up. Stevie laughed. He would definitely need throwing in the bath when they got home, clothes and all, but what the hell. The fresh air wasn't taking any of the pain away, but it was nice to splash around on some soggy land and get mucky with nature.

When they got home, they stuck the flowers in conventional vases, and then when they ran out, in milk bottles and the cream jug. Once Danny was tucked up in bed and well on his way to Sleepyland, Stevie took up Paris's plight of unrequited love again, but still her head wouldn't play the game. There was no conviction in Brandon's proclamation of love. She only wanted to warn Paris that he was bound to bugger off at some point, if not right then, and the omnipresent bluebell scent in the room only served to remind her of kissing Matthew, or being besotted by Mick. Or even to take her further back, with memories of those sunshine-filled May picnics, when she was someone who still believed in fairies and magic and that princesses got their princes. And that there were such things as happy endings.

Chapter 9

Two days later, when the bluebells had started to wither, Adam watched Stevie enter the gym, swinging her bag, and present her entry card at the front desk. She had spotted him, he knew, but was trying to pretend she hadn't by whistling a merry tune and looking everywhere but in his direction. Pathetic really. She had been here every morning since she joined; he had checked her records to find out when that was precisely. The date alone had made it pretty obvious why she was pounding away on the treadmills, although she wasn't going to lose a lot of weight building up a mad sweat and then going off and eating half the restaurant like he had caught her about to do on what he now realized was her first day. *Yeah, great start.*

Her friend's hair had looked infinitely better then, he had noticed. In fact, she looked quite a classy piece, having got rid of the weird pink. *She* had had hers done too, but he *so* wanted to drum it loudly into her obviously less than bright skull that it wouldn't do any good. She should have thought of making such improvements *before* she drove her man away. Did she think she was seriously going to lure him back by cutting off a few dead ends? Not when faced with the mighty attributes of his beloved Jo. She could not even hope to come near to Jo, who could knock any woman off the planet with her looks. She would be far better following *his* plan of action but she wasn't going to listen to him, she had made that perfectly clear. In fact, from her snotty attitude, he actually had the impression that she thought some of this might be his fault! How, he hadn't worked out yet, and he wasn't going to ask the little madam how she'd drawn that conclusion. Well, he just hoped she didn't cock up his plans for reclaiming his woman. He was going crazy without her. He could hardly sleep for the nervous excitement that her homecoming tomorrow was giving him.

Stevie went into the gym with a heart that was stuffed full of blame and looking for a target, but Matthew was as protected and cloaked as the starship *Enterprise* during a Klingon attack. Her head just wouldn't let her attack him, because surely he was a victim in this – emotionally outmanoeuvred, a sitting duck. She wasn't even starting to allow herself to think what she wanted to do to Jo, but she had to grudgingly concede that even Joanna MacLean was a sort of victim too, and you didn't need to be a genius to point to the source of all this heartache: that Scottish animal, masquerading as something human and respectable behind that desk, the wildman who had come into Stevie's life and tried to wreck it. Oh yes, she had seen the blame in his eyes, the belief that this was somehow her fault. She didn't know how he worked that one out, but then again, his type never took responsibility for their own actions.

That cocky look he was giving her just made her want to storm over there and tell him that if *he* hadn't been such a psycho-nutter, if *he* had treated his wife like a woman should be treated, if *he* hadn't brought her low with mental torture and physical violence, she would not have had that air of vulnerability which had been obviously irresistible to her soft-hearted, gentle, uncritical Matthew. In comparison with *him*, Matthew had looked like a knight in shining armour, and no woman could resist that.

This mess was all Adam MacLean's fault. She despised him.

MacLean was trying to pretend he hadn't seen her, which was good because she didn't want to talk to him either. What on earth could they possibly have to say to each other? Besides which, she didn't want to talk to anyone today, not even Catherine. She was too busy with her preparations for tomorrow, and trying to cling onto her dwindling reserves of inner strength. The house was extra-sparkling clean, the fridge was stocked up with lovely goodies and treats, and all Matthew's favourite nibbly things. The bills due had all been paid, the banking was done, although the joint-account status had been a bit of a shocker, but she would sort that one out with Matthew later. All that was left was to get on that treadmill and start running, in the hope that by some miracle she would have lost a stone by the time Matthew landed tomorrow, and also that she might burn off some of the hatred she felt for that red-haired gorilla.

Adam did a sweep of the place an hour and a half later and saw that Stevie was still pounding away on the treadmill. He almost felt sorry for her, before remembering it was her fault they were all in this position. He noticed that she was glaring in his direction and so he glared back. Then she suddenly buckled, lost her footing, tripped over her own trainer and fell on the treadmill, which transported her backwards, made her do a reverse roly poly then rudely deposited her with a thud on the floor. Buster Keaton couldn't have choreographed it better. A couple of people started to come over to help, but they were mainly pensioners around at this time, and Adam beat them to it.

His long legs thundered over to her. She was a customer, after all, and he had a responsibility to her. Even if she was the one who had wrecked his relationship with the most wonderful woman in the world, he still had his professional duty to do.

'Are you awwwwrrright?' he asked, helping her up.

When she realized who it was helping her up though, she shrugged him right off. People were looking at her and she felt a total idiot and, even though she knew it was a huge cliché, Stevie really did want the ground to open and swallow her up whole and get her out of there via an underground network. It was her own stupid fault, she knew, for not eating enough. In the past five days she had eaten little more than three bites of that ham and Brie panini, and was surviving mainly on the milky coffees she had been drinking on a half-hourly basis. It wasn't as if the caffeine would interfere with her sleep patterns, because she wasn't getting any sleep. As a result, she felt totally wired all the time, a condition not helped by the adrenaline surging through her veins, generated by the anxiety of waiting for this week to be at an end.

Now the only thing she could feel was embarrassment. People were going to go home tonight and say, 'Ha ha, this woman fell off the treadmill today big time – it was hilarious,' and just to add total humiliation to the mix, Bigfoot had tried to lift her up. Her nose felt clogged up and was swelling before everyone else's eyes, and she wasn't going to be eight stone and beautiful by tomorrow. She would still be plump, but with blonder, shorter hair and a big, fat, swollen, split-open, red nose. There was no way she was going to cry in front of *him*, though, however defeated she felt. In fact, thinking about it, this was his fault as well. If she hadn't looked over and seen him staring at her, she would not have lost her running rhythm. Bloody Scottish jinx. Was he making it his new mission to screw up her life totally?

'Let's get you tae the First Aid room,' Adam said.

'I'll fix it at homeb,' said Stevie, cringing with embarrassment as a big splodge of nose-blood landed on the floor. She hadn't a tissue or even a long sleeve, and was forced to accept the soft white hankie he offered her from his pocket. His best one too, he thought. He wouldn't see that again.

'Dank you,' she said grudgingly.

'Come and sit down for a minute.'

'Doh. I just wand my bag and do go homeb,' said Stevie, sniffing and then wincing because it hurt to do so. 'I'b bring dor hankie back dext timeb.' That is, if she could bear the indignity of everyone pointing her out as the in-house entertainment.

She did look hellish pale, thought Adam, and a wee bit woozy. He would be failing in his duty if he didn't advise her not to get into her car, even if home was just down the road.

'I really don't think you should drive for a wee while,' he said, attempting to take her arm again. 'Trust me, I'm Firrrst-Aid trained.'

'I'mb fine,' she insisted, pulling back as his hand made contact.

'Well, I cannae force ye, of course,' he said, holding up his hands in a gesture of defeat.

'Really? Ad there's be thinking dat's your sbeciality!' said Stevie, and with as much dignity as she could muster in the circumstances, she turned on her heel and headed towards the changing rooms, leaving a stunned Adam thinking,

Now whit the hell did the stupid woman mean ba' that?

Chapter 10

Matthew packed the little red-hearted G-string into the side of Jo's case, sighing as he remembered the fun they'd had with it the previous night. Jo came out of the bathroom, brushing her teeth as if she had sensed that his brain was occupied with some very naughty thoughts about her.

'All set for tomorrow, darling?' she said.

'No, I want to stay here for ever,' he said, adjusting himself as his pants suddenly felt very tight. She noticed the impressive bulge and her eyes rounded.

'Well, it'll be like this from now on, won't it?'

'Exactly – only colder.'

'I'll think of lots of ways to warm you up,' she said smokily and his pants got even tighter. In fact, they were in danger of exploding. He hadn't thought it was possible to sweat as much as he had done this week. If he died tomorrow, he would have enough memories to keep him happily entertained for all eternity. Although really, he shouldn't joke about dying tomorrow, because he just might, if Adam MacLean got hold of him. That thought made his pants suddenly have more than enough room in them.

'Will you be okay, going to pick up your stuff from your

house? Do you want me to come with you?' he asked Jo softly.

'I'll be fine,' she said. 'It's not as if Adam knows about us.'

'If he did, then he'd be pretty angry, right?' said Matthew with a gulp.

'He'd be waiting for us at the airport with a flame-thrower if he did,' said Jo. She stroked his face soothingly. 'But he doesn't, so relax.'

'No, of course not – how can he know?' said Matthew, more to himself than to Jo, but wondering if they sold Kevlar body armour in the airport duty-free shop all the same.

'So, you're going to tell Stevie tomorrow to move out then?' said Jo.

'Well, I'll have to give her a bit of time to get packed up and find somewhere else. She has got Danny to think about.'

'Poor little Danny,' said Jo, sniffing sadly. 'This is going to be awful for him too. I can't bear to think about it. She'll probably . . .' Jo cut off and shook her head.

'She'll probably what?' urged Matthew.

'Nothing,' said Jo. 'Forget it.'

'No, what were you going to say?'

'No, it'll come out wrong if I say it,' said Jo. 'Just leave it.'

But Matthew wouldn't.

'Well, I think that you should be very careful how you handle Stevie,' said Jo. 'She may turn . . . feral.'

'She won't. She's not like that,' said Matthew. Jo gave him an 'I know better than you about women' look.

'Trust me, I'm not trying to be awful,' she said. 'God

knows, this is going to be a living hell for the poor darling. It's just that . . . well, she herself told me how it was – last time.'

Matthew had to conclude that, actually, Jo might be right on that one. He rewound to some old conversations he'd had with Stevie about how she had reacted to Mick's infidelity. There had been lots of shouting, ripping things, throwing things, emotional blackmail, even a bit of stalking, and generally going nuts – totally out of character for the gentle person he knew and had loved. *Had loved*. He noted that he was already thinking of her in the past tense. It was just as well that all he was going to tell Stevie was that he needed some space and it might be better if she moved out for a while. Once she was out of the way, he would pretend to get together with Jo, who would move in soon after, of course. Playing it that way meant that they (hopefully) wouldn't have to worry about coming home to a bunny stew.

After this week, he hoped Stevie would be out of the way pretty soon because he could not wait long to carry on at home where he and Jo would leave off in Majorca. It had been so good to wake up with her after a long night instead of skulking about, snatching moments when Stevie's back was turned. He didn't know at what point he was going to tell Stevie the wedding was off. He was sort of hoping she would draw that conclusion for herself and save him the hassle. It was a cliché all right, but all *was* fair in love and war. He had to keep thinking that or he would never be able to look at himself in a mirror again.

Obviously, Adam MacLean might not quite see it in those black and white terms. Jo was going to tell him that she wanted some space too, and then join Matt at the Queens Hotel in town, when she had packed up a few essentials. She hadn't been quite so keen on his first suggestion of the B&B on Lunn Street, but what the hell – it wouldn't be for long, then any money worries would be over. No doubt Jo would go for a quickie divorce on the grounds of MacLean being a violent git, and the latter would have to pay her out once their house was sold. Matthew presumed then that she would buy half his house in Blossom Lane and all money pressure would be right off him. Then they could really start to enjoy themselves from a steady financial platform. Plenty of holidays in the sun like this one, plenty of cosy romantic meals for two at home and cuddle-ups on the sofa, plenty of tiny little *Agent Provocateur* red G-strings to pull off with his teeth. His perfect life was just around the corner.

'So, what do you want to do on your last night?' he asked.

She sidled suggestively over to him, reaching behind her to unzip her dress. It fell to the floor and she stepped out of it, wearing nothing but some very small black see-through briefs.

'What do you think?' she said. 'I bet Stevie never wore anything like these for you, did she?'

Matthew groaned.

Stevie who? was his last coherent thought of the day.

Stevie tucked Danny up with his teddy and read him a story about a Useless Troll with a very grisly ending, which he listened to with little-boy rapture, sucking his pyjama collar, until she extricated it from his mouth. She kissed him good night and thought, The next time I see you will be the day I see Matthew too. Then the phone went and it was Catherine doing her mother hen impression.

'You all set for tomorrow? How are you going to play it? Are you going to let him know you know?'

'No. I'm just going to be really nice. Not shout or bawl, just be calm and collected and cool.'

All of which she knew was going to be pretty difficult, since she had discovered that Matthew had taken out most of the money in their joint savings account, money that he hadn't actually put in. They had planned to take Danny to Euro-Disney with it that summer. He had probably spent it on *her*, but Stevie would try her best not to mention that.

'Don't let him get away with it entirely, he'll think you're a soft touch,' said Catherine, who was amazed at her friend's self-control. She had been witness to the crazy state she had been in when she found out that Mick was playing about. She half-expected Matthew to cop for that as well as his own misdemeanours because people did that sometimes, carry a load forward if they couldn't get emotional satisfaction the first time – and Stevie had a lot of unfinished business in that past relationship.

'Yes, I take your point,' said Stevie, 'but I want to listen to what he has to say. If he carries on pretending he went to Aberdeen and that's obviously the end of the matter, then I'm just going to try and forget this ever happened.'

'And will you really be able to do that?' asked Catherine with a gasp.

'I'm going to have to,' said Stevie, with steely resolve.

Chapter 11

After a night of fractured sleep, Stevie rang the airport and found that Matthew's plane had left on time, which meant that it was due into Leeds/Bradford airport just before midday. Allowing time for luggage and motorway delays, she reckoned he would be home between two and three o'clock. It felt like an eternity between now and then, and the anticipation filled her veins with a very unpleasant anxious sensation.

She prayed that there wouldn't be two people in his car when he drew up outside their house because she wasn't quite sure what her reaction would be. She didn't think she could be quite as level-headed as planned, in those circumstances. She just hoped Jo went straight home and was murdered by Adam MacLean. She presumed that was what part of his so-called 'plan' entailed – and for a split second she was dangerously on his side. Then she remembered how his cruelty had driven Jo into Matthew's arms. Jo, who had cuddled Danny on her knee and read him stories in her soft voice. Jo, who had cried on her shoulder and brought her flowers to say thank you for listening. Jo, with whom she had traded private stories of her life. Jo, who had helped her plan her wedding. Jo, who had ruined her son's first chance of a proper family with a proper dad. Jo, who had been so desperate for love and attention that she had chased her out of Matthew's heart without a second thought. It truly was a dog-eat-dog world.

Matthew's eyes darted madly around the airport from left to right, then up and down as if it wasn't beyond the realms of possibility that Adam MacLean might swing down from a rope SAS style, dressed in black and carrying a machine gun. Or even explode up through the floor like a force from hell. Jo, on the other hand, didn't seem half as perturbed as he expected her to be in the circumstances.

'Relax,' she said, when she spotted that his head was jerking everywhere like a lunatic in an asylum hunting imaginary flies. 'If Adam was here, there are plenty of security men to overpower him and he would only end up in prison again.'

Which would be small comfort on the mortuary slab, thought Matthew, although he didn't voice it. He did not want to admit being frightened. After all the brownie points he had earned being Jo's Sir Lancelot, he didn't want to lose them all by being Wimp Boy.

They picked up their luggage from the carousel and then made their way to the Leeds/Bradford long-stay car park. Matthew did a thorough check that there was nothing ticking under the car wheels and as he slid into the driver's seat, perspiration ran in rivers down his forehead. He made Jo stand well back until he had twisted on the ignition, then felt almost like crying with relief when all he heard was the engine and not a *boo-boom* and St Michael's voice asking him to wait in the queue at the Pearly Gates.

They both looked very healthy and brown – too much so for it to be attributed to a sun-bed, plus they were both far too blissed out to have been exercising on a Welsh treadmill or crammed up in an Aberdeen conference centre. Matthew was wondering if this really was going to be worth the fall-out to come, when Jo's long fingers came out and squeezed his inner thigh.

'Drop me around the corner when we get there, usual place.'

'I thought you said he wouldn't be at home!'

'He shouldn't be, but his shift pattern might have changed. Anyway, I have to see him some time, it's better that it's now.' She gave him a big brave smile.

'I'm scared for you, sweetie.'

'Don't be,' she said. 'But . . .' She left a long dramatic pause, which made his sweat glands crank up again. 'If you haven't heard from me by six o'clock, call the police, just to be on the safe side.'

'God, now you really are scaring me!'

'He threatened his first wife with a chainsaw.'

'Chuffing hell!'

Jo shook her head. 'He won't get the better of me, though. Not this time, I promise.'

She looked so determined that Matthew found himself smiling proudly. What a remarkable woman. She had come so far since they had first got together; back then, she was little better than a fragile shell with no confidence. A beautiful woman who really did think she was as ugly and useless and unlovable as MacLean had driven her to believe. He really had saved her, Matt thought with a proud inner glow that warmed him right through. They were so good together – as soul-matched as Cathy and Heathcliff, Tony and Cleo, Bonnie and Clyde. Jo MacLean was the most fantastic creature he had ever met. And after they had both done the necessary business this afternoon, nothing would ever part them again.

When Matthew's car pulled up outside the house at thirteen minutes and twenty-eight seconds past two, Stevie was relieved to see that he was alone. She manufactured a smile, which trembled on her lips as she jumped across the room from the window to stage herself casually at the computer just before the door opened.

'Hey there!' she said, pulling her smile as wide as possible in a semblance of 'woman overjoyed to see missed fiancé' and sprang up to give him a welcoming hug. She noticed immediately how stiffly he reciprocated it.

'Did you have a nice time?' she said breezily, trying to overcome the lump of panic that was clogging up her windpipe. 'Hey, I see you've been at the sun-beds there. Great leisure facilities, eh?' She did the lie for him.

'Yes, they were. Fantastic, in fact. Nice way to unwind – sitting in the . . . on the . . . er . . . sun bed. Especially after the long hard boring meetings.'

'Must have been tiring. Bet the journey back was hell,' she said as chirpily as a canary on Prozac.

'Yes,' he said, stretching and yawning with exhaustion at the imaginary long drive from Scotland.

'Cup of tea?' she said.

'No, I'm okay. Stopped off on the way at some motorway services at Scotch Corner.'

Liar. She herded her rebellious thoughts back into line
and stretched the smile a little further, not too much that it
was gushing, but enough to be warm and welcoming and
unaccusing. It was harder than she had thought, trying to
be Mrs Nice Person whilst someone was lying their head
off to you, and what's more, you knew they were and you
were sifting through everything they said for substantiating
evidence. It was the little details to give credence to his
story that were the most hurtful of all: *stopped off at Scotch
Corner; long boring meetings; sun beds . . .*

'Stevie.' He started scratching the back of his neck.
Something he did when he was nervous, usually when
opening a bank statement.

'Yes?' she said, still wearing that ridiculous smile onto
which she was hanging tenuously, because this was it, this
was the moment. The way he said her name suggested that
what was to follow was not good news.

'Stevie, when I was away, I did a lot of thinking. Alone.
Lying under the sun . . . er . . . bed.'

Lying being the operative word.

'Oh, did you?' Smile, smile. *Thinking and shagging. And
spending my son's holiday money!*

'I don't know how to say this so I'll just come straight
out with it . . .'

Oh God, oh God . . .

'I'm listening,' she said, presenting her bravest and most
understanding face.

'I think . . .'

Oh, please don't say it, Matthew, please don't!

'. . . I think we should take a bit of time out. Before the wedding.' Damn, I didn't mean to mention the wedding, Matt thought. Now I've made it look as if it's still on.

Which was exactly what Stevie was thinking.

'Before the wedding' – that means it's still on! Thank You, God!

She tested him. 'You mean, like, split up?' she said.

'No . . . yes . . . no . . .'

Damn! Her total reasonableness threw him. He had expected her to start crying and pleading and throwing things, then he would have had licence to storm off. This was so much harder, her being calm and nice and giving him nothing to kick against.

'Okay, if that's what you want,' she said, nodding. 'I totally understand.'

'Eh? Oh, right then.' *Bloody hell! That was easy!*

Maybe it was because she was one step ahead of him, knowing the 'game' that she found some strength. As if she was in Danny's *Harry Potter* and had just eaten a slice of rejuvenating pumpkin pie.

'So how do we do this?' said Ms Chirpy the drugged-up, happy-sounding canary.

'Er, well, let's think.'

Like you haven't thought already, Matthew!

He tapped his lip with his finger whilst considering the options.

'Maybe if I move into a B&B for a few days, just to give you a chance to get your stuff together,' he said, as if it had just come to him.

'My stuff?' echoed Stevie, a little breathlessly.

'Yes. I think it might be for the best if you ... er ... moved out for a bit.'

'Oh yes, I see – of course "my stuff",' she said, stretching her smile that bit further. Her thoughts were screaming at her from the sidelines to think positive and focus on the fact that he hadn't asked her to cancel the wedding. This was all still salvageable if she stuck to her plan of being 'nice-accepting lady'. 'Right. Okay then. Yes, you're probably right.' God, this was starting to hurt so much.

'Just for a while,' he said, which again wasn't what he meant at all, but it was easier to let her go with a little hope in her heart. It staved off the histrionics, at least.

'I'll obviously need to take some money out of the Euro-Disney trip account for a room or rent or whatever,' she said, not letting her face slip and upping the sweetness levels to offset the contentious subject of 'their' money. She couldn't wait to find out what he had to say to *that* one.

'Oh, er . . . I had to borrow some of it.' He wriggled a bit and looked more sheepish than a freezer full of mutton on an Australian farm.

'Did you? What was that for?' Plastic smile again, but the urge to wring his neck was getting pretty strong too.

'Petrol and stuff in Scotland. I'll pay it back. Obviously. Emergency.' He actually had the good grace to go red now.

'Oh, yes, okay. If you could, considering what it was for.'

'Absolutely, straight away.'

Stevie nodded, although she had heard that one just a few times too often from him to believe it any more.

'Well, right then,' she carried on, leashing her anger

with desperate effort. She had to be in control, their future happiness together depended on it. This, after all, was a much wider picture than a lost fifteen hundred quid and a couple of lust-driven lies.

'I'll go and get a few bits together then,' he said nervously, edging upstairs.

'Yes, why not.' The smile weighed heavy and was getting painful to keep up. She wanted to let it drop, right onto the floor where she could stamp it flat and vomit all over it.

Matthew backed off upstairs and at least she took some comfort from the fact that she had rattled him with her coolness and self-possession. She had done something right at least. This time.

She could hear him padding about upstairs, opening drawers, and she followed him in her imagination. He would pack that beautiful blue silk shirt, and the chinos that always made his bottom look nice, and his best suit so he could take Jo out for a posh meal somewhere. He liked to wine and dine, and he always looked so handsome in a suit, especially by candlelight.

She found she was not quite strong enough to hold all the tears back. They started to leak out of the corners of her eyes, faster than she could wipe them away, but wipe them away she did as soon as she heard his footsteps coming down the stairs, faster than a small child's on Christmas morning. Then he crossed to the drawer and got out his mobile phone. He had left it there deliberately, of course, she knew, but she didn't react.

'Look, I'll be in touch soon, promise,' he said, carrying a very large case and some suits in covers.

'Yes, well, you take care,' she said. She needed three big lads and some scaffolding now to hold up this smile. She came forward and hugged him and tried to let go first – it was *basic psychology* that the one in control always did that – and she *just* managed it, but she had to fight back the urge to hang onto him for ever.

'Goodbye, Stevie. Give my love to little Danny.'

'I will,' she said, thinking how final 'goodbye' sounded. Why hadn't he just said 'bye'? There was a difference. Then he was gone, without one glance of recognition that she had had her hair done or was half a stone lighter.

She didn't wave his car off, she just sat on the sofa and let that infernal smile drop into a reverse of itself – a deep, downward arc. Then, when she could no longer hear the sound of his engine, she let her head fall into her hands and sobbed her heart out.

Chapter 12

Matthew had worn a path into the carpet by the time he heard the footsteps creak up the staircase outside the hotel room. He checked his watch for the eighteenth million time – *six minutes to six and six seconds* – threw open the door before the soft knock had ended and fell upon a wide-eyed Jo.

'I was so worried!' he said, taking her in his arms. He had his mobile in his hand, ready to ring the police. It had been a close call.

'Sorry,' she said, sniffling. 'He was there. It was pretty gruelling.'

He pulled her away from him and studied her, looking for signs of violence but thankfully there was nothing, only pale lines on her face where tears had cut through her make-up. Then again, MacLean didn't hit her where it showed, did he?

'Are you okay? He didn't—?'

'No,' Jo said, snuggling further into him to take his warmth and comfort. 'Not really.'

'What do you mean, "not really", darling?' said Matthew, rearing a little.

'Well, at least I got away. Let's just say, he started getting a bit rough.'

She winced as his hands fell on her shoulder and she let him gently unbutton the top of her shirt to find small deep fingernail-shaped crescents on her shoulder, and bruising already forming around them.

'The swine! I'm getting the police.'

Matthew pulled out his mobile, but Jo stilled his hand.

'No,' she said. 'It's over. I don't want any more police. I've seen too many of them in the past. I don't want to file another report. Nothing ever comes of it anyway, except he gets more annoyed. Please, darling. Let's just get on with the rest of our lives now. I'm free of him.'

She looked at him with her heavily fringed dark treacle eyes glistening with tears and he relented.

'Oh baby!' He squeezed her tight and then let go temporarily when someone else knocked on the door. Matthew opened it to find three porters standing there with six massive suitcases. 'Wow!' he said.

'It'll be a relief to get them over to your house,' Jo said, adding pointedly, 'sooner rather than later.'

'Stevie is going to move out as soon as she can,' said Matthew.

'How was she? Upset?'

'No, actually,' said Matthew, shaking his head, as if he didn't quite believe it himself. 'She was . . . er . . . very understanding. Very understanding indeed.'

He thought back again to how calmly she had smiled goodbye. She hadn't even blown her top when she found out he'd ransacked the joint account, considering he had only put fifty quid in it towards the holiday in the first place. Had he looked at Jo at that moment, he would have seen something cross her face like a cloud. A cloud that was full of the grey shades of confusion that said, 'Now *that is odd* . . .'

The scent of Jo's hair chased the image of Stevie away and Matthew found himself looking forward to the night, instead of backwards at the afternoon. Still, it niggled him that something wasn't quite as it should be, and Stevie ranting and raving would have unsettled him far less than her smiling at him.

Chapter 13

Eddie walked in from work and straightaway asked his wife,

'So, how did Stevie get on with Buggerlugs today?'

'Don't ask,' said Catherine, giving him her customary peck. They had kissed each other hello and goodbye for eighteen years now and saw no reason to ever break the habit. 'Apparently Matt came in, packed a bag and sodded straight off.'

'Never! Where's he gone?'

'To a B&B,' she said. 'He didn't give her the name of it. Told her he wanted a bit of space before the wedding.'

'The wedding? Still on then, is it?' Eddie shook his head. 'Blimey.'

'He's moved out for a few days.'

'Just a few days?'

'Until Stevie moves out.'

'What?'

'He wants her out.'

'Eh?'

'I couldn't have put it better myself, babe,' said Catherine, who was wondering when the Doppelgänger had taken over Matthew's soul because this was so not like the nice guy she knew. He was everything Mick wasn't, so why was he acting just as idiotically as him? Had it been anyone else but Matthew, Catherine would have advised her friend to get out and draw a line under it all without so much as a backward glance, but Matt was a great bloke – steady and quiet, well, at least he had been before he went batty. He was fond of Danny too, and that was something of paramount importance to Stevie.

'What's she going to do?' asked Eddie, stripping off his orange skip-deliverer's tunic. He was a plasterer by trade but he'd done a day here and there helping out his old friend Tom Broom in refuse and recycling since they had left school. Tom made even big Eddie look like a midget but he was a really sound bloke. Like Matt used to be.

'She hasn't a bloody clue,' said Catherine.

'Well, you'd better ring your Auntie Madge and tell her that Stevie won't be going to Pam's wedding on Saturday.'

'I'm doing nothing of the sort,' said Catherine. 'Stevie's going and that's that. It'll do her good.'

'Nay, Cath . . .'

'Eddie, apart from the fact that Pam would kill her if she didn't go, I've told Steve that she needs to be seen enjoying herself and getting on with life, not moping about. That's not going to attract Matt back to her, is it?'

Pam was Catherine's rather formidable cousin. She was getting married to William, the really nice guy who ran Gym Village, and they had all been invited. The tartan-ribboned invitation was on Catherine's pin-board in the kitchen, as it was in Stevie's; her own and Matthew's names on it bracketed together as a still-present couple. The groom was a native Scot and getting married in full tartan regalia, and it promised to be a jolly affair.

Eddie scratched his head. It was all harder to understand than a David Lynch film.

'What if Matt goes and takes that Joanna? Have you thought about how that would make Stevie feel?'

'Don't be daft, he wouldn't dare! And even if he did think about bringing her, she wouldn't be that iron-faced as to come. Besides, I reminded Stevie how she'd promised Danny that he could stay at ours that night with Kate. She wouldn't dream of letting him down.'

Kate, who loved the little boy to bits and pieces, and was adored in return, had volunteered to babysit him, along with her other brothers and sisters. Volunteered after being offered a lump sum, that was. Danny was going to top and tail in little Gareth's pirate-ship bed and he'd had his Mr Incredibles bag packed for a fortnight waiting for it.

'That's below the belt,' said Eddie, wincing.

'I know, I'm a total witch,' said Catherine with a very self-satisfied grin. 'But it worked. She's going. I'll ring Auntie Madge and get her to jiggle the seating arrangements a bit though.'

'Cath,' said Eddie kindly, 'are you sure it's the right thing for her?'

'Sure as eggs are eggs,' said Catherine. 'Think about it. If Matt had truly known what he was doing, he would have cancelled the wedding. He'll come to his senses, I'm totally convinced of it. He'll be holed up in a grotty B&B wrestling with his conscience and having a last-minute commitment panic. Soon as he sees that Stevie is fine without him, he'll want her back.'

'And where's this Jo then?' said Eddie. 'Has she gone back to her husband or what?'

'My guess is that she did. I tried to get Stevie to ring MacLean to find out, but she wouldn't. Do you think I should?'

'No, I bloody well don't,' said Eddie. Much as he loved his wife, it niggled him sometimes that she always thought she knew better than anyone else. He had a feeling that one day she was going to get it so very wrong. Or maybe, by getting Stevie and Matt together in the first place, she already had.

Chapter 14

Adam MacLean spotted Stevie on the weights. She had her headphones on and was watching the television screen. Now which channel would she be tuned into? he mused. Sky News? The Music Channel? Or *Morning Coffee* with Drusilla Durham and that smarmy Gerald 'The Man' Mandelton bloke talking about cakes?

He wondered how the day before last had gone at her end, when Matty Boy returned home. Not too well, if her serious, pale face was anything to go by. If only the daft woman had listened to him, this stupid business might all have been over and done with now. No doubt she had shouted at Finch, pleaded with him, screamed, cried, and embarrassed him back to his Jo faster than if he was Sir Roger Bannister and his backside was on fire. How *not* to win your spouse back in one easy lesson.

He could see that her teeth were gritted as she tackled far bigger weights than were on her toning programme. He should have gone over and told her she needed to do more reps on smaller weights, otherwise she would end up like a miniature Hulk Hogan, but he sent Hilary over instead because he would not have been able to resist asking how things were and she, no doubt, would have replied with some cocky remark that made him even more disgruntled than he was already.

The seven nights in bed without Jo's body beside him were hard enough, but the last two had hurt more than all of them put together, knowing all her wardrobes were empty and her jewellery and toiletries and make-up were gone from cupboards and drawers. Poignantly, she had left her long, pink toothbrush behind. It leaned against his own in the glass.

He knew he had played it like a master when she walked through the door looking beautiful and tanned and glowing and telling him how wet Wales was. Like he had tried to say to Mrs Universe over there – *basic psychology*. Jo had been shaking when she left him, and even though she had gone out of his door with her suitcases, climbed in her car and driven off – no doubt to the arms of her lover – he would have bet his own car on the fact that Round 1 had been to him.

'Mummy, is "happily" an adverb?'

'Yes, it is, love,' said Stevie, changing his wet pyjama top. Now his Superman short bottoms were teamed up with a Shrek T-shirt, 'as in "Danny Honeywell chews his pyjama collar *happily*".'

'Sorry, mummy,' said Danny.

'It's okay.'

'Can I wear my Dannyman top instead?'

'It's in the wash, pet.'

'Mummy?'

'Yes, Danny?'

'Where's Matthew?'

'Weeelll . . .' she began, then realized she hadn't a clue how she was going to answer that, or even if she could because her voice felt as if it would be too wobbly to deliver the words, if she opened up her mouth. She wasn't quite sure where tears came from, but they seemed to be taking a fast-speed train up to her eyes these days, and the pressure of holding them back physically hurt.

'He's just living somewhere else for a while and we're going to live somewhere else for a while,' she said, trying to make it sound like a jolly adventure.

She knew this wouldn't be enough to satisfy his inquis-itive little mind though and, sure enough, four seconds later he asked, 'Why?'

'Because that's what grown-ups do sometimes.'

'Why?'

Oh farts!

'Because they sometimes live apart to see if they miss each other. You see, when they get married, they want to make sure they live happily ever after.'

'"Happily" is an adverb, isn't it?'

'Yes, Danny,' said Stevie, seizing him and putting him on her knee and cuddling him tightly. 'Yes, "happily" is an adverb.'

She put him to bed after reading him *The Useless Troll* yet again. He knew what the ending was and still delighted in hearing the gruesome 'sting'. Stevie wished she knew what the ending to her story was, and whether it was one she could look forward to with as much enthusiasm, although she also hoped her ending would be less hideous. Then again, with her luck, it would probably be worse.

Admittedly, she had not done a thing as regards finding somewhere else to live. The thought of leaving Matt's house was awful, but she knew she must – and soon. It would be far better, she supposed, to play the game and make all the necessary arrangements and then have to cancel them at the eleventh hour when Matthew came to his senses than dither and risk Danny and her being thrown forcibly out. That wouldn't exactly help any future reconciliation plans.

It had been Matthew who had badgered her to move in with him, with the 'two could live as cheaply as one' philosophy, although she had ended up paying most of the bills and the mortgage since she'd been there. She had even cleared a few of his arrears, thanks to a nice profit from the sale of her old house. She had also recently paid for her own wedding dress, Matthew's wedding suit (which cost more than her whole outfit, accessories included), Catherine's bridesmaid dress, Danny's pageboy outfit, the rings and the deposits on the reception, flowers and honeymoon. At least the money for the balances was safe in her own account, thank goodness.

Matthew's plans to contribute were tightly bound up in procrastinations, not that she minded because life with someone was about sharing, wasn't it? After Mick, she had thought she would never trust anyone enough again to unlock the door to her heart and throw it open. Until Matthew. Maybe she should have realized she wasn't destined for happiness and that keeping the chain on might have been a safer option.

So Stevie settled down with a coffee and the *Properties* section of the local newspaper. Buying somewhere wasn't an option at this stage, just in case Matthew came to his senses and asked her to come back, so, as far as rental accommodation went, it had to be somewhere nearby for Danny's school, which ruled out most of the houses available. Of those that were geographically suitable, one was a seven-bedroomed barn conversion and the other a one-bedroomed flat in an infamous drug-riddled street. Of course, the cottage across the lane was featured, as always, but the bond alone was enough to have most people voicing the message to the landlord, 'Hope the sun shines for yer, mate!'

Stevie made a mental note to ring some estate agents very soon, but the thought filled her with dread and she knew she was stalling, waiting for a miracle to rescue her. The miracle that was, unbeknown to her then, just around the corner.

Chapter 15

Jo was drying her hair at the dressing-table after a dribbling shower. Matthew watched her fondly, the expression of a love-struck Labrador pup on his face.

'What's the matter?' she said, catching his eye.

'Nothing, I'm just looking at you.'

'Well, stop it,' she said, and carried on wafting the hairdryer and trying to pretend that she wasn't being scrutinized quite so thoroughly.

Coming up behind her, he planted a kiss on her neck.

'Not now,' she said, wriggling away. 'I'm late for work.'

'*We're* late for work,' he said, 'but at least we can occupy a car-sharing parking space. They're always in plentiful supply.'

'Great,' said Jo sarcastically, which made his little Tigger bouncing heart deflate a little.

'You okay?' he said.

'Well, no actually,' she said, winding the cord around the hairdryer as if she was wrapping it around someone's neck. 'I don't enjoy living out of a suitcase one bit. I just want to move into your house as soon as possible.'

'I know it's hard, sweetie,' said Matthew sympathetically

because he recognized that it was a lot easier for a bloke living in a hotel room than a girl with all her essential accoutrements. 'We'll be in there soon enough.'

'How soon is "soon"?'

'Well, I have to give Stevie a few days at least.'

'Of course,' said Jo, putting down the hairdryer and coming over for a snuggle. 'I'm sorry, I'm being selfish even asking. Forgive me, it's just that if I think too much about Stevie, I'll start to feel awful. I know she didn't deserve what we did to her and that's what makes this so hard. I betrayed my friendship with her to get you, and the awful thing is that I would do it all over again if I had to. It doesn't make me feel very good about myself. Sorry. This must be a terrible time for Stevie. I've been trying to think of what we could do to make all this easier for her.'

Matthew's arms closed around her tightly. Building a relationship on the ruins of another wasn't what either of them had wanted, but it had happened. The whole Stevie thing had brought tears to Jo's eyes many times, because neither of them were the sort of sick people who went around hurting others for fun. It was just that when love like this called, you didn't hide and pretend you were out, you flung open the door, invited it right on in to sit in your most comfortable chair and fed it your best tin of biscuits.

Jo sighed and rubbed the back of her long, swan-like neck.

'I'm so stressed out. I'm waiting for Adam's next move and I just want to be safe in your house with you rather than in some place where he could easily get to me if he wanted.'

'I understand,' he said, rubbing her shoulders and making her purr. 'I'll ring her later and push her along a bit.'

'What if she starts playing "not answering the phone" games?'

'Then I'll call round,' although he didn't want to.

'Maybe she'll be at the wedding tomorrow – you can ask her outright then.'

'The wedding?'

'Yes. Will and Pam's wedding,' said Jo.

'You are joking. I can't go to that now!' said Matthew, shaking his head.

'Whyever not?'

'Well, they're more Stevie's and your ex's friends than mine and yours for a start.'

'Don't be silly,' said Jo. 'I'm sure you and I were invited on our own merits and not just as "plus ones". Don't put yourself down like that. You knew Will from the gym, didn't you, before you even met Stevie. And I've met Pam and Will a couple of times and got on very well with them.'

'Well, I suppose,' conceded Matthew weakly.

'Plus I've bought a new suit I have every intention of wearing.'

He didn't look convinced so she came at him from another angle.

'Matthew, the sooner Stevie sees us as a couple, the sooner she'll realize it's over for you and her. She has to know.'

'Stevie won't go to the wedding. I'd put my life savings on her not going after all that's happened.'

He knew Stevie too well. She wouldn't want to face the

world at the moment. At least he hoped he was right, because he didn't want her turning up, going all Glenn Close, and making a scene.

'So, what's the problem?'

'Well, I'm thinking about Adam.'

'Matthew,' began Jo with a dry laugh. 'I have no intention of hiding away. I'm not the one that wrecked my relationship – I've got nothing to be ashamed of.'

'We don't have to go. I'm sure we wouldn't be missed if we didn't turn up. You and I could do something special together instead.'

'People have to know some time that we're an item, Matthew! Stevie will be far less hurt thinking tomorrow is our starting-point. We're both free agents now, aren't we? No one can say it's wrong for us to be a couple now.'

'Well . . . er . . .' started Matthew, who hadn't actually spelt it out to Stevie yet that he wasn't coming back, but Jo wasn't listening. Her brain had run on ahead.

'It's fairer on Stevie in the long run. Okay, it won't be very nice for her at the beginning, but as soon as she knows you have found someone else, the healing process will kick in for her.'

Matthew was more worried about what MacLean would 'kick in' when he heard that someone was moving in on his wife.

'Trust me, Adam will be less "upset",' said Jo, loading the word with meaning, 'to see us getting respectably together in front of him tomorrow than poking around to discover we've been having an affair behind his back for the past few months.'

'What if there's a fight?' said Matthew, thinking about his skull and Adam's fist connecting with it.

'Darling, William's family won't let anyone ruin his wedding day. If Adam starts any trouble at all then he'll be out on his ear. As for Stevie, well, I've been thinking, maybe we could find her somewhere ourselves. I've seen some lovely rentals out in Penistone.' She nibbled his ear on the final 'nnn'.

'Aaahhh! I think she'll want to stay in the area,' said Matthew. 'Danny's school and all that. But that is so kind of you for looking.'

'Come on, it's the least I could do. She's a nice person and little Danny is sweet too,' said Jo, and she smiled up at him through her long mascara-ed eyelashes. His legs felt weak, as if someone had taken all the bones out and replaced them with a Birds trifle.

'Look, let's talk about it on the way to work,' he said, kissing the tip of her little pointy nose. He picked up her briefcase for her and they walked out into the corridor to find the lift out of order and the prospect for Jo of four flights of steps in very high stilettos.

'Bloody hotel!' she said. 'How much did you say you were paying for this per night?'

'Don't ask,' he sighed, following her fuming passage down the stairs. He was just at the top of the second flight when he realized what she had actually said:

'How much did you say you were paying?'

Chapter 16

The day of the wedding dawned. Danny woke up with a heart full of excitement for the hours to come. In the next bedroom, Stevie woke up with a heart full of dread for the hours to come. The day could take so many possible forms:

1) Matthew doesn't turn up
2) Matthew turns up and ignores her
3) Matthew turns up with Joanna
4) Matthew turns up with Joanna and announces his engagement
5) Adam MacLean murders everyone

None of them was especially good.

Eddie bee-beeped outside at half past eleven and Danny moved as fast as if he had a nuclear rocket secreted down the back of his pants.

'Mummy, it's Uncle Eddie, it's Uncle Eddie!'

'Never!' said Stevie, smiling at his jubilation, which trebled when he looked out of the window and saw Boot's massive and ugly profile in the back seat.

'Mummy, Boot's here! Quick!'

'They aren't going to drive off and leave you, Danny. Hang on, let me get some shoes on.'

'Come on,' he urged, dancing around like Michael Flatley with a bladder problem. Eddie wolf-whistled when Stevie came out to the car in her very long rainbow-striped dressing-gown and a pair of trainers.

'Oh, get stuffed!' said Stevie, knowing she was hardly wolf-whistley material in this, or at all. Only blind, insane or desperate builders from high-up scaffolding had ever whistled to her, and that was usually because of her generously proportioned chest.

'Stevie, what the bloody hell have you done to your conk?'

Stevie's hand shot up to her still-tender nose in horror. 'I fell at the gym. Oh God, can you see it? Is it really noticeable?'

Eddie waved it away with a flap of his hand. 'No, is it heck. Slap a bit of make-up on it, nobody'll notice.'

'I did that already.'

'Oh, sorry,' said Eddie, twisting round to the little boy as a means of escape. 'Ready, Sunshine?' Danny had already clambered in the back and was fighting off a very licky Boot.

'Boot!' reprimanded Eddie. 'Get down!' Boot immediately lay down with his chin on Danny's lap and the little boy's face registered heaven as he stroked the big black head that looked as if it should be guarding a gateway into hell somewhere. It was part of a scenario Stevie had wished for him so many times: brothers and sisters, a house full of rough and tumble, everyone piling in a people-carrier with a big sloppy dog and a big sloppy dad. Except that it wasn't her kids or his big sloppy dog or his big sloppy dad but those of her best friend.

'Oy you, cheer up,' said Eddie, seeing the shadow of sadness suddenly cross Stevie's features. He reached through the window, took her hand and squeezed it in his bear-like paw. 'We'll look after you today and we're going to have a great time, and no one will notice your conk because the rest of you will be so gorgeous.'

He meant well.

'You wearing a kilt then?' asked Stevie, clicking on a smile.

'Get lost!' said Eddie. 'I don't want women lusting after my legs.'

Stevie laughed. 'See you at one outside the church then.' She rapped on the window to Danny and said, 'You be good!'

'Ah, he's always good,' said Eddie. 'He's a cracker like his mam.'

She blew them all a kiss and then went inside the house in the hope of making herself look the cracker of all crackers. Just for once.

'Well, this is as good as it gets,' she said to her reflection an hour later, which nodded back its approval. She had lost weight since she tried the red suit on in the shop; it fitted her not so snugly and the cut made her waist nip in nicely. Offset with slim black patent heels, a matching bag and a large-brimmed red and black hat, she looked okay, if she said so herself. An extra blob of foundation almost covered up the scab on the bridge of her nose and took some of the bluish hue of the bruise away. The taxi pipped outside and she quickly grabbed the wedding present and locked up the front door on her way out to get it.

'Saint Peter and All Angels,' she said, just as the text message came through from Catherine to say they had just arrived and were waiting outside for her. *No sign of x + x*, was how the message ended, which was good, if it lasted.

It was a beautiful day for a wedding, sunny and no wind to blow hats off and skirts up, Marilyn Monroe style. The bells were pealing from the pretty little Maltstone village church where Catherine, resplendent in navy blue and a very gorgeous cloche hat, and Eddie in a dark grey suit and a tartan tie, were waiting for her outside as promised.

'Oooh, lady in red, you look swanky,' said Eddie, coming forward and giving her a little kiss.

'So do you, kind sir,' said Stevie, although even if Eddie had been wearing Armani he wouldn't have managed to lose that 'I hate suits' look. His hair, as usual, refused to play ball, sticking up at all angles and making him look like a mad uncle with a secret laboratory.

'Stevie, you look lovely,' said Catherine, giving her a cheek peck and a little squeeze. Then her smile dropped. 'What on earth happened to your nose?'

'Oh hell,' said Stevie, covering it up with her hand. 'I fell in the gym. On the flaming treadmill. Guess who helped me up.'

'Ouch!' said Catherine, who didn't have to guess. 'Bet that hurt more than the injury. I think you have to be the most accident-prone person I know, Steve.'

'Idiotically clumsy, you mean.'

'No, I don't mean that at all. Look, the nose thing isn't really noticeable – I'm sorry I mentioned it,' said Catherine, trying quickly to mend the fast-growing hole in Stevie's composure. 'It's only because I stared at you from point-blank range. Your hat throws it right into shadow . . .'

'Shut up about her beak,' said Eddie. 'Between the pair of us we'll have her running off over the gravestones like Zola Budd! Come on, let's get inside where it's dark and no one can see anyone's nose,' and he presented his arms to both ladies and led them down the church path. It made a change from being led down the garden path, thought Stevie with grim humour.

They were so busy talking in the queue for hymnbooks that neither woman noticed him at first. It was only when it was Stevie's turn and the distinctive voice said, 'Brrride or Grrroom?' that she jumped and took a long sweep upwards from the big hairy legs appearing out of the bottom of a heavily sporraned kilt to the mashed but surprisingly cleanshaven face, and then further on to a very, very cropped hairdo.

As if he hadn't looked hard enough before. Even his name sounded full of testosterone. He was probably going to start smashing bottles on his teeth in a minute.

'Pardon?'

'Brrride or Grrroom?'

He even managed to make that sound threatening. As if she was in a Belfast pub and he was asking 'Catholic or Protestant' and any answer would result in a kneecapping.

'Broom,' said Stevie, swallowing.

'She means "bride",' said Catherine, coming to her rescue.

'All three of us are,' continued Stevie, making it sound as if they were a united force. Like Charlie's Angels.

'Right, that side there then,' he said, pointing left, and handed over three hymnbooks and order of services.

'Thank you, so kind,' said Stevie, sounding like her Auntie Rita who had been a bit of a slapper, by all accounts, until she married Uncle Reg, who was a barrister, and overnight became all posh and correct.

Catherine and Eddie twittered on in the background as she filled him in on who that was. They filed down to the middle of the church, Catherine first, Eddie in the middle and Stevie on the end.

'What's he doing here?' Stevie asked finally.

'Haven't a clue. He must know William. Oy, Steve, did you see his legs?' asked Catherine in a whisper that seemed to echo all the way up to the altar.

'Shhh!' said Eddie, which echoed as much.

'I thought he'd got furry oak trees under his kilt,' said Catherine, snorting from the effort of trying to keep the laughter in.

'Where's his hair gone?' said Stevie, wondering if there was a connection with its absence and the break-up of his marriage. Some bizarre Scottish ritual, perhaps.

'He's stuck it on his legs, I think,' said Catherine, having a major fit of giggles under her hat.

'Will you two be quiet!' said Eddie like a teacher on a school trip, although even he had a good look when usher-time was at an end and Madman strutted down the aisle to take up his seat on the groom's side. He was obviously trying to get his physical house in order, thought Stevie. Ah well, better late than never. Surely, he must have realized before that he wasn't anywhere near Jo's equal in the looks stakes, not compared to someone as handsome as Matthew. It pained her to think how stunning a couple Matt and *she* would make, with their matching dark hair and brown eyes and long legs, and treacherous hearts.

'Big lad, isn't he?' said Eddie. 'Wouldn't want to be on the wrong side of him.'

'Like me, you mean,' said Stevie, who then had to shut up because the organ started playing the first notes to 'Here Comes the Bride' and Pam swaggered down the aisle in a fishtail white velvet dress, her hair piled up on her head with white flowers in it and a light furry cape dressing her shoulders. She was a big lass and a meringue frock would have looked 'a bugger', as she had so delicately put it, but in that get-up she looked gorgeous and sexy as she walked down the aisle on her dad's arm – uber-slowly because he'd had a stroke and walked with a stick. Pam didn't care about the pace, though; it just gave her maximum opportunity to milk that last journey as a single chick and more time to wave and wink and smile at her friends and relatives, in her own unique Pammy way.

'Dearly beloved . . .' began the vicar and Stevie gulped. It was exactly four weeks to her own wedding and she hadn't a clue if it was still on the cards. Her head was clinging onto the possibility that it was, but a very strong and sensible voice within was telling her that she needed to wake up and smell some very strong espresso.

She managed to get through miming to 'Love Divine', which was pitched for either Barry White or Aled Jones in his *Snowman* days and no one in between. At least she had licence to dab her eyes at the readings then burst into full Teardrop City with everyone else as Pam and William sauntered back up the aisle as husband and wife, smiles bursting their faces open. There were no bridesmaids. Pam didn't want anyone more glam than her stealing her thunder. Not that they would have been able to out-do Pam's huge personality – and her huge everything else. And little, tiny, skinny William adored her. You could tell by his face during the ceremony that he could not believe his luck. No one, not even Matthew, had ever looked at Stevie with such intensity of feeling. *And no one ever will*, said a nasty little voice in her head that appeared to have a Scottish accent.

So, in the absence of bridesmaids, the best man linked up with Madge, Pam's mum, William's doll-like mum linked up behind with Adam MacLean, and Pam's dad walked out at a more leisurely pace with his own mother. Stevie noticed MacLean flash her a look and she flashed one back as hard. They both transmitted 'what the hell are you doing here?' in international eye language. Then, as if that wasn't enough to contend with, the first person she saw as she followed the others outside for the photos was Matthew. The plus point was that Jo wasn't with him. The minus point was that he had the suit on that he was supposed to be wearing for his wedding to her.

'Oh shit!' said Catherine. 'Have you seen who's over there?'

'Yes, I've just seen him,' said Stevie, suddenly feeling quite nauseous and light-headed.

'No, not him.'

'What?'

Catherine did a discreet stabby point and Stevie followed it to see Jo there, in a black suit with red accessories, looking tall and slim and stunning. Stevie was thrown into total shock, and pins and needles prickled at her limbs. She wanted to run across the graveyard and go home. No, she didn't, she wanted to charge at Jo with her head down like a bull and start clubbing her to death with an urn.

'Keep calm,' said Catherine, tapping her lightly on the arm. 'You're the one that hasn't done anything wrong. Let them be the ones to make fools of themselves.'

'She obviously hasn't gone back to MacLean then, so that answers that one,' said Stevie. 'Then again, why are she and Matthew ignoring each other?' She should have felt heartened by this but something was interfering with her ability to do that. Jo was, after all, a designer and this scene was looking distinctly designed.

'They're probably trying not to incur the wrath of the hairy-legged one,' said Catherine.

Stevie watched as Adam's eyes fell on Matthew and stayed there for a long, long second. His body locked like a Rottweiler's before an attack, then he snapped out of it quickly to be pulled into a smiling photographic tableau. Then, as a natural consequence of seeing Matthew, he looked around for Jo. He found her, he stared, he swallowed and then was once again part of the happy wedding scene.

This must be as hard for him as it is for me, thought Stevie, recognizing that blanched, brave look.

She let her eyes casually drift over to Matthew, who pretended that was the first he had seen of her and, how she managed it she didn't know, but she waved genially and smiled like the Queen, and then carried on eye-flitting, as if she was merely perusing the crowd. Jo's red and blackness was harder to deal with. Stevie couldn't bring herself even to glance in that direction so it was wiser to pretend Jo wasn't there. Her suit seemed to keep creeping into Stevie's peripheral vision though, and she had to keep constantly finding places for her eyes to rest away from Jo and Matthew and MacLean. It was exhausting.

'Last photo – group shot of friends!' announced the photographer, about three million years later, when all the old people were starting to ask loudly, 'How much longer before we sit down and have something to eat?'

Oh God, thought Stevie as all the people in her worst nightmare seemed to converge onto the lawn. Catherine protectively dragged Stevie between herself and Eddie and moved forward into the throng. Jo was posing at the other end, Matthew was in the middle and Adam was nowhere to be seen, which meant he was probably somewhere behind her.

'That's one for the album – not,' said Catherine wryly, giving her a nudge.

'Right, has everyone got lifts back to the Ivy?' enquired big Adam MacLean in full duty mode. He didn't have to shout to be heard. His voice showed up on the Richter scale between the San Francisco earthquake and a Def Leppard concert.

'We haven't,' replied Eddie, who had left the car at home so they could all have a drink. He hadn't said it that loudly, but it appeared that Adam also had the ears of a bat (as well as the face of a bashed crab, thought Stevie with a smirk) and he expertly organized them into a car with William's ancient Uncle Dennis. Stevie took a sly look over at Matthew, who appeared to be making a pretence of saying, 'Hi,' to Jo and asking her if she had a lift, if the extravagant hand gestures towards the church car park were anything to go by. It was like watching someone conduct something complicated by Rimsky-Korsakov.

'There, that wasn't too bad, was it?' said Eddie as they were crammed together in the back of a treasured old car that belonged in a museum, driven by someone who belonged in the same place.

'What?' said Catherine. 'Are you thick? If she'd shook any more, her blood would have turned to yogurt.'

'I think I might skip the reception and go home,' said Stevie, who felt nauseous, something that couldn't be blamed on Uncle Dennis's wild driving. Tortoises and snails were overtaking them on both sides.

'No chance,' said Catherine. 'You're doing great. Think of "your plan".'

'Did he look at me at all?' asked Stevie, thinking how the last time she had asked Catherine that, was at the sixth-form disco about the cool and gorgeous Oliver Thompson, resplendent in a burgundy jacket and black trousers. She had gone totally off him twenty minutes later, after finding him dancing like a nerd to 'Are Friends Electric'. Ah, the fickleness of youth!

'I honestly don't know,' said Catherine. 'I was trying not to look at him.'

Behind her back, Catherine's fingers were crossed on the lie. She did not tell her friend that on the couple of occasions she had looked over, Matthew seemed only to have eyes for Jo. It was all she could do not to march over there and bang their heads together.

Alas, the Ivy wasn't *the* Ivy, but it was a very nice country hotel less than a mile away, with a small golf range and a rather magnificent entrance hall, where trays of sherry and malt whisky were awaiting. Stevie's hand was shaking so much that she managed to spill most of her sherry down her skirt. She did a quick sweep of the room to make sure no one of importance had seen her be so clumsy.

'Calm down,' reprimanded Catherine. 'You look like you've got the DTs.'

Adam was laughing, circulating and being jolly Ginger Man. He looked totally different with all that hair off, thought Stevie. She wouldn't have said 'softer', because no one with that nose and scar could have looked remotely soft. 'Less hideous', was the assessment she preferred.

Jo and Matthew were at opposite ends of the room. She was talking to some other women, poised and elegant and not spilling her sherry. Matthew was chatting to the best man. Stevie tried really hard not to look over but her eyes kept gravitating towards him. She noticed that he was trying equally hard not to let his eyes wander over to Jo, but, like herself, he was failing.

'Hi there!' Pam burst in and kissed them all. She had a champagne glass in one hand and a long menthol cigarette in the other.

'Congratulations,' said Stevie. 'You look fab.'

'So do you actually, Stevie. Have you lost weight?'

'A bit,' said Stevie.

'Sorry to hear about you, hon, hope it all works out for you.'

'Oh er, yes. Don't worry,' said Stevie, plastering on a smile and manipulating a change in subject. 'So, where do we put your presents? I hope you like this.'

'God knows, me mam's got that bit organized. Course I'll like it. I'd like it even more if it were a pair of slippers. I tell you, my pissing feet are killing me in these shoes. Don't know how I'm going to manage to dance.'

Pam, the less than traditional bride, then swanned off with a 'see ya later' on her massive satin heels and left them standing in a quiet triangle.

'Sorry, but I had to tell her about you and Matthew,' said Catherine with a little apologetic smile. 'I didn't think you'd want to be sitting next to him if he turned up, so I asked my Auntie Madge to alter the seating plan.'

'I would never have thought of that,' said Stevie. Sitting next to Matthew would have been torture. She squeezed Catherine's hand gratefully. 'Thanks.' It was so typical of her thoughtfulness; no wonder they'd been friends for so long. You would always want to hang onto someone like her.

'You need to sort this wedding thing out with him, quick,' Catherine went on. 'I don't want to upset you and so I won't say anything else, but in the next few days you have to find out where you stand.'

'I know,' said Stevie.

'I'd chuffing cancel it if I were you,' said Eddie, taking a big glug of the Barnsley Bitter he'd had to buy because Catherine had nicked his sherry to give to Stevie. 'He's definitely not the bloke I thought he was at all.'

No one answered him, but, yes, they were all thinking the same.

'Laydeees and gelmen, would ye kindly make yer way tae the dinen arearrr,' came Adam MacLean's cannon of a voice.

'If he's doing a speech after, no one will understand a flaming word,' said Catherine, giving Stevie a little tension-busting giggle.

They looked at the seating plan and Stevie found that she was sandwiched between Eddie and *Oh no – A. MacLean!* Luckily, her mind was playing tricks on her and it was actually A. MacLeod, who was a young spaghetti-string of a teenage boy who kept pulling at his collar as if it was strangling him.

Matthew was somewhere further down the table on her side and out of spying sight and Jo was halfway down an adjacent table, between two middle-aged men in kilts who seemed more than happy with the seating arrangements. She certainly didn't look very victimy, considering she was sitting five people away from her psychotic soon-to-be ex-husband, who was behaving with remarkable dignity in the circumstances, Stevie thought. He actually seemed very jocular. She didn't notice him glance over at Jo once, and by crikey, she was watching for it.

'Stop looking at them,' hissed Catherine. 'I would kick you but I'd snag your tights.'

'Sorry,' said Stevie, and tucked into her turkey main course. It was a full-blown Christmas dinner. Pam had wanted a Christmas wedding, hence the fur cape, but she didn't want to risk the weather, so she had the best of both worlds – sunshine and turkey, except for the lone vegetarian kid to her right, pushing a nut roast around on his plate. She had never seen an unhealthier-looking pallor on anyone. She almost wanted to kidnap him and force-feed him some chops and see if they might turn his own chops a better colour.

There was Christmas pudding and mince pies to follow, then when coffee was served, the newly-weds cut the cake – a massive three-layered chocolate creation that apparently had more rum than butter in it, according to the best man's speech, during which everyone laughed and the air seemed charged with love and smiles.

Stevie's wedding wasn't going to be as big or nearly as grand as this, but her dad was giving her away and she was having frothy pea soup, roast beef and Yorkshire puddings, and raspberry meringue roulade or fudge cake for afters at the White Swan, a lovely pub out in the countryside near Penistone. Matthew's brother was flying in from Canada to be best man and she had picked pink roses for her bouquet. Everything was in place, and so far, he hadn't called it off.

'*So why is he wearing his suit now at someone else's wedding? And looking gorgeous in it for someone else, not you,*' said that annoying voice in her head again. She wished it would contract a serious and sudden case of laryngitis.

Her thoughts came back to the table as glasses were raised to 'the Happy Couple'. Stevie raised hers along with the others and tried hard to smile convincingly. Matthew was sleeping with someone else and she was in the process of moving out of his house. How feasible was it that they were going to be 'the happy couple' themselves in three weeks' time?

There was no ordinary disco for Pam's night entertainment, oh no. She had a Ceilidh band and a dance demonstration team clad in Highland clobber, stripping the willow and reeling about, not unlike Uncle Dennis had started to do after three sherries.

'He'll have to leave his car behind, by the looks of it,' said Catherine, as he fell off his chair without breaking the rhythm of his hand-clapping.

'This is a dance called "Blooo Bunnets"' said a hairy accordion player, who looked like a smaller, 'before' model of Adam MacLean.

'Blue Bonnets? I used to do this at school,' said Eddie.

'You? Doing country dancing?' said Catherine with an amused squeak.

'Aye, I was good an' all. All the lasses wanted me for a partner.'

'Get on up there then, lad.' Catherine pushed him towards the dance floor.

'Knickers! I can't remember how you do it.' He retreated shyly.

'You don't have to – they show you.'

'I'm still not.'

'Go on, you know you want to.'

'Get off, you big bully!'

As Catherine and Eddie continued their giggly fight, Stevie watched as Matthew started to edge slowly towards Jo. It took him another four minutes before they engaged in conversation. Maybe they were pretending to 'get it together' at the wedding, not having a clue that she and Adam MacLean already knew what had been going on between them.

'I see contact has been made,' said Catherine, nodding over at the treacherous twosome.

'Yes, I noticed. I'll bet they're making a show in front of MacLean and me that this is their actual starting-point.'

'The next dance is "The Birds and the Bees",' said Accordion Man. 'Come on, now, let's have you up herrre, laddies and lassies.'

A flurry of sherried-up aunts and uncles hit the floor.

'Looks fun,' said Catherine. 'Do you want a go? Eddie'll partner you.'

'Eddie won't,' said Eddie.

'Where's the bonny bride hersel'?' shouted someone from the demo team and started chanting to get Pam up dancing. 'C'moan, it's good luck tae dance this wan.'

'Right – well, if I'm going to make a twat of myself, then *everyone* is. Come up, get up,' slurred Pam. She stubbed out her fag and then shovelled Eddie and Catherine and Stevie forwards, like a giant snow-plough. Everyone hit the dance floor because Pam had said so.

'Stevie, you can road-test Will for me,' said Pam, shoving her new husband in front of Stevie at the end of the formation. 'Adam, get your Scottish backside over here!'

'I don't know what to do at all,' said Stevie.

Will whispered, 'Join the club, Stevie, but you know what she's like. Just do this one dance then she'll leave you alone, I promise.'

'Now's your chance, big boy, to seduce me with your fancy footwork,' said Catherine, giving her husband a saucy wink.

'Don't blame me if you end up moaning in the morning that you've had no sleep,' said Eddie.

'Oh promises, promises,' said Catherine.

Pam dragged Adam opposite to her and he and Stevie glared at each other diagonally.

'We're a six, we need to be an eight,' said Eddie.

'Hark at Fred Astaire!' said Catherine.

'Oy! We need another two over here!' shouted Pam.

A spare 'two' was pushed over from where it was clinging onto the next 'eight' hoping no one would notice it was superfluous.

'*Oh God,*' said every single one of them, even half-sloshed Pam, as Matthew and Jo took up their awkward positions next to Eddie and Catherine. However long this dance lasted, it was going to be too long.

The demonstrators ran through the sequence. It all looked quite simple in a twizzling-about way. In real life it proved to be slightly more difficult.

Pam cocked up and ended up going the wrong way, taking Will as her partner. This cast Stevie in the path of Adam MacLean, and as Pam barked, 'Never mind, carry on,' Stevie was forced to link his arm and be spun around at G force.

'So, how's yerrr nose?' he asked, as they changed direction. He pointed at it as if she might have forgotten where it was.

'Fine, thank you – and yours?' Stevie asked, not knowing quite why she had asked that. Then again, at that point she was trying to coordinate skipping backwards with not being sick.

'Okay last time I looked,' he said humourlessly, tripping forward and catching her hand. He was surprisingly nifty on his feet for an Aberdeen Angus, Stevie thought.

'So, ready to hear whit I have tae say yet? You don't look as if you're making much progress your way.'

'And you are, I suppose?' said Stevie, quirking her eyebrow.

'Aye, I most certainly am!'

Stevie twirled around him with a little sarcastic, 'Ha!' and followed it with, 'No, thank you. I think I'll pass on this and every other occasion to discuss your "master plan".' Her arm brushed against Jo as she skipped down the back of the formation to meet Matthew. It was like being touched by an electric cattle prod. Stevie jerked to the side, bouncing into Will, and would have fallen over if Adam MacLean hadn't grabbed her elbow. By comparison, Jo's steps were perfect. She and Matthew looked like John Travolta and that Stephanie woman in *Saturday Night Fever* who were so spiritually and bodily synchronized. As if Stevie needed any more proof of how gauche she was by comparison.

Adam cast her off and she did a figure of eight around Pam and then bumped clumsily into Matthew, who stared straight ahead of him in a 'God, get me out of this quick' kind of way. Then Adam caught both of Stevie's hands at the top of the line and trotted down the middle of the other three partners with her. They were huge hands. Hands that smacked women. It made her feel ill to touch him and she tried to pull them away but MacLean hung on firmly.

'So ye're no gonnae listen, I take it?' he grumbled out of the corner of his mouth.

'Not in this lifetime,' panted Stevie.

Adam sneered, like Elvis having a bad day.

'Well, let's hope you're better at ho'ding onto your man than you are at dancing,' he said gruffly as he let Stevie's hands go and relinquished her to Will, who spun her round 'Gay Gordon' style for the last few bars of the reel. As soon as the final chord had sounded, Adam and Jo and Matthew were gone from the dance floor, three people united in their desperate desire to get right away from the lumpy woman with her sherry-stained skirt and scabby nose.

Catherine led her friend gently off into the shadows, leaving her flushed-face, exhilarated husband applauding. He had truly found his dancing legs and was skipping about like Rob Roy with fleas.

'How awful was that?' said Catherine. 'I thought it would never end.'

'Trust Murderous McKilt to be in our group,' said Stevie, all sorts of sad and angry thoughts blasting through her body. 'I didn't expect to end up dancing with him when I set off with Will.'

'Well, you got back with your original partner in the

end,' said Catherine. 'Maybe it's symbolic,' she added, trying to give Stevie a bit of hope, however weak it might sound.

'Maybe,' said Stevie.

Oh poor love, thought Catherine, watching her friend's eyes follow Jo to a quiet table for two in the opposite corner. Matthew joined her tentatively a few moments afterwards in a move choreographed slickly as the sweetly named Birds and Bees dance.

Catherine could tell Stevie had had enough by now, but she continued to clap with the others at another jolly reel, watching the pairings split and repair. Eddie still hadn't left the dance floor. Having refreshed his passion for square-dancing, he was presently flinging his bulk about with Auntie Madge and wondering if they sold men's kilts on eBay.

'I think I'll slip away home now,' said Stevie. 'I don't think my stiff upper lip can take any more.'

Catherine nodded and kissed her on the head.

'I'm proud of you. You've acted like an absolute lady. Have a long lie-in tomorrow and pick Danny up when-ever. He won't thank you for being early.'

Stevie didn't doubt it. It didn't appear that she was high up on anyone's list of 'people to be happy to see'.

Stevie asked the lady on Reception to phone her a taxi, then she sat on the big squashy couch, listening to the jolly strains of the music next door. The taxi wasn't long in coming but no sooner had she got to the glass exit doors than Matthew's voice came from behind.

'Stevie, Stevie, wait!'

She turned around, a hopeful flutter in her heart, but he wasn't making much eye-contact, which wasn't exactly an encouraging sign.

'Sorry, bad timing. Your taxi's here, isn't it?'

'Yes, it is,' she said. Her heart was thumping like a tom-tom issuing a distress signal.

'Stevie, is it okay if I pop around tomorrow? About nine?'

'In the morning?'

'No, in the evening, when Danny's in bed.'

'Yes, yes, of course.'

Outside, the taxi driver gave an impatient jab on his horn.

'Okay, see you tomorrow then,' said Matthew, then he waved weakly and disappeared quickly back inside to the party.

'Yes, see you tomorrow,' said Stevie to his cold slip-stream.

Chapter 17

A fortnight ago, Adam had never even seen the bloody woman, and now it seemed that everywhere he went, she was there as well. If her hatred of him hadn't been so obvious, he would have thought she was stalking him. His gym, the wedding and now the supermarket on a quiet Sunday morning. Was there no peace?

He had been careful not to drink too much at the wedding last night. He didn't want to give *her* or Matty Boy or Jo a speck of ammunition to use against him and he needed to keep control of the situation at all times. He had behaved impeccably and had even used the loo out in Reception so he wouldn't bump into Matthew and scare him into making a mess of what looked like a very expensive suit.

He had been quite surprised at how controlled *she* had tried to be too, although she was really a bag of nerves, any fool could have seen that. What was it she had said when he asked her which side of the church she was to sit on? *Broom?* He had nearly laughed aloud at that. *Broom!*

He also noticed how much her eyes were taken up with the three other main players in this ridiculous production. Admittedly, he himself had been fascinated to watch

Matthew and Jo stage-manage their 'coming together', just before 'The Birds and the Bees'. He had suppressed a wry smile at their guile, although seeing Jo flirt with another man in that way poked at something ancient and violent within him. She and Matty Boy had stayed together all evening after that, careful not to give away any clues to their already established intimacy by making every move look casual, though this had been sabotaged somewhat as Jo kept having to sneak out her purse to pay for the drinks that Matthew went up to the bar to get. She wouldn't have liked that one bit, and might have just won him Round 2 by default, which offset some of the feelings that were twisting in his gut like a blunt, rusty knife.

He saw that Matty Boy had run after his estranged partner when the time had come for her to leave, although he was gone less than a minute. Adam wondered what all that was about. Couldn't have been much, because he went straight back to the table and there was a moment of discreet but heavy-duty talk between him and Jo. Not that he was watching them much. He was trying really hard to look as if he was unbothered and jolly. It was all part of his master-plan.

Dragging his thoughts back to the here and now, he watched *her*, hovering around the salad vegetables here in the local supermarket. She was wearing jeans and a green sweatshirt which complemented her ruffled blonde hair. She looked quite neat now and she had certainly scrubbed up *nae bad* in that little red suit and hat at the wedding, he had thought, although she must have wanted to die when Jo turned up in a reversal of the same colours. Jo looked so gorgeous that he would not have been able to stop himself kissing her and carrying her home, if she had given him the slightest encouragement. Something inside him had creaked when he saw her looking so long and lovely in that beautifully expensive suit, although commonsense told him that it was his stomach making that sound through hunger. His heart knew different.

No little boy with *her* again – so who had she palmed him off onto today, Adam wondered. He just bet the Mother of the Year awards were stacked high on *her* mantelpiece. Mind you, the kid was better off away from a mother with a temper like that. It must have been sheer luck that he hadn't been hurt in the crossfire when she threw pans in temper at Matthew.

She must have just come into the supermarket for she had only collected the one item so far – *and what an item!* She hadn't seen him because she was concentrating on trying to guide a trolley with a demonically possessed front wheel, so the advantage was his. It was wicked, but he couldn't resist charging deliberately into her trolley with his own, full of many bottles of spirits, mainly whisky, which rattled in rude protest. Then he gave her a look of mock surprise that wouldn't have fooled the king of village idiots.

'Well fancy meetin' yooou here. Adjusting to single life verrry quickly, I see,' he bellowed, pointing down to the very long cucumber standing erect in her trolley. She blushed immediately and threw the nearest thing to hand in beside it to dilute the embarrassment. A tray of stir-fry.

'Oooh yum yum,' he said puckishly. 'Cucumber stir-fry, my favourite.'

'Was there something you wanted, Mr MacLean?' said Stevie haughtily, trying not to blush any harder.

'No' really,' he said, trying not to be so amused that she was redder than the vine-ripened tomatoes nearby. She would be fun to torture, he thought. It might take his mind off what her man was doing with his woman.

'Only I've far more important things to do than stand here being insulted by you.'

'I wonder what they could be?' he smiled like a barracuda, raised his eyebrows and cast a look at the impressive cucumber.

She *sooo* wanted to batter him round the head with it.

'My fiancé is calling around later,' Stevie said, ignoring his pathetic childish innuendos. He looked interested now and less piss-takey.

'Oh really?' he said, folding his arms. 'Whit forrr?'

'I don't know, but he's coming when my son is in bed so he obviously wants to talk. I'm quietly optimistic,' which she was, surprisingly enough. After she got home from the wedding, she had looked up 'winning your partner back' on the internet and picked up a thread about 'the power of positive thought'. Apparently, the trick was to visualize what she wanted to happen and focus on that. It was worth a try; anything was worth a try. So by that token, she had been telling herself since then that Matthew *was* coming home tonight for good. He had finished with Jo at the reception because she was so boring and uninteresting and had bad breath, and now they were back on track to get married and live happily ever after. And Adam MacLean would be kidnapped by aliens and whisked off to Saturn for painful medical experiments.

'Well, good luck,' said Adam MacLean, 'but will ye take a piece of advice?'

'No,' said Stevie and started to wheel away, but he grabbed her handlebar forcefully and made sure she wasn't going anywhere.

'Well, I'm givin' it tae ya anyway, so take it or leave it. *Basic psychology.* Play it exactly the opposite tae how he'd expect you tae behave. It's yoor only weapon.'

Whether or not he meant to imply that her looks or her personality wouldn't do much in a head-to-head with Jo, that's the way she took it.

'Yes, well thank you, Professor Platitude,' she huffed belligerently. 'I look forward to your next lecture with great eagerness. What will it be, I wonder? Jung's theory of the Absolutely Bloody Obvious?'

Not that he'd know who Jung was. Probably thought she meant the old DJ whose first name was Jimmy. And with that, Stevie and her enormous cucumber weaved off in the direction of the celery, whilst her trolley headed for Fresh Meats.

She turned up at Catherine's just after half past eleven to find the kitchen in chaos and Danny tucking into a full English breakfast.

'How the hell did you get him to eat that?' said Stevie, after she had given him a big 'hello' kiss. 'I can hardly get him to eat anything except for Coco Pops and chicken – and his flaming collars of course!'

'Ah, the wonderful mystery of children,' said Catherine. 'Violet doesn't eat eggs usually, she's only eating them because Danny is, and he's only eating them because Kate is. James obviously eats nothing because he never gets up.'

'Does Violet eat them when Kate eats them then?'

'Naw, doesn't work like that – they're related,' said Catherine with a sniff, leading her pal off for a coffee in a quieter corner after swiping bits of uneaten bacon from the twins, Sarah and Robbie. 'Mmm, why is it that food stolen from kids always tastes so good?' she said, smacking her lips in neo-orgasmic delight. 'Oh, by the way, Danny's got a snaggy toenail, Kate said, but he wouldn't let her cut it off. He said the Toenail Pixie will get it later, is that right?'

'He's scared of getting his toenails cut, so I do them in the middle of the night when he's asleep. He thinks a pixie comes and does it,' explained Stevie.

'I don't know how you think of these things,' said Catherine. 'I haven't a creative bone in my body.'

'Oh, I don't know, I think you've created quite a lot,' said Stevie, looking at the kitchen scene, which looked like a Waltons family reunion, with Danny playing the special guest-star part. 'He looks so happy here,' she said, as he giggled at Eddie who was trying to pretend that one of them had stolen the sausage that he had just fed to Boot under the table.

'You worry too much,' said Catherine.

'He was in front of the headmaster last week for smacking Curtis Ryder.'

'. . . Who was trying to pull his trousers down,' said Catherine sternly, because she knew where this was going. 'That's why Curtis Ryder got a thump, not because Danny's doolally because Matthew's gone. The lad's standing up for himself, like you always tell him to. Take a chill pill, gal'. And she shoved a packet of medicinal chocolate digestives at her to break open with her nails.

'I don't know how he'll react if Matthew and I don't get back together, Cath. He takes disappointment so badly.'

Catherine gave her a comforting tap tap on the shoulder. 'All kids take disappointment badly, Steve. It's not just Danny; he's a normal little kid with little kid funny little ways. Some carry comfort blankets, some suck their thumbs, sleeves or collars – it's what they do at four. You are a GOOD MOTHER. He gets more love and attention from you than most kids do with two parents, and if the worst happens, he'll cope. He'll have to, and so will you.'

Catherine knew, of course, what was mostly on her friend's troubled mind as she continued, 'Stevie, he didn't know Mick and he hardly got used to Matthew. He won't be damaged.'

'But he asks me, if his daddy loved him, why did he die and leave him? Then he'll see that another man who supposedly loved him has left him too. It's laying down a pattern for him. He'll be in therapy by the time he's six, thinking he's been rejected by two fathers.' Stevie suddenly stamped her foot as a bubble of frustration burst inside her. 'You know, I'm really angry at Matthew for putting Danny through this more than I am for myself. All the time we were living together, supposedly happily becoming a family, he was carrying on with *her*. Didn't it even cross his mind that Danny was getting closer to him every day and would get hurt?'

'Well, blokes don't think past their dicks half the time,' said Catherine, 'and we don't know when they started getting it together, do we? I'm sure Matthew wouldn't have moved you in if he wasn't serious about you, which makes me think it's a pretty recent thing so there's a good chance it will be like a cheap firework and die quickly. Good news you're getting angry, though. It's far more healing than getting upset.'

'Thanks for helping me out so much and for having Danny, Cath.'

'Don't be daft, he's no trouble at all – it's just one more plate on the table for me. In fact, the kids behave better when he's here. Outsiders divert them from killing each other. Anyway, I think I owe you a few, after all you've done for me in your time.'

Catherine's family, close as they purported themselves to be, were never that keen on helping in practical ways. Before Kate was old enough to extort massive babysitting fees in exchange for the job, it had been Stevie who looked after them sometimes, to give Catherine and Eddie a few hours' break together. It had been Stevie who did most of the vacuuming and washing and ironing in the background when Catherine's babies arrived, whilst the relatives were sitting on their fat backsides drinking tea and cooing. Catherine never forgot that.

'Matthew's coming round later when Danny goes to bed,' said Stevie. 'He came after me yesterday and caught me up in the foyer, just before I got my taxi home.'

Catherine stopped mid-pour. 'Did he say what for?'

'No, he just made arrangements to come over and then disappeared. How were *they* after I'd gone?' She knew Matthew hadn't been slaughtered en route back to the table

because she'd checked the local news on Ceefax first thing
that morning and there was no mention of 'Mad Highland
Nutter Axeman Kills Love Rival at Wedding'.

'Much the same,' said Catherine, plonking the biscuits in
front of Stevie. 'They were just talking, nothing else.'

'Did they leave together?'

Catherine didn't answer, which answered the question
anyway.

Stevie sighed heavily. 'Do you know, one minute I think
he might be coming round to tell me he doesn't want me
to move out, and then the next . . . I mean, if they left
together, that means it's still on between them, doesn't it?
He's not alone at that B&B, is he?' *Oy, you, think positive!*
reminded her inner mantra, but it was so very difficult.

'I don't know, Steve, but there's no point in driving
yourself barmy speculating; you'll have to wait and see
what he has to say. Have you eaten? You hardly had a thing
yesterday.' She pushed the biscuits almost up Stevie's still-
tender nose.

'I've not got much appetite. I went into the supermarket
first thing this morning to see if I could find anything to
tempt it back, and only bumped straight into that flaming
man MacLean again, didn't I.'

'Didn't have anything embarrassing in your trolley, did
you?' Catherine laughed gently. 'Like a monster pack of All
Bran and loads of toilet rolls.'

'Worse,' said Stevie.

'Oh God, no! Not pile cream!'

'Not even close.'

'What?'

'Only the world's largest cucumber.'

'No!' Catherine let loose a peal of horrified laughter.

'His trolley was so full of booze the wheels were nearly flat. Typical piss-head Scot.'

'A cucumber! NO! Did he say anything? Sorry!' she apologized for not being able to control herself. She was shaking with laughter.

'Yes, he made some crack about "adjusting to single life quickly".'

'NO!'

'Then he forced me to listen to his advice that I should play this exactly the opposite to what Matthew might expect of me.'

'That's what you're doing, isn't it?'

'Yes,' said Stevie, 'but I'm a woman and he probably doesn't think I have the capacity for such logical thought. Chauvinistic butt-ugly thug.'

'Actually . . .' began Catherine, then snapped off what she was going to say.

'What?'

'Nothing.'

'Oh go on, say it.'

'You'll hate me if I do.'

'Try me.'

'Well, Eddie thought he seemed a nice bloke,' said Catherine tentatively. 'Genuine.'

'Oh, come on, Cath, he's bound to have developed a super-charm gland, looking like that,' said Stevie with a mirthless laugh. 'Otherwise he couldn't have pulled someone who looked like Joanna. Think about it.'

'I thought he was quite attractive close up,' said Catherine, 'especially with all that hair off. And he has fabulous legs. Bet his thighs are . . .'

'Stop, you're making me ill.'

'He was looking after all the old relatives. He seemed to know all the steps to the dances.'

'It's something he'll have learned in the Highlands. It's how they unwind after biting the heads off live Sassenachs for breakfast. Hitler probably knew a few swanky moves. Apparently he could be quite charming too.'

'You're being silly now.'

'I don't like him,' said Stevie. 'You won't convince me he's a really nice bloke.'

For once, Catherine didn't try. The last person she had said was a 'really nice bloke' was Matthew, and look how that seemed to have turned out.

Chapter 18

Danny was tired out and asleep by half past seven, which left one and a half hours of absolute nerve-jangling torture in which the hands of the clock seemed to stay so still that at one point Stevie lifted it to her ear to see if it was still working. The time went trebly slow from nine o'clock until five past, when Matthew's black Punto pulled up outside. For the seven millionth time, Stevie quickly checked her precisely chosen casual clothes in the mirror and looked to see that there was no lipstick on her teeth. Matthew knocked on the door, which indicated a big marker of their estrangement, and Stevie was careful not to jump too quickly to open it. *Slowly, slowly*, she paced herself. She opened, smiled, invited him in and then went to sit in the big winged armchair.

Adam's words suddenly reverberated very loudly in her head. '*Play it exactly the opposite tae how he'd expect you tae behave.*' Not that she was going to play it any other way, but he made her push it that one notch further. Matthew would have expected her to be tarted up to the nines ready to seduce him back. He would have expected her to sit on the sofa in the hope that he would join her and not be able to resist snuggling up. He would have expected her to have the kettle on and offer him tea, so she did none of those things.

'What can I do for you?' said Stevie with a small smile.

'Well, firstly I came to see if there was any post,' said Matthew.

'It's on the hall table waiting for you,' said Stevie, still clinging on for grim death to her friendly nice-lady smile.

'And secondly . . .' He raked his hand through his thick dark hair. 'Sorry, it's a bit awkward. I thought you should know, because I don't want there to be any lies between us' – which made Stevie gulp down the biggest sarcastic laugh her voice box could hope to create – 'I . . . er . . . asked Joanna out last night.'

'Joanna? But she's married,' said Stevie, taking her place on the stage to receive her Oscar for 'best shocked actress'.

'She's . . . er . . . split up from Adam at last. As I found out last night. So . . . er . . . I'll need the house back as soon as I can.'

Stevie felt shaky and sick. 'What? You're moving her in already – after one night?'

'No, of course not. Don't be silly.' Matthew's hand went nervously to his hair again and then he started rubbing his neck. He really wasn't very good at lying.

He must think I'm an idiot to believe all this, thought Stevie, suddenly filled with a boiling rage which took over her mouth, totally bypassing her brain.

'Well, actually, I was going to tell *you*, Matthew, that I've found somewhere and I'll be out by Wednesday. I can't make it any earlier than that, I'm afraid, so I hope that will be okay with you?'

'Oh yes . . . great.'

Great? He actually said great. The rage temperature shot up a few more centigrade. She was not even letting herself think of what she was saying; she just wanted to show him she was in control and okay and bigger than this. Even if she wasn't. Even if inside she was vibrating with anger and fear and hurt, outside she would look as if she could cope. Stevie stood up, surprised that her legs had been strong enough to support her.

'I'll pop my keys through the letterbox when I leave. Let's say, by Wednesday noon.'

'Five o'clock would do,' said Matthew, seemingly unable to cover up the sweat of his relief. If he'd had a handkerchief handy he would have probably mopped his brow at this point, Stevie thought. Like Louis Armstrong singing 'Wonderful World'.

'Okay, five o'clock then.'

'Right. Brilliant.'

'So let's get your post,' Stevie said, rising to her feet. 'Where are you staying?' She clung on to the amicable smile. It was like hanging onto something burning; it hurt and she couldn't wait to let go of it.

'Oh, just one of the hotels in town.'

Hotel. So it wasn't a grotty little B&B after all then. She wanted to ask which one, and whether Jo was staying there too, and watch him squirm because, had she had any life savings left, Stevie would have put them on the perfidious pair being holed up together in a double room in this mysterious and nameless 'hotel in town'. But that's what he would be expecting her to do, cross-examine him, so she didn't. She played outside his expectations. There was something she did need to ask, though.

'So, about our wedding,' she began, her voice croaking like a frog on forty Woodbines a day.

Matthew didn't say anything; he just looked at her with big, apologetic, brown eyes.

Stevie gritted her teeth and said, 'I thought so. Well okay,' she managed, with a 'let's get on with it then' hand clap. 'You tell your parents and your relatives, I'll do the rest.'

'Sorry,' he said, as if he had just accidentally stood on her toe and not smashed up her life with a sledgehammer.

'To be expected in the circumstances. Especially if you're asking other people out,' she said, her upper lip so stiff, she doubted it would soften in three tons of Lenor.

'Bye, Stevie, you're such a lovely, understanding person,' he said, and he shocked her with a big grateful hug after he picked up his post and stuck it in his pocket, which at least proved to her just how surprising the unexpected could be. She extricated herself, battling the urge to stay there and fill herself with the smell and the feel of him and to beg him not to leave her.

'Bye, Matthew.'

She lasted five seconds after the door closed before breaking down. How could she have been so stupid as to think a nice hairdo and a few pounds off would make any difference? Hadn't she learned *anything* from last time?

When she first suspected Mick had been having an affair, she had post mortemed herself to shreds. What was she?

Too porky, too blonde, too unfit, too arty, too short, too straight-haired, too blue-eyed, too incredibly clumsy, too crap at cake baking? What was it that had caused Mick to turn his attentions to another woman? Then she had found out who he was having an affair with. A barmaid – Linda: hook nose, yellow teeth and proud owner of incredibly fat ankles.

'*This hasn't happened because you've got a slightly bigger bum than you should have, girl*,' said a nice, kind part within her, eager to give some comfort. It hadn't stopped her from wanting to know just why it had happened then, to pin his actions to a reason. Why was it so hard for blokes to understand that all an ex might need to go forward was a two-minute explanation? Why did they hold up an aggressive crucifix against the demon of 'closure'? Even, 'I ran off with Linda because I happen to have a thing about women who look like bulldogs,' would have been better than the not-knowing *why*. But the cowardly swines saw no advantage in facing up to what they had done and so women started ripping into themselves trying to find the answer, as they would their house if a ring had been lost and leaving no stone unturned to find it. No wonder they started boiling rabbits and sewing prawns into curtains. Well, Stevie wasn't going to go mad this time. She wasn't going to hide Matthew's clothes, follow him in his lunch-hour, starve herself or give him her full emotional repertoire in a misguided, desperate attempt to get him back. All that would do was drive him further away, as she knew to her cost with Mick.

Stevie crunched herself up into a small ball and sobbed

quietly, so Danny wouldn't hear, though she wanted to keen and howl at full belt like a wolf at the moon and let out all the pain. And what the buggery bollocks had made her say she had somewhere else to go? In three days' time too? '*So what are you going to do now?*' the sensible part of her brain shouted at the smartarse side. The smartarse side was not forthcoming with any answers.

She couldn't stay at Catherine's, although she knew the Flanagans would shift and jiggle to accommodate her and Danny. There would be no space to work, plus she wouldn't be able to work anyway from the guilt of inconveniencing them. Her mother lived too far away for Danny's school and anyway, Edna Honeywell only had a one-bedroomed flat, and a life in which there was even less room for them both. As for her father – well, he wasn't even in the short-list of people to ring with this one.

Stevie sobbed some more, letting herself wallow in rare self-pity. Five months ago, she had had her own house, a nice full bank account and a fabtastic boyfriend who loved her just as she was. So how had she got to this place – grossly depleted savings and three days away from being homeless? She hated to admit this, but there was only one person who just might be able to stop everything slipping away from her. Stevie went out to the recycle bin in the garage where all her scrap paper was kept awaiting collection, scavenged around until she found what she was looking for, and then she rang the number on the retrieved business card.

'Hellooo,' said a voice full of nails and razor-blades.

'Hello, Mr MacLean. It's Stevie Honeywell. I think I'm ready to talk.'

Chapter 19

It was with a certain amount of cockiness that Adam MacLean swaggered up the short path and rang the doorbell of 15 Blossom Lane the next morning, at nine thirty, as arranged, and it was with a certain amount of humility that Stevie received him. He accepted her offer of a cup of coffee and followed her into the kitchen where a percolator was already chewing on some beautiful-smelling beans. The room looked completely different when it wasn't covered in flour, he thought. She had obviously tightened up her act a bit since Matty Boy left. It was gleaming actually, and so was the front room that they went into when the coffee was ready, give or take a bit of mess that made a home comfortable – Spiderman slippers, jotters and pens, a big tub of Lego and a very strange head made out of a sock sitting in a jam jar with grass for hair. Adam sat down on a sofa that was meant to hold four people and took up nearly half of it. On the coffee-table there was one of those infernal books that daft women read, called *The Carousel of Life* by Beatrice Pollen. He picked it up, gave the back cover blurb a quick dismissive read and put it back down again in such a way that gave Stevie no doubt of his opinion of it.

'So?' he said, rather smugly. 'You changed yerrr mind.'

'It wasn't an easy decision.'

'I can bet.'

They even managed to make their coffee sipping look like a duel.

'What was it then that finally made ye ring?'

'He – Matthew – came around last night.'

'Aye, you said he was coming roon, when I saw you in the supermarket. With the giant cucumber.'

Stevie bared her teeth a little but didn't rise to the bait. Instead, she continued icily, 'He told me that he and *her* had got together at Pam and Will's wedding.'

'Oh?'

'And I have to get out of this house by Wednesday and cancel my wedding.'

'Oh.' It was quite a sympathetic 'oh' for him, who seemed to deduce from the speed at which she started slurping coffee then, that she was possibly quite upset about having to do that.

'So where will ye go?' he said.

'I don't have a clue. I'll have to start looking bigtime. And packing. God, I don't know which to do first.' Her voice went all funny and she coughed it away.

'So do ye want tae know what I think noo?' said Adam MacLean, who was wearing jeans and a cornflower-blue shirt that exactly matched his eyes.

'Go on,' she said.

'Ah think you and I should pretend to start winchin.'

Winchin? What the hell did that mean? She needed an interpreter to converse with the bloody man.

'I'm sorry, you've lost me.'

'Winchin. It means "go-ing out to geth-cr".'

'Who?'

'You and me.'

'You and me?' Stevie laughed, waiting for the punchline, because that was a joke, wasn't it? And not a very funny one either. She was being serious and he was messing about.

'No, it's not a joke,' he said. 'This is part of my master-plan.'

'Your *master-plan*?'

'Is there an echo in here?' he grumbled. Stevie ignored him and he went on, 'First of all, I didn't fight the decision for Jo to leave me. I just let her go. I knew that would affect her far more than if I acted like she might expect me to.'

Stevie didn't ask how Jo would expect him to act. That seemed pretty obvious. It had to involve something dangerous that hurt a lot.

'And you want us to go out together?'

'My God naw!' he protested a bit too enthusiastically. 'Just to pretend.'

'You're barking mad.'

'Quite possibly, but have you any sane solutions?'

That shut Stevie up because she hadn't.

'Any chance of another coffee, please?' he asked. 'With a wee bit more mulk this time, if I could?'

'Yes, of course,' said Stevie, and went half-dazed into the kitchen. Adam picked up another *Midnight Moon* book from the table under the window. Another by Beatrice Pollen – *The Silent Stranger* – she must be *her* favourite.

Obviously, this Pollen woman was some sad old grand-maw of a writer with a loveless life who lived her dreams through characters with names like Maddox Flockton and Devon Earnshaw. Jeez, who thought o' this crap?

Devon flirtatiously pushed back her luxurious auburn hair, exposing her long creamy neck. Maddox grabbed her, ignoring her protests as he rained kisses onto that neck until she surrendered to him and groaned aloud, 'Maddox, Oh Maddox!'

Bollocks, oh bollocks, more like, he thought, closing the book and putting it back where he had found it by the window. Then his eye caught sight of the sign on the house opposite, just before Stevie returned to put a giant cup down on the coffee-table for him. It had been a joke Christmas present and was one-step short of a horse trough.

'What's that hoos? Is it tae let?' He pointed to the big cottage opposite.

'Yes,' said Stevie, roughly understanding what he was saying.

'Why don't you get that wan?'

'You are joking!' said Stevie with a laugh belonging to Mrs Rochester. 'I couldn't afford that in a month, sorry, year, sorry millennium of Sundays.'

'Will Housing Benefit not cover it?'

'Housing Benefit?' said Stevie indignantly. 'What on earth makes you think I would get Housing Benefit?'

'I . . . er . . . just presumed, seeing as you're at the gym every day, that you didnae work.'

'Well, I do work actually, thank you!' said Stevie.

'What do you dae?'

'None of your bloody business!' Like she was going to tell him that after he had tossed her book down as if it was some worthless piece of crap and then have him do a snidey laugh thing.

'Sorry I asked,' said Adam, holding his hands up in a gesture of peace. He took a sip of coffee and, contrary to her silent wish, didn't burn his throat in agony. 'So, how expensive is it?'

Stevie sighed and got out the newspaper to show him some brief details. 'Too expensive for me, and my *salary.*'

'Christ awmighty!' said Adam as the figure shot out at him from the page. 'Be cheaper tae move into a Hilton Penthoos.'

'Precisely.'

'Hmmm.' He rubbed his smooth, freshly shaven chin in thought. 'Although the Hilton doesn't have such a good view as that hoos has.'

'Pardon?'

'And because you can't afford it, that's even more reason for it to be the perfect place.' He was thinking out aloud. *This was starting to look verrry interesting.*

Stevie shook her head. 'I haven't a clue what you're talking about, Mr MacLean.'

'If you lived there . . .'

'I couldn't anyway, even if I had a million in the bank,' butted in Stevie, shaking her head quite defiantly. 'There is no way I could stand to see *those* two in *this* house every day and every night, and furthermore—'

'Hold your wheesht, woman!' Adam growled. 'If you lived there, you would absolutely cause them mental hell. "How could she stand to live there opposite tae us? How could she afford it?" they'd ask. Then I turn up wi' floooers . . .'

Floooers? 'If you mean "floors", at a rough guess I think it might have them already, Mr MacLean. And possibly ceilings. Maybe even a wall.' *What is the man on!*

'Och! Not flairs, *floooers*.'

Stevie's face, with its mask of utter bewilderment now, told him she wasn't getting any of this and he took a fierce intake of breath before further clarifying, none too patiently either: 'Fl-ow-errrs. If I came with fl-ow-ers, we'd mash their hids . . . *heads* totally wi' all the questions we'd raise. Think aboot it. Not only have we not reacted as rejected partners should naturally in accordance wi' the laws of heartbreak, but then we start oor own relationship – *pretend* relationship,' he emphasized for clarity. 'I think the wee green-eyed monster would be oot daing . . . sorry, *out doing* his damage within a very short time. *Basic psychology*. No one wants to be that replaceable, that quickly.'

Okay, he had a point, Stevie thought, but at what cost to her own sanity?

'Like I tried to say to you before – *basic psychology*,' he said again, tapping his frontal lobe skull-casing. 'I expect Matthew thought you'd totally freak – as, I know, did my Jo of me. But we didn't, we haven't given them what they wanted. Trust me, their brains are trying to process the strange wonderful creatures that we are and cannae. We are *haunting* them. They are expecting more from us. They're waiting for us to flip and revert tae type, but they aren't gonnae get it and that will unsettle them more than anything will. Tell me that Matty Boy isn't expecting you to kick up a fuss.'

Stevie thought of all she had told Matt about the break-up with Mick, how crazed she had acted in grief. He had listened to her patiently then, with love and understanding. She couldn't have known then that her confession would be stored and one day used as a weapon against her. Now he would use her past actions as an excuse to extricate himself from her as quickly as possible.

'Yes, he'll expect it,' she answered quietly.

'Aye, well, there are reasons why Jo will expect the same.'

'Obviously,' said Stevie.

He didn't like the way she said the word, full of implication.

'Guid. Then, they'll no' anticipate this turn of events in a million years.'

Stevie considered everything he had said. She hated to admit that he might be right, but she was going to have to, because she was desperate. Crackers as the whole scheme was, it was worth a try. Well, it would have been if she'd had the money to do it.

'I'll ring the landlord aboot the place opposite—' MacLean started to say.

'Excuse me,' Stevie tried to interrupt. *Didn't he listen? Didn't he hear the bit about not being able to afford it? Had the sound of all those bagpipes affected his eardrums?*

'If you'll agree to consider moving in there, we'll come to some arrangement about the money that disnae see you short,' Adam interrupted back. 'I might be able to batter the landlord down on price.'

Yes, she could imagine he would be very effective at battering. She had a sudden scene in her head of some old, defenceless landlord in a headlock saying, 'Yes, yes, I'll compromise – please just get off my windpipe!'

She nodded her head warily. This seemed to incense him.

'Look, lady, I'm doing this primarily for me and Jo, not you and *him*, but unfortunately we're all knotted up in this together. This isnae a charity thing, if that's what you're thinking.'

'As if!' Yeah, like that thought had crossed her mind.

'Well then? It's the only way, and trust me I've thought of every possible solution. So if you would be so kind as to give me your telephone number . . .'

Stevie scraped the bottoms of the barrels of her brain for any other alternatives, but came up with zilch. As he said, mad as it was, this was worth trying. Anything was worth trying. Even entering an unholy alliance with McBeelzebub here. She *had* to get Matthew back, so she swallowed her pride and it felt bitter and lumpy on the way down.

'Okay, you're on,' she said, with a heavy sigh of resignation.

Once she and Matthew were reunited, they might even laugh at this one day, surrounded by grandchildren and sipping Horlicks by a fireside, with Mr and Mrs MacLean long resigned to the trashcan of history. She scribbled down her mobile number on one of the five million pads she had littered about the place, in case of sudden literary inspiration, then Adam left quickly – a man with a mission, locked on course.

He rang her an hour later, during which time her nerves had knitted themselves into a scarf of knots.

'The landlaird willnae budge o'the price,' he said.

'Pardon?'

'Theee land-lord will not budge on the price,' pronounced Adam slowly.

'Oh well, that's that then.'

'I'll cover what you can't afford. We'll sort out the details later. I've signed the lease and I've got the key, which I'll drop around to you this afternoon, so if you've anything heavy to carry across, I'll do it for you then, because you start moving in today. Ring your man tomorrow and tell him the place is empty a day early. Now go pack!'

Then he put the phone down before Stevie could manage a single word of protest.

Chapter 20

Adam arrived with the key just as Stevie was disconnecting her computer. Together they walked across the road to inspect her new temporary home, whose formal address, according to the lease, was Humbleby Cottage, the houses on that side of the road having only names, no numbers. Humbleby was something of a misnomer, because there was nothing the least bit humble about it from the outside aspect and even less from the inside, as they were to find when they unlocked the door and went in. Adam hadn't (unfortunately) banged his skull on the beams and fatally injured himself. They were deceptively high and his head cleared them easily, although maybe it wouldn't be wise for him to start pogo-ing to any punk records whilst he was there.

The cottage was chocolate-box pretty. The kitchen was roadside with a huge Yorkshire stone inglenook fireplace, an old working Aga and original wooden floors with thick patterned rugs over them. Thankfully, the modern world had been allowed in too and there was central heating and double-glazing with security windows throughout. There was the bonus of a good-sized, well-equipped separate study with hundreds of bookshelves, a lounge with an even grander fireplace, and a darling little sunroom around the back looking out onto a long private cottage garden, which apparently had been maintained by a gardener in the absence of a tenant. Upstairs was a huge spacious girly bathroom and two massive, pretty bedrooms with exposed beams.

For some reason, Adam had smiled slyly when he said, 'Only two bedrooms, eh?'

She hadn't even dared to ask what *that* might have meant.

A domestic service had been going in once every three weeks to dust it down, so the cottage was ready to move into without Stevie having to clean it or scrub out the cupboards. It was immaculate and fully furnished with some very nice stuff.

'Whit do you think?' said Adam.

'It's lovely,' said Stevie. She would have to be very careful and try not to fall in love with it. Her relationship with the house would have to be a casual one. Although she was beginning to doubt her ability to fall in love with anything again. As soon as her heart touched something, it seemed to scare it away.

'Right – got anything heavy I can move for you?'

'I haven't got a lot of things,' she replied. 'I sold most of my furniture with my last house because it wouldn't fit in Matthew's.'

'You must have something, mon!'

'Just my computer for now.'

'Let's go and get it then.'

So off they went back to Matthew's house and he carried

her computer over and set it up for her in the little study. It would be a change to work in some generous space for a while, she thought, after being cramped in the corner of Matthew's tiny dining area.

'Work from home, dae you?' he asked as he was twiddling with leads.

'Yes,' she said, without furnishing him with further detail.

'On this?'

'Yes,' she replied. He didn't need to know any more and she had no intention of enlightening him and earning his ridicule.

'So, what's next?' he asked, when the computer was up and running.

'Well, I've got some books.'

'C'moan then,' and he marched back over like a Black Watch soldier on parade. She hadn't unpacked most of them from her last move so they were all still conveniently in boxes under the dining-room table. Matthew had been going to buy her some shelves for her birthday, but he had not had the spare money and the date had come and gone. He had bought her some smellies from Marks & Spencer instead – the sort of soap collection one would buy for a spinster aunt with dodgy olfactory workings.

'They're a bit heav—'

'Nonsense,' Adam said, and lifted the first one up as if it was an empty crisp packet, then he came back for the other two and carried them as effortlessly. The bloke was an ox. He should have been out ploughing fields, not running leisure facilities.

'What noo?' he asked, not even a bit out of breath.

'Nothing really. The rest will just be suitcases and black bags. I can manage those myself when I fill them.'

'Right, I'll be in touch,' he said, and then he dropped the cottage keys into her hand and went without further ado.

After he vroomed off, Stevie rang Catherine to tell her how the previous night had gone with Matthew.

'I still can't believe how he's treated you,' her friend said, when Stevie filled her in on the details, 'and then to pretend he wasn't going out with Jo until the wedding! He's got such a nerve. What will you do?'

'Well, if you've a spare half an hour, I'll show you,' Stevie replied.

'Show?'

'Can you get your butt over here? You won't regret it.'

'I'm in the car already.'

Five minutes later, Catherine was there and Stevie led her silently and mysteriously over the road. Catherine gasped when she produced a key and slid it into the lock of her favourite house ever.

'You're not moving in here? You can't afford this, can you?' she said with breathless excitement.

'Yes, I am, and no, I can't,' said Stevie and proceeded to tell her the Adam MacLean part of the story.

'You lucky cow bitch from hell living here,' said Catherine.

'In other circumstances, maybe,' said Stevie.

'Well, even for a little while it'll be nice,' said Catherine, whose eyes couldn't move fast enough around the inside of the house. 'Bloody hell, Steve, it's like a Tardis. It's even bigger than it looks from outside – it's massive, in fact, and it's absolutely gorgeous. No wonder it's so expensive.'

Stevie nodded. Yes, it was beautiful, apart from the view from the kitchen – for the home she was leaving would sit there framed in the window like a taunting picture: *Ner ner ner ner ner, you don't live here, but guess who-o do-oes*.

'Well, for the record, I think it's a bloody good idea of Adam MacLean's,' said Catherine.

'Do you?' Stevie was surprised at that. Catherine wasn't usually one for wild schemes and mad impulses, or for siding with people who beat up women for a hobby.

'Yes, I do. I'm not condoning violence, don't get me wrong, but I think Jo and Matthew both deserve a taste of their own medicine,' she went on.

'Will they get it though?' said Stevie, who had made tea for two in her new temporary home and opened up a celebratory packet of chocolate shortbreads. Not that she had anything really to celebrate. Yet.

'Well, it's worth a try,' said Catherine and nudged her lasciviously. 'You and Adam MacLean, eh?'

'No, *not* me and Adam MacLean. There is no me and Adam MacLean. I want to hang onto my teeth and ribs a bit longer, thank you. Besides, the man is barely house-trained. Trust me, I wouldn't give the bloke so much as the time of day if I wasn't so desperate.'

'Fantastic legs, though. I could imagine them—'

Stevie held her hand up and staved her friend's verbal flow.

'Please, no Adam MacLean sexual fantasies. I'm trying to hold onto the contents of my stomach.'

'Well, he doesn't come across to me as the violent nutter *she* said he was. Plus, can you really believe her word on all this? Miss Butter-wouldn't-melt?'

'He's "acting" the non-violent type for our benefit, that's the point. He can't risk losing his temper because he needs me as much as I need him. But I don't trust him as far as I could throw him.' Which wouldn't have been very far at all. The bloke was a walking sofa.

'Is there a house phone? You'll have to give me your new number.'

'I'll sort it out tomorrow – well, the day after tomorrow,' said Stevie.

'Why, what's happening tomorrow that's so important?'

'Tomorrow I'm going to cancel all the wedding stuff.'

Catherine abandoned her biscuit and came over to give her a hug. 'I can do all that for you,' she said.

'No, no, it's all right,' said Stevie, with cry-shiny eyes. 'I do appreciate it, but you've got enough to do.'

'Naw, now the kids are all at school or nursery, I actually find time to breathe. I feel a bit lost, to be honest,' said Catherine with a sad little smile.

'I have to do it myself,' said Stevie. 'I have to face facts that this wedding is not going to happen.'

'God, Stevie, you are so strong.'

'Trust me, I'm not,' said Stevie, with a little laugh. One kind word would have turned her eyeballs into Niagara Falls.

'The offer will still be there in the morning, but I won't bully you for once,' said Catherine, stroking her friend's hair as if she were Boot, whilst thinking to herself, What an idiot you are, Matthew Finch!

Stevie and Catherine had been friends from nursery school, although it hadn't started out that way. They had both fought viciously over the Cinderella crinoline in reception class and had to stand facing the naughty wall together. Somehow after that they had become friends, bonding over the Play-Doh shape machine and a few Spangles. The friendship grew from strength to strength, even when Catherine got pregnant at seventeen to a trainee boxer, Eddie Flanagan, although he was hardly the candidate the heavyweight boxing community had been holding out for. Eddie had about as much edge as Boot. Stevie had been prepared to hate him for coming between her and her best friend, but you couldn't dislike Eddie, not even if you were on mind-altering drugs. Catherine and Eddie married and went on to have kids and animals, whilst Stevie had taken the university route, during which time their friendship took a pen-pal turn for three years. Then Stevie came home and worked through a succession of dead-end jobs by day whilst she pursued her dreams of becoming a writer at night. Whenever she felt like giving up after a post-box full of rejections, Catherine was always there, spurring her on with her commonsense and fighting talk. She was the sister Stevie wished she had had, and could be very scary when crossed.

'Right, come on now, this isn't knitting the baby a bonnet,' said Catherine, who had knitted quite a few baby bonnets in her time. 'Let's get ready to rumble.'

Stevie carried her clothes on hangers straight over the road because there didn't seem much point in packing them only to have to unpack them at the other end all creased up. For herself, she picked the pretty pink bedroom at the back, which overlooked the garden. The front bedroom was larger but she did not want the first thing she saw when she drew the curtains every morning to be the house where her fiancé and his new lover lived. She carried her toiletries over in one of the cardboard boxes she had cadged from the Happy Shopper around the corner. She took the soft white towels she had recently bought too, leaving Matthew with his ancient ones that were more like wafer-thin loofahs. She would have left him a couple of hers, until she visualized Jo using them.

Shoes took up one of the new suitcases she had bought for their honeymoon. Catherine took the plastic-covered wedding dress over. Stevie hoped she might get some of her money back on that but either way, it needed to be got out of sight as soon as possible. She was stripping her bed when Catherine walked in on her from bagging up some of Danny's toys.

'What are you doing?' said her friend, standing over her with her hands on her hips.

'Well, they won't want to sleep in my sheets. I was just changing them.'

'Don't be so soft, Steve. Stick them in the laundry basket and leave them. Let them make up their own bed and lie on it.' Then she shook her head at the irony of her words. Catherine had her 'do as I say or else' face on, so Stevie obeyed.

She took her Le Creuset pan-set from the kitchen and her new super-steamy iron and the ironing board that she had bought only a couple of weeks ago. There was just the rest of Danny's room and bits and bobs to pack up, and then they had to call a halt to the day's mission, as it was time to pick up the children.

'I'll come round with Eddie about seven o'clock,' began Catherine, shutting up Stevie before she started protesting. 'I'll bring you a couple of spare duvets and some sheets and pillows to tide you over, and he'll carry the microwave over for you.'

'I can't take the microwave.'

'Who bought it?'

'Well, I—'

'Who bought it?' Catherine said again, being extra stern.

'I did,' Stevie relented grudgingly, 'but for both of us.'

'You can't split it so you take it. Besides, the cottage doesn't have one,' said Catherine, who was beginning to realize that Stevie's financial contribution to the arrangement had been a lot greater than was fair. It looked as if Matthew hadn't paid for much of anything at all and there she was, thinking he had been so generous. Certainly, on the times they'd gone out to dinner, he was very extravagant with his money. She had taken that as a strong indicator that he was a good provider. Something else it appeared she was wrong about.

'Look, do you want *her* baking her spuds in it, whilst you and Danny do without?' urged Catherine, watching Stevie still deliberating over the microwave.

That was the clincher. Catherine really should have been a psychologist. Or a Kray.

'Okay, I'll take it then.'

'Don't you dare try and lift it yourself. I know what

you're like, Stevie Independent Honeywell, it'll weigh a ton! Promise?' admonished Catherine with a heavy wag of her finger.

'Yes, Sergeant Major, sah, I promise!' said Stevie, saluting her. Then she went to pick up her son and tell him, with a softening ice cream en route, about their new domestic arrangements.

Danny's new bedroom was much, much bigger than the old one, plus he had a double bed in it, which was 'cool', and once he was full of chicken nuggets and was arranging his toys in his new space and had put Mr Greengrass Head on the kitchen windowsill, he seemed easily content with the changes. It was a real relief for Stevie who hadn't known how he would react. She'd had visions of him screaming and clinging to the door whilst she tried to drag him over the road and crying, '*I won't go, I won't go!*' but he trotted over quite keenly and said, 'Wow!' and 'Cool!' a lot, which was always a good sign.

She and Danny had taken some other bits and pieces over, then Eddie and Catherine arrived and helped to move the boxes of Stevie's videos and CDs and DVDs. Eddie transported the microwave and Danny's portable TV. There was a huge TV in the cottage and speakers all round the room. Eddie, a gadget maniac, fiddled and foddled and found out how to switch it to cinema surround.

'Curtains closed, a big bag of popcorn and a Harry Potter on here, lad, and it'll be better than the pictures,' said Eddie, which had Danny's face lighting up like a Christmas tree. He was viewing all this as much of an adventure, as

Charlie Bucket did his trip to Willy Wonka's Chocolate factory.

'Or a Johnny Depp,' said Catherine with a conspiratorial wink. She intended to take advantage of a couple of nights in here herself with a Blockbuster special and a bottle of vino, a cheesecake and two forks.

'Can Gareth come and play in our new house?' said Danny.

'Course he can,' said Stevie.

'And Josh Parker?'

'Er . . . we'll see,' said Stevie, exchanging horrified looks with Catherine, before moving swiftly on.

Catherine quickly made up Danny's bed, whilst Stevie got him washed, pyjama-ed up and toothpasted. He was tired, little lamb, after all the excitement of his busy day. In his Superman pyjamas under his giant Superman fleecy blanket and cuddling his Superman doll, he was asleep in minutes.

'So, are you sorted then?' said Eddie, who had been finishing off a thank you bottle of lager from the Happy Shopper, whilst he relaxed in the reclining bit of the sofa that he had just discovered. He looked so comfortable, he could have been part of the furnishings.

'I just need to clean over there tomorrow and that's that,' said Stevie, raising her own bottle of lager in thanks to him.

'Clean?' screeched Catherine.

'I don't care what you say, I'm not having Jo slagging me off because there's a bit of dust where I've moved things,' returned Stevie. Okay, this might be 'acting to type' but there was no way she was going to let anyone call her a mucky sod. 'There's not all that much to do but I'm doing it. Then I'll get on with the . . . other business.'

'What other business?' said Eddie.

'Cancelling the wedding,' said Stevie.

'Oh sorry!' said Eddie. 'Me and my big mouth. Again.'

'Don't be daft, it's got to be done. Better than him jilting me at the altar, I suppose.' A cold shiver ran down her spine as she wondered how close she had come to that happening.

Catherine smiled kindly at her. 'You look worn out. You should get to bed yourself.'

'I don't think I'll sleep, to be honest.'

But Stevie did, and it was a sleep of far better quality than she had had for quite a long time. As if it was a gift to rest her soul for the ordeals in store for her the following day.

Chapter 21

Danny was a little disorientated when he was awoken by his Spiderman alarm clock and found he was desperate for a wee. Stevie was in such a deep sleep that when she felt herself being shaken by the shoulder and a little voice saying, 'Mummy, someone's stolen the toilet,' she actually believed it for a moment and sat up bolt upright with a rush of panic. Her eyes came into focus on soft tones of pale pink and old cream painted on uneven plaster walls rather than the familiar white woodchip wallpaper and that wonky black and red 'boy' border – so much nicer, gentler colours to wake up to. Then she realized where she was and that a toilet burglar probably had not targeted them after all.

Once the loo had been re-discovered, Stevie set about making breakfast. She caught sight of her former home through the window, which was an odd, almost out-of-body experience moment. She tore herself away and concentrated on pouring out Coco Pops for two, deciding that she could not afford to let emotion get in the way of the task in hand and ruin everything. Although if – *when* – she and Matthew got back together, she wasn't sure she could move into that house again. That would be too painful. She would insist they sell up and move on. A fresh start.

As soon as she had dropped Danny off at school, she headed across the road with her cleaning kit. She gave the place a quick dust, a vacuum, and a double extra going over in the kitchen, not that it really needed it, other than the dull square where the microwave had sat. Between the work-surface paraphernalia, the space it had occupied was as obvious as a missing front tooth. She did consider rearranging everything to make the gap less obvious, but decided why should she? If she didn't make a hollow in his life, her stuff sure as hell would. Any little points of satisfaction that thought brought, though, were soon offset by the fact that Matt would probably miss the coffee percolator more than her. He had loved the post-dinner ritual of fancy coffees and all the fresh cream mints she used to buy in Thorntons.

There was an empty, echoey feel to the house that was inexplicable because Matthew's stuff was still there. In fact, apart from being a lot cleaner and shinier, it looked just as it did the day she moved in at New Year. It was as if she had never been there and part of his house, part of his life.

Stevie wound the cord around her Dyson, ready to take it across the road. Matthew would just have to cope with his ancient cylinder in the under-stairs cupboard, which had been hard-wired into believing its primary function was to blow out more dust than it sucked in. Tough, but necessary because she *knew* that he would expect her to leave behind all this stuff, because that's what good-hearted old Stevie would do. She might beg, plead, cry or hang around his workplace desperate to talk to him and change his mind, but she was incapable of thinking of her own needs before his. Nice Stevie could not bear to see him surviving on sandpapery towels and incompetent electrical equipment. *Well, he had a little shock coming then!* Twisting the engagement ring off her finger, Stevie put it on the work surface. Then, remembering that she herself had paid for the flaming thing, she snatched it back up and stuck it in her pocket. Not that she would ever wear it again, but she could all too easily visualize Matthew flogging it and then taking Jo out for dinner on the proceeds.

She took one last look at Matthew's house, which she had kept warm and full of treats and comforts. Matthew's house, which she had intended to share with him as Mrs Stevie Finch. Then she forced herself to leave it, locked the door behind her and posted the key back through the letterbox. That one small action was huge in its implications. She tried to see it as a comma in their relationship, but it felt more like a big fat full stop.

The first thing she did on entering Humbleby Cottage was to pick up her mobile. Taking a big breath, as if she was about to dive underwater, she rang Matthew's number. It clicked onto answerphone and she noticed how the recorded message was slightly different to his usual one. He sounded chirpier, cocky as a greedy cat in a cream factory. She wondered if he really was too busy to answer or was just ignoring her. She prepared herself for the long beep to end.

'Hi, it's Stevie,' she said, pitching it neither too up nor down. 'Just to let you know that I've fully vacated the house now and posted the key back through the letterbox, so it's all yours. Take care, bye.' Then she hung up and let all the air out of her lungs before taking up her notebook to make the first of all the other dreaded calls.

'Hello, "Kiss the Bride",' answered a jolly voice.

'Is that Ros?'

'Yes, this is Ros, who's speaking, please?'

'It's Stevie Honeywell. I bought one of your wedding dresses, I don't know if you remember me. It was long, to the floor, white silk, criss-cross breast panel.' She had brought the dress and accessories home from the shop so that she could show them to Jo, if that wasn't a kick in the teeth.

'Ah yes, I remember, we had to have it considerably shortened.'

'. . . And a pink bridesmaid dress, size ten, and a pageboy outfit. You've still got those in the shop.'

'Yes, I've just altered those too for you.'

'Er . . . yes. Well, the thing is, there isn't going to be a wedding any more, so I wondered if I could have a refund.'

'Oh dear,' said Ros, 'I am so sorry. Is there no chance that maybe in the future . . .?'

Stevie didn't answer either way, just in case she would influence some self-fulfilling prophecy that happened to be lurking about in the cosmos. She merely shook her head slightly whilst thinking, Even if there were, I couldn't wear that dress now with all its bad memories.

'Oh dear,' said Ros again in a not too encouraging way. 'Well, the thing is, we did have to have a lot taken off the hem.'

God, I'm five foot two, not Jimmy Krankie, thought Stevie.

'I haven't worn it at all. Isn't there anything you can do? The shoes haven't even been out of the box and the veil is still wrapped up.'

Surely, other short people get married?

'Well, I did say that I would buy everything back for forty per cent if you wanted to sell it after the ceremony. That's the best I can do, I'm afraid. I've had to alter everything so much, you see.'

'The shoes and the veil haven't been altered though,' said Stevie bravely.

'Yes, but they've still been sold to you. Oh dear, it is sad.'

Obviously not sad enough, though.

'Is that really your best offer?' said Stevie, suspecting it probably was. 'It's cost me a small fortune.'

'I'd make him pay for it,' said Ros, still dreadfully sympathetic.

'Alas, that isn't an option,' said Stevie stiffly. Matthew hadn't contributed a penny towards the wedding and was swanning around in the seven hundred quid suit she had bought for him, not counting the shoes. Why hadn't she made him stump up? Why was she so stupidly unsparing?

'I'm afraid that really is my best offer,' said Ros, as if it embarrassed her terribly to say so.

'Okay,' said Stevie resignedly. 'Can I bring the dress and other stuff in today?'

'Yes, of course,' said Ros. 'I totally understand how you'll want it out of sight. Oh, it is such a shame, I am so sorry,' and she sounded it too. Sorry enough almost to cry, but not sorry enough to barter.

'Thank you for your help then,' said Stevie.

'A pleasure,' said Ros with a voice as soft and as sweet as June rose petals, belying a heart that was as soft and sweet as a concrete block.

Stevie decided not to make the other calls before getting rid of the dress and all the accessories that 'Kiss the Bride' supplied. She threw them all straight into the back of her car and headed into town, finding a parking space not too far away. There was an embarrassing walk through the arcade to the shop, as if everyone she passed knew she was taking the stuff back because she had been rejected for someone prettier with longer legs and who was no doubt better in bed as well.

Ros was dressing a dummy with a pageboy's outfit when she walked in. A little Scots boy with a kilt, wouldn't you just know it.

The 'poor you' look she gave Stevie when she entered the shop and set the bell tinkling, sent tears flooding up to her eyes.

'Aw, my dear,' said Ros. 'Come and sit down, whilst I check the dress over.'

It was amazing how cold and warm someone could be at the same time.

Satisfied that the dress hadn't been worn and that all the accessories were as perfect as Stevie had described, Ros wrote a cheque for exactly 40 per cent of the amount on the receipt. Right down to the twenty-four pence.

'Well, if it's any consolation, you'll have all this

excitement of picking another dress one day, I'm sure of it, dear,' said Ros with a big summery smile. 'He's a mad fool, but then they all are. Men.'

'Thank you, Ros,' said Stevie.

'I'm sorry I couldn't help more.'

'It's okay,' said Stevie, who found she was actually so relieved to have the stuff out of the house that in the end, she would have taken less if pushed. Not that she would voice that to Ros. She would need all the money she could get to pay Adam MacLean for living in the cottage.

'Have you had to cancel everything then?'

'*No, I thought I'd keep the cake and flowers for a laugh,*' she almost wanted to scream, but instead she answered calmly, 'Well, no. I've got that delightful task in front of me. You were first on my list.'

'Aw, I hope you have a friend there to help you. It's not something you'd want to do without support, is it?'

'No,' said Stevie with a loaded sigh, wondering how much support she would get from her mother, who was next on her list to ring.

'Good job I haven't bought my outfit yet then,' said Edna Honeywell with a big sniff. 'Anyway, I never liked him.'

'That's a lie, Mum – you said he was nice.'

'Too good-looking. You'd never have kept him.'

Thanks.

'He's not gone for good, Mum. We're just having a short break.'

'So what's *she* like?' Edna went on, not hearing what Stevie was telling her. 'I presume there is someone else.'

'There's no one else, Mum. We just want to be sure so we're putting the wedding off for a bit,' said Stevie, thrown off-kilter by her mother's powers of perception. She didn't want her parents knowing what the situation really was, because she knew this storm would blow over and she and Matthew *would* end up getting married later. Positive thoughts like this kept her spirits buoyant. It was crazy but somehow *she knew* he would come home to her heart again. This was merely a temporary glitch in the greater scheme of things, albeit a massive temporary glitch.

'There will be another woman, mark my words,' said Edna. 'They don't leave unless they've sniffed another bitch. Have you told *him* yet?'

'I'm going to ring Dad next. Will you let Auntie Rita know?'

'Yes I'll let our Rita know but I'll have to get off the phone soon, I was just on my way out.'

'Oh, going anywhere nice?' asked Stevie with a hopeful attempt at continuing the conversation for just a little longer.

'I've got a Salsa class at half-past.'

Stevie might have known. Her mother always did have a class on the go. She had been doing Great Female Poets during pregnancy and fallen in love with Stevie Smith's work, hence the choice of name for her daughter. Luckily the Greek Legends course had been cancelled otherwise Stevie would now be living life as Aphrodite Hera Honeywell.

'Okay, mum, I won't keep you.'

'Well, anyway, I'm sorry for you, lass. It can't be easy.'

'It isn't easy. Danny's fine, by the way.'

'I was just going to ask!' snapped Edna. 'I don't know, you can cause an argument in an empty house, can't you?' she continued. 'No wonder your fella buggered off.'

Stevie ended the call politely before it degenerated into all the other conversations they had, where she ended up feeling surplus to requirements. Edna Honeywell made Ros's heart look like a goosedown pillow.

Stevie told her dad that she and Matthew had decided to take some time apart and re-think things through. She gave him her new address.

'Nay, lass, never,' said Jack Honeywell, strangely drawing the same conclusion as her mother. 'He wants shooting. Can't keep it in their trousers, some lads,' which was rich, considering he had kept *it* well out of his trousers when he left her mum for Thick Neck. Then he cheated on Thick Neck for Cyclops, who lost her left eye in a fight years ago after being biffed in it with a bingo dabber. Neither woman had felt the slightest obligation to welcome Stevie into the step-family fold.

'Are you all right? Are you coping?' he asked solicitously.

'I'm fine, Dad. I've moved out. Danny's fine too by the way.'

'Good, give him a big kiss from his granddad. I nearly called in last week. We were passing coming from Thelma's (Cyclops's) son's house. Good job we didn't, if you'd moved.'

'I only moved last night.'

'Oh.'

Stevie finished the conversation before it ended up like all the other calls to her dad, which made her feel insignificant and second-best to her step-family, and that if it weren't for the connection of blood, there would be no connection at all.

Next was the cake woman.

'I've already made the fruit cakes in the hexagonals you wanted. I'll have to keep the deposit and just not charge you for the icing,' she said grumpily.

'Thank you,' said Stevie, who didn't feel up for a fight. Was she just being ultra-sensitive, or was the world really such a hard, bitter place, she wondered. Did people think she was doing this for a joke, organizing a wedding and then cancelling it because there was nothing good on the telly? The wedding world was far more cold hard cash than it was warm hearts and flowers. Talking of which, the florist was next call. Thank God for gay male florists.

'Oh, you poor darling,' said Donny Badger before spitting, 'Bastard!' like an irate cobra. If she had gone into the shop in person, she had no doubt he would have taken her in the back room and be plying her with biscuits and tissues by now, which might have been rather lovely because she so badly wanted someone to be nice to her. It was slightly disconcerting, the way everyone assumed she had been traded in for a better model. There seemed to be an awful lot of sceptics in the world. Maybe that's why her *Midnight Moon* books did so well, because her heroes and heroines were honourable and faithful and didn't hurt each other. True fantasy then. Stevie didn't want to turn into a hard-bitten cynic who didn't believe in love in real life any more.

However, it was looking more and more as if any love that existed out there was never going to be for her.

'Look, love, what's your address again? I'll put you a full refund of your deposit in the post.'

Stevie started to give her old address, before correcting herself. She should have got a forwarding form from the post office for her mail, although her post going across the road would at least give her the excuse to have contact with Matthew again. In saying that, she wasn't 100 per cent sure that she wanted to have it whilst her nerves were in this raw, torn state. It would be like picking at a sore, rubbing salt in the wound – all the clichés seemed to fit.

The photographer hadn't taken a deposit and was grumbling that he had turned someone away on that date for her. '*It's not my fault!*' she wanted to scream at him.

The vicar offered counselling, which she kindly refused, but he was very sweet. The manageress of the White Swan promised to send the deposit back, if she didn't tell anyone, she said warmly, although any faith recovered was lost again with the horrible old printer who had just completed the order of services and said he had just put them and the invoice in the post, so she would have to stump up.

After him, Stevie couldn't face making another call. She composed a general letter on her computer to send out to the people on her side of the guest list.

The wedding is off, sorry folks.
Matthew is shagging Jo MacLean.
Love,
Stevie x

Well, maybe not. The second draft was less blunt.

> *Due to unforeseen circumstances,*
> *the wedding between*
> *Matthew and me has been called off.*
> *Please don't ring. I will be in touch.*
> *Sorry, folks.*
> *Hope you are all well.*
> *Love Stevie (Honeywell) x*

It wasn't exactly literary genius but it was to the point and would do. She wondered how many of their guests would be of her mother's opinion and say, 'Well, I'm not surprised, he was far too good-looking for her.' It was one of many thoughts to torment her as she got on with the business of alternately addressing envelopes and wiping away the fat tears that were dropping from her eyes. Then, when she was done, she posted the letters as she went on her way to pick up her son from school, hoping no one at the school-gates would notice how red and puffed-up and sad her eyes were. Thank goodness, there was always a bout of conjunctivitis going around to blame it on.

Chapter 22

In the Queens Hotel, and after a very nice evening meal, Jo had just finished packing.

'I know this is an awful thing to say, but thank goodness Stevie's left the house,' she said, shutting the last case. 'I did wonder if she would start playing silly games.'

'Well, she's actually got out a day early for us,' reminded Matthew.

'That was sweet of her in the circumstances but it wouldn't do her any good at all psychologically, being in that house any more,' said Jo. 'I *so* cannot wait to get into a decent bed. I hope she hasn't left the place in a real mess for you.'

'I wouldn't have thought so, knowing Stevie,' said Matthew. 'Wonder where she's living?' It was a question that had been circling his head like a lost homing pigeon since he picked up the message that morning. He hadn't really believed her when she had told him on Sunday that she had somewhere else to go, and so when he heard her on the answerphone, he was amazed. Of course, he hadn't picked up the actual call because he was convinced she was ringing him to ask for extra time, or worse, to cry and beg him to come back.

The porter started to load the cases into Matthew's and Jo's cars like a Tetris expert.

'You drop those off and come back for me,' said Jo. 'Just in case there are any nasty surprises waiting.'

'I shouldn't think—'

'I'll stay here and have some coffee, darling,' said Jo, brooking no argument. She gave him a long, warm kiss that reached all the way down to his toes before zooming back up to his groin, then she waved him off and headed back to Reception.

Matthew parked the car outside his house in Blossom Lane then entered it tentatively in case a massive booby-trapped hammer arced down and smacked him cartoon-style on the head. To his relief, nothing happened, but then he hadn't even considered that Stevie would have done anything malicious until Jo had put the thought into his head. Everything looked nice, tidy – as it should be – and there was lots more room now that Stevie's work corner had been freed up and her boxes of books had gone. The hotel was plush but he had missed the comfort of his house and he couldn't wait to climb into his lovely cosy bed with a lovely cosy Jo that evening.

He took the suitcases upstairs and found the undressed bed.

Oh hell, he thought as it put paid to his plans to carry Jo over his threshold and then straight upstairs to tangle her up in the sheets. Then again, it was probably a bit much think-ing Stevie would make up a bed in which she knew he might soon be making love to someone else. *Still, he could-n't believe she hadn't done it for him*. He got a nip of guilt for being so mean and batted it away. He knew that if he stopped to think how horrible they had been to Stevie, it would ruin his first evening at home with Jo.

He went back to the hotel for the rest of the cases, hoping that maybe Jo would have settled the bill. The hol-iday had cost him a fortune and he thought she might have stumped up for her share but no, she had merrily let him pay for the lot and thereby ruined his chances of borrow-ing a cash advance against his Visa for the mortgage. He couldn't hope that Stevie would pay it for him any more now.

It wasn't that Matthew didn't earn a good wage because he did. It was just that he had managed to accumulate quite a lot of debts that accounted for most of his outgo-ings. It was a typical story: boy gets a few Visas and goes a bit mad, boy gets a huge consolidating loan, boy blows consolidating loan on big-woofer stereo and plasma TV and designer clothes instead. Life was really too short not to have nice meals out and look the very best he could whilst he was young. A work colleague had dropped dead from a congenital heart defect when he was twenty-five; if there wasn't a lesson there, where was there one?

When Stevie moved in and offered to pay half the bills, he was determined to use the money he would save to finally become debt free, only to find that spending money on nice meals and flash clothes was even more fun with Jo. And he couldn't stop buying her presents, especially when he found out how she said thank you. The long and the short of it was that he just liked to spend money, except that he did not have any to spend any more. At least, not his own.

Stevie didn't earn a fortune but he'd rather taken advantage of her selfless generosity, and whilst she was paying all the bills, thinking she was helping him to clear off some of his debts, he was actually wining and dining Jo. He hadn't quite told either of them just how bad things were financially – a man has his pride, etc – but Stevie had been quite sweet about the little she knew anyway. She used to stuff his pocket with money if they went out with friends and he would produce it like a wizard and play the benevolent sybarite. He suspected Jo might not be quite so accommodating.

On the drive back to the hotel, he was thinking that he would need to approach the financial problem with Jo sooner rather than later because this holiday had just about wiped him out. His resolve doubled when she swanned regally out of the hotel to wait in the car, leaving him to settle the account there too. There was an embarrassing moment when his Barclaycard was declined and he had to hunt around for his emergency Goldfish, which he was glad she hadn't been witness to. If the bloody basic bill wasn't bad enough, he discovered all the ironing services she had charged to the room, and she had just wasted another fifteen quid on coffee and farty little chocolate truffles whilst he had been engaged in taking the suitcases back to the house. Still, when she got her share from her divorce from MacLean, they would be laughing financially. Speculate to accumulate and all that.

He was like a kid who couldn't wait to unwrap his Christmas present when they got back to Blossom Lane. He lifted her over the threshold and shoved the door to with his foot so as not to interrupt his smooth passage up the stairs, but giggling she broke away.

'Don't leave the suitcases in the car,' she said.

'Later,' he said sexily, moving back in for more kisses.

'No way, my jewellery is in them,' she said, pressing him back out.

'Oh okay,' he said good-humouredly and went out to the Golf that she'd parked in his carport whilst his Punto stood behind it on the drive. There were lights on in the cottage across the road, he noticed. *Lord, some people have more money than sense!* Still, he wouldn't swap with them for what he had waiting for him behind his door.

Jo was running her finger around the surfaces when he got back inside.

'Well,' she said, 'I'm surprised. Had it been my man moving another woman in, I'd have made sure it was an absolute tip.'

'Stevie's not like that.'

'I don't mean to sound cruel, Matt, really I don't when I say this. Nice happy Stevie might not be like that but, as you know, unhappy scorned Stevie can be very nasty.'

'Hmmm,' said Matthew, although he knew that was slightly out of order. 'Nasty' was not a word he could truly associate with his ex. Even when she told him how mad she had gone during the Mick business, she had not done anything that could truly be classed as 'nasty'. Not making up a bed for him and his new lover hardly constituted cutting all the crotches out of his suits, although he realized he hadn't checked them. Sprinting quickly up the stairs, he threw open the wardrobe doors and flicked through them. Nope, all intact. *Phew!* Like he'd doubted her really! He knew Stevie like the back of his hand, although he had thought she would be more upset about them splitting up than she was. Admittedly, her total acceptance of the situation had surprised him. And even though he knew it was unreasonable, it had slightly annoyed him too.

Jo followed him up at a more leisurely pace and sussed out the wardrobe space situation.

'So that's one suitcase worth, where do I put the others?' she said with a teasing smile.

'We'll figure it out,' he said. 'Personally I think you should throw all your clothes away and be naked for ever.'

She laughed, and he thought, Bloody hell, she's in my bedroom at last. He felt as thrilled as he did when he was in the same situation with Tina Tinker when they were seventeen and his mam and dad were away for the night.

'I see the bed's not made.' She poked the naked quilt.

'Do you care?'

'What do you think?'

'I think I want to see you undressed on it now.'

She slowly unbuttoned her shirt, and the sensations that started to missile his brain knocked all thoughts of Visas and Mastercards and bank loans and overdrafts into Kingdom Come.

Chapter 23

Nothing could have prepared Stevie for the sight that met her eyes as she went to close the kitchen blinds. She could not possibly have ever found a big enough piece of padding to protect her heart against it, not even on the World Wide Web. She jumped back from the window as if it had just given her a belt of electricity and hid in the shadows, wanting to move away but unable to. With a gruesome compulsion, she watched the smart red Golf drive cosily into Matthew's carport then his black Punto pull up behind it. Both drivers got out smiling, and then her ex-fiancé scooped up her treacherous ex-friend in his arms and carried her Prince-Charming style into her ex-home. They were giggling, probably singing a song from *Oklahoma* as well, because that's what it looked like – Hollywood happiness – the sort you dream of but only one person in a million ever gets, and it is never you. The door seemed to close slowly and magically behind them, and at that very moment it felt as if someone had whipped away the top layer of Stevie's skin and everything that possibly could, hurt and throbbed. What the hell had possessed her to follow Adam MacLean's hare-brained scheme and move into this cottage, when she had known she would feel like this as soon as she saw *them* together? It was going to kill her, day after day after day. She could appreciate how Prometheus felt now, having his insides eternally picked at by a big bird for stealing fire from the gods. Except it was her that was being both stolen from and punished, and no prizes for guessing who the big bird was.

Mesmerized, she stayed there watching for sights of more animation, and was rewarded, if you could call it that, for her patience with the sight of Matthew speeding out again to get their suitcases, rushed and clumsy like some Ealing Comedy newlywed. Then she watched as the bedroom light went on upstairs, and then watched as it went off.

Her high-performance imagination made a best friend and a powerful enemy. When dealing with the Parises and Brandons at work, it had a good place, but here it tortured her with a horrible and vivid slideshow projection. They would have fallen onto the bed now, not even noticing that it hadn't been made. An orchestra was welling up behind them, the couple that were meant to *be,* the heaven-made match who would ride every tidal wave life threw at them, like champion golden Australian surfers. They would buy each other anniversary cards, years from now, with poems on page 3 that précised to 'we showed 'em, didn't we?' and their 'our song' would be something by Shania Twain. They would spend their lives bonking like beautiful body-perfect minks: Jo savouring Matt's toned, lightly muscular body and his big shoulders whilst Matthew marvelled in her velvet skin and her cellulite-free arse. These were

Stevie's thoughts as she stood in her *Joseph and his Technicolor Dreamcoat* dressing-gown and Totes Toasties, and continued to sip from a mint Options, which had long since gone cold.

She honestly did not know if she could go on. Her life was a shambles, her fiancé was a love rat, her friend was a love rattess, she couldn't face writing any more and she was in a house she couldn't afford. Not only that, but she had not yet formally sorted out terms and conditions with a bloke she owed money to who had no qualms about bashing women he supposedly liked. So what would he do to women he couldn't stand the sight of? And what if McPsychopath demanded his oats instead of money – and she didn't mean the Scott's Porage variety? Then again, she had to go on, because she had a wee – a *little* boy sleeping upstairs, wrapped round a cuddly Superhero, who needed his mam to be strong and to feed him and provide for him and give him a home other than a cardboard box on a street somewhere. Even if she was an old boot of a mam that had surprised no one by being dumped. Thank God she was only drinking cold hot chocolate and wasn't up to her forehead in gin because by now she would have had her Roy Orbison CD on and be upping the Kleenex shares by fifty quid each, and be in a very dangerous state of mind.

She did eventually doze off in bed that night, but only in between many wakings up that meant she bobbed in the shallow waters of sleep rather than surrendered to the deeper warm currents that rested the mind. Her dreams had a Hammer House of Horror certificate.

★

Stevie had read, and indeed written, about people who compartmentalized their pain, who put a jolly face on and confronted the world, even though their heart was cracking inside them, only to sob into their pillows when they were safely alone, but she didn't really believe anyone could manage it successfully. She found, however, the next morning, that she was living proof of the phenomenon. She scurried around the kitchen like Doris Day, for Danny's sake, tra-la-la-ing as she poured out Coco Pops and orange juice and made 'fresh cwoffee'. She kept the kitchen blinds open to a minimum, just enough to let some sunlight squeeze through them, but at an angle that didn't allow her to see anything of the house opposite, or the goings-on of the people within it.

As soon as Danny was safely in school, her whole body seemed to sag, not helped by the fact that a day of trying to sort out Paris and Brandon's fates awaited her. She knew another wasted morning of rubbish-quality writing would be the outcome, and that the only possible solution of working off some of the half-grief, half-murder feelings that were munching away inside her, lay up the road in Well Life.

It was the first time she had been since doing her Norman Wisdom routine on the treadmill, but contrary to her belief, no one nudged each other as she got on it or pointed her out. There were no, 'That's her's whispered a bit too loudly or sniggering behind hands; she was once again consigned to the anonymous. Grabbing a towel, she put her bag in the locker and climbed aboard the treadmill carefully. She had forgotten her headphones so couldn't divert her thoughts by listening to Jeremy Kyle trying to sort out complicated dysfunctional lives on the overhead TVs. Maybe she should give him a ring.

She tried to blank her mind and keep her pacing rhythm true to the background music blasting out through the speakers, until she realized the track was 'Loneliness' and a connection sparked between her and the song. From then on, every time she heard it in the future, an accompanying image of herself lonely and rejected would loom up in her head, sadly trying to achieve the impossible by running on the spot. Her eyes started to leak again to her absolute horror, and she tried to build a quick surreptitious eye-wipe into her routine, which nearly upset her balance. She had decided to rest the machine for a couple of minutes when she saw Adam MacLean heading directly towards her.

Oh farts!

She acted out a scene of 'something in my eye . . . oooh good, it's gone now' whilst waiting for the inevitable.

'Sohowryegeinun?' he said, in the mistaken belief that big volume would make her understand what the hell he was saying. Seeing her look of utter confusion, he began again slowly, as if he was talking to a daft old aunt. 'So how arrre you getting on?'

'Fine,' she replied. 'I've just got something in my eye.'

'Aye, the place is full of flying things.'

She suspected that might have been sarcasm, but he wasn't giving any clues.

'Any news aboot yoor man?'

'He's . . . er . . .' Her voice started to wobble and she coughed. 'He moved in last night with . . . er . . .' She couldn't have said her name if there was a million pounds riding on it.

'So it's time to start a plan of action,' Adam said, after a big gulp.

'Right,' she replied warily. She rubbed her neck, which was straining because of the angle it had to achieve to talk to him up there.

He picked up on that and asked, 'Have ya time for a wee cup o' tea?'

'Um yes,' said Stevie, following five paces behind him to the coffee bar, where he grunted something about sitting down at a table (she thought) and then said something equally incomprehensible to the girl behind the counter who seemed to understand perfectly. It was obviously a prerequisite of his staff to be bi-lingual, she concluded. English and Caveman.

Stevie sat with her hands in the prayer position in between her knees. She was trembling. It wasn't unlike the sensation of waiting outside the headmaster's office for a roasting, which she had only had to do the once, and that was a case of mistaken identity. To be there for a legitimate reason was bad enough, but to be there when you were innocent of the crime alleged (apple scrumping) had been terrifying. Fortunately her case for the defence was believed ('It couldn't have been me, I've got a fear of heights and I'd vomit if I climbed a tree'), especially after it was validated by Miss Crackett, the PE teacher, who had once been witness to her being sick from the top of the ropes. She was rightly exonerated, but that experience had left its scar. She had never been able to abide injustice.

Adam put down two cups of tea and a jug of milk and some sugars on the table and then sat down opposite to her, blocking out most of the light from the window behind him like a solar eclipse. He tipped the milk over hers first but she refused. Likewise the sugar.

Jeez, she doesn't take sugar! he thought.

Jesus, he's got manners! she thought.

Then she remembered he probably had a first-class degree from the University of Charm and quickly withdrew any thoughts of goodwill.

The tea was molten and burnt her mouth. Adam watched her gasp, gulp, fan her mouth in barely covered amazement, and asked, 'Are ye sure ye're no' a self-harmer?'

'It was extra hot!' she snapped. 'Where did it get brewed – hell?'

It wasn't outside the realms of possibility.

'So have you any ideas whit you'd like to dae next, before I tell ye what I think?' he said.

Stevie shrugged. In truth, she didn't want to do anything but pack up and escape to some place on the other side of the world. A nice thought that rocketed up freely, only to be brought down by the weight of practicalities.

'We have to sort out money,' she said tentatively. 'It all happened so fast we didn't get an agreement.'

'It's okay – if you don't pay, I'll throw you oot,' he said with a smile that didn't quite reach up to his eyes.

Her lungs inflated sharply.

'S'okay, only joking,' he said, seeing the look of horror flash in her eyes. 'I'm no worried aboot aw that, we'll sort that later, really. It'll give me an excuse to come around to the cottage some time soon and be seen. Talking of which, have they seen you yet?'

'No,' said Stevie, shaking her head. 'I sneaked my car into the garage and I've only used the back door when I've gone out anywhere.'

'Guid – sorry – *good*. Now, let me think.' He stroked the red stubble coming through even though he had only shaved a few hours earlier, and stared up into space as if hoping to see the answer materialize there in front of him.

'We have to leave them a tantalizing trail of crumbs. They have to realize that you're living there before he knows there's anything going on between us two. Not that there is,' he added sharply.

Like she'd have jumped in and blushed and giggled and tried to correct him!

'So here's what I think,' Adam went on. 'Did you get a forwarding order for your post?'

'No, not yet. I—'

'Paarrrfect,' said Adam. 'Now, here's what I want you to do . . .'

Chapter 24

'Darling, where's the iron?' Jo called upstairs to Matthew, now alone in the bath that they had been sharing until five minutes ago.

'Under the stairs with the ironing board. Sorry, darling, didn't you hear me?'

'Yes, I know you said that, darling, but it isn't there.'

Matthew heaved himself out of the bath and into his robe to go and check for her. He padded downstairs, leaving bubbly footprints, and poked his head inside the cupboard, where Jo was waiting and gesticulating like an airhostess demonstrating a safety procedure.

'But it's always there,' he said, scratching his damp head.

'Stevie will have taken it, won't she?' said Jo, shaking her own damp head whilst smiling with some annoyance. 'Like she took your microwave and any towel that was half-decent.'

'Oh yes . . . er . . . she might have. It was a big fancy thing. She only bought it a couple of weeks ago.'

'Gr-eat,' said Jo. 'So what do I use now? Please tell me you've got a spare.'

'Look,' said Matthew, who thought she looked uber-sexy in sulk-mode, 'we'll pick up one tomorrow. You've got stacks of other clothes you can wear,' which, incidentally, had taken up her side of the wardrobe and half of his and they would still have to buy another at some point. If he managed to find some space on a Visa, that was.

'I haven't anything that's pressed though. Aw, I really wanted to wear that dress, too,' Jo pouted.

'I wanted you to wear that dress, too, darling,' said Matthew, moving in for a long, slow kiss. She had worn it the first time they had made love in Stevie's car. It had very happy memories for him and he was hoping for an action replay in the back of his Punto on the way home from the restaurant.

'Okay, I'll find something else,' she sighed. 'I can't blame Stevie for taking a little revenge. I'm only glad it wasn't more.'

'Put anything on. We're only going out for something to eat at Giovanni's, not the Ritz,' he laughed and tweaked her gorgeously cute nose.

'Matthew Finch, I shall always look my best even if we are eating fish and chips out of newspaper on a park bench.'

Matthew wished they were. He had just paid fifty quid off his credit card and he was going to be loading another hundred on. Did they really need to celebrate their first full day of living together by spending so much?

'We could stay in and eat each other,' he suggested, which he would prefer, financial reasons or no financial reasons.

'No, I want to see and be seen – with you, obviously,' she said, smiling a smile that would melt him into spending every last penny he didn't have. *Did life really get any better than this?* Then his mobile rang.

He was in such a dreamlike state that he never checked the caller ID and clicked straight onto answer.

'Hello, Matthew Finch.'

'Hello, Matthew, it's Stevie.'

Damn!

'Oh hi, Stevie,' he said, tightening. Jo mouthed, 'What does she want?' to which Matthew shrugged innocently as if he had just been accused of something.

'Sorry to bother you, it's just a quick call. It's about my post.'

'Oh of course, your post,' he said aloud for Jo's benefit.

'I have informed people of my new address, but just in case any stray letters slip through the net . . .'

'Course, I'll forward them to you,' he said, butting in, anxious to get her off the line. Jo was looking distinctly territorial and it was making him nervous, and slightly horny too. He grabbed a pen and notepad. 'Okay, give me your new address and I'll post them on.'

'Er . . . well . . . there's no need,' said Stevie.

Hell, she wants to call and get them, he thought, and quickly jumped in to head her off at the pass.

'No trouble at all. So where are you?'

'That's what I'm trying to tell you,' said Stevie. 'You can just pop them through the letterbox if you wouldn't mind.' She took a huge breath to prepare herself for dropping the bombshell. 'I'm in the cottage across the street.'

'You're what?' Matthew drained so white that Jo poked him with her sharpest nail to get his attention to find out what was going on, not that Matthew felt it as he headed for the window to peer through the curtain. Sure enough, there at the other side of the street, was the figure of a person also on a mobile waving at him, although the voice was loud and clear in his ear. It was the most uncomfortable stereo experience he could remember.

'Hi, there you are!'

'W . . .' he said, but the word, whatever it was, refused to be formed.

'Anyway, that's all for now. So thanks, and er . . . good night.'

Matthew didn't say a word. He just clicked off his phone and answered Jo's flurry of questions with a flat, disbelieving voice.

'That was Stevie. She wants her post. She's moved into that cottage.'

'Which cottage, where?' said Jo, flicking back the curtain herself but seeing only a square of light from the big pretty house opposite. 'There?' she said. 'No, not there – tell me not there!'

'Yes, there.'

'How there? Why there?'

'I don't know.'

'What's she playing at?'

'I don't know.'

'Well, it's obvious isn't it? She's flipped!' said Jo, shaking her head wearily. 'I knew this had gone too smoothly to be believed. Matt, you have to talk to her. She's nuts. Poor, poor Stevie. Does she really think you'll go back to her if she stalks you? She's doing what she did with her husband all over again, isn't she?'

'I don't know,' said Matthew, who didn't. It was certainly

going to be an expensive way to tail him and for no end. He should have seen this coming, really, because she did have some history as a bit of a hanger-on when it was obvious the relationship was dead. Maybe he should go over and talk to her about it and spell it out that he really was not coming back. Jo was right, though, it certainly explained why she had 'let him off' so lightly. She had obviously been saving her energies for this pièce de résistance. *Did she see Jo's car arrive? Did she see him carry her inside? So then, did she realize Jo had actually moved in? How mad would that make her feel? Had she copied his keys? Could he smell prawns?* The questions got too big and he suddenly wanted to get away from it all.

'Come on, let's just get ready and go out. We'll deal with this later, but for now, let's go eat.'

'And drink,' said Jo, who threw down the useless, thin, bendy Ryvita of a towel that was wrapped around her hair but had absorbed nothing. Then she skipped upstairs to her extensive designer wardrobe, throwing behind her, 'I'll need champagne to drown out this little revelation!'

Matthew groaned.

Stevie breathed slowly in and out as she had done in labour to steady herself. She could barely press the disconnect button on the phone for trembling. Then, when she felt able to cross to the window again, she snapped the blinds shut, cocooning herself safely away from the rest of the world, and leant against the wall for some badly needed support because this was the closest she had ever come in her life to fainting. Then she stabbed in the text lettering *Mission accomplished*, and sent it to Adam MacLean.

Chapter 25

A parcel arrived for Matthew just as he and Jo were setting off for work the following morning. He threw it in the porch to deal with later because he did not have the time to open it then. He locked up the house and looked across at the old cottage before getting in the car, half-expecting to see Stevie framed in the window, staring back wistfully at him. Or tapping an axe in her hand. Or holding a rabbit and a big stew pot. As it was, he saw only a cottage with all the curtains drawn and blinds dropped, but knowing that Stevie was moving behind them still made him feel uncomfortable.

Jo had been right, scorned women were dangerous, irrational beings and she couldn't have moved in across the road for any other reason than to wreak havoc in his life. He should have realized she had trouble dealing with rejection. By her own admission, Mick's leaving had driven her half-mad. Certainly, her little phone call had put a big damp cloth over their whole evening. All roads of conversation bent back to Stevie and her new living arrangements, however much they had tried to get on with enjoying the meal. They hadn't succeeded and Matthew had driven straight home, with no detour down Lovers' Lane. It had not been ninety-two quid well spent.

Matthew had struggled to get an erection in bed because the thought of his ex-lover living directly across the lane had got in the way and stirred up all sorts of feelings that had fingers in all sorts of emotional pies. He had managed to perform in the end, because who couldn't when they were in bed with someone as gorgeous as Jo, but it wouldn't have gone down as his best performance. Although it was still bloody good.

Jo was taking him shopping at lunchtime for an iron and a microwave and some towels that didn't scratch her skin off, and some decent sheets. He pocketed the invitation to get a new Platinum Visa that arrived with that morning's post from one of the few remaining banks with whom he didn't have one. His emergency Goldfish was starting to drown.

Catherine was already at the garden centre café when Stevie rolled up. Catherine had suggested lunch out, away from Blossom Lane and the gym. She thought some country air and carbs might do her friend good. They hugged hello and plonked themselves at a nice table with a view of the stream, heavily populated by ducks and a gangsta goose.

'So how's it going, dare I ask? Got back into your writing yet?' asked Catherine, after they had sent the young waiter off with an order for caramel lattes and two pasta carbonaras. Stevie's shiny-eyed silence made any verbal answer unnecessary. Catherine reached over the table and gave her hand a comforting squeeze.

'Stevie, I've not really a doubt in my head that Matthew will come back to you after he's realized that Jo is a cold, calculating bitch who probably deserved to get clobbered by Highland Hairy Legs, but—'

'But what?'

'But is he really the person you thought he was, to put you through this? Would you ever be able to trust him again?'

'I want him back, Catherine,' she said steadily. 'We'll sort it out between us afterwards, I'm sure of it.'

'It will happen,' said Catherine, who was totally convinced of it. 'Both Eddie and I think that Matthew's weak rather than wicked. Anyway, what's the update?'

There was a brief pause whilst the coffees arrived. Then another brief pause whilst Catherine sent them back for being lukewarm.

'At these prices I should get third-degree burns off this!' she said to the waiter, who went off hunched over with humiliation, as if his mum had just smacked his legs.

'I met Adam MacLean in the gym yesterday,' said Stevie.

'And?'

'He told me what to do and I did it.'

'Which was?' said Catherine eagerly, rotating her hands as if to wind her friend's clockwork up.

'To ring Matthew and tell him if I had any post to drop it off at the cottage opposite.'

'Hang on a mo,' said Catherine as the waiter came back with two fresh coffees and stood there dutifully whilst she tested the temperature. She nodded her approval and he went off smiling with relief, as if she was the man from Del Monte.

'So, Matt knows where you're living then – oh wow!' carried on Catherine, as they spooned off the froth and drank the lovely sweet coffee. 'And how did he take it?'

'I think he was too shocked to say anything then, but I had a peep through the kitchen blinds this morning and saw him staring over – sorry, *glaring* over – at the house before he got into the car. He didn't look very pleased at all.'

'Good!' said Catherine. Then the pasta arrived.

'Not good really,' said Stevie. 'I don't want him to hate me. I want him to love me.'

'Bloody hell, Steve,' said Catherine crossly. 'He doesn't own the whole town – you can live where you like! Tough tits if he doesn't like it. There's Danny's school to think of, more than his inconvenience.'

'Yes, you're right,' said Stevie, marking those points down for possible regurgitation later. 'Although, it does look a bit obvious why I've moved there, doesn't it? He'll think I'm stalking him.'

'Not if you ignore him he won't, and certainly not if you're seen on the arm of another bloke.'

'Don't remind me.' The prospect of that part of Adam MacLean's so-called 'plan' was starting to make her feel ill. For a start, they would look the world's most ridiculous couple, and what would they talk about? His experiences in Barlinnie? The best way to garrotte someone? She despised people like him – pathetic bullies who used their size and looks to intimidate. The fact that she could join forces with someone who actually deserved to be deserted by his partner spoke volumes of her desperation to get Matthew back, and as soon as she had, she hoped Jo and Adam MacLean would disappear back to hell.

The two women filled their mouths with the spaghetti and the waiter picked that moment to pop back to make sure everything was all right, to which they both nodded vigorously and made primeval noises.

'They teach them that at waiter school,' said Stevie after she had swallowed. 'To wait until everyone has their mouths stocked before asking it. They love it. It's a perk of the job.'

Catherine laughed. It was good to hear Stevie make a joke.

'It's actually perfect, you moving across the road,' Catherine said. 'Old Thunder Thighs is right, you know. It *will* confuse them both. They'll be on constant red alert waiting for something to happen. He's quite a clued-up bloke, isn't he?'

'Yes, well, we'll see,' said Stevie, who had yet to be totally convinced. She was sure she would be in for just as many nasty surprises from MacLean.

'So when's the next attack?'

'I don't know,' said Stevie. 'I think the idea was to wait and see what the fall-out from stage one was. Sort of a softly, softly approach.'

'It's like *Mission Impossible*,' said Catherine.

Stevie nodded, knowing what Catherine meant, but her words did sound a depressing, prophetic note. She really was starting to wonder if fighting back was just going to make everything so much worse.

Matthew went into the house, forgot the box was there and tripped right over it, which only added to his mood of annoyance. Not that opening the box did anything to take those feelings away.

'What are those?' said Jo, looking over his shoulder as he unpeeled layers of tissue around some very pretty, be-rib-boned stationery. It was funny to see his name there still together with Stevie's. It felt like years ago since they had been together choosing the paper and the lettering and the picture on the covers, when, in real time, it had been less than three months.

'Order of services and an invoice for ... HOW MUCH?'

Jo eased it out of his hand.

'You aren't going to like this but hear me out,' she said calmly. 'This bill is in Stevie's name. You need to take it across the road now and let her deal with it.'

'I'd feel a bit rotten doing that,' said Matthew with a stab of guilt, not saying that it had been he who picked such an ornate and expensive design.

'As I say, hear me out,' admonished Jo softly. 'The reason you need to do what I say is that if you are nice and offer to pay for these, Stevie will misread your actions and see hope where there is none. You have to be cruel to be kind here, Matt. You need to be hard with her. Go across the road and insist she pays for these. Don't play her game, for all our sakes – especially Stevie's, darling. Just give her the box and come straight back. Don't let her use it as an excuse to engage you. You won't be doing her any favours in the long run. Trust me. We don't want her to be hurt any more than she is already, do we?'

'Yes okay,' said Matthew, before any of his more hon-ourable thoughts questioned Jo's logic. He hoisted the box up, marched across to the cottage, and rapped loudly on the door.

When Stevie saw Matthew approach, she put two and two together to make a very accurate four. She straightened her back and opened the door, half-closing it behind her so Danny wouldn't see or hear. The straight-backed, unthreat-ening sight of her stole a hundred knots of wind from his sails. She looked so *together*, and her stiff body language was not saying to him, 'How nice to see you, I'm so glad you called.'

'These arrived for you,' he said, thrusting them forwards.

'The order of services, I presume. Yes, the printer said they were on their way,' she replied, without making any attempt to take them from him.

'Well, here you are.' He rattled the box at her, but her hands stayed by her sides.

'You could have saved yourself a trip and just put them in the bin,' she said flatly. 'I have as much use for them as you do, Matthew.'

'There's . . . er . . . an invoice.'

Despite her attempt at indifference, Stevie found herself unable to disguise the flare of contempt in her eyes, which hit him at point-blank range and stirred up something within him that didn't make him feel very good about himself. He deflected it back, attack being the best form of defence, etc, and surprisingly found he didn't need to fake his annoyance.

'Why are you here, Stevie?'

She could have been glib and explained that the birds and the bees visited her mother and father one day, but decided to play it straight.

'You wanted me out, quickly, and this house was available.'

'But why here? Why this street?'

'Matthew,' she began calmly, without surface emotion, even though she was bubbling inside with a cocktail of anger and frustration with base flavours of hurt and despair, 'this was the only house I could get that was near to Danny's school. You didn't exactly give me the luxury of time to shop around, did you? Besides, you have made it perfectly clear that you have another life now, and so have I – one that you're not part of any more. I am a free agent too now, remember, and can live where I like.'

She whipped the invoice from the top of the box.

'My wheelie bin's full so I'll deal with this and you deal with those. Please let's keep this civilized, Matthew. Thank you for bringing the bill.'

And with that, Stevie slowly but firmly shut the door in his face.

Matthew hadn't been expecting that. He felt as if he had been slapped, even though she hadn't been aggressive or shouted or tried to use the parcel as a way to keep him there, as he had been led to believe by Jo that she would.

There was no pleading, no trying to win him back. It has to be a double bluff, he thought. Then again, she was acting 'indifference' awfully well. Too well, actually. If he didn't know Stevie so intimately, he would have thought she really meant what she had just said. She couldn't have forgotten him that quickly really, could she?

He was well aware that Jo was staring at his progress through the window opposite as he walked back over with the box, so he was jolly glad Stevie had taken the invoice. He was, after all, thinking of her emotional welfare in the long run. So why then did he feel like an absolute shit?

Stevie patted her heart and wondered how she could have spoken so coolly with the acrobatics it had been doing simultaneously in her chest. She had not a clue how she had held it together, but she had and she was proud of herself. Any weakness, any show of hurt, would have proved all his suspicions right but she had given him none. Her little victory did not stop her feeling inordinately sad, though. How could she and Matthew be such strangers to each other, when less than three weeks ago they had made love in the bed he now shared with another woman? She started to think about the details of that last time, how he had been mentally in another place whilst his body had been beside her, although he had put it down to being tired and she'd had no reason to disbelieve him. She had even given him a long massage to ease him to sleep. With the clear eye of hindsight, she realized that it wasn't an act of love after all but a red herring shag to put her off the scent that he was about to go on holiday with another woman.

The thought opened the catch to a big box of hurt that sprang its lid and filled up her heart to bursting-point. He had cared for her once – very much, she knew – so where had those feelings gone? Why hadn't she felt him slipping away?

She supposed she had better let Adam MacLean know; they had agreed to keep each other up to speed, after all. She checked on Danny and then dialled his number.

'Hlloooadmcln,' he said.

'Hello, it's Stevie Honeywell,' she said.

'How can I help you?' he said brusquely.

'Just an update. Matthew came over with a parcel for me and asked what I was doing in the cottage.'

'Do tell me more,' Adam said, as if the drama of it all was killing him. Not.

'Well, I told him that I had my life now and he had his. I think he was quite surprised.'

'Oh, right.'

Stevie snapped. 'Mr MacLean, you asked me to keep you updated. That's exactly what I'm doing. Sorry to have bothered you.' Then she hit disconnect before he came back at her with any more of his hilarious dry Scottish wit.

Adam MacLean had been about to say, 'Yes, I know you did and I appreciate it,' when she had a hissy fit and slammed the phone down on him. It was obviously *that week* every week with her. Luckily they weren't in the same room or she would probably have thrown a vase at him, that being her usual trick when she didn't get her own way, apparently. She should have been grateful he spoke to her at all; everyone else had had a grunt today, if they were lucky.

That morning the bed had seemed much emptier and colder than before and it hit him hard and low that Jo might just have gone for ever. Then he sprang out of that cold lonely bedroom and he knew that it wouldn't happen, because he wouldn't, *couldn't* let her go – and even if he had to marry that bloody Stevie woman to make Jo intrigued or jealous enough to come back to him, then he would – although he hoped to heaven and back that it wouldn't come to that. Then Adam opened his birthday cards.

Chapter 26

Catherine flopped on the sofa and stuck her feet up on the footstool.

'Here you go,' said Eddie, and placed a large glass of white wine in her hand.

'Thank you, my big gorgeous darling,' said Catherine.

'Flaming Norah! How many have you had already?'

Catherine laughed and took a mighty swig that she felt snake down to her tum and then rocket back up to her brain. 'God, I needed that. I mean, much as I love my kids, I do so enjoy this time of night when it's just you and me,' she said, snuggling down into the big cushions on the sofa and grabbing the TV mag. There was a Dalziel and Pascoe on in half an hour on cable, and the curry was due to arrive in twenty minutes from the Koh-i-noor. Bliss!

'All right if I go out with Large White and Judd tomorrow for a couple of jars? I'll be back by eleven,' said Eddie. Not that he had to clock in and clock out, but he had a faulty male wire that compelled him to ring home and give info and not be on an elastic band. In fact, all the considerate things that according to *Men are from Mars . . .* he shouldn't have done if he had a willy.

'Yeah, course,' she said. 'You don't have to ask me, love.'

'I know,' he said and smiled over and she smiled back and they settled into an easy relaxed silence whilst the box entertained them.

'Funny though,' said Eddie eventually.

'What is?' said Catherine, holding out her drained glass for a fill-up. Eddie reached down to the side of him and recharged it for her.

'Well, I've been thinking, if you did mind about me going out for a night, say if you were the possessive type, you wouldn't exactly let me go to a health spa for a week, would you?'

'You're going to a health spa?' said Catherine.

'Am I hell. I'm not talking about me, I'm talking about that Jo and the big Scottish bloke. How come he never let her out of his sight but he was okay about her going to that health spa? You know, the one she never actually went to.'

'Hmmm, I see what you mean, yes,' said Catherine.

'I was watching him at the wedding, you know, and he looked an okay bloke to me. I don't buy all that wife-beater stuff. Something wrong somewhere.'

Catherine nodded. Her thoughts had been running along the same lines, but her brain reminded her how wrong they had been about Matthew. Maybe they weren't such good judges of character as they believed. Still, interesting point. She should tell Stevie.

Catherine lifted the phone to dial Stevie's number when it rang in her hand and she picked up to find the very person she wanted to speak to. It happened quite a lot to them.

'Listen,' said Catherine excitedly, 'Eddie's brain grinds slowly but exceedingly small and he's just come up with the point that if Adam MacLean had Jo on such a tight leash, how come he was okay about letting her go to a health farm for a week?'

'I don't know,' said Stevie, mulling it over. 'It's a bit weird, I suppose, isn't it?'

'Yes, isn't it.'

'But then Adam MacLean is weird full stop. He probably had a "plan" to do with that, too.'

'No! Do you think?' Catherine said.

'Most likely. Maybe he suspected something but gave her some space to smoke her out.' It wasn't information Stevie attached any great significance to, but, nevertheless, she filed it in her mind under 'B' for MacLean. Then she went on to tell Catherine about that day's adventure with Matthew and the parcel, pausing periodically to allow a few choice expletives to air from her friend. Stevie found it gave her some comfort to be free temporarily to hate the man out loud whom she still wanted so very much within.

Across the road, all thoughts of cancelled weddings were now in the wheelie bin with the box of stationery. With an arm around his sleepy lover, Matthew flicked lazily through Ceefax at the news, then the football results, then the numbers for the previous night's lottery draw. Not that he expected anything; he had only won about three tenners ever, or so it felt. At one point he had been buying Thunderballs, EuroMillions, Hot Picks, Extras, Daily Plays and then the Irish Lottery too until he realized he really,

really couldn't afford to carry on, and resigned himself to the occasional Lucky Dip and a regular line twice a week. He had just changed his numbers to his and Jo's birthdays and the date they first made love. Numbers that were now on the screen in front of him.

'That can't be right,' he said, dislodging Jo for a moment in order to get out his ticket from the drawer.

'What's the matter?' Jo asked. She was just about asleep with the delicious combination of a very nice white wine, a very nice warm room and a very nice man stroking her arm very nicely.

'I've won the Wednesday lottery!' said Matthew, checking the screen numbers against his ticket numbers. A cold hand grabbed his innards tightly as he thought it was out of date, then realized to his relief that it wasn't. Jo, now fully awake, snatched it out of his hand and double-checked it.

'Five, you've got five. My God, how much is that?' she shrieked.

'I don't know, I don't know!' he said. He didn't like to hazard a guess.

'How do you find out?'

'I don't know, I've only ever won tenners.'

Jo looked at the back of the lottery ticket. 'You have to ring Camelot! Quick, hand me the phone!'

Matthew handed her the phone. The line was engaged, so was his head. He could clear all his debts and start a clean slate. He would tear all his Visas up and live within his means. Then again, it was sensible to keep one or two to pay for purchases and holidays, for the extra insurance they gave. A holiday in Barbados for instance, Jo in that white bikini during the day, that little red G-string during the evening and nothing at all during the night.

'Try again!'

'Still engaged!'

'Here, let me try!'

'Anything?'

'Engaged again.'

'Matt, go and get some champagne.'

'What?'

Jo kissed him. She was fizzing like a bottle of Bollinger. 'Go and get some champagne. We have to! Oh please. Let's toast our luck.'

She looked at him in that sultry big-lashed way of hers that was full of lust and promise of even more lust. Goddammit, she was gorgeous. He didn't need champagne to make his heart any more thrilled. He would have got the same effect from a carton of Um Bongo if it was shared with Jo. But she had other ideas.

'Please, darling. If ever there was a champagne moment, this is it.'

'*Twenty quid for some champagne,*' said the part of his head that governed his pant-area. '*You're going to have thousands in the bank in a couple of days, you can please the lady with a bottle, surely?*'

'Okay,' he relented, and she jumped up and down and clapped her hands like a little girl.

'Bring back two,' she said. 'We'll get horribly drunk and ring in sick tomorrow and then spend all day in bed and plan what we're going to do with the money.'

Matthew already had his shoes on.

'Don't ring again until I get back,' he warned sexily. 'Or I'll have to smack your bottom.'

'Ooh, promises, promises,' she said.

'You're my good-luck charm, that's what you are,' he said, pulling her into his arms and kissing her lovely juicy lips.

'You'd better not be long,' she purred. 'Although I might have slipped into something more comfortable by the time you get back. My, it's so hot in here,' and she unbuttoned her shirt a couple more notches.

He shot out of the door to the car with a smile as big as his erection, although both reduced a little when he saw the light filtering through the blinds across the lane. A kind thought slipped through all the black ones that said he really should give Stevie some money from his winnings towards the cancelled wedding and what he owed for Danny's holiday.

But then again, if she could afford to live in that cottage . . . And Jo said he had to be cruel in the short run to be kind in the long run.

In a trice Matthew had justified keeping his winnings for himself and Jo, and he drove to the off-licence for their champagne.

Chapter 27

There was a message waiting for Stevie after she had come back from an Adam MacLean-free hour on the weights at the gym.

'*Bea darling, it's Crystal. Just ringing to see if everything's okay,*' which was her boss Crystal Rock's (yes, really) way of saying, 'Where the fucking hell is your manuscript? It's overdue and I never have to chase you – so what's wrong?'

Stevie bit the bullet and rang her back immediately.

'Darling!' Crystal said, when her latest PA (Danielle?) put her through. Stevie tried to learn their names, but none of them seemed to last more than a week. Crystal was scare-ee, although somehow she and Stevie had always managed to get on just fine.

'Hiya, Crys, sorry I've not been in touch.'

'I was worried about you, darling,' said Crystal, who had a voice like an expensive smooth cocktail.

'I was just ringing to allay your fears and say that my manuscript is nearly ready.'

'Nearly? Oh now, darling, you've been neglecting me for your wedding plans, haven't you?' said Crystal, with a heavy threat tangled up in the light banter.

'There isn't going to be a wedding,' said Stevie, who was quite aware she was using her distress to buy herself some time. She couldn't lose this job, and if she could sell her soul to MacLean in exchange for her man, she could sacrifice her pride for her work. She could virtually see Crystal shifting forward at her desk and putting her Pomeranian, called 'Eiffel', down on the floor, as she did when chat became serious.

'No wedding? What on earth do you mean?'

'Matthew has . . . has found someone else.'

'Oh darling, the absolute . . .'

Stevie winced at the word she used, although even she had to admit it actually sounded quite classy being issued via Crystal's Swiss-finishing-school-educated voice-box.

'Look, it's fine. When *can* you get it to me?' said Crystal in a rare moment of leniency.

'I'll email it Tuesday first thing. It's nearly finished, I promise,' gushed Stevie, issuing a silent prayer of thanks upwards. She was out of the frying pan.

'I'll expect it, darling. Oh, and start thinking about the next one. We've had an absolute glut of Mediterranean heroes and yet our own Scots and Irish boys have been totally neglected.'

'I'll do an Irish.'

'No, I've given Paul the Irish. I want you to take the Scot. Call it *Highland Fling* – you know the format. But let's have some red hair and Gaelic testosterone and plenty of it.'

'Absolutely,' said Stevie, who suddenly felt herself being catapulted out of the pan and thrown into a very hot fire. *How the hell could she make a sex symbol out of a red-haired Scot when she would be imagining that . . . that man?* He would end up killing the heroine with a giant-handed slap in Chapter One – and how flaming romantic was that?

Matthew rose from bed feeling incredibly sick. Sick in head, stomach and heart. The line to Camelot hadn't been engaged after all, it had been faulty, although they hadn't known that when they were ringing excitedly at five-minute intervals. After seven more attempts, they cracked open the first bottle of champagne, and after that was drained they started dancing. After the second bottle of champagne, to which they had added brandy and brown sugar to make cocktails, Matthew had carried Jo upstairs and attempted to make love to her, failing dismally – not that either of them cared. They were going to be rich – well, rich enough to have a bloody good spend and a fantastic holiday *au soleil*. More importantly, he could put off that ever-looming money talk with Jo. The fates were smiling on him.

He was woken up by Status Quo playing in his head, a stomach like a cement-mixer and Jo shaking on his shoulder to say she had eventually got through to Camelot to find he had won five hundred and fifteen quid, which he could collect from a post office.

Five bloody hundred and bloody fif-bloody-teen quid for five bloody numbers. They weren't the only f-words that crossed his mind and that was from a man who hated swearing.

'A record number of winners on that draw,' Camelot had said, with a copious amount of sympathy.

Four hundred and seventy five quid 'profit' then, if you

took off the price of the champers. It wouldn't even make a small dent in what he owed so there wasn't much point in chucking the money to a Visa company. It would be like throwing a microscopic blob of plankton into the mouth of a ravenous Great White shark. No, they might as well enjoy it with something frivolous. Ironic really – having to spend the money on something to take the pain of such a win away.

Jo brought him Paracetamol and coffee and he threw them up so she brought more. She was such a sweetheart and he loved her for caring, especially because she was as sick as he was and kept saying over and over again to him that it really didn't matter. He rang in work for them both, getting much sympathy for the food-poisoning excuse he used, but was too ill to care if he was believed or not. Then he crawled into bed, falling asleep as soon as his arm had encircled the gorgeous, but limp, woman at his side.

'Hello,' said Stevie, picking up the phone.

'Adam MacLean. Hreyooo?' boomed *his* voice. Why did he have to be so loud all the time?

Stevie felt her whole body stiffen. 'Fine, thank you. How are you?'

'Okay. So, anything to report?'

'Not really,' said Stevie, 'unless you want to know that his car is still outside. So they haven't gone to work today presumably, although that's a very trivial detail and I'm almost sorry to have mentioned it.'

She could sense his jaw muscle tighten and twitch with annoyance at the other end of the line and she got a little thrill out of that. Yes, writing about a Scot in her new book might be fun. She could have him jumping like a puppet to her call. She could have him trampled by a beautiful white horse, ridden by the gorgeous young strawberry-blonde heroine. She would call her Evie. Evie Sweetwell.

'I rang to say I think we should initiate the next stage,' he said, smilingly polite, although he was probably crushing the skull of some small animal to offset the pain of trying to be nice.

'Whatever you say, Mr MacLean.'

'Can you get a babysitter tomorrow?'

Uh-oh, this was sounding ominous. A siren was going off in her head and there were so many warning flags they were doing a very long Mexican wave down her spinal column.

'Er . . . not sure, why?' she asked, but knowing Catherine would help out in a crisis. Kate wasn't courting at the moment and saving up madly for whatever seventeen year olds save up for and would gladly welcome twenty quid, full access to a blackcurrant cheesecake and a sly couple of Bacardi Breezers.

'Because I think you should go oot, it being Saturday night an' all.'

'Me – out? Where?'

'With me.'

Oh farts! 'With you?'

'Get yer best clobba on, lady,' said Adam MacLean. 'I'll pick you up at seven-thirty. We're aff to the picturehoos.'

Chapter 28

'So, what are you going to wear?' said Catherine.

'Dunno, what you do think?'

'That green crossover top, definitely. That was Matthew's favourite so that's bound to strike a chord if he sees you.'

'*If*? How do I make that a definite, so all this will be worthwhile? What if they don't see us? What if they don't happen to be looking out of the window watching us go off together? I mean, it's highly unlikely they will be, isn't it really? It's mad, totally mad.'

'It's a mad world though, Steve. And if they don't see you, then you have to keep going at it until they do.'

'I was afraid you'd say that.'

'Well, it's all part of the plan!' Catherine laughed, although she was getting less keen on the idea of a Stevie and Matthew reconciliation every day. Even though she wanted her friend to be happy, she also wished she would stuff it home to Matthew that there was life without him, and if it took Adam MacLean to help her do that, then so be it. She hoped Stevie wouldn't give in too easily when Matthew came crawling back to her because he would, nothing surer. Catherine wanted Matthew to realize what he was missing in Stevie, although she was becoming increasingly confused as to what Stevie was missing in Matthew.

'I've to be ready for seven thirty.'

'Well, Kate will be over for seven.'

'Great – I'll direct her to the cheesecake and the other food stocks. She's a good girl.'

'She's an extortionist. Twenty quid! I'd do it for nothing if there was a cheesecake involved.'

'I'll get her a taxi back. I won't let MacLean drive her.'

'Thanks,' said Catherine. 'Ooh, those legs though. If I babysat for you, I'd let him drive me home.'

'You're one sick woman, Catherine Flanagan.'

Catherine laughed. 'Nervous?'

'What have I to be nervous about? I'm only going out with a wife-beating psychopath.'

'I don't think he's anything of the sort,' said Catherine. 'I think the bloke has got some bad press. We believed everything Jo said – and look what a calculating cow she turned out to be. We only have her side of things. I tell you, Steve, I took a long hard look at him at Pam's wedding, and he looked like a pretty decent guy to me.'

'Pretty?'

'You know what I mean.'

'Oh Cath, come on. There can't have been that much smoke without fire. You only have to look at him to know he's not Mr Fluffy!' Stevie gave a disbelieving laugh. 'Have you seen that scar on his face? What the hell could have caused that? He didn't get *that* making daisy chains.'

'Well, he was certainly Mr Fluffy with Pam and Will's old relatives.'

'All show!' said Stevie, who remained unconvinced. 'He was playing to an audience. He would have kissed babies too if there had been any. Politicians' tricks – and we all know how wholesome they are, don't we?'

'You really don't like him at all, do you?'

'No,' said Stevie, 'but we need each other, it seems. And at least being at the pictures means I don't have to talk to him.'

. . . Which had been Adam MacLean's precise thought when he proposed the venue. The cinema was central, popular and he would not have to converse with *her* much. Plus there was a good chance someone would spot them together and report their presence back to Jo. Even though she might not want him herself now, she wouldn't want anyone else to have him either. He knew what a jealous creature she could be, a fact that would work very much in his favour here.

Matthew was actually filling the kettle when he noticed Eddie's van at the other side of the lane dropping off his daughter. Kate had babysat for them a couple of times, which was the only reason she ever came round. Stevie must be going out, he concluded. Probably to Catherine's. *But then she would have taken Danny with her, surely?* Stevie never went out by herself, unless it was to Catherine's. So where was she going? On a Saturday night too.

He mentally slapped himself; it wasn't any of his business – they were separated. He was with Jo now, so why should he even be interested?

But still . . .

★

'You look nice,' said Kate, trying not to fall over as Danny wrapped himself around her very long giraffe-y legs.

'Do I?' said Stevie.

'Green looks great on you,' said Kate. 'I wish I were blonde.'

'You are!' laughed Stevie. Kate was naturally the platinum blonde that people aspired to, but she persisted on dyeing her long, long hair Goth-black with various shades of wild colour shot through it. At the moment, the *couleur du jour* was electric blue. She carried it off with the confidence of youth and looked stunning.

'Going to help me demolish this then, Dans?' asked Kate, her big sapphire eyes rounding at the sandwich fest and cheesecake which Stevie had left out for her. 'Have you had your tea?'

'Yes,' said Danny. 'I had beans off toast.'

'Beans *off* toast?' Kate looked to Stevie for further explanation.

'He means beans minus toast,' Stevie sighed. 'My little boy has suddenly decided he doesn't like bread.' In the same way that halfway through a McDonald's a couple of months ago, he had decided that he didn't like chips any more and hadn't touched a potato since. At least he was an Atkins-friendly child.

'Bread's really good for you, Dans. Especially this brown stuff. I eat loads, it's *cool*,' said Kate, giving Stevie a wink and stuffing a sandwich in her mouth.

'Is it? Do you?' said Danny in amazement. 'Mummy, could I have one like Kate's got, please?'

Stevie was quite sure that Kate could get Danny to eat horse manure if she tried.

As the second hand began its slow descent towards half past, Stevie was feeling more and more nauseous. The evening stretched excruciatingly long and hard in front of her and she had thrown the free newspaper supplement away so she didn't even know what was on at the 'picture hoos'. No doubt she'd have to sit through some all-action movie with a big macho hero who shot lots of people with huge guns whilst a little girly, accidentally caught up in the action, teetered behind him with stilt high heels and massive knockers.

'I think he's here,' said Kate, peeping out of the window.

'Shit!' said Stevie.

'Mummy!'

'Sorry, Danny,' said Stevie, slapping her hand over her mouth.

'Where are you going?'

'It's . . . er . . . a business meeting about Mummy's writing,' said Stevie. 'You go in there with Kate, darling,' and she ushered him towards the lounge before he could see MacLean and get nightmares.

'Come on then, Dans, let's go and watch a DVD with the cinema surround on full vol,' said Kate, taking him into the lounge. 'Give Mums a kiss.'

'Bye, darling, be good for Kate,' said Stevie, although she knew he would be an absolute angel for Kate. Then, as soon as the lounge door closed, there was a battering-ram-type boom at the front door. Stevie grabbed her jacket and handbag and reached for the handle, noticing how much her hand was shaking as it stretched out in front of her. She opened it to find Adam MacLean colour-co-ordinated with her in a pale green shirt and stonewashed jeans.

'Both of us in mint – nice touch,' he said appreciatively. 'I took a slow walk from the car to the door,' he went on. 'Now we'll take a slow walk back to it.'

'Okay,' said Stevie. He opened the car door for her (for show obviously), closed it behind her and then climbed in the driver's seat. The CD switched on with the ignition – Alvin Stardust. She had been expecting something a lot heavier: the Prodigy maybe, or some other group with a lead singer who bit the heads off live rodents.

They didn't speak at all. Stevie wished she'd brought a knife to cut the atmosphere between them, though actually, just bringing a knife would have been sensible. Adam drove steadily despite his car being such a long, fast, sleek number. She knew the myth about men and big cars, although she doubted very much that Jo was the sort of woman who would have entertained a man who was short in that area. Matthew was nicely endowed – not too big, not too small – and from the size of the rest of Adam MacLean, he looked as if he might have a bit of a monster in his trousers. Then she wondered why on earth she was thinking about Adam MacLean's willy and cut off those thoughts there and then.

They arrived at the car park, which was just around the corner from the cinema. Still not speaking, they crossed the road and joined the queue for the ticket booth.

'Whit do you want to go and see?' he asked.

There were two films showing. One was something like *The Strangulator* – no prizes for guessing that would be his choice, thought Stevie – or a psychological thriller with Denzel Washington, who, Stevie thought, was quite dishy and would certainly take her mind off the fact that she was on an obligatory evening out with *him*.

'Er . . . what do *you* want?' said Stevie diplomatically.

'It's up to you.'

'Well, the, thriller's got good press,' she suggested, hoping he would say that he was off to see *The Strangulator* and would meet her in the foyer after the film was over, but (*bugger!*) he simply said, 'Aye, that'll dae then.'

Stevie rummaged in her bag for her purse but he said, 'I'll get these. You awa' and get the popcorn.'

'Okay,' said Stevie, thinking, Popcorn? This is looking too much like a real date! However, she then realized that he didn't want her to think she was getting away with not paying for anything.

'*He thinks I'm a freeloader!*' she said to herself. '*Right, I'll show him!*'

She was served, just as Adam appeared with the tickets. She was struggling with a 'small' popcorn the size of a mop bucket and a 'large' which was roughly a skip, and had cost as much. She had plumped for the special offer and got two drinks as well. Not having a clue what he wanted, she had chosen Diet Cokes seeing as a gallon of Bells and Irn Bru wasn't an option. He had the nerve to look taken aback.

'I wes actually joking,' he said.

'Well, unfortunately I'm not yet fully acquainted with the nuances of your wit,' said Stevie, grappling with a sweet smile as well as with the enormous feast.

'So which is mine?' he grunted.

'This big one, of course!' said Stevie. *Is he joking or does he think I'm a hog?* She had just found out it was possible to dislike him a little more.

'Ba' Christ, it'll take me aw night to eat this.'

'I didn't want you thinking I was mean,' said Stevie purposefully, with a tight smile. It was, after all, *his* race renowned for parsimony, not hers. 'Which brings me around to say that I do very much want to get the financial side of our arrangement sorted soon too. I don't want to be in for any nasty shocks.'

'Aye,' he said without elaboration, then turned his back on her and led the way into the darkened cinema.

'Here,' said Adam, picking one of the big cushioned seats with the row in front of them a distance away. 'I paid extra for the superior seats. Ma legs get aw crunched up in the ordinary wans . . . ones.'

He did have very long legs, thought Stevie, who reckoned both hers placed end to end must equal the length of one of his. He must have to go to special shops for his jeans. 'Big Ignorant Scottish Bastards 'R' Us', possibly.

The lights dimmed and the adverts and trailers came on and Stevie took a long look around. The place was full of couples, silhouettes of their heads coming together as they passed a joke or a sweet nothing, so it felt odd to be part of them, and yet not part of them. How many others here were sitting with people they couldn't stand, and who they knew couldn't stand them either?

She and Matthew loved the cinema. Quite a few times he had rung her from work to say, 'See if Kate can babysit and we'll go and see a film.' Then they would invariably make a night of it and have supper somewhere afterwards and blow the expense. Like he would do with Jo now.

A rush of tears blindsided her and she coughed them down. Then she felt Adam MacLean nudge her to inquire if she was choking on popcorn. It was like being hit by a bus.

'No, unfortunately for you, I'm fine,' she said, and he laughed a big 'ha'.

They munched and watched in entertained silence. Denzel was gorgeous and the plot was twisty and thrilling. It was obvious from the off who was the bad guy but that fact didn't detract one iota from the enjoyment. At the end, the lights came up and Adam got up, stretched, and knocked all the stray knobs of popcorn off his shirt into his container. Between what he and Stevie had left, there was enough to feed a third world country for a week.

'That was quite good – well picked,' he said.

'Yes, I enjoyed it,' said Stevie. 'The film, I meant,' she added. Just in case he thought she meant his scintillating company.

She really doesn't like me very much at all, he thought with faint amusement, although he couldn't for the life of him think why that was. Had he not treated her with anything but absolute courtesy, that first meeting excepted? None of this situation was his fault. He had gone over his relationship with Jo with a finer than fine-tooth comb in his head, but he still couldn't work out where he'd gone wrong. It was torturing him, not knowing why she preferred a prick like Matthew Finch to someone who had treated her like a queen. It was Miss Stroppy Drawers here that hadn't made Matty Boy happy and he had strayed. It was *her* fault, not his. Slatternly, verbally abusive, prone to violent outbursts when she was drunk, and they were just at the beginning of the list. If she was adamant about flinging blame about, she should look nearer to home.

He led Stevie out and back to the car, where the cheesy seventies CD blasted out 'Wig Wam Bam' and 'Do You Wanna Touch'. It seemed to her that his music taste was as dubious as everything else about him. They both sat in stone-faced silence, each wanting to get away from the other as soon as possible.

'Want me to run your babysitter hame . . . home?' he offered, as they turned into Blossom Lane.

'No, it's all right, thank you. I'll get her a taxi,' said Stevie, a bit too quickly.

He was laughing now and shaking his head. The nicer he was to her, the more it seemed to annoy her. That made him want to be even nicer, because getting under her skin was the only bit of fun he was having at the moment.

'Okay, spend your money,' he said, 'but don't say I didnae offer.'

They pulled up outside the cottage. The lights were on downstairs in Matthew's house and the curtains were still open.

'We'll sit here for a wee minute,' Adam MacLean said, 'and give them a chance to see us.'

Great! thought Stevie, but then again, the sooner they were seen, the sooner it would all come to whatever head it was going to come to and be over.

'After aw,' Adam went on, 'that's what lovers dae . . . do, isn't it? Sit in the car and talk and kiss and stuff.'

'There's no way I'm kissing you,' said Stevie, horrified.

'Don't worry yerself, lady,' said Adam, jerking backwards. 'I'm just trying to make this as realistic as possible. Without stooping to bodily contact. Agreed?'

'Agreed,' said Stevie.

He grunted.

'Would this be a good time to talk about money then?' said Stevie.

'Look,' he said, sounding a little bit strained, 'I'll work out some figures. I certainly can't afford to pay for the entire cottage and my mortgage for very long . . .'

'I'm not asking you to! That's my point!' Stevie burst out.

'Stop yer blethering, woman! I know you're no' asking me to!' he snapped, then made an open-palmed gesture that suggested he was trying to calm himself. He had massive hands that looked more than capable of landing a painful wallop.

'Look, if it bothers you that much, I'll make it my priority, okay?'

'Yes, it does bother me, Mr MacLean,' said Stevie, 'so I'd appreciate it if you would, thank you.'

'My name's Adam, by the way. Might sound a wee bit odd if we're trying to convince people we're a couple when there's you calling me by my title and surname.'

'Okay . . . Adam,' she said. It sounded rather intimate to call him by his Christian, or rather heathen name, especially after she had gotten used to calling him 'MacLean' for so long. Well, that and a selection of fruitier alternatives.

'So, is Stevie short for Stephanie?'

'No, it's just Stevie. Like the poet.'

'Stevie Smith?'

Crikey – he's heard of her. 'Yes.'

She's surprised I've heard of Stevie Smith. She thinks I'm bloody illiterate! Cheeky wee . . . Adam tried to contain his annoyance but it leaked out in the way he drummed his fingers on the steering wheel in an angry little tattoo.

They waited a tad longer, but there was no activity from across the road. Matthew and Jo had probably gone to bed and left the light on in their hurry to get upstairs and bonk each other's head off. Both she and Adam started to say together that maybe they should go, and likewise, together, they thought, So this evening's been for nothing, after all.

'Maybe better luck next time then,' said Adam.

Oh, God forbid a next time! Although that thought was quickly pushed out of the way by a more serious one as Adam got out of the car. *Where's he going? Oh, please don't tell me he wants to come in for coffee!*

However, he was only doing his gentlemanly-type duty in opening the door for her, then he got back in the car after a gruff and sarcastically toned, 'Good night and thanks for the popcorn!' and after doing a three-point turn in the little lane, he zoomed off with a frustration-laden squeal of tyres. Stevie flinched. She hated loud noises of any kind – bangs, shouts, pops – they upset her, made her feel insecure, took her back to childhood days she would rather not think about. *He couldn't wait to get away from me, as much as I couldn't wait to get away from him,* she mused, staring into the space his car had just occupied.

Suddenly her heart was in her mouth, for out of the corner of her eye, she saw a figure at Matthew's window, obviously alerted by the noise of the car.

'*Steady*,' she told herself, and raised her hand, waving a fond farewell at the car that had already gone, not that whoever was at the window would know that. Then she slowly opened the cottage door and walked in, with another lingering stare up the lane for good measure.

After Kate's taxi had ferried her home, she made a quick call to Adam MacLean who was more than surprised to hear from her.

'I think we were spotted,' she said excitedly. 'Well enough to set the cat amongst the pigeons, although I could be getting it out of perspective.'

'Calm down, woman, and talk English,' said Adam. 'I cannae underston' you.'

Which is rich coming from a person who makes Rab C. Nesbitt sound intelligible, thought Stevie.

'Your tyres made a bit of a noise as you sped off,' she said, enjoying making the point. 'You must have alerted them across the road because someone . . .'

'Jo?'

'I don't know, I didn't dare look, but there was definitely someone watching through the window. I pretended to be waving goodbye to you, although you'd already gone. Rather loudly.'

'Awright, awright, I get your point. Anyway, it obviously did the trick,' said Adam, fending off her obvious criticism of his driving abilities. 'That's good news. I just wish they'd seen me too and, you know, linked us together.'

Stevie caught sight of the invoice for the wedding stationery and a beautiful little plan hatched before her eyes.

'I think I know a way to do that if you've got what I need,' she said, trying to fight off the strangest feeling that what she planned to do next felt dangerously akin to fun.

Chapter 29

Stevie's idea was as simple and delicious as a stuff-in-the-oven part-baked loaf and was ready to be implemented three days later on the Tuesday when she got a quick call from Adam to say that he was finally in possession of the required item. She met him briefly at the gym where he handed it over, and after an accident-free half-hour walk and periodic sprint on the treadmill, she went home to plug away at her new work brief until Matthew got home from work.

The realization that this plan of Adam's might not be as daft as she had first thought and might actually work had brought such a light feeling to her heart that she had found herself able to sort out Paris and Brandon's final chapter at long last. Their wonderful, idyllic ending was created from a happy, hopeful bubble in her brain, and it was quite an impressive one, if she said so herself. Blissfully, the manuscript was emailed over to *Midnight Moon* HQ by start of business that morning, as promised. Stevie was resolute that she would never cut it so fine again. You could only let people like Crystal down once, and then you were toast. Ashes of toast, even.

It was a big relief, to be back on track writing. The pretty room she was using as an office made a major contribution to that. It was spacious but cosy and peaceful, with a bonny view of the long garden. Nosy roses poked in through the windows, which had been thrown open to let in some fresh air, along with the comforting rumble of the odd train in the near distance. It was the sort of room she could imagine sitting in and writing her big blockbuster. Not that she wasn't grateful for her position at *Midnight Moon*. She and 'Alexis' and 'Paula' were privileged in that they received a monthly salary in advance of any royalties, and that gave them a steady income. Crystal also pushed a few magazine articles her way, paying her a separate amount for those, and Stevie bumped up her savings by writing some long, traditional poetry for a greetings card company. She had been doing a lot of extra work to finance her wedding. Now it seemed she had been working for months for nothing.

Stevie took a walk into town to get some fresh air and stretch her legs and do the final but hardest job – letting go of the wedding rings. She was going to sell them on to the jeweller who was well-known in the area for giving the fairest prices. The man offered her one hundred and twenty for the two wedding bands, which would cover half the cost of the order-of-service booklets, and a further one hundred and five for the engagement ring. Stevie took it without even trying to barter him up to a better price. It wasn't as if she could ever have worn it, not with the memories it had collected. If – *when* – she and Matthew got back together, she would choose a new one, not pearls next time though. She should have listened when her mother had inspected it and said, 'Pearls mean tears, I hope you know.'

When she got home, she chased away the dip in her spirits by scribbling some rough notes for *Highland Fling*. She decided to make her heroine small and feisty and the 'hero' mean and moody. Possibly give him a scar, one that had been very painful to receive. The heroine would outwit him at every turn. *Ha!* Once she had pictures of 'Damme MacQueen' and 'Evie Sweetwell' in her mind, the ideas started to come through thick and fast. She felt she just might have a winner on her hands.

Chapter 30

In stark contrast, Matthew was finding it hard to concentrate at work. He had acted upon the letter asking him to apply for a Platinum Visa by ringing *this number for an instant decision*, only to be told that he had been instantly rejected.

'So why the hell did you invite me to get one if you were going to tell me I couldn't?' said Matthew, taking their decision extremely personally.

'Sorry, sir,' said the levelheaded operative, who'd had this conversation many times before. Then she went into automated spiel about how he could find out his credit rating. Matthew knew exactly how he could do that. He also knew that the fact he had been refused their Visa would show up on his rating and influence future lenders. He hung up when she was in mid-flow and immediately felt guilty about being so rude and acting so out of character. Then again, he seemed to be doing quite a lot of things lately that were out of character and of which he didn't feel particularly proud.

One of his Visa bills had arrived that morning. The holiday cost had been added on to the amount outstanding, plus the charge for a cash advance that he had totally forgotten about, which had taken him over the limit. This needed settling immediately, so the urgent block-capital-written message emblazoned across the top had commanded. Plus something was niggling him and that wasn't helping his mood either. He just happened to be about to close the curtains on Saturday night, when he saw Stevie standing on the doorstep of the cottage waving someone off. She had her best green top on and a big *dreamy* smile, the sort of smile you didn't wear for a friend, either. Why that had affected him so much, he didn't know because it was none of his business; she was no longer in his life. He was with Jo now. He had put it out of his mind numerous times, but it seemed to be on elastic and kept bouncing back.

The sunlight was streaming through the window when he got home that evening, highlighting how grubby the kitchen had become since Stevie had left. The work surface was full of crumbs and the floor badly needed a good scrub. He'd have to get a cleaner in. Jo wasn't the type to put on an apron and wear down her long, deliciously scratchy fingernails doing domestic chores; she wasn't a 'Stevie'. There wouldn't have been much point leaving Stevie for her if she was.

Jo relaxed in the bath for half an hour whilst Matthew rustled up something tasty in the kitchen. She had been through so much and he wanted to cosset her and spoil her. That wasn't to say that he didn't miss coming home to sparkling work surfaces and delicious cooking smells, especially tonight, when his spirits felt as if they had been steamrollered, but what he lost with one hand, he gained with the other and twice over. How could he compare what he had rejected to what he had now? Jo was a different creature entirely, one built for pleasure and luxury, not for comfort and reliability. Jo and Stevie – it was like comparing a brand new sports car with a Vauxhall Cavalier. Although that was an unfortunate simile, he thought straightaway. He'd had a faithful Vauxhall Cavalier for years and loved it, and the new sporty black Punto he had traded it against in the end hadn't been a patch on his old car friend.

Whilst the pasta was boiling, he thought he might just snap around with a duster and tidy a few things away. Jo's detritus seemed to have taken over every surface like a virulent ivy, and how the hell could they roll around on the mat in front of the fire, like he intended to do that evening, when it was dull with dust and mysterious house 'bits'. He went into the cupboard for the vacuum cleaner. Where on earth was the Dyson? *Oh bloody hell!*

Stevie waited a good three-quarters of an hour after she had seen Matthew come in from work before going over the road. She had to be seen to be extra casual. Luck was on her side as Matthew's head seemed to be zipping across the window as if he was moving things from one place to another.

'I'm just popping across the road. I'll be ten seconds, poppet!' she called to Danny.

'Okay, Mummy!'

Stevie lifted up the Visa bill that Adam had given her,

and walked slowly and deliberately across the road. She had been dying to steam it open, but hadn't fallen prey to the temptation.

He's seen me, she thought, on noticing how Matthew jumped back from the window. That hurt a lot. Did he really have to insult her by pretending he wasn't in? What had she ever done to him to deserve this? The small act turned her jellied nerves to steel. She put the envelope through his letterbox without ceremony and returned home, not looking behind her. Then she texted Adam to tell him that she'd done it. Then she waited.

As soon as Matthew had jumped back from the window, he felt cross with himself. It was a stupid, puerile reaction, a ridiculous thing to do and she must have seen him. '*She didn't deserve that*,' said the old Matthew. The nice, friendly, kind one with a conscience that he had stuffed away in order to allow himself to act in the way he had been doing for the past few months. He had wanted Jo so much, there was no easy way to get her, there were bound to be casualties. *All's fair in love and war*. He recited the mantra when the doubts crept up on him and his own brain started to mutiny and call him a selection of choice names. *All's fair . . .*

The letterbox clacked and the single envelope dropped on the doormat. He stole up to it, as if it might contain something harmful or demanding, then, tentatively, he lifted it to see it was just a Visa bill for Jo. He wondered how much her outstanding amount was, and if there was enough credit left on it to buy a badly needed vacuum cleaner. He stuck it on the mantelpiece to give to her later and thought no more about it.

Thought no more about it, that was, until half past midnight, when his cooling brain was resting on the pillow, sifting through which head rubbish to throw into dreams, which bits of the day to put in the 'in' tray and which in the 'out'. When its attentions came to Jo's letter, it stopped its manic business abruptly and nudged him rudely awake.

Why did Stevie have Jo's post?

Matthew went downstairs and got the envelope bearing Jo's old address, the one she shared with her husband. He couldn't work it out. The only way Stevie could have got this was if MacLean gave it to her. But why would he do that? How come they knew each other? What did it all mean? What was he up to? What was she up to? He didn't get it. His brain started to ache from trying to work it all out.

Matthew didn't get any more sleep that night, and not even the big bread-knife he tucked under his pillow brought him any feeling of security.

The next morning he waited until Jo was dressed before he handed over the envelope to her. She looked at it, then immediately threw it down as if it was contaminated.

'How did you get this?' she asked. 'Did Adam bring it round? Shit, he knows where we live, doesn't he?'

Jo looked nervous and frightened, and Matt immediately leapt out of his seat to wrap her up in a big safe cuddle.

'Well, there's the mystery. Stevie posted it.' He felt her stiffen even more.

'Stevie? *Stevie?* How the hell did she get it?'

'I don't know.'

Jo ran to the window. 'What is she up to?' she said, screwing up her face as if she was casting a hex. 'Or should I say *they*?'

'They who?'

'My ex and your ex. They both have an axe to grind, wouldn't you say?'

Matthew laughed. 'You can't seriously be insinuating that Stevie and Adam have got together, can you?'

'Don't be ridiculous,' Jo jeered. 'Adam wouldn't look at someone like Stevie Honeywell.'

Matthew had been about to ask what was so wrong with Stevie, but the hard look in Jo's eyes told him that might be unwise.

'I'm going to go over there and ask her how she got this,' he said, rolling up his sleeves, nervously rather than aggressively.

'Don't be silly!' snapped Jo. 'That's exactly what she wants you to do.'

'But I want to find out if he knows where I live!' Matthew gulped. *Oh God!* He would come home from work tonight and find a horse's head in his bed.

'I don't know how he could know that,' said Jo. 'I told him you lived at the other side of Wakefield.'

'He could have followed us. You said it yourself – he's nuts, isn't he?'

Jo was about to say something, but swallowed it. Instead she started to nod slowly in agreement.

'Yes, that's possible, I suppose. Then again, I think he

would have done something a bit more drastic than this. Not exactly his style – grievous bodily letter delivering, if you know what I mean. And Adam wouldn't have got the wrong house.' *Which means he's up to something.*

'So what's going on then?' Matthew querried.

Jo thought of what had happened when she had returned home from Majorca and told Adam she was leaving him. She should have realized from his reaction that he had something more up his sleeve. *Hmmm.* Her previous suspicions *had* been correct after all. How stupid had she been, to think that Adam really had let her go?

She flapped her hand, as if dismissing the whole other side of the street.

'Look Matt, I'm sorry, but I am not playing psychological games with Stevie because that's what she wants me to do. It's not fair on her. She obviously needs help.'

'You seem very sure that's what she's doing.'

Jo nodded slowly. She felt suddenly empowered, thrilled. *Adam still wants me.*

'I know how women think, Matt, because – surprise, surprise – I'm a woman myself.' She cocked an eyebrow. 'Wanna see some proof?'

'Yes, please.'

Once again, Jo and Matthew were late for work.

Adam MacLean rang Stevie at ten.

'What time does your wee boy go tae his bed?' he asked.

'About half past seven,' said Stevie. 'He's always asleep for eight.'

'I'll be round at nine,' said Adam. 'Feel free not to cook anything.'

And Stevie thought, Even when the guy's talking English, he makes no sense at all.

Chapter 31

The anticipation of having Adam MacLean come to the house was worse than having a real date because at least on one of those, the chances were you were going to be with a person who liked you, not with someone just aching to criticize and score points. Was she supposed to cook or what? She could throw him a bone, she supposed, and watch him gnaw it whilst she had a sandwich. *Like she was going to give him the satisfaction of calling her inhospitable!* She wasn't the most fantastic cook in the world but she could throw together a very nice chilli. Stevie made rather a huge one for that night and poured a big slodge of red wine in it. At least if he didn't eat, she could freeze it for herself. And eat it over the coming decade.

With Danny tucked up in bed, Stevie put a light blue blouse on and her jeans. On the slim off-chance that Matthew happened to see them, she would look out to impress but with a foot in casual. Perfect. Had posting Jo's letter done the trick? Had that one small stone caused big ripples in their happy water life? If so, they would be watching out for activity at her front door. If not, then she might have to think about shagging Adam MacLean in the street. *Ugh, joke!* Matthew was an intelligent guy, intellectually if not emotionally, and he could put two and two together – and, with any luck, make five in this case. There must have been a few questions floating around in his brain by now, surely?

Knock knock knock, It was quite a soft knock for him. Considerate that Danny was in bed, maybe? *Yeah, right!* She wasn't ready to give him any benefits of any doubts yet; he had hardly earned the privilege. Stevie crossed to the door and opened it to a huge bouquet of flowers, which quite took her breath away.

'Hi,' said a porridge-rich voice from behind a big pink rose.

'Oh hello,' said Stevie. God, they were beautiful, expensive. If a lover had genuinely given these, she would have fainted. Then recovered to bonk him five seconds later, which obviously was not going to happen in this case. Not without a frontal lobotomy anyway.

'Can you see anything across the street?'

'No,' said Stevie. 'Their cars are there but there's no sign that they're in.'

'Oh, the swine,' said the rose.

'Do you want to walk around the block and come back?'

'No, in case they are in and have seen me. Then it would look mighty odd, me bringing floooers then taking them away again.'

'You should have squealed your tyres. Your driving capabilities seem to attract the most attention.'

'Are ye going to invite me in or no?' said the rose loudly, getting more and more annoyed.

'Certainly, do come in,' said Stevie with a courteous and tinkly little laugh for the benefit of any viewers who might have been watching over the street. Adam handed the flowers to Stevie. They weighed a ton and she buckled under the weight of them. She stole a look across the lane, but nothing. She noticed that, once again, she and Adam had colour co-ordinated.

'Same blue claes,' he said, which she presumed meant 'clothes', in the absence of anything else they had co-ordinated in, apart from the number of eyeballs. *Was he really from Great Britain? In fact, was he really from Earth?* Adam walked straight into the dining area to find it was neat and tidy, which saved him having to tell her to keep it so. The owners had been most specific about that. He had lied to them and said that his 'lady' was extremely house-proud. He then walked through to the kitchen, which was also scrubbed, he noted, as he did a slow warder-type walk around it – not a hint of flour or chocolate anywhere. There were lovely spicy beef waves coming from an enormous cauldron-like pot on the hob and his stomach keened in response to it.

'Well, at least they'll see the car if they don't see me,' said Adam.

'Yes,' said Stevie, thinking, Okay, the preliminaries are out of the way, so what do we do now for the next hour or so?

'So – money,' said Adam, answering her unasked question.

'Great!' said Stevie. *At last.* Now she'd find out just which percentage of the flesh nearest her heart she would need to cut out in order to pay him.

'May I?' He gestured towards the table.

'Yes, of course,' said Stevie, and he sat down at a chair there and got out a folded piece of paper from his pocket.

'Do you want something to drink?' she asked. 'Tea, coffee, wine? Sorry, no spirits.' She added that last bit with an over-sorry smile. She didn't want to give him the opportunity of fuelling up on whisky and starting a singsong and/or a fight.

'Wine would be nice, thank you,' he said.

'White or red?'

'Red, please,' he answered, almost sure it would arrive at the table with the £1.89 label still on it. She surprised him with a very rich little South African Pinotage, fragrant and heavy on the summer fruits and berries. He nodded appreciatively.

'Nice,' he said.

'Yes, isn't it?' she drawled. I've surprised him, she thought. He thinks I buy crappy wines to get me drunk cheap and quick.

'Look, here are my calculations.' Adam smoothed out the paper. 'I've taken a three-month lease and we'll assess the situation after that, if it takes that long, but if you can pay me, say, four hundred pounds a month, I can cover the rest. Can you manage that?'

Stevie stared at him. She had been expecting so much more, a thousand a month at least and dubious sexual requests. As much as it shamed her to say it, if it would have guaranteed Matthew coming back, she would have considered stumping up on all fronts, and back.

Four hundred was reasonable, too reasonable, but for all

she couldn't stand the man, she wouldn't have cheated him.

'Mr MacLean . . .'

'The name's Adam.'

'Sorry . . . '*Adam*.' She made the weighty pause before his name sound like an insult. 'I can afford more.'

'No, I said I'd take four hundred – that'll dae.'

Stevie shook her head. 'Sorry, I'm not a charity Mr . . . Adam.'

'Charity, by Jings! Whit on earth are you talking aboot, woman?'

'Seven hundred. I know what this place is costing. That's what I can afford. Seven hundred a month.'

'Four.'

'I can do eight at a push.'

'This is bartering in reverse!' said Adam, pushing his hand back through his hair. 'Are ye mad?'

'Obviously yes, to be here in the first place,' said Stevie calmly. Four hundred was so low as to be suspicious. She would rather not be in his debt so much.

'What do you do for a living that you can afford to throw your money aboot?' said Adam.

'None of your business,' said Stevie, 'and I'm hardly throwing it away. I'm living here and it's a lovely, big, expensive house. Eight hundred, Mr MacLean, that's my final offer.'

Adam MacLean sat back in the chair and slowly folded his arms. He looked faintly amused.

'So if I say no, what are ye going to do? Refund me to death?'

She didn't answer. She just stared him out until he broke eye-contact and smiled resignedly.

'Okay, if it makes you feel better, let's say seven hundred. That is *my* final offer. I can take a cheque.'

Stevie produced one she had made earlier, like Valerie Singleton, and Adam put it down on the table, slowly moving his head from side to side.

'Crazy lady,' was his only comment.

'Would you like to eat something?' said Stevie. 'I made a chilli. It'll help pass the time. Unless you want to play Scrabble.' *Neanderthal could be quite a high word score.*

'Food would be very nice. I am actually quite hungry,' said Adam. He crossed to the kitchen window and peered through the blinds. There appeared to be no activity at all in Matthew's house. The night was closing in, the curtains weren't drawn, and no lights had been turned on. Despite the presence of the cars, it looked very much as if they were out. *Och nooo!*

Adam excused himself and went upstairs to the loo. The front bedroom door was closed with a KEEP OUT SUPER-HERO'S ROOM door hanger on the handle. Stevie's bedroom door was open and he poked his head inside to find it was tidy also, and subtly scented like a sweet summer garden. A *Midnight Moon* book was on the bedside cabinet, by Alexis Tracey. The bed had a big puffy quilt like his Granny Walker used to have. He and his sisters would creep in and bounce on it and his granny would turn a blind eye, because she knew they didn't have much else in life to make them smile.

'Want a hand?' he asked, appearing in the kitchen

doorway once again and filling it more than the door did.

'You can stick that garlic bread in the oven if you want,' said Stevie, pointing to a tray with a herby loaf covered in cheese gratings and salsa. *Home-made garlic bread*, Adam thought.

His eyes must have lingered on it a bit too long, for she said, 'What's wrong? Not to your taste, Mr MacLean?'

'Not at all,' said Adam, taking the bread and putting it in the oven. 'It's just that the first time I saw you, you appeared not to have an affinity with cooking.'

'I was baking,' said Stevie. 'I can cook okay, I just can't bake. For some reason, if it involves flour, it just doesn't happen for me. The kitchen seems to explode.'

'Oh I see,' said Adam. He watched Stevie scurry about trying to locate the rice in one of the cupboards.

'Mind if I try oot the cinema surround?' he said, thumbing towards the lounge.

'It's your house,' Stevie sniffed.

'I'm trying to be polite,' he smiled wearily.

'Go right ahead,' said Stevie in her best part nice-hostess and part bugger-off voice.

Whilst the rice was cooking she stole a look across to Matthew's house. '*Why aren't you in? Where are you, you bastard! Don't you realize what I'm doing for you?*' she said in the direction of the unfaithful house, which was now keeping Jo safe and warm. Well, lukewarm, for life at the cottage was much more comfortable temperature-wise. Matthew kept the central-heating thermostat very low. It gave them the excuse to cuddle up lots. *Where had all that love and affection gone?* Maybe it was hiding dormant in the walls, waiting for her return. It couldn't just disappear into nowhere, could it?

The buzzer telling her that the rice and bread were ready rescued her from unwelcome tear-duct activity. She dished up and was about to carry it to the table when Adam came in to help her. She hoped she had made him enough; after all, she had only done three ton.

'This is quite nice,' he said, tucking right in. He sounded surprised, as if he only thought her capable of tackling boil in the bag cod and crispy pancakes.

'Why, thank you,' she said, with an ultra-sarcastic smile, but he seemed too absorbed in his food to notice.

He asked her again what she did for a living, and once again she told him she wasn't telling him. Then he asked her how her son had taken to the move and she answered that he had been remarkably 'cool' – in the warm sense – about it. Then she changed the subject because Danny was not part of all this. She didn't want him any more confused than he had been already, and she didn't want Adam MacLean talking about her son; he was off-limits. Adam MacLean, however, was nothing if not persistent.

'How old is he?' he asked.

'Four,' said Stevie.

'Does he go to Lockelands School around the corner?'

'Yes.'

'Hard work at that age, aren't they?'

'He's a good boy,' said Stevie. The clipped monosyllables weren't putting him off, obviously.

'So Matthew's no' his daddy then?' he asked mischievously, for he had already worked out the answer to that one.

'No,' said Stevie, clearly irritated. 'I've only known Matthew for two years.'

'Ah, so your wee boy was two when you met.'

'My goodness, you can do sums as well. Where do your talents end, I wonder?'

Adam growled and spooned a little more chilli his way. 'He a local boy?'

'Matthew? Yes.'

'No, your wee boy's daddy.'

'Yes, he was a local boy too.'

'Wes?'

Okay, she would end all the questions now.

'Yes, "wes". I'm a widow, Mr MacLean. My husband died when I was two months' pregnant, if you must know. Danny never knew his father.'

Adam stopped mid-chew. What she had said sank in and he had the grace to look slightly ashamed of himself for thinking her a loose piece. Jo had twisted that particular detail. She'd told him that Danny didn't know his father because Stevie wasn't sure who he was. He started to eat again.

'I'm sorry.'

'Yes, well, that's life. Or rather it isn't,' said Stevie with a black little laugh.

They chewed on some more and Stevie filled up their glasses.

'So how long have you actually lived with Matthew then?' asked Adam.

'Well, I was introduced to him about two years ago, as I say, but we first went out as a couple eighteen months ago.

I moved in with him at New Year,' said Stevie. 'I really thought I was doing the right thing. You have to take chances sometimes, don't you? Even if you do keep getting it wrong.' She gulped back any more leakages of information. 'So what about you and . . .?'

Nope, she still couldn't say the name.

'The same. I've known her just over eighteen months; lived together for fifteen.'

Stevie put down her fork. It was the first proper meal she'd had in ages, even though she had barely cleared half of the small portion she had given herself.

'You'd think after aw that time, you'd know someone enough not to get hurt like this, if that makes any sense?' said Adam.

'Yes, it makes perfect sense,' said Stevie, knowing exactly what he meant. She had been with Mick just over eighteen months, too, and thought she knew him inside out. Before that, there had been Welsh Jonny, a hideous flirt of a police officer whom she discovered having email affairs with half the known world – all at least fifteen years his senior – from a menopausal Lulu look-alike in London to a tan-tighted granny in Tyneside. They split up after eighteen months, no surprise there then, when he upped and left her for TTG just as her retirement lump sum came through. It made Stevie quite ill to think that Jonny had probably been fantasizing about Thora Hird when they'd made love. She'd give him a ring when she was eighty if she was still single and try another eighteen months, she'd joked to Cath, although she knew she probably would be. It appeared Stevie had invented the 'eighteen-month itch'. Maybe they would name it after her like a disease:

Honeywell Syndrome: *state of being so dissatisfied with your partner after a year and a half that you feel the need to bog off with someone else in the most hurtful way possible.*

There was a single ladleful of chilli left. Stevie offered it to Adam, but he refused.

'That was awfa nice but I am so full,' he said. 'Thank you.' He stood and started clearing plates. Stevie tried to protest, but he counter-protested and won.

'Coffee?' she said, as he started loading the crockery into the dishwasher.

'Naw, you're okay,' he said, meekly for him. 'It's obvious there's going to be no joy tonight. I'll away.'

Stevie nodded. She was disappointed too. She had so wanted to aggravate the inhabitants of 15 Blossom Lane with Adam's visiting presence as much as the latter himself did. Probably more because she genuinely loved Matthew; she didn't just see him as a possession that was not allowed to leave, as MacLean saw Jo.

'You'd better put those flooooers in water,' he said, in a tone that suggested she was ungratefully at fault for not doing it immediately. 'Are there vases in the hoos?'

Stevie had found two in the cupboards whilst the rice had been cooking. She would tend to them; after all, it was no fault of the flowers that they had been bought by Adam 'Control Freak' MacLean.

'Yes, I'll do it soon. Thank you for reminding me,' she

said tightly. She would set her stall out early and make sure he knew she wasn't one for doing what *he* dictated.

'Nae bother,' he said. 'It would have been actually worth it if they'd seen them, though. Cost an absolute fortune.'

'Would you like me to pay half?'

'No, you're okay.'

'I'll wave them over if I see them arriving.'

They both smiled unwittingly at each other. Then they realized what they were doing and stopped it immediately.

'Start thinking aboot the next step,' said Adam, returning at warp speed to gruffness.

'Your cheque,' reminded Stevie, handing it over.

'Yes, thank you,' he said, shoving it in his back pocket.

'Oh, and here.' She handed him a flat packet of hand-kerchiefs.

'What's this?'

'You lent me a hankie, remember? I couldn't get the blood out. So, there you go. They only sold them in threes.'

'You didn't have to go and do that.'

'Yes, I did.'

Hmmm,' thought Adam MacLean and walked to the door. She was trying awfully hard to prove she wasn't a freeloader. Too hard, in his opinion, and she was wasting her time because he knew exactly what sort of person she was.

'Good night then, Mr . . . *Adam,*' said Stevie.

'Good night, and thanks again for the food.'

He got into his car. It was dark now and it was obvious Matthew and Jo weren't in after all. He drove off slowly, turning right at the end of the lane, not seeing the couple rounding the corner on the left. They had taken a long walk into town to see the Denzel Washington film and then broken the journey home by calling in at a bistro. The woman's eyes closed in on the numberplate.

'God, that was Adam! What was *he* doing in here?'

'It's okay,' said Matthew, putting his arm around her shoulders. He was the picture of heroic calm although inside his nerves were jangling. *Treble shit, he's come looking for me. I'm dead . . . HEEELLLPPP!*

The dishwasher was contentedly humming, washing away the evidence of Adam's unsuccessful visit. How many more of them to go before Matthew and Jo saw them? Maybe they were destined to miss them by a whisker every time. Maybe she and Adam would both be eighty and on their four-millionth bouquet and chilli before Matthew spotted him knocking at the door. By then his cataracts would be so bad he wouldn't have a clue it was Adam, though.

Stevie couldn't have said that the evening had been 'pleasant', but then again it hadn't been 'unpleasant' either. The big man's manners were surprisingly nice, and there had even been a flash of vulnerability at one point. Then again, she was too soft, too emotional, and any chink in Adam MacLean's armour had been put there for her to see. He was manipulative, that much she did believe from Jo. She had something he wanted and he had to keep her sweet and on side.

Stevie started to head up to bed. She clicked off the light, then immediately put it back on again because she knew that she wouldn't sleep. Maybe half an hour torturing

Damme with some psychological twists and turns from Evie might help. Just half an hour.

There was no sign that *he* had been near the house at all when Matthew and Jo got home. No forwarded post through the letterbox, no booby traps, no death threats written in blood on the door. As Matthew closed the curtains on the day, across the road, the light shone from the downstairs cottage window. One eye of light that suddenly went off once and then on again. It was as if it had winked at him.

Chapter 32

Stevie saw Adam twice in the next week, but only in passing. He nodded to her from a distance when she was on the lat pulldown in the gym and she nodded in return. Then he nodded again a couple of days later when she was leaving, and once again, she nodded back. It was like the birth of another language, because there was something in each nod that told the other person that no, they had nothing to report.

They hadn't instigated any more action. First, they wanted to see if the seeds they had planted had sprouted over the week. But eventually it looked as if they might have to re-open Parliament because the couple across the road continued to travel to work together each morning in perfect loved-up harmony, still walking the ten steps' distance from the front door to the car holding hands and making Stevie's stomach heave with jealousy and hurt. The pain seemed to get worse, not better.

On the seventh day since seeing Adam MacLean in the lane, the tension had actually started to leave Matthew's shoulders and he let himself finally believe that he was not suddenly going to be accosted by Jo's estranged husband, or his own ex-partner, because he still couldn't quite believe she had accepted the break-up with so little reaction. In fact, on one occasion he had actively encouraged her to make a move after seeing her buzzing near the kitchen window and so had darted straight out to deliver some post that had arrived for her. He knew she had seen him, and he *knew for absolute definite* that at the very moment when he reached the letterbox she would open the front door as if by total coincidence and force him to engage in conversation. However, no, he was wrong. Not a sausage.

He almost wished she would flip and start throwing things at him because he wanted to bring this to a head finally. He was certain she was up to something and it was driving him mad trying to work out what it could be. He had a theory but it was too ridiculous to take seriously.

The post was occupying a lot of his mind recently. Every day seemed to bring a new bill, a new demand, and his mortgage payment had bounced. He was perpetually on the brink of asking Jo to contribute financially, but how did you broach a subject like that with a woman who spent every lunchtime in Harvey Nichols? Especially after what he'd told her about his bank balance.

He decided to soften her up and went shopping in his lunch-hour and bought fillet steaks and champagne and raspberries, white chocolate, cream and cognac and accompanying nice-meal vegetables. Expensive, but he hoped it would be a worthwhile investment for him. He ran Jo a bath after work and told her to stay in there until he called her, then he brought her up a glass of chilled champagne and popped a truffle into her mouth and kissed the chocolate from her lips, and retired to the kitchen to work at a feast fit for the queen of his heart that she was.

She came down in her robe to find the table lit by candlelight and a beautiful romantic supper waiting for her. He topped up her glass, chinked his own to it, and said, 'Cheers.'

'What's all this for?' she said with surprised delight.

'Because I love you,' he said, pulling out the chair for her, and tucking her under the table.

Then, after the main course, he served her raspberries soaked briefly in cognac resting in a cloud of cream whipped with the melted chocolate, with coffee to follow. Her eyes were full of heaven tasted. Matthew was a seductive cook. He just hoped he had been seductive enough. He led her to the sofa, snuggled, and caressed her.

'Jo,' he said, then taking her hands between his, 'I want you to divorce MacLean as soon as possible. I don't like the thought of you being married to him at all.'

She answered him by pressing her body hard against his and kissing him urgently. 'He's not in the way.'

He squeezed her to him. 'Serve MacLean his divorce papers, please.'

'There's no point.'

He stopped kissing her neck and looked confused. 'Why not?'

'I'm not married to Adam.'

He pulled back from her. 'What?'

'I'm not married to him. Surely you knew?'

'No,' he said, with a great sweeping puzzled inflection at the end of the word.

'MacLean is my maiden name, pure coincidence. Common enough, though, I suppose, if your ancestors are Scots. We just lived together.' She snuggled into him once again. 'So you see, he is out of my life totally; we have no bindings to each other.'

'Oh, I see.' She hadn't mentioned it. He would have remembered that one. And hadn't she always referred to MacLean as 'her husband'? 'But don't you have any financial commitment to him? The house, for instance?' he asked cautiously, in case she realized why he was asking.

'Alas no!' said Jo. 'I didn't have any money to put towards the house when we lived together. Adam took everything I had – he was very clever. Told me he was "looking after it for me" and that was the last I saw of it. That's why it's so great to go out at lunchtimes and spend, spend, spend, and be with someone who looks after me for all the right reasons, who doesn't try and tell me what to do or take what I have.' And with that she kissed him with a fervour that threatened to pop his lungs like twin balloons landing in a patch of nettles.

'Oh . . . er . . . great!' Matthew said, when he was eventully forced up for air, although his head was screaming, '*Bugger bugger bugger* . . .' He had been counting on Jo's share of the divorce money. He had already spent a chunk of it in his head on a conservatory and a return trip to Majorca.

She raised her head and walked her long-nailed fingers

saucily up his chest. 'Anyway, why did you really want me to divorce him?'

'Er . . .'

'Because you want to marry me yourself, maybe?'

He took her lovely face in his hands. Well, it hadn't featured in his immediate plans but, seeing as she had come to mention it, yes, waking up to Jo MacLean for the rest of his life would be better than any Euromillions jackpot win. Well, almost. But he knew that he'd have to do better than a roast-beef dinner at the White Swan for her.

'Jo, I would marry you tomorrow but I'm not asking you until I'm able to give you the wedding I know you'd want. Classic cars, morning suits, lobster for the wedding breakfast . . .'

Jo's head started to run with the theme: 'Mmm, seven bridesmaids and pageboys. Red roses filling the church . . .'

'No expense spared for you, my love,' he said. 'So, alas, we'll have to wait.'

'Your investments are due to mature soon though, surely – so you said.'

'Ah yes . . .'

Which was not entirely a lie. An insurance policy his mum had set up for him was due to mature on his thirty-fifth birthday at Christmas. It would yield about five thousand pounds, but he had slightly exaggerated the figures to impress her at the early courting stage. Well more than slightly. Added two zeros at the end actually.

'We could honeymoon in the Med. Cruise maybe? Italy, Sardinia, we could go back to Spain again, Oh Matthew, it will be wonderful!'

'Jo, there's something . . . Ahhh!'

Her hand started to knead him *there*. He had to tell her the truth about himself tonight. There had been too many lies and deceptions and he wasn't really that kind of person. Her fingers were delicious and then he heard the rasp of his zip. Suddenly she was out of his arms and kissing a molten trail down his shirt.

'Stop, please, Jo . . . oh!'

Mañana – as the locals had said so often in Majorca.

Chapter 33

The children broke up for a lovely sunny May half-term at the end of that week and Stevie took time off from writing about other people's love-lives to do nice things with her boy. They had a day at the seaside and the zoo, and she made a million egg and potted-beef sandwiches for a major picnic with Catherine and the kids in Higher Hoppleton Park. Then, on the Friday, Stevie and her son had a burger in town and mooched around trying to find a present to take to his friend Josh Parker's fifth birthday party the next day. She didn't really want to go, for more than one reason, but Catherine's little boy Gareth had been invited too and her friend was forcing her along. She said it would occupy her mind and stop her moping at home, and Josh was, after all, one of Danny's special friends. He was a lovely kid, and his mum, Jan, was very sweet. There was just one tiny problem, which stopped her socializing with the Parker family.

She settled on a badge-maker because Danny had one and it was a toy that he frequently played with, sadly not the case with the 80 per cent of his toys that lay untouched since his last birthday and Christmas. Mostly ones with irritating little bits in that became detached from the rest of the pack and ended up embedded in her foot or snarled up in the vacuum cleaner. She had ashamedly binned a few toys with missing pieces that rendered them unplayable with, and there was nothing worse than trying to reconcile stray pieces with their mother toy. She had felt quite wasteful about it until Catherine had admitted probably sneaking the equivalent of Toyland into the wheelie bin over the years. The badge-maker, however, remained cared for and the pieces were always dutifully returned to the box after a craft session. He had umpteen 'superhero' badges reflecting his various egos. His favourite alter ego was 'Dannyman'. He had designed a badge which was blue based, like Superman's, but instead of the S there was a D. Stevie had adapted a pair of pyjamas for him with the same design.

Her brain found a tenuous link to Danny's pyjamas and Matthew. One day, Matt had stuck a paper M on his chest and he and Danny had chased each other around the house saving the world. She had laughed so much she had cried. Just like she was starting to do now, in the middle of flaming Woolworths.

It was useless. Matt was slipping further away from her, and Adam's silly 'plan' wasn't doing anything to stop it happening.

'*Remember, he hasn't actually seen you together yet. Matt needs to see you and MacLean together . . .*' said the part of her brain that apparently was still holding out some hope.

Stevie fished her mobile out of her bag whilst she was standing outside Argos and rang Adam MacLean. He answered after five rings.

'We need to hammer this home once and for all,' she

said, talking over his hello. 'They need to see us together next time for definite. How do we do it?'

And Adam, who had been about to ring her with the next stage of his plan, outlined his suggestion.

'You're going to do *what*?' said Catherine incredulously down the phone.

'Follow them,' said Stevie.

'Why can't he just keep leaving his car outside your house? They'd soon realize something was going on then, surely?'

'Yeeesss, but we've tried that and so far it hasn't worked very well. We have to force them, once and for all, into seeing *us* together. So he's hiring a car on Sunday so we can follow them in secret and then surprise them by turning up where they do.'

'Bit hit and miss, surely?'

'Well, with the luck we're having, probably, but they seem to go out quite a lot and they will definitely go out on Sunday.' She knew that because Matthew hated Sunday evenings in the house. He had always dragged her out when they could get a babysitter. 'Come on, let me treat you,' he would say. Although most of the time she had ended up paying. She wondered how many times he had done the 'empty wallet' trick on Jo. Probably never.

Catherine grimaced a bit. 'It just seems so much desperation and hard work. Are you sure it's worth it, love?'

Stevie cut her off there and then, refusing to face the fact that every plan they made gave a spark of hope – then seemed doomed to fail.

'Yes. I want him back, more than ever. I miss him so much, Cath,' she said, and it was true. Each morning it was becoming harder not to look out of the window and see him get into the car. It pierced her to see them together, but she still wanted to snatch every sight of him that she could. That morning she had stood there, not caring if he caught her watching or not, tears streaming down her face, until commonsense pulled her backwards, just before his door opened and unravelled all her good work so far.

Jo had kissed him when they had got into the car, as if sensing they were being watched and was staking ownership of her man. Jo, who had been her friend, the woman who had gone shopping with her, eaten at her table, cuddled her son, exchanged secrets. It was almost a worse deception than Matthew's.

There couldn't be any such thing as karma, otherwise why were they so happy after causing so much destruction, when all Stevie had done was love and her heart was shattered?

Chapter 34

Stevie opened up her eyes to a Saturday morning full of a whole Junesworth of sunshine bursting through the curtains. It had all the promise of a gorgeous, warm photographer's delight of a day. A gorgeous, warm but awful day. Her wedding day.

By the time she came out of the shower, Danny was up, grinding his fists into his eyes to knock out the sleep and then he smiled.

'Morning, Mum,' he said, and she picked him up and cuddled him. He smelt of sleep and beds and he rained kisses on her cheeks and lips. He was so beautiful, she wanted to squash him. His love for her was so sweet and uncomplicated. Why wasn't adult love as pure and faithful as this?

'How many hours to Josh's party, Mum?' he said, as she put him down.

Hell, she had almost forgotten all about it.

'Three hours, I think,' she said, although she would check the invitation pinned up on the noticeboard to make sure.

'Cool,' he said, and went off for a wee.

★

She left the kitchen blinds closed and set the table in the sun lounge instead. The last sight she wanted to see this morning was the couple across the road sticking their tongues down each other's throats on a day that should have been hers and Matthew's. Was he thinking about what today should have been too, or had it been wiped from his memory? He had probably forgotten and was having wild sex right at the very time that he should have been getting his last shower as a single man. Stevie presumed he and Jo were having sex all the time. She found that she was almost getting obsessed, thinking about the two of them in bed together and *their* sex being the stuff of films, with no fumbling for condoms, wet sticky patches or embarrassing squelchy noises. There would only be fluid, powerful, rolling-about stuff and simultaneous orgasms and sweat that smelt of musky perfume. She hauled her thoughts away from across the street and back to the important issue of how to break it to Danny that they had run out of Coco Pops.

Across the street, Jo and Matthew had just finished having sex and were now relaxing in the glowing aftermath. She was nestled in the circle of his arms and talking about weddings. Theirs.

'I think I fancy a carriage drawn by white horses, and a chocolate wedding cake like Pam's only a lot bigger – three more tiers.'

Matthew just wanted to lie there and stroke her, not talk about spending money. He had fallen asleep the previous night totting up how much exactly he owed, and it was a lot. At present rate of payback, the debt would be a millstone around his neck for fifteen years, not counting the extra to pay for the wedding that Jo was busy planning. Rough figures intimated that would cost at least twenty thousand, and that wasn't counting the extravagant honeymoon. He felt slightly sick.

The clock said it was nine-fifteen on Saturday 3 June. If he had stopped at giving Jo MacLean his hankie in the car park that day instead of becoming involved, he would be getting married in a few hours. Contentedly so because nothing was actually wrong with Stevie: she was a good girl – generous, kind, warm, considerate, funny, sparky . . . and there would be less of a hole in his financial situation. He shuddered and pulled Jo into him. How could he be thinking like that? He didn't like it one bit.

'What's the matter?' she said.

'I should have been getting married today,' he said.

'What – and you're upset that you're not, is that it?' Jo pulled away from him.

'Don't be silly – hey, come back here!'

She let him drag her back but lay huffily in his arms.

'It's not very flattering being in bed with someone whilst he's thinking about marrying another woman,' she pouted.

'I'm not,' he protested. 'Sorry, it was tactless and insensitive of me even to mention it. Come on, what can I do to make it up to you?'

'Well, there is something,' she said with that look in her eye. Then she lay back as his head disappeared under the duvet.

*

Josh Parker's party was being held in the function room in the annexe part of Well Life. There was a bar there and Stevie was all too aware of how well utilized it would be by all the dads who had been dragged along. One in particular, worst luck.

Catherine had arranged to meet her outside and her welcoming smile slid further off her face the closer Stevie got.

'Christ, you look like shit,' said Catherine.

'Thanks,' said Stevie. 'It's not the best I've felt.'

Catherine was overcome with guilt. Maybe it would have been better for Stevie to sit in the cottage and mope or get drunk on gin until she hit oblivion. She could have taken Danny to the party for her and let Stevie pretend the day wasn't happening. She was thinking about it the previous night then got sidetracked when the kids fell victim to some nameless bug that was circulating. Well, all of them except for Gareth, which was lucky, because he was excited about the party and she wouldn't have wanted him to miss it.

Catherine linked her arm and they walked in together, and immediately Stevie voiced the, 'Oh God,' that Catherine was thinking. The function room was not only full of balloons, but party poppers were piled up in small mountains on every table. The disco music was blaring out by the dance floor and the bar was thick with dad-customers. Josh's own father, Richard, waved over with a balloon in his hand, seemingly specially prepared. He looked like it was *his* birthday when his eyes first locked on Stevie.

Stevie hated balloons, she hated party poppers and she hated Josh's noisy dad more than both of them put together. A legacy from her own mum and dad's shouting days, she suspected, when she had cried herself to sleep, waiting for her fragile world to be split apart. It was almost a relief when it eventually happened. At least the screaming stopped.

Matthew had never come with her to any of the parties, so she had usually been on her own amongst a sea of couples, and what was it about some men that the title 'thirty-something single mum' was male-speak for 'easy prey'? At the first party they had ever been to, Richard Parker had leapt on Stevie's reaction to a popped balloon with a 'hilarious' tirade of many more. She had tried to laugh it off, but after two more hours of having her eardrums tormented, her nerves and her temper were in shreds. Ever since then, he had been there at every children's party squeaking balloons near her, exploding party poppers behind her, however deep she was in conversation with anyone else, however much she ignored him, until she wanted to scream at him to leave her alone. But how could she do anything but try to be a good sport? She didn't want to show Danny up or embarrass herself with an over-reaction, and if Jan Parker found Stevie telling her husband to 'sod off', what would she think?

She would probably presume that Stevie was at fault, because wives never quite believed that their partners were the instigators of trouble with another female, did they? Then they would end up not talking and the bad feeling might filter down to the kids, all because some stupid idiot didn't know when to stop. Yet he would remain blameless in it all, ready to torment another day. So Stevie suffered in painful silence and hoped he would get tired of the joke but he never did, and the more beers he had, the funnier he thought it all was. Today he looked as if he had had quite a lot to drink already.

'Stand close to me,' said Catherine. 'I'll tell him to piss off, even if you don't. No wonder his mam called him Dick!' and with that, she squashed Stevie on a corner table out of the way and went to get the first round in. Josh, Gareth and Danny were dancing – the lady entertainer was demonstrating 'The Ketchup Song' – but Stevie's smile at them was quickly knocked off by a big bang in her ear. She squealed and spun around.

'Gonna get you later big time!' said Richard Parker, staggering slightly behind her and waggling his finger. His rubbery lips moved over each other as if he was chewing a toffee but couldn't quite locate it in his mouth.

'Excuse me!' said Catherine forcefully and barged him out of the way with her expertly agile mum-hip. She plonked herself down next to Stevie, handed her a drink and said, 'I bet you just love me now for forcing you here, don't you?'

'It's okay, Danny's enjoying himself.'

Then Gareth threw up.

'Oh sod, I thought it was too good to be true,' said Catherine. Mothers converged onto the dance floor with tissues and dragged off little brothers and sisters who wanted to go splashing in the puddle of watery vomit.

'I'll get your bag,' said Stevie, wishing, and feeling really awful for doing so, that it had been Danny who had thrown up and given her the excuse to go home. Did that make her a terrible person? Probably. The murderous thoughts about Jo she had tried to keep a lid on that morning were making her feel a bit unhinged. But Danny wasn't going anywhere; he was having a ball and it would have been so unfair to take him home and upset his day too. It wasn't his fault his mum was too much of an old trout to keep a man, and what would they do instead because she didn't want to go out or do anything but curl up into a ball and sleep the day away.

'Oh Steve, I've cocked this right up for you, haven't I?' said Catherine.

'It's not your fault, Cath,' said Stevie. 'Gareth's poorly and that's that.'

'I should never have nagged at you to come. I always think I know better than everyone else.' Wasn't it me who more or less forced her to go on that first date with Matthew when she was going to back off? thought Catherine. Eddie had been right when he accused her of interfering too much in other people's lives.

'Mummeee!' cried Gareth.

'Look, go,' said Stevie, pushing her away. Catherine was dreadfully reluctant to leave her friend, today of all days, but she was trapped. Eddie was working and Kate, not 100 per cent well herself, was looking after the other kids, so there really was no alternative.

'Go!' Stevie ordered again, and so Catherine blew her an apologetic kiss and went.

Out of the corner of her eye, she saw Richard Parker

staring over. Where was his bloody wife? She was sure that if Matthew had made a beeline for a woman every time he saw her, she would have picked up on it. Then again, this from a woman who hadn't seen what had been happening under her nose with her man and Jo. A sweep of the hall showed her that Jan was in the dining area, too busy even to look up. A balloon brushed past Stevie's head, then another landed and almost knocked her drink over, and so with her nerves stretched to breaking-point and unable to bring herself to do anything about it, Stevie endured the next hour.

Then the children conga-ed into the dining area, and after making sure Danny's plate was replete, Stevie stole off to the ladies. She just wanted to go home but there was another half an hour to go and Danny would never forgive her if she dragged him away before the party bags were ready. Her thoughts were so much on where she might go afterwards to keep herself occupied that she didn't see the figure hiding behind the corner when she emerged from the loo.

Bang.

Stevie screamed.

'Told you I'd get you!' said Richard, with eyes very glazed and holding a clutch of more balloons. He swaggered forwards a little, straying too far into her personal space, pointing to her chest. 'What I find amazing though, is that you're scared of *these* balloons when all the time you've got *those* big balloons under your jumper.'

Stevie's mouth fell into a long O. She was too stunned to react and stand up for herself, but it didn't matter because seconds later it was done for her. From nowhere, big Adam MacLean appeared with a not very friendly expression on his face and he boomed so loudly into the top of Richard Parker's bald patch that it left an echo hanging in the air,

'Hey pal, are you bothering this lady?' Even Stevie blanched at the tone of his voice, which was a weapon of mass destruction in itself. She was witnessing the side of him now that she hadn't seen yet but had heard lots about, but despite it, boy was she glad to see him.

'Er . . . oh . . . er . . . sorry, no offence!' *Mumble mumble.* Richard shrank and scuttled away back into the party room and Adam let him. Contrary to what Stevie might have expected of him, he didn't grab him and mince him between his fists or do a Steven Seagal and launch him through the nearest glass window. The confrontation ended there. Then again, Adam was at work and a little worm like Richard Parker throwing balloons about obviously wasn't worth risking his job and another assault charge for. Funny, that. She didn't think they'd employ someone with a crim-inal record for GBH in such a posh place, and Adam had spent time inside a hard Scottish prison for violence, so Jo had told them.

'Thank you,' she said, relief washing over her like a warm shower.

'Don't get excited, I wid have done it for anyone,' he said in his usual gruff and dismissive way. 'What were you doing out here alone with him anyway?'

Why is this my fault? thought Stevie. Her head sud-denly flooded with voices: her mother saying *'No wonder he buggered off!'* and Mick's mother screaming at her, *'If you'd*

been more of a wife, he'd still be alive!' and pictures of the way
Adam MacLean always looked at and spoke to her as if she
was to blame for Jo leaving him. She wanted to scream
aloud, 'I'm not to blame for this, I'm not!' Then she
thought of waiting outside the headmaster's office, being
accused of climbing high trees and pinching apples, and it
was then that Stevie's last remaining nerve snapped, and it
appeared that it was the one holding the lid down on her
tear supply because they moved at Exocet missile speed up
to her eyeballs. And, like an Exocet missile, there wasn't a
damn thing she could do to stop them.

'I only went to the loo. Please, Adam,' she said, without
the customary pause before his name, 'not today.' She
wiped at her eyes with the flat of her hands; they were
dripping out water like a pair of taps with faulty washers.
'I don't care if you fight me for the rest of your life, but
please, *please*, I beg you, not today.' Her throat failed on
the last word and she turned away before she could make
any more of a fool of herself in front of him, and melted
back into the party room, grateful that it was so dark
inside.

When the party was at last over, Stevie and Danny went
down to Blockbusters and got out the *Crocodile Dundee*
trilogy and a big bag of popcorn. They transformed the
lounge of Humbleby Cottage into a cinema, closing the
blinds and diverting the sound through the surround speakers. Then they snuggled up on the sofa with the popcorn
and Cola. Really, it was a lovely hot day and it was a shame
to be inside, but today, Stevie didn't want to see the sunshine. She didn't want to know that she would have been

outside the church bathed in it now, having her photo-
graphs taken, laughing and being beautiful and throwing
her bouquet. Neither did she want to think that tomorrow
she and MacLean were going to tail the faithless exes in a
hired anonymous car, like Starsky and Hutch, in a bid to
win them back. *Who was she kidding?* Matthew and Jo
hadn't taken their bait, it was useless. A tsunami of despair
engulfed her and dragged away her last remaining hope
with its massive ebb.

'Are you okay, Mummy?' asked Danny, holding up a
nub of popcorn near her lips.

'I'm fine, love. I think I'm just getting a bit of a cold,' she
sniffed.

'You've got cry all over your cheek.' Danny's little hand
came out to wipe away the escaping tears that threatened to
flow so fast that she would be dissolved by them. It would
have been so easy to collapse into them but she didn't want
her little boy to see her as a weak, blubbering mess when
she was supposed to be the strong one. Sometimes it was so
hard to keep it together, though. Sometimes she just
wanted to let go, surrender her power to someone else
who would look after her, deal with things and make
everything all right. But that was a luxury she was not
afforded, so, with a monumental effort she managed to
rein her tears in, just as there was a knock on the door. *Oh
no, no, no!* She didn't want to see anyone. Maybe she could
pretend she wasn't in. *Boom boom boom*. Whoever it was
knocked again more insistently, and there was only one
person who did knock like that. And she didn't want to see
him more than she didn't want to see anyone else.

BOOM BOOM BOOM!

He'd break the damn door down if he carried on, the loud insensitive swine.

'Stay there, pet, I'll be back in a minute,' Stevie said, closing the lounge door behind her before opening the outside one. If it was who she thought it was, Danny must not see him under any circumstances. Unfortunately for her, it was.

Adam MacLean was standing there on the doorstep in his smart work clothes: a white shirt and a blue tie with a WL motif on it.

'Hellooo,' he said, sounding quite contrite for him. Jeez, she looks terrible, he thought.

'Hello,' she said coldly, the bloodshot shining eyes betraying her air of composure.

'I . . . er . . . came to say I'm sorry for sounding a wee bit aff.'

'Oh right,' she said. He seemed a bit taken aback that she didn't seize on the opportunity to say that he'd never sounded anything other than 'aff' and not thought to apologize for it before. There looked to be little fight left in her.

It was over.

'Adam, this isn't working,' she started to say.

Then time stood still. The world stopped revolving for five seconds but it was just enough to allow her to catch her breath and decide how best to capitalize on this gift of a perfect moment. For there across the lane, Matthew Finch was perfectly framed in the window. He was looking at her. And Adam's car. And Adam himself. On her doorstep. Smart in a shirt and tie.

Now or never!

Stevie arranged her tired features into a smile that twisted as sexily as she could at one side, then she reached forward for Adam's tie, reeling him slowly in, and down, and then kissed him gently on the mouth.

Adam didn't resist. There was only one reason she had just done that and it wasn't because apologetic butt-ugly Scotsmen turned her on.

'They're watching, aren't they?' he whispered loudly.

'You don't think I'm doing this for fun, do you?' she confirmed through gritted teeth. He pushed her inside the house as if he was eager to get her alone for questionable reasons and they slammed the door together and stood behind it, each of them wiping at their lips with the back of their hands like three year olds that had experienced their first kiss and were thinking, *I'm NEVER doing that again*.

'Aw this planning and the chance just falls into our laps,' said Adam, fighting back the desire to whoop around the kitchen. For one horrible moment there, he had nearly been in danger of hugging her.

'I know, I know,' said Stevie quietly because her heart was pumping so fast it wasn't letting her breathe properly. Had she had more air in her lungs, she would have danced with him, leapt on him, hugged him, *yes him*. Then Danny appeared in the doorway with his collar sucked up into his mouth and freeze-framed because there was a giant in the room who looked like a ginger Mr Incredible. Far from being scarred for life at the sight of MacLean, Danny's only comment, after letting the soggy collar drop from his mouth was, 'Hi.'

'Hi there,' said Adam, waving awkwardly.

'Who are you?'

'Oh God!' began Stevie, but Adam dropped to his haunches.

'I'm Well Life Man,' he said. 'See?' And he showed off the letters on his tie. 'I just dropped by on a mission to ask all people who work at home to come and be fit, but shhhh, you haven't seen me, okay? If anyone asks, I'm Adam MacLean. Like Superman is Clark Kent, understand?'

'Cool!' said Danny, nodding. Yes, he knew exactly what he meant.

Well, he couldn't have picked a better persona than a Superhero to ingratiate himself with my son, Stevie thought. She was observing exploitation at its best. That's what his handle should have been: 'Manipulatorman'.

'Danny, go and watch Dundee and let me and Mr . . . Well Life talk about . . . er . . . having a coffee.'

'Okay,' said Danny, grinning. *Wow, a secret Superhero in the kitchen. Cool!* 'You're not going yet are you?'

'No, I'll say goodbye before I go,' said Adam, waving again and raising his best 'shushing' finger. Then, when Danny had gone, he crossed the window to steal a quick look across at Matthew's house.

'He's still there,' he said, smiling over at Stevie, as if he was saying something suggestive instead. 'Quick, come here.'

She came there as requested, but she didn't expect him to enclose her in a great big embrace and tip her back Hollywood snog-style.

'Right, you can get off me now,' said Stevie eventually.

'Bit longer, we're still being looked at.'

'Both of them?'

'Can't tell. I'll pretend to kiss you. Put your hands in my hair.'

He brought his cheek close to hers, she started stroking his hair. They would have looked magnificent in profile, very *Gone with the Wind*.

'Right, he's moved away,' said Adam, letting her drop ungraciously to the floor.

'Ow!'

'Oops, sorry.' He extended a hand and helped her up.

'There obviously isn't a word for chivalry in Gaelic then.'

'Look, lady . . .' He nipped off what he was going to say because he didn't want to add any more grief to her day. She had probably had enough of a bad one and he hadn't helped.

He had been at work checking on the CCTV camera when the little boy had been sick, then recognized the woman rushing towards him – the one with the ex-candy-floss hair. He had moved the camera around, aware that he was looking for *her*. Sure enough, there she was, sitting alone, out of the way. He focused in on her face, saw how unhappy she looked. Some dickhead was throwing balloons at her, insensitive to her annoyance, actually relishing in it. Adam got on with some work, then switched on again soon afterwards to find the dickhead was still annoying her. Then he had checked again later and saw her walk out of the function room. He watched the man dump his beer and follow her out and then, obviously in a professional vein, Adam had felt obliged to find out what was going on in person.

When he found her cornered in the corridor, she looked so utterly defeated and helpless, and something flagged up in his subconscious that today was the wedding day that never was. He didn't know why he had been so hard on her outside the loo, when it quite obviously wasn't her fault. He had wanted to stride in and rescue her from that slimy little man, but something had twisted inside him and he had ended up accusing her of causing it all. He hadn't liked seeing her so vulnerable and it confused him. Her pale little face had haunted him all afternoon and he knew he wouldn't have slept, had he not driven over to see if she was okay. It was the right thing to do after he had behaved so rudely.

'Is Well Life Man staying for tea?' said Danny, appearing round-eyed with fascination in the doorway again.

The two grown-ups looked at each other. Stevie's thoughts had never been so perfectly at war. On the 'No' side was:

1) this was Adam MacLean
2) she didn't want Danny getting confused
3) she didn't want Danny getting eaten

But on the 'Yes' side was:

1) Adam needed to be there at least another hour for maximum effect

2) the damage had been done – he and Danny had met

3) Danny appeared to remain psychologically intact

4) she was doing all this for Danny as much as for her-self

The argument was clearly won.

'We're going to have fish and chips!' said Danny.

'Ooh, one of my three hundred favourites!' said Adam, rubbing his hands together.

It looked as if he was staying then.

'Cool,' said Danny, stroking Adam's tie as if it was as precious as a national treasure. 'I love Superheroes, you know.'

'Is that what you're going tae be then, when you grow up? A Superhero?'

'No,' said Danny, as if that was the most stupid question in the world. 'I already *am* a superhero. I'm *going* to be a window cleaner.'

'Oh I see.' Adam suppressed a grin. 'So, have you got a name, fellow Superhero?'

'I'm Dannyman.'

'Glad to meet you, Dannyman,' said Adam, holding out his hand. Danny's little mitt was swallowed up in it.

'So when did you last save the universe then?' said Adam.

'Thursday,' said Danny, and off he trotted to watch the rest of *Crocodile Dundee*.

Chapter 35

Matthew stood at the window and tried to process the information his eyes were sending to his brain. Stevie with a man. Not just any man. A huge ginger man. And not just any huge, ginger man. *Him*. She had pulled his head down towards her with his tie. So it wasn't a casual call then. How bloody long had *that* been going on? Matthew asked himself. This was supposed to be their wedding day and she was snogging MacLean! His brain was busy speed-reading the events of the past few weeks for any enlightening information. The irony of his thought processes was lost on him.

So that's how Stevie got hold of Jo's Visa bill . . . That mysterious connection had been bugging a back part of his brain since it happened. He moved closer to the window. The scene being played out in front of him raised a hell of a lot more questions than it answered.

He had been waiting to see something bizarre from MacLean and Stevie. Her ultra-cool reaction to being rejected hadn't been normal, but he didn't expect *this*! Was this why his leaving had seemed to cause such little interruption to her life then? Had they embarked on their affair first? *Stevie and MacLean? NO! HOW?* Is that why they were dancing together so clumsily at Pam and Will's wedding – double-bluffing to throw him off the scent? There were so many question and exclamation marks bombarding him, he thought his brain might go into punctuation overload and pop out of his head like a jack-in-a-box. Then, just as he thought it might be a hallucination, there they were engaged in Part II by canoodling in the window – and not right next to the window, as if they were showing off to a would-be audience either, but back from it, lost in each other. It couldn't be! They weren't a match. She was what – five foot two – and he was the bloody BFG! Well, a BVG – a Big Violent Giant! Although they had looked pretty matched up, snogging like that. Too much so for comfort.

Matthew was shocked, puzzled, confused, bewildered. Matthew felt like he had just been punched in the stomach.

'Sorry, it'll just be fish and chips,' said Stevie. 'I haven't been shopping these past few days, I've been a bit . . . preoccupied.'

'It would be better if you went for the fish and chips,' said Adam. 'It looks then as if I'm already established in the house.'

'Okay,' said Stevie, seeing the sense in that. 'Danny, get your shoes on, pet.'

'Aw, Mummy, can't I stay here with Well Life Man?'

'No, of course not,' said Stevie.

'Pleee-ease!'

'He's okay,' said Adam, not immediately seeing the problem. 'We can talk about hero stuff.'

'Cool!'

'I don't want my son used as a tactic, Mr . . . Adam,' said Stevie quietly near his ear. Well, three foot beneath it, which was as close as she could get without stilts.

'He won't be. If the wee guy disnae want to go, I'll look after him till ye get back. I don't mind at all.'

'Absolutely no way. No chance. Impossible.'

Stevie shook her head again and in such a way that it switched on a three-million watt light bulb in Adam's head.

'You think I might hurt him, is that it?'

'Well, I don't know you all that well, do I, to leave my child in your capable or incapable hands?'

'Surely you wouldn't think that your child isn't safe with me?' MacLean looked genuinely taken aback, as if she really had hit him where it hurt.

No, she didn't think that at all, really. Ignoring the fact that he looked like a primitive heavyweight boxer-cum-maniac-savage, in her heart of hearts Stevie didn't think Adam MacLean would hurt her child. Even if he could duff up a duplicitous adult bitch in the comfort of their own home.

'Please, Mummy!'

'Here, take this,' said Adam, stretching a ten-pound note out to her.

'Don't be silly,' said Stevie, pushing it back. 'I owe you one for helping me out earlier anyway.'

Adam ignored her and stuffed it in her handbag whilst she was preoccupied with calming down her son.

'Please, Mummmeee!' whined Danny.

'No, you come with me.'

'Awww!' Danny's face creased up and threatened tears, but Stevie did not give an inch.

'Look, Superheroes need er . . . privacy to set the table. We'll only be five minutes. Come on, get your shoes on.'

'Please, Mummy!' With the non-negotiable obstinacy of a four year old, Danny was not going anywhere.

'C'moan, leave him, you'll only be five minutes,' said Adam.

Danny turned on his most charming blue-eyed smile. Stevie knew when she was beaten.

'I'll be less than five minutes,' she said, making it sound more like a warning than a statement of fact.

Her boy would be okay. Her maternal instinct had no doubts on that score. But still, she ran up the road like a hungry Linford Christie.

Across the road, Matthew had just about shut his jaw when he saw Stevie come out of the house, on her own. That meant she had left Danny and MacLean alone together. *She would do that? After all she knew about him?* Then again, it hadn't stopped her snogging him, had it? Or worse. My God, he was a true charmer, that much was true, and Stevie must be very vulnerable at the moment, especially today, the perfect time for such a manipulator to take full advantage of her. Matt felt a huge pull to go over there and check everything was all right. He really would never forgive himself if MacLean hurt Stevie too. Or Danny.

'What are you looking at, babe?' called Jo from the sofa, where she was painting her toenails.

'Er . . . nothing, darling.'

It crossed his mind to tell Jo her ex had just been snogging his ex, but he couldn't gauge what her reaction would be. Recently her selfless, caring consideration for Stevie's welfare had segued into jealous sulks every time her name came up. So Matthew kept to the safe path, buttoned his lip and came away from the window. He didn't want to spoil this lovely weekend they were having, although a letter from the bank to inform him that his loan payment had bounced had rather done that already. *Could he please rectify the situation immediately?* Oh, and he had been charged fifty quid for the letter.

There was a queue at the chip shop as a fresh batch of fish had only just gone in. The shop-owner made a joke about it, and though Stevie smiled politely, she didn't find it in the least bit amusing. Her nerves were as tight as harp-strings.

I shouldn't have left him with MacLean, she thought after foot-tapping in the queue for what felt like an eternity. She was on the verge of exiting empty-handed when the chip man eventually said, 'Right now, love, what can I get you?'

She ran back with the warm parcel in her hands, her head playing the most awful tricks on her. *Danny and MacLean alone together!* What sort of mother was she? To make it worse, she could hear sounds of distress that grew louder the nearer she got to the cottage. They weren't in her over-active imagination either – her boy really was screaming.

Stevie sprinted to the door and threw it open to find

Danny squealing and MacLean attacking him. She threw
down the parcel on the nearby dining table and launched
herself at MacLean, climbing fearlessly on his back and
trying to get a grip on his cropped hair. Failing, she started
clobbering him with her handbag instead.

'Get off my son, you animal!' she screeched.

'Ow!' said Adam, the one word recognizable amongst
the guttural exclamations of pain.

'Mummy, what are you doing!' said Danny, watching
her in a most unharmed way.

Stevie stopped mid-batter. 'Are you okay, love?'

'Yes, Adam was showing me some Well Life Man
Superhero moves.'

Stevie slid down off Adam's back. 'Sorry,' she said
meekly, 'I thought . . .'

'S'okay,' said Adam, rubbing his head and wincing. 'It's
just a bit of jujitsu. It means "the gentle art". Maybe you
should come tae a few classes. That's a heavy wee bag ye've
got there.'

Stevie didn't mean to burst into laughter, but then it was
a very odd day. The sort of day, in fact, that made the Big
Dipper at Blackpool look like a baby ride. Adam's laugh
joined hers, and then they both stopped abruptly. That was
twice they'd shared laughter now; it was in danger of
becoming a habit.

Adam arranged the fish on the plates and fish bits for
Danny, whilst Stevie shared the chips out.

'No chips for you, Dannyman?' said Adam.

'I don't like chips,' said Danny.

'Wannae try some of mine? Potatoes are really good for

you, you know. They teach you that at Superhero School. Carbohydrates – give you energy. Isn't that right, Mammy?'

'Erm . . . yes,' agreed Stevie.

Danny's face registered total amazement. 'Really?'

There and then, the little boy rediscovered a fondness for the potato.

'She's been for fish and chips,' said Matthew. He had unconsciously gravitated back to the window and become so engrossed in what he was witnessing that he hardly realized he was thinking aloud. Stevie was running back to the house as if the devil was on her heels – *as if she couldn't keep away from him* – which annoyed Matthew even further. 'So he's eating there . . .'

'Who is eating where?' said Jo. Realization dawned on her face and soured her smiling expression. 'Oh I get it, you're spying on *her*. Why? Why are you so interested in her all the time?'

'I'm not. Nothing could be further from my mind. Just thinking something through for work. Just looking into thin air, not over there. Pah!' said Matthew, desperately trying to head off an argument. Not wanting her to see MacLean's car, he whizzed the curtains shut. 'Look, that's how much I care about *her*. Let's go into the garden, my love. Shall we open a bottle of wine? I think I could do with a glass.'

'Yes, that would be nice,' said Jo, uncurling her lip. 'Oh that reminds me – do you think ordinary champagne or vintage for the wedding toast?'

'Er, let me think about that one,' said Matthew, and

reached for the last remaining bottle of Chablis in his once impressively-sized wine cache.

'So what was going on at the party then, with that idiot?' said Adam, helping Stevie to clear the table as Danny took an Alp of ice cream into the lounge.

'Oh, he's one of the dads,' Stevie started to explain. 'Once upon a time he found out that I can't stand loud noises – party poppers, crackers. . . .'

'Tyres squealing . . .'

'Precisely, and I hate – *loathe* – balloons. So he thinks it's hilarious to torment me with them every time he sees me.'

'Could you no' tell him to bugger aff?'

'I don't want to cause trouble,' said Stevie. 'I can live with it. It was just that today he stepped over the mark. Said something a bit offensive.'

'Whit?'

'Oh nothing. It's probably just me over-reacting.'

'No, c'moan, whit was it?'

'No, really I can't, it's embarrassing.'

'C'moan, tell me!'

Stevie pulled in a deep breath and told him.

'*Whit*? Cheeky swine!' said Adam. He felt offended and angry for her. Why were some blokes such pigs? If he'd known that, he'd have . . . he'd have . . .

'I would have batted it away, but today being today, well, it didn't help, I suppose,' Stevie went on, forcing out a smile.

'Was it your . . . er . . . today?' Adam struggled and coughed over the key words.

'Yes,' said Stevie, quickly changing the subject. 'Anyway, coffee?'

'Aye, please.'

She put the box of chocolates on the table that Crystal had sent her after reading the Paris and Brandon manuscript. She had loved it, apparently.

'Oooh, choccies! And very expensive choccies tae!' said Adam with delight, and aimed for a knobbly-looking nut one.

'Present from my boss,' said Stevie.

'So what do you do again?'

'Not telling.'

'Oh come on, spill the beans. It cannae be that bad.'

She opened her mouth to tell him, then recalled that look he had given her book. It had been one of *Midnight Moon*'s bestsellers too. No, she wouldn't tell him. There were only so many batterings her ego could take at the moment.

'Have as many chocs as you like. An extra sorry for trying to scalp you,' said Stevie, putting a cafetière on the table.

'No real damage done, so far as I can tell. I've a heid like a coconut,' he said with a twinkle and rapped on it with his knuckle. 'That smells nice – what sort of coffee's that?'

'Madagascan vanilla. I get it from the coffee shop in Town End, where they sell all the gorgeous puddings. I've a spare packet if you want to take it home with you. I always go a bit mad in the shop and overbuy.'

'Thanks, that would be very nice,' said Adam, watching as Stevie crossed to the cupboard. Then he snatched his eyes away, suspecting he might have actually been on the verge of assessing her in a boy-girl way.

'What flavour do you want?' Stevie started to read the labels. 'Vanilla, Irish Liqueur, Maple Syrup and Walnut . . . er . . . Death by Chocolate?'

'Oh, Death by Chocolate definitely.'

No surprise there then.

Stevie handed it over to him. 'It'll make your house smell like a cake shop, that one.'

'I'm no' bothered aboot the house,' said Adam quietly. 'I don't want to be in there without Jo really, and there are just too many reminders of her around. If she doesn't come back, I'll sell it.'

'Where would you go?'

'I'd have to stay around the area for my job. I like it here, we made friends – you know, people like Will.'

'He married my friend Catherine's cousin.'

'Aye, so I gathered. He's a great guy. For a Lowlander.'

They sat in contemplative silence for a moment, both realizing that they might actually have to start making alternative plans for their lives soon, if Jo and Matthew didn't come back to them. Adam was going to move, it seemed. What would Stevie do? Where would she go?

Adam took the initiative and poured the coffee before it climbed out of the cafetière itself.

'I don't think we need the hired-car adventure tomorrow now, do you?' he said, as he was halfway down his drink.

'No, I think today's probably done the trick,' said Stevie, and she giggled suddenly without planning to. The sound resonated like a bell in the air. It was a sound that belonged to someone with a great capacity for joy, a merry heart. It jarred with the image he carried of her and was thus indigestible, and it made him feel uncomfortable for a reason he didn't understand. Grabbing up the coffee packet, he said stiffly, 'Think I'd better make a move.'

'Yes, of course,' Stevie responded, wondering what she had done to send him back into Gruff Land.

'I'll ring you to discuss what we do next. Let me know if you hear anything.'

'You'll have to say goodbye to Danny. You promised,' said Stevie.

'Of course I was going tae,' he snapped back. They glared at each other, enemies again, until she broke contact and called Danny through.

'I'm off, pal,' said Adam, bending to him, and then gently jabbed his cheek with his enormous fist.

'Awww. Are you coming back soon?' said Danny.

'No doubt I will see you again,' said Adam, flashing a quick look at Stevie, but she wasn't looking at him. She was too busy trying to work out what her son was making of it all, checking that he wasn't confused or upset by Adam's visit. Adam understood that and respected it. More than she could ever know.

'Shall we colour co-ordinate when I call again?' he asked her once he had stood again to his full height.

'I'll be in yellow and pink,' said Stevie.

'Well, maybe not,' said Adam with a cough. Then he left.

★

There was no one across the road watching Adam go, although he did leave with a tyre squeal just in case they needed to know he was on his way. He could still feel where Stevie had scratched his head, but he smiled as his hand came up to rub at the slight raised weal. You would-n't have thought there was such a tigress in her tank to look at her. Therein lay the trouble. He had thought he had known her, before he had even laid eyes on her. Her rep-utation had preceded her and, respecting the source of the gossip, he had taken it as gospel. Really, tonight was the first time she had acted anything like Jo's reporting of her. *But wasn't that understandable, if she thought he was hurting her son?* So far, he had to admit, there hadn't been much evi-dence of her being a fraction of the lazy, unhinged, crockery-throwing harridan Jo had said she was, and the selfless defence of her child wasn't the action of a mother who was borderline abusive.

He wished his mammy had been like Stevie in full flow, in the times when they got hurt. Especially the day when his da had been skelping wee Jinny with a heavy, drunken hand for weeing the bed and Adam had stepped in to stop him. He wasn't a big boy then, but he was getting stronger by the day, and for the first time Andy MacLean had strug-gled to overpower him. So he had gone for the hot poker and burnt his son on the face. Branded him like an animal. Said that every time he looked in the mirror from then on, he'd remember how he raised a hand to his daddy. And his maw had stood there like a scared ghost, watching it happen. She had not stepped in, like he'd seen Stevie do, mad for the safety of her wean.

He was a hell of a big man now but that still hadn't stopped Stevie going for him. She had run at him like a ram and had not given a single thought to what damage he could have done her. And he had the strength of a bull and could have done her a lot.

And when they said he'd be scarred for life, he'd thought, Surely my mammy'll leave him noo? But she didnae.

Chapter 36

'If you could give me a little more time, I get paid in a week,' said Matthew down the phone, believing he was whispering and not aware that his fellow office workers could easily overhear him.

'I'm sorry, Mr Finch, but I can't stop the interest being charged, nor can I authorize to refund you the overdue fee for the reasons you've given me for non-payment. Plus as you are paid monthly, you will have to find two months' mortgage from that single salary. Have you thought about that?'

'Of course I've sodding thought about it. I can't think of anything else!' snarled Matthew.

'I'm sorry, but I won't be sworn at,' said the mortgage advisor, and she put the phone down on him.

'Bloody bitch!' said Matthew, a little too noisily.

'Personal calls, Mr Finch?' said a starchy voice behind him.

'Just the one urgent one, Colin, just the one,' said Matthew, inwardly cringing. It would have to be *him* – Colin Seed, Head of Personnel, doing his rounds. Creepy Colin, Seedy Colin, Colin the Cardigan and, rather cruelly given the recent circumstances, Norman Bates. He couldn't have been more than ten years older than Matthew, but he looked near to retiring with his Shredded Wheat comb-over, ill-fitting brown suits that struggled to close over his paunch and a face guaranteed to cure hiccups. He spoke to every man as if they were naughty schoolboys and he was their headmaster. Even Matthew, who was the thirty-four-year-old Head of Concessions.

'Of all people to be there when you're on the phone to someone not work-related,' said Matthew, telling Jo about it on the drive home. 'That bloke is always lurking about. He's got a real personality problem.'

'Who were you ringing?'

'Oh . . . er . . . just the bank, to see if a cheque had been paid in that I was expecting. Interest owed to me.' *Damn, what made him lie again?*

'Why didn't you use your mobile?'

'Can't find it,' he said. Lying again. He had finally cancelled it in a desperate economy measure. That, and cancelling his gym membership, would save him a hundred quid a month easily.

'Anyway, why do you think the man's got a problem?'

'Well, you only have to look at him,' said Matthew. 'He's a total numpty. He was born middle-aged, he's never had a girlfriend and he's never likely to get one either.'

'He could be gay,' said Jo.

'No chance. He likes to hang around women too much. Not that he'd know what to do with one. Unless he found a blind one into trainspotting.'

'Bitchy! I've always found him quite amiable in passing,' said Jo, slapping Matthew gently.

'Well, you are a very beautiful girl and will no doubt have charmed him where everyone else has failed.'

'Aw, sweetie,' said Jo and stroked his hand, making his skin purr with pleasure. 'He's probably just lonely.'

'Seedy? Yeah, probably is,' said Matthew. 'Anyway, I think he'll be leaving soon, thank God. They've wanted him to go over and run the New York offices for ages, but he lived with his mum and that stopped him going. She died a couple of months ago and left him a stack.' Lucky bugger, thought Matthew. What he wouldn't give for a windfall like that. And the chance to go and live in New York. He'd gladly swap places with Seedy for all that – brown suits, fat gut, comb-over, Hallowe'en face and all.

'Poor man,' said Jo, with a heavy sigh.

'Poor man, nothing! He's a frustrated git who is jealous of anyone who looks as if they are getting a shag,' said Matthew, 'and the reason he is nice to you, darling, is because you are simply gorgeous and he probably wants to eat you all up, like I do.'

'Thank you,' said Jo, giving him her most beautiful smile. 'Talking of eating, shall we dine out tonight and celebrate how lovely I am then?'

'Oh what the hell, why not,' said Matthew, who found he really did not want to be at home amongst the negative energy of a stack of unpaid bills, or drawn to the window to see what was going on across at the cottage. Not that anything Stevie did could affect him, you understand, she was out of his life. That's what he found he had to keep telling himself anyway.

*

Adam MacLean rang her just as she was making up a cup of Horlicks to take to bed. It was ten o'clock and Matthew and Jo were just coming home from somewhere. Stevie watched as Jo slammed the door of the car and fumbled angrily with the house lock, leaving Matthew in her wake and looking very sheepish. He flashed a look towards the cottage to see if anyone was witnessing his humiliation and for once Stevie didn't step back from the shadows. Why shouldn't she be at her window, closing her blinds? If Matthew wanted to play with fire, let him get burnt. She hadn't done anything to skulk into the shadows for.

'Hi there,' Stevie drawled into the mouthpiece, looking very dreamy as she was talking. *Let Matthew Finch observe that as well – ha!*

'It's me, Adam,' he said, thinking she couldn't have realized. She was talking like Emmanuelle.

'I know, I'm being watched.'

'They cannae hear you!'

'No, but the voice comes free with the expression.' Honestly, what did he think? That she was actually trying to seduce him? She watched as Matthew followed Jo into the house and closed the door meekly behind him. Boy, what Stevie wouldn't give to be a fly with big ears on *that* wall.

'It looks to me as if my neighbours across the street might just have had a row. She's stomping about and he looks totally whitewashed,' reported Stevie.

'Guid. Wonder if it's anything to do with us?'

'No doubt we'll get to know in due course if it is.'

'Have you got your invite?'

'What invite?'

'For Will and Pam's barbecue.'

'No.'

'Well, it's on its way. You know what I'm going to say, don't ye?'

It wasn't hard to work out.

'What? You and me to go together?'

'Absolutely.'

'Colour co-ordinated?'

'As long as it's blue. No yellow or pink.'

'When is it though? It all depends if I can get a babysitter.'

'Saturday. Apparently, the weather at the weekend is going to be gorgeous and the good news is that you don't need to find a babysitter because the kids are invited too. Pam's organized a Bouncy Castle and a magician and thousands of e-numbers-worth of sweets and pop. Will asked me if I minded him inviting Matthew and Jo and I said not at all. In fact, I positively encouraged him to do so.'

'I don't know if I dare.'

'Oh, you dare,' said Adam with a sort of jolly threat. 'And what's more, we'll take centre-stage on this one, lady. Just you wait and see.'

Jo had never really forgiven Matthew for carrying no cash with him at Will's wedding. She had got sick of dipping into her purse to pay for all the drinks at the reception that night, but she swallowed it because she thought it was a one-off genuine mistake on his part. But tonight was unforgivable! First she had to bear the embarrassment when his card was declined, then she had to stand by as he looked hopelessly through a wallet he knew was empty, as if he was Paul Daniels and would suddenly shout, 'And that's magic!' and flourish up two fifty-pound notes. They were starting to attract attention for all the wrong reasons, and so she whipped out her Amex to reclaim some dignity, only to have to bear the *in*dignity when that too was declined. Luckily, she had her chequebook and in anger and embarrassment, she had written out the wrong amount and had to do another. She would never go in that restaurant again, at least not with Matthew. How dare he treat her like that? Funny how he always had money on him when he went shopping for those poncey male moisturizers and face packs. Adam would not have been seen dead with a mud-pack on. *And* he had paid her Amex bill every month. Foolishly, she had not considered that he might have cancelled his direct debit and that she would have to stump up for it from now on. She had taken his generosity for granted for so long. Not even the prospect of Matthew's half a million to come could salve the humiliation of this evening.

'Please, sweetie, I'm so sorry. I'm so stupid. Please, let me make it up to you,' Matthew pleaded in bed and started to smudge his mouth down her body, but she pushed him away and presented him with her back.

'Matthew, just go to sleep,' she said. Sex might have had a big place in Jo MacLean's life, but next to money, its importance was negligible.

Chapter 37

'Have you got your invite?' said Catherine, with a just-dropped-the-kids-at-school Tuesday-morning phone call.

'It's just arrived now in the post.'

'And?'

'Yes, before you ask, I'm going with Adam MacLean.'

'Fandabidozy!'

'Is Matthew going?'

'They've been invited. Apparently, Will asked Adam first if he minded and he said no, and Pam asked me to ask you if it was okay.'

'Yes, it's fine.'

'I said that. In fact, I insisted she invite them because I just know that you two have a plan up your sleeves, don't you?' laughed Catherine.

'I wouldn't say it was a plan exactly. We just want them to see us together.'

'About time too,' giggled Catherine. 'Anyway, what are you going to wear?'

'I'm going shopping for something new.'

'When?'

'Towards the end of the week, probably.'

'Can I come?'
'Absolutely.'

They met for their shopping trip on Thursday, mainly because Stevie needed to get in a couple of days' hard writing on the story of Damme and Evie. Even with his (battle) scar, the big Scot was turning out to be an incredibly powerful character – against her will, it had to be said. He was evolving all on his own. Obviously, as a *Midnight Moon* hero, he had to be wonderful, but Damme MacQueen definitely had the McX factor. Evie presumed his roughness was not consigned to his exterior, and he thought her beauty was only skin deep – it was sexual Semtex. They were far too good for Crystal's conveyor-belt fiction and Stevie wished she had saved him for the long romantic novel she so wanted to write. She was having a great deal of fun writing the lovers' verbal battle scenes, each one of them misjudging the other totally.

Was that what she and Adam were doing? she had thought more than once recently. She had seen the scar on Jo's leg, witnessed her tears and fears but really, it was all circumstantial evidence, as they said on *A Touch of Frost*. Stevie had made herself a firm promise that she would butt out of the Honeywell/MacLean alliance at the first sign of violence, but there had been not even a hint of it so far. Could Jo have been telling lies? Did women have the same capacity for deception that men had? Was there really that much smoke without fire? Not that it mattered really, since Stevie's involvement with Adam was merely a means to an end, as was his involvement with her. She couldn't give a

damn what happened to either him or Jo after she and
Matthew got back together. Really.

Catherine picked out a very floaty summer blue dress
from the rack. 'Try this on.'

'Wow, that's perfect,' Stevie said. Just the colour Adam
had said he was going in too – although she would be
dressing for Matthew, not Adam, a nudging thought
reminded her.

'Go try.'

Stevie go-ed and tried. Then she came out of the changing rooms and gave her friend a modest twirl.

'That's the one,' said Catherine.

'Do you think?'

'Deffo.'

'Well, that's totally spoilt the morning then,' said Stevie.

'Nothing says you can't buy the first dress you see,' said
Catherine. 'Anyway, now we'll have more time to acces-
sorize and scoff buns.'

'Well done, that woman,' said Stevie, and went off to pay
lots of money. She had so much spare this month. Even
with the big wodge of rent money out of her account, life
was infinitely cheaper living without Matthew than with
him.

Salvation came for Matthew in the form of a letter from
Goldfish, which arrived on the same day as his formal
invite to Pam and Will's barbecue. They had upped his
Visa limit by two grand, so he immediately took out a
cash advance and paid the mortgage arrears off before the
interest crippled him any further. It was no big deal, he

told himself. Some people lived all their lives robbing Peter to pay Paul, although he wasn't sure how much longer he could do that because Peter hadn't anything left to rob and Paul was going to send some big mates round with knuckledusters on soon. He called the bank and made an appointment to see his account manager, in the hope of getting a consolidating loan. Then he planned, once and for all, how he was going to tell Jo the truth: that he wasn't just in that house as a stopgap until his 'family' investments matured and allowed him to buy a nice pile in the country. That he couldn't afford a fancy dancing wedding and the meals out every night would have to stop because he was *poor, poor, poor*. She would not be happy, but the scene at the restaurant had brought things to a bit of a head. He hadn't expected Jo to react quite as badly as she did, and it made him aware that he needed to tell her everything, now, whilst things were the worst financially that they could possibly be. She loved him, she would understand. Of that, at least, he was totally convinced.

Jo still wasn't talking to him. They hadn't had sex since the weekend and nothing he did, or tried to do, had warmed up the frosty air between them. He saw her enter the office after her lunch-break, waved over and smiled, but she sailed past him, carrying a posh-looking carrier bag, and his expression dropped to that of a kicked puppy. He sighed and got out his Visa, then made a call to 118 118 to find out the number of an Interflora, then rang 'Floral Fixation' and ordered an extravagant bouquet to be sent to a Ms J.

MacLean in *Design*. He did not notice that Colin Seed was well in earshot behind him.

Meeting up deliberately early so they could have a quick natter at the school gates, Stevie filled Catherine in on all the details since their last meet. She had, of course, rung to tell her that Matthew had seen them together, but trying to have a long intense conversation with children on both sides continually interrupting meant only the gossip skeleton was delivered, in preparation for the flesh to be put on now.

'You look better than you did,' said Catherine, adding cheekily, 'In fact, you looked bloody terrible at Josh Parker's party. Adam must have rejuvenating lips.'

'Don't be obscene!'

'Anyway, I'm glad he sorted Dickhead and his balloons out for you.'

'Yes, he did,' said Stevie, not realizing she was smiling. She had played that little scene over and over again to herself on a continuous loop – Adam MacLean coming around the corner just at the very moment when she felt at her most helpless. She had used it in her book where Damme arrived, just as the evil Richard had Evie pinned in a corner. The difference being that Evie's heart had started fluttering, whilst her own had . . . er . . . started fluttering actually. *Stop that. That is a ridiculous thought, and not a true recollection*, she mentally slapped herself. That was the trouble with having the imagination of a romantic novelist: the story world and the real world blurred and crossed over in some cases. She had ended up on more than one occasion seeing things as she wanted to see them and not as they really were. Men being the prime example.

'So as we were saying,' prompted Catherine, waving her hand in front of Stevie's face to check she was still with them, '. . . about Adam. How did it feel to snog him?'

'I didn't snog him, Cath. I just kissed him very lightly once, and then we both went inside and started wiping our mouths.'

She had only been so playground puerile because she saw his hand come up to his mouth first and therefore she needed to prove that kissing him was every bit and more disgusting than he seemed to find it. Although it hadn't been disgusting at all, she was forced to admit. He had very soft lips not that she wanted to dwell on that particular detail.

'Steve, is all this worth it?' Catherine asked suddenly. 'Kissing men you can't stand, buying expensive frocks . . .'

'Yes, Cath, it is,' Stevie said, picking up her carrier bag with the lovely blue dress in it. She had lost Mick to Linda, there was no way she would let history repeat itself by losing Matthew to Jo.

Chapter 38

There was a slight panic on the Friday as unforecasted rains came: great heavy flash floods and sparking lightning that Saturday brides and barbecuers alike stared out at in dismay. Stevie and Danny, walking home from an after-school visit to the park, were caught in a spectacular shower that drenched them totally, and they ran home half-laughing, half-screaming like mad things, then peeled off their saturated clothes and climbed straight into a big bubbly bath together.

Luckily, the clouds were gone the next day, except for a few wispy mares' tails and the air was already very warm and shimmery above the garden. By mid-morning, brides everywhere reached for their lipsticks with relieved smiles. Stevie had worked in the sunny garden all week, and a splash of freckles had appeared all over her nose and cheeks as if flicked there by a paintbrush. The light tanning of her skin made her eyes seem as blue as that day's skies and they shone with anticipation and excitement. She toasted a little further as she and Danny spent most of the day in the garden weeding out the potatoes that plagued the flowerbeds and digging out the dandelions, and the physical work took her mind nicely off the nervous anticipations of the evening to come. Then Danny fell asleep under the umbrella whilst she was mowing the grass, and as it was probably going to be a late evening for him, she let him sleep on until it was time to get his bath and then his party shirt on. Catherine had arranged for Eddie to pick him up and take him to the Flanagans' house so he could go along with the rest of the children.

'That'll give you another two hours to make yourself beautiful,' she had said with a wink, and Stevie had retorted, 'I'll need more than that!'

'Not in that frock you won't,' said Catherine. 'All the work's done for you.'

And so, as soon as Danny ran joyfully down the lane in his red dragon party shirt to Uncle Eddie and Gareth awaiting in the car, Stevie jumped in a bath armed with exfoliators, hair treatments and her trusty razor blade – a woman with a mission.

Apart from the fact that her hand was shaking when she put her eyeliner on and she had to redo one total socket, Stevie was quite pleased with her self-treatment, although she knew she couldn't compete with Jo's salon-perfection. Catherine was right, the dress was beautiful and fitted as if it had been made for her. She had dropped over a stone and a half in weight since all this business had started and the nipped-in waist only served to accentuate the curves below and above it. The dress pointed out the best bits even further, and teamed up with some strappy gold sandals that would probably cripple her in an hour, and a blue flower holding back her hair at one side, she looked fresh and rather lovely.

She had met Adam briefly at the gym the previous day. He was zipping about busily but found her at the weight bench to say that he would pick her and Danny up at seven-thirty. He was going to drive, because he didn't want to drink enough to put himself over the limit, and he wanted his head clear. When Stevie told him that Danny was going on ahead, she thought he had looked slightly disappointed. But then again, Adam MacLean, *Family Man*, would have shoved Matthew's nose a little further out of joint, she thought cynically. She hoped Danny wouldn't be upset by seeing Jo and Matthew together but, as Catherine had said, she couldn't hide it from him forever that life moved on.

At seven she heard a taxi beep and peeped through the upstairs window to see Matthew and Jo climbing into it. He was wearing a loud Hawaiian shirt that would have looked ridiculous on anyone else but on him, it looked fun and summery and his shoulders looked big and broad in it. *She* had on a white strappy sundress with incredibly high black sandals. The whole ensemble looked very simple, but stunning, and Stevie's nerve took a bit of a nosedive. Then again, she knew there was nothing she could have done to look better than she did with what she had available. Stevie felt *right*. Right shade of lipstick, right shoes, right hairstyle. This was it: *shit or bust*, as her Auntie Rita used to say, pre-posh husband.

She spent the last half an hour trying to keep her fingernails out of her mouth. She had French manicured them herself and they looked quite nice, although they weren't long talons like Jo's because she had to keep them short for typing. She was so nervous that when Adam was thirty seconds late she was all for ringing him to say she wasn't going – but just as she was doing the five-billionth check that there was no lipstick on her teeth, she heard a car pull up outside. Her legs wouldn't move. She heard the car door shut, she heard his steps, she heard his heavy rap on the door. *Maybe if she pretended she wasn't in . . .*

Telling herself off for being so pathetic, Stevie got up, went out into the hall and opened the door. Adam was wearing the same colour shirt as her dress. He looked big and blue and a bit handsome, and she found that her breath got all snagged up in her throat and she gave a little involuntary gasp.

He, meanwhile, gave her a discreet look up and down, then said quietly and as if surprised, 'You look nice.'

'Oh . . . er . . . thanks,' coughed Stevie, who was quite thrown, seeing as she hadn't expected a compliment from him, not in a million years. She thought it only polite to give one back. 'So do you, actually.'

'Aye, well, enough of the Mutual Appreciation Society annual day oot, let's get tae the party,' he grumbled, suddenly impatient. Stevie, who found she was a lot more comfortable with Adam MacLean in hostile mode than being a pretend nice-person, took a deep breath and climbed into the passenger seat.

The journey to Will and Pam's house was too short. They had to park up at the end of the street as there were so many cars. Stevie's heart was boom-booming and she was trembling with tension. When Adam turned off the ignition, he didn't look too keen to get out of the car himself.

'You okay?' he asked.

'No,' said Stevie.

'You . . . we'll be fine.' Sounds of laughter and music filtered into the ensuing silence that hung between them. 'I'm a wee bit scared myself for the record,' he added eventually.

'Are you?'

'Aye.'

And scared as she was, it was Stevie who said, 'Well, come on, we know what we're doing. Let's get on with it,' and with that she opened the car door.

Contrary to what she thought might happen i.e. that the world would stop revolving and there would be a silence so profound that if a pin dropped it would deafen everyone within a forty-mile radius, what actually transpired was that Adam rang Pam's doorbell, Pam answered, kissed and hugged them both and shoved them out into the back garden. There, they fell straight into the welcoming company of Catherine and Eddie, who were halfway down their first lagers. Adam, with his advantage of height, did a quick sweep of the merrily drinking crowds, but there was no sign of the lovebirds. He shook his head and Stevie was a paradoxical mix of relieved and disappointed.

'They're just around the corner to the left,' said Catherine in a low whisper. Then she started doing an odd eye-blinking thing to Stevie, as if trying to deliver a message in Morse code. Bizarre as it was, Stevie understood it. But then they had been friends for four thousand years.

'Oh . . . er . . . Adam, I know you've seen Catherine but you haven't really said a proper hello yet so, anyway . . . erm . . . this is Catherine and Eddie, my best friends. Cath, Eddie – this is Adam.' Hands were shaken and smiles exchanged. He had quite a nice smile, Stevie noticed, as he flashed it at Catherine. Modest, warm and genuine.

'Can I get you a drink, mate?' said Eddie.

'Naw, thanks. I think we'll head awf and get one ourselves in a wee minute,' said Adam, taking another look around and waving at someone.

'You look bloody lovely,' whispered Catherine to Stevie.

'Do I? I could be sick with nerves!'

'You look like a proper couple. You're both glowing. Interesting, that.'

'Oh shut up. I just wish they'd see us and be done with it. Where's Danny?'

Catherine pointed over to the Bouncy Castle. He was with Catherine's brood and having the time of his life.

'He won't come over even if you shout. You are one of the forgotten, like us,' said Catherine, and gently pushed her forward. 'Go and be seen, my love.'

'Come on,' said Adam, and he reached down and took up her hand. Stevie stared at it enclosed in his big square one and rounded her eyes at Catherine, who gave her a sly thumbs-up and a schoolgirl-giddy smile. Then, as if she was attached to a very energetic Doberman Pinscher, Stevie lurched forwards as Adam proceeded to move.

'There they are,' said Adam, tightening his grip. 'Stay

calm and if you want to pretend you haven't seen them, keep your eyes right on the conservatory.'

It was Catherine, watching in the background, who recorded what happened next. As she was to tell it later to Stevie, Jo and Matthew were walking slowly back into the throng engaged in beautiful couple conversation with an equally tall and willowy pair. As Jo's lovely head swung around, her eyes touched upon her ex, holding hands with Stevie, and her whole body seemed to stiffen to the extent that, for a moment, she was almost one of Pam's garden statues. Matthew followed her eye-path and saw them too. He hadn't imagined it then, they really were a couple. Here was the indisputable proof. Both of them watched as Adam moved fluidly towards the drinks table. Then he bent to Stevie as if to ask her what she wanted, and she placed a hand at the back of his neck as she was speaking into her ear.

Beautiful! thought Catherine, watching the little touch that spoke of more intimacy than if they'd started shagging on the grass in front of everyone. Then Adam poured her a drink first and himself one second, then they very gently chinked their glasses and, after a respectable time, with a protective arm curled around her, Adam steered her back in the direction of her friends. Their movements were Bolshoi Ballet perfect.

Matthew's mouth hung so widely open, it would have been easy to think the shock had dislocated his jaw. Never in his wildest dreams had he imagined that if they were together, they would be so brazen as to be seen in public. And what's more, they were acting as if they had been together years, easy and comfortable in each other's company. *And she was holding his hand!* He stole a tentative look at Jo, who now knew what he did, and he was suddenly afraid at what that information would do to her. He could see her trying to act natural but she was a mess of nervous, annoyed gestures; the fingers on the hand not holding her glass were working at each other, her eyes were blinking and it was costing her a considerable effort to keep them away from her ex. Her smile was stiff. She looped her arm possessively through Matthew's and forced him back into the conversation, but his brain was scrambled egg and he wasn't contributing much other than the strained village idiot grin of the disengaged.

'You did good,' said Adam, kneading at the back of his neck. It felt as if someone had been using his muscles to do macramé.

'I feel shaky as hell,' said Stevie.

'We're okay. The worst is over and the good news is, I think it's working.'

'Oh, that was a beauty. Nicely understated,' said Catherine, butting in. 'Well, they definitely know now you're a couple, and they both looked far from happy about it.'

'Really?' Adam and Stevie said in unison.

'Everyone all right?' said Pam, making her usual big appearance. 'Stevie, I have to ask, when did you get to be so chuffing gorgeous?'

Pam might as well have put her on a rotating pedestal with neon arrows pointing to her. Stevie blushed and fobbed the compliment off, as the others teased her. Adam found himself looking at her through man glasses and realized with a shock how lovely his companion appeared to everyone. Of course, he had given her a cursory once-over when he first saw her, but now he studied the detail of her – the tousled golden hair, the sky-blue eyes, the curves you could time eggs by. He wrenched his eyes quickly away, not wanting to look at her like that. That was not in his plan at all.

Pam was laughing like a drain. She took Stevie's drink from her and gave it to Adam.

'I'm taking this one away for a bit. I'll bring her back safe and sound in a moment, promise,' she said, threading her arm through Stevie's and proceeding to lead her off. 'Come here, you – I want to show you something.' They walked off towards the conservatory because there was no saying 'no' to Pam. It was a family trait – you just didn't argue with a née Manning girl.

'What are you showing me then?' asked Stevie.

'Oh, this and that,' said Pam enigmatically. 'Come and look at my new conservatory.' She picked off two glasses of champagne from a tray in the kitchen and led Stevie off to the big sunshiny room. Pam didn't do 'little'. Except Stevie. Stevie was a small person she was very glad to know.

'So how's married life?' asked Stevie, after she had admired the huge comfy and colourful bouncy sofa in the room. If Pam had been an object of furniture, she would have been that sofa.

'Fuck married life. Tell me about you and Adam MacLean. How long has that been going on?'

'Oh . . . er . . . not long,' bluffed Stevie.

She would have to be careful in this interrogation. She didn't want to lie to Pam, but neither did she want to blow it by spilling the beans that they were actually only pretending to be together. Pam's mouth was as big as an aircraft hangar.

'I have to say you could have knocked me down with a feather when I heard about you and Matthew, Steve.'

'Me too,' said Stevie.

'You didn't know it was coming?'

'No, not a clue,' said Stevie.

'He'll be sorry,' said Pam, shaking her head. 'When he comes to his senses.'

'I doubt it,' said Stevie. 'Jo's pretty spectacular.'

'She'll be even sorrier. I never took to her, you know. Neither did Will. Too far up her own arse,' Pam said with a derisory sniff.

'No?' Okay, Stevie got a thrill that Pam and Will hadn't liked Jo, especially because Pam was not the type to say something just to make her feel better.

'Something cold about her, I always thought. Eyes like a dead haddock. Cut her up like a stick of rock and the word ME would be written all the way through. Not what I would have thought Matthew would go for at all, the stupid man. I do so like Matthew.' Pam belched and tutted, 'God, I'm such a class act! That's posh drinks for you.'

'Pardon you,' said Stevie, grinning.

'I don't know Adam as well as I know Matthew, but he strikes me as a really nice guy and I hope it works out for you both. Will thinks he is a great bloke and you look really good together. Bloody odd but good.' She clinked her glass against Stevie's. 'Shall I save you my wedding dress?' She roared with laughter.

'Let him get divorced first,' said Stevie.

'What you on about, girl? He's a free agent – he *is* divorced.'

'Divorced from Jo? What, already?' Stevie was confused.

'No, you barmpot. Divorced from his first wife. He's not married to Jo. MacLean is her maiden name. One of those coincidences that probably started the conversational ball rolling between them,' Pam huffed.

'I never asked, I just presumed . . .' said Stevie.

'No, he was married a few years ago to someone else and she pissed off with her boss. Gold digger, by all accounts, but very good-looking. She took Adam for every penny she could, so Will said. Wouldn't surprise me if Jo MacLean was the same, so thank God they weren't married because I bet she would certainly try to rip the financial arse out of him. Apparently she wanted this big, fancy wedding thing but Adam, understandably, was a bit scared.'

'Scared? Adam MacLean!' scoffed Stevie, then added a quick re-balancing, 'Er . . . I mean, my Adam scared?'

'Awww, "*my Adam*", that's so sweet,' said Pam, mocking her in a friendly, amused way. 'Yes, scared. I suspect he wanted to make sure he had got it right this time, after losing everything he had to that Diane, I think her name was. He didn't want to rush it. Personally, I think deep down he knew Jo wasn't right for him and that's why he was stalling.' She suddenly grabbed Stevie and hugged her like a little doll. 'Awww "My Adam"! I'm keeping you from him. Come on, you get back to the wee laddie before he gets withdrawal symptoms.'

Pam pushed her through the door. 'Enjoy yourself, Stevie. You deserve a bit of loving, and Adam MacLean looks like he needs a good woman for once,' and with that Pam weaved off to interfere in someone else's love-life, always with the very best of intentions.

Cutting across the grass, Stevie turned her face bravely towards her nemesis. Jo was staring at her with narrowed arrogant eyes that wanted to slice her up into little pieces. Then, as Stevie shifted her eyes to Matthew, he suddenly broke from Jo's side as if he was coming over, only to be stopped by Jo's hand on his arm. Then she said something incredibly intense to him but tried to disguise it as normal conversation. Matthew looked withered. Jo was actually telling him off. This bizarre, crazy plan of Adam MacLean's to get under their skin *was* working.

'Welcome back,' said Catherine. 'Did Pam apply thumb-screws?'

'No, she tried to bribe info out of me with champagne. Her methods are more subtle since she got married.'

'We're going off for something to eat,' said Catherine. 'Coming?'

It wasn't a question but a command. Catherine was a née Manning girl too.

'She's quite a girl, Pam, isn't she?' said Adam as they started walking towards a huge grill where a group of blokes were cremating meat.

'Do you know her well?'

'No, not well. We've just met a few times at parties. I

know Will better. He was my deputy at Gym Village before I deserted to the enemy to manage Well Life.'

'Pam seemed to be under the impression that you and Jo weren't married.'

'No,' said Adam, suddenly stiffening. 'Not yet.' He looked over at Jo, whose eyes flickered over to his and then locked with them, defiantly trying to outstare him. For a moment there was just the two of them. The rest of the crowd melted away. She was so beautiful, so tall and slim and lovely, and cruelly beautiful.

There was always a part of his mammy Adam had never had. Isa MacLean was tall, slim, lovely – and so, so cold. She worshipped Andy MacLean, who abused her, but never quite managed to love as much the son who adored her. And the more he loved, her hoping she would, the more apparent it became that she would never really let him into her heart. Maybe that's why he was drawn to beautiful women who were destined to hurt him – women like Diane and Jo, who held back enough of themselves to drive him half-mad trying to reach them, making him exhausted by his efforts to gain their love. He failed every time.

The four of them got some hot-dogs and then Adam went back for a steak, asking Stevie if she wanted anything too, like a proper attentive date would.

'No, thanks. I'm just nipping off to the loo,' said Stevie, disappearing back to the house. As Adam got a steak, he spotted Danny coming off the Bouncy Castle and making his way over to the familiar face he had just spotted. Adam kept his eye on the little boy as he tugged at Matthew's trousers, then Matthew ruffled up his hair and bent to hug him. Then Danny crossed to Jo and hugged her with gusto as if he knew her too, but Jo subtly removed him and then, with smiling irritation, pushed him away, back into the crowd. Adam's heart was suffused with sudden anger and pain. Watching Jo made him think of himself and his mammy, and he was glad Stevie hadn't been witness to it. She wouldn't have let anyone push her boy away.

Adam bounced towards the little boy who was now looking lost.

'Danny,' he boomed, which seemed to annoy Jo from the way she threw her drink down her throat.

'Well Life Man!' screamed Danny with undisguised joy.

'Shhh! Whit did I tell you? It's Adam!'

'Sorry,' said Danny, clamping his hands over his mouth. Then he threw his arms around Adam's legs, as far as they would go anyway.

'Your mammy's just away to the washroom,' Adam said, bending right down until they were at eye-level. 'Were you looking for her?'

'No, I just wanted some pop.'

'Come on, I'll get you some.' Danny slipped his hand inside the big man's paw and they trotted off to the drinks table.

'So, you having a good time, wee man?' said Adam, twisting off the top of a bottle of cherryade and sticking a straw in it.

'I've had a big cheeseburger,' whispered Danny. 'Uncle Will cooked us it. He did us onions as well.'

'Here, want some of my steak? It'll give you special protein powers.'

'Ye-ah!' said Danny and Adam laughed as the small boy took a huge greedy bite.

'Good, is it, son?'

'Cool. Mr Well Life, what do you think is morer important to a Superhero,' said Danny, when he had finished chewing his present mouthful. 'A cape, a good heart or tights?'

Adam threw back his head and laughed.

'I think tights are very important, and so is a cape, but I think a good heart is probably the answer,' he said finally.

'I think so too. Are you coming home with us?' said Danny, taking a long slug of pop.

'Oh, I don't know about that, fella,' said Adam, filling a pint glass with lemonade for himself.

'We used to live with Matthew but we don't any more,' said Danny, as if divulging a great secret. 'We've only got two bedrooms now, but if you wanted, you could have my room. It would be so cool. Anyway, see you,' and off he trotted, back to the other kids who were settling on the grass in front of the magician.

Something started buzzing around in Adam's head, like a mosquito in the dark. He couldn't quite locate it to swat it and look at it fully. It was irritating him. Maybe if he waited, it could come back to him . . .

Stevie had taken a slow walk back to Adam. She had watched him find Danny in the crowd and take him off for a drink. It was instinctive, not the action of a man out to use a little boy to impress an ex or keep her onside. He had thrown back his head and laughed at something Danny had said and there had been real warmth there. She found herself smiling at him in thanks for being nice to her son. Coupled with the conversation she had just had with Pam, it occurred to her then that maybe she didn't know the real Adam MacLean at all.

Pam bumped into Adam by the cheesecake. She was swaying quite a bit now.

'Having a good time, Scotty?' she asked.

'I certainly am,' he said. 'Fabulous cheesecake – is it homemade?'

'Of course, but not by me, by the baker on Lamb Sreet,' and she let loose a laugh that could decimate a building. 'So how are you and Stevie getting on?'

'Great,' said Adam.

'Good girl, is Stevie.'

'Aye,' he said.

'Be nice to think she was seeing someone who didn't break her heart for a change. That bastard Mick . . .' Pam shook her head in unmitigated disgust. 'I don't know how she held it all together really. Brilliant stuff she does. Have you read any yet? Then again, you're a bloke so probably not. But for Matthew to go and do the same as Mick – to Stevie, of all people! She wouldn't hurt a fly, Stevie. Never known a girl have as much bad luck with blokes!'

Adam pretended he knew what she was talking about and nodded.

'He didn't give her a penny – Mick, you know. Then he left her with all that shit to sort out. Stevie's an absolute diamond, though, and I love her to bits. You look after her,

Adam MacLean, or you'll have us to answer to.' She thumbed towards the crowd in the general direction of Matthew. 'His loss, your gain, that's what I say. I really like Matt, but he is being such a knobhead at the moment. In fact, I'm going to speak to him, right now. I'm going to tell him—'

'Oh no, you're not!' said Will, appearing from the side and leading his wife masterfully off inside the house for some soft drinks and a cheese sarnie. Despite appearances, Will could handle Pam quite efficiently when he needed to.

And as Adam's brain processed this new, albeit confusing, information, it occurred to him that maybe he didn't know the real Stevie Honeywell at all.

For the remainder of the party the pretend lovebirds managed to give the perfect semblance of a truly together couple. They spent a fair bit of time apart with their separate groups of friends, but the clues were there in the times they sought each other out – in the small touches, the considerations which spoke far more than grandiose displays of snoggy-type affection. Then all too soon it was time for them to go home. Adam had been talking to Will and the gym guys, once again battling the merits of Well Life versus Gym Village, when he looked over and caught Matthew staring over at Stevie, who was chattering happily away to Catherine and a well-sobered-up Pam. It wasn't the look of someone who had lost all his feelings for her, and Adam didn't know why, but it annoyed him. He made his way over to Stevie, put his arm possessively around her

and squeezed her, then bent his head to her to say that they
were being observed. She felt for his hand and decided to
put on a good show in that case. Stevie had never been one
for holding hands, so she knew that if Matthew was watching this, it would strike a loud chord. Being swallowed up
by Adam's big meaty mitt, though, wasn't anything like the
rare slim-fingered Matthew-hand experience. Adam was
stroking her knuckles with his thumb absently whilst they
were talking to Catherine. It felt as intimate as a kiss, almost
more so, and for that reason, she felt herself pulling away,
just before Danny came along, yawning. She gave
Catherine and Eddie and her host and hostess a goodbye
hug, then they wended their way back to Adam's car.

Danny was asleep as soon as he was buckled into the
back seat and Stevie wasn't far behind him. She hadn't
drunk much alcohol; the first glass of champagne had gone
straight to her head and she didn't trust her actions if her
feelings were booze-distorted, so she'd mostly drunk tonic
water. Still, she felt dizzy and exhilarated. She'd had such a
lovely time and it had been more successful on the
Matthew/Jo front than she could ever have thought possible. Jo had spent most of the evening trying not to look
cross and Matthew just looked weary. His disgruntled face
and Jo's obviously snipey asides had added very much to the
enjoyment of her evening, and if that made her a bitch,
then so be it. She had caught Matthew staring over at them
quite a few times, and once she thought he had been about
to come over, until Jo had stopped him. What would he
have said, she wondered.

And Adam had been . . . well, lovely actually. Even

though he was faking the affection, it had been nice to imagine what it would be like to be wanted and touched and fussed over by someone who had her interests at heart. Matthew had liked to be touched and fussed over, but he rarely gave back the affection he expected. Every day, Stevie was becoming more aware of how much she had given out and how little she had received in return. It made her feel even more lonely and unwanted and stupid than she did already.

Adam drove in silence. The buzzing little mosquito had landed and he had swatted it in his head and examined it. It had been a very interesting little bug.

He carried Danny into the house for her, and deposited him gently on his bed. Stevie took off her son's shoes and threw his cover over him. Then she asked Adam if he wanted a coffee and he said that he wouldn't mind. She put a half-packet of ground beans through the percolator, then they went into the lounge and flumped down. Stevie reclined on the sofa and kicked off her sandals. Surprisingly, she had only been aware of her feet hurting since she had walked in through the door. She wiggled her toes and relaxed.

'What sort of coffee is this then?' asked Adam, taking a great big dreamy sniff.

'Chocolate ice-cream. It's nice iced, with a big blob of cream on the top.'

'Sounds lovely.'

'It is.'

They drank in a silence that was surprisingly compan-ionable. For a while, she almost forgot she didn't like him. However, that wasn't to last.

'You seem to like these books,' he said, picking up a Beatrice Pollen *Midnight Moon* from a stack at the side of his chair. 'I wouldn't have thought someone like you might be into crappy romances like these.'

Had Stevie been a puffer fish, she would have swollen up to twenty times her normal size then and grown spikes.

'Yes, but you don't know me at all to judge me, do you?'

Adam couldn't believe she had snapped at him. He had actually meant what he said as a compliment!

'No,' he said, thinking back to his conversation with Pam, 'you're right, I don't. But I think I might get to know you quite a bit better soon.'

'Oh, do you really think so?' drawled Stevie, as all thoughts of goodwill towards him disappeared in a puff of smoke. Cocky git! The party was over, so was the pretence, and now he was back to being the local Loss Ness Monster representative.

'Yes, I think we need to capitalize on the impact we've made tonight.' He calmly sipped from his cup in stark contrast to Stevie, whose eyebrows appeared to be doing a tango.

'Meaning?'

'Meaning, it's working so we have to give it our all.'

'So, Mr MacLean, how exactly do you propose to do that?'

'Easy, *Miss Honeywell*. Tomorrow I'm moving in with you.'

Chapter 39

'Well, that was another great evening!' Jo grumbled, throwing her clutch purse down on the sofa and ripping off her shoes. 'I can't believe Adam would even *think* about going out with *her*. Obviously, he's doing it out of spite. What does he think he's bloody trying to prove? I mean, as if I'd be jealous of a fucking ugly fucking dwarf!'

'You think he's trying to actually do that? Make you jealous?' said Matthew, wincing at her foul expletives. Not even Jo with her posh accent could make them sound acceptable to him.

'What else? He can't actually like her, can he? He's obviously using her and the stupid bitch can't see it.'

'Don't be cruel,' said Matthew with a weary huff. 'Stevie hasn't done anything wrong. She's a good person.'

'She can't be that great if you left her at a minute's notice,' sneered Jo waspishly.

'I didn't leave her because she was horrible,' said Matthew, but quietly because Jo was being quite scary and her comment hit his conscience in the bull's eye.

'You're standing up for her?' Jo looked at him with an expression so twisted it made her sweet face look quite ugly.

Matthew decided not to say that he was worried to death about Stevie and would have to step in soon to stop her from making the biggest mistake of her life. He knew it would cause this row to get even bigger and he was too tired, physically and emotionally, for that tonight. His head felt heavy and mixed-up and fit to burst. It was as if Jo was two different people sometimes and he was seeing less of the sweet, lovely one every day.

'All I'm saying is that she didn't deserve what she got from us and does anyone deserve to be a punchbag for *him*?'

'Oh, don't be stupid! Adam wouldn't—' Jo snapped off what she was going to say and flew into a different fury instead. 'How dare he? With her! How long has it been going on, that's what I'd like to know.'

'Does it matter?'

'Yes, of course it matters! No one is unfaithful to me. No one!'

She thought once again of how easily Stevie had let Matthew go. And she thought of how undramatic the scene had been when she had told Adam she was leaving. He had listened without saying a word and made no attempt to follow her when she went upstairs to pack her cases. He had even carried them downstairs for her and put them in the car. She saw that sadness was heavy in his eyes, but he still had done nothing to stop her going. In the car, she had pressed her nails into her arm in frustration and anger, hardly feeling the pain. *How dare he let her go so easily?* She had despised him as weak at the time but now she was sure this was all part of some greater plan, and it excited her. No one had ever let Jo go without a fight.

'Jo, please explain to me why exactly would you be cross that Stevie and Adam have got together? How can you be bothered, after all he put you through?'

Jo's mouth opened and then shut tight again. Then she started up the stairs, saying, 'I'm going to bed, Matthew. Come if you want.'

As he heard the bedroom door open, Matthew knew that her back would be waiting for him in bed and tonight, for the first time, he really didn't care.

In his cold, echoey, four-bedroomed house that night, Adam started to pack a suitcase. It was young Danny who had reminded him that there were only two bedrooms in that house – something that Finch would know. If he moved in, Finch would presume the obvious – Danny in one bed, he and Stevie in the other. Their plan was working better than he could ever have expected it to. He had seen how many times Matthew's eyes had drifted over to Stevie at the barbecue. As for Jo, she was hurting; Adam was definitely getting to her. He could tell that by the way she sneered at him through the happy, party crowd, as if she was enjoying the thought that he might be suffering. Like a wasp, Jo stung to kill when she was threatened. Then he had witnessed how she'd treated the boy. It had altered everything, seeing Danny try to cuddle her and Jo shove him off as if he was something abhorrent. Something about the events of that night had shifted all the pieces around in his heart.

Then he thought of how slowly Stevie's head had turned towards him when he had made the suggestion that he move in with her to Humbleby. He didn't think it was possible for anyone's eyes to open that wide without popping out and detaching from their optical nerves. It was all he could do not to burst out laughing, but he feared she would have whacked him with the nearest *Midnight Moon* rubbish.

'One last big push and I swear to you that if they haven't broken up in seven days, I'll move out again. But I promise you they will have.'

'Of course you're joking!' said Stevie breathlessly.

'Naw,' said Adam. 'I've never been more serious in my whole life.'

It was obviously against her better judgment but she had soundlessly and slowly nodded her assent and continued drinking her coffee. Who would have thought they would ever have had to resort to these measures?

Chapter 40

At 15 Blossom Lane, the next day was a very strained affair. Matthew made Jo an early breakfast in bed as a peace-offering, although he wasn't quite sure what he was apologizing for. He went out for a huge stack of Sunday newspapers and settled himself on the dining-room table as Jo went back to sleep. Was it his imagination or were there more debt articles than ever in the supplements? *How to manage your money? Should I get a consolidating loan? How to stop spending . . .*

His bowels started to cramp up as he read. He really could not afford, in all senses of the word, to delay the money talk with Jo any longer, so he wished she would hurry and wake up. She was still asleep when he called up at lunchtime, so he slunk back downstairs and reached for another newspaper with only a bacon sandwich and a bag of Cheesy Wotsits for company.

He heard signs of her rising just after four and waited patiently, chewing his nails, whilst sounds of the fully-turned-on bath taps filtered downstairs. He was almost physically deformed with anxiety by the time she came

downstairs, an hour later. His heart sank as he saw she was
dressed to go out.

'Are we going out for something to eat?' were her first
words to him.

'Now – say it now!' urged a voice in Matthew's head.

'Er . . . Jo.' He took her hands and pulled her softly
down on the sofa. 'I can't. I'm a bit broke at the moment.
I'm sorry.' *There, that was easy enough!*

'Broke?' She looked confused. 'What do you mean,
"broke"?'

Matthew took the sort of breath one did before a
bungee jump off the Grand Canyon.

'The thing is, for a while . . . it would help if you could
give me something towards the household bills – you
know, the mortgage and . . . stuff.'

She stared at him as if he had just grown a pair of horns.
Then she stood abruptly up. 'You are fucking joking, I
take it. Now, like I say, are we going out or do I pack a bag
and leave now?'

'We'll go out,' he said.

'I'll get my shoes,' she said.

Oh bollocks.

As Matthew was dreaming that night of a big Visa card
with Colin Seed's cardigan on chasing him around work,
Adam's car was pulling quietly up outside Humbleby
Cottage. Danny was asleep in the big bed that his mum
would share with him for the next seven nights. Stevie
would have preferred to stay in the back room, but the
front bedroom had a lock on the door.

'Hi,' she greeted Adam nervously.

'Hi,' said Adam, bringing in a suitcase and a sports bag, which he dumped by the door.

'I've put you in my room,' said Stevie a little awkwardly. He raised his dark red eyebrows and she bristled in response. 'I will, of course, be sharing with Danny. I've told him you're having some decorators in and are just lodging here for a while.'

'Fine,' said Adam. 'I'll no' confuse the boy.'

'Good,' said Stevie.

'I'd have taken the sofa. You didn't have to move out for me.'

'I fell asleep on the sofa once after working late. Trust me, it's not at all comfortable even for someone my size, so . . .'

'You never said what it is that you actually dae for work?'

'Anyway, if you take your case up I'll put some coffee on,' said Stevie, ignoring him.

'I'll take that as an "I'm no' telling you, so bugger aff".'

'That's it in a nutshell, Mr MacLean. You know where your room is, of course.'

He laughed. 'Yes, ma'am,' he said, and saluted and obeyed.

The room smelled of something sweet like wild strawberries swirled in with the perfume she wore. He had noticed it on her at the barbecue – light and floral and violety – so unlike the heady, exotic, spicy scents that Jo preferred. Stevie had put fresh linen on the bed; lovely cool cotton sheets. She had left big white fluffy towels folded neatly on top of the duvet and she had cleared some wardrobe and drawer space for him too. This was not a woman who lounged about all day watching TV through a layer of dust, he thought, and wondered again what it was exactly that she did do all day then. He could have asked Will but he didn't want to cheat. He wanted to crack her secret himself. It amused him to puzzle on it.

He came down to the beautiful smell of coffee hissing and spitting in angry protest through the percolator.

'What sort is that one?' he asked, 'It smells divine.'

'Crème caramel,' she said. 'Have you eaten?'

'Don't worry yoursel'.'

'We had a big chicken for lunch. There's plenty left, if you want a sandwich.'

'Thanks, I might just do tha—'

'I thought you might,' she said, putting down a substantial plate of sandwiches in front of him, garnished with crisps and salady bits. 'You don't look like the sort of bloke who says no to food.'

'Not unless you baked the bread yourself,' he said.

'No, you're safe. It's from Morrison's.'

And then they watched a late-night murder mystery and munched chicken sandwiches and chocolate digestives until bedtime, like an old married couple who warred a lot.

Chapter 41

The first thing Matthew noticed as he opened the curtains the next morning was Adam MacLean's car outside Stevie's cottage, and it didn't take an idiot to work out that he had been there all night. He presumed that's why Jo was extra-agitated and stomping and crashing about and in a generally foul mood. They both knew there were only two bedrooms to that house. Neither of them said a word about it but it was obviously on their minds, and they were both cross that it was on the other's mind, none of which helped to lift the mood of a day that had already been spoilt by 7.30 a.m.

They journeyed to work in the same uncomfortable silence that had stood like a concrete block between them the previous evening during dinner.

'Look, please, can't we be friends?' Matthew said, pulling into the work's car park. 'I hate this atmosphere between us. I'm sorry about mentioning the money and I don't care what's going on across the road. Let them get on with their lives and let us get a sandwich at twelve and go and sit in the park and talk.'

'I'm going shopping,' said Jo, petulantly through a very dry pout.

'I'll come with you,' he said, smiling at her. 'Would you like that?'

'No, Matthew, I wouldn't like that,' said Jo flatly. 'Today I want some space. I've got things to do.'

'I'll walk five paces behind you,' he tried to joke but she rounded on him fiercely.

'For Christ's sake, stop stifling me!' And she leapt out of the car and went into the building alone. He sat in shock because she had always led him to believe that she liked to be made a heavy fuss of. Rather like a spoilt, demanding Persian cat.

Matt waited for Jo in the foyer at the time when her lunch-hour was due to end, hoping to catch her for a quick kiss-in-passing at least. He wished so much that he could have turned the clock back and not mentioned the money. He hoped it was that which was making her hostile towards him and not the Adam and Stevie thing, which had taken up a big unwelcome block of his own headspace, too, however much he was trying to deny it. He had an appointment with his bank account manager fixed up for the next afternoon, and had he waited for the outcome of it, he might never have had to tell her that he had a few financial problems. Then all he would have had to do was tell her one final lie – that his investments weren't as great as he had been led to believe. How he was going to break the news that they were approximately half a million pounds light was a bit of a teaser though. He had got so carried away exaggerating, trying to impress her. *Oh God, what a mess!*

There was something different about her as she came in from town, then he realized it was that she didn't have any shopping bags.

'Why are you waiting for me?' she said, with the big scared eyes of a spooked deer. She didn't break her stride, forcing him to trot along at the side of her.

'I thought we might snatch five minutes.'

'Not today, Matthew. I don't feel like I want your company today.'

'Please, darling.' He grabbed her arm to stop her. She ripped it away with disproportionate force and ran up the escalator. It was all very odd. She looked like she did when she had first started speaking to him, when she had been scared of Adam. Matt couldn't get a handle on it at all.

However, coming through the revolving door into the building immediately behind her, Colin Seed knew he could.

Chapter 42

It was Catherine's youngest daughter Violet's birthday that same day.

'Vio can't wait to see her new pyjamas!' said Danny that morning, skipping his way to school.

'Oh Danny, you didn't tell her and spoil the surprise, did you?' said Stevie.

'No, I didn't,' said Danny indignantly. 'I just said that it's something she can wear in bed.'

'Great,' said Stevie, shaking her head.

The Flanagan matriarch picked Danny up from school to whisk him away for a party at Burger King, allowing Stevie time to get stuck into *Highland Fling*. She had sent Crystal the synopsis and was waiting for a call to see if she liked it. Knowing Crystal as well as she did, she rather thought she might. It was turning out to be the best *Midnight Moon* she had ever written. There was a knock on her door just after six and she opened it to find Adam on the doorstep.

'I didnae like coming straight in.'

'Well, it's going to look pretty weird if you start knocking, considering you're supposed to be living here.'

'Aye, I suppose so,' said Adam and he bent, placing his cheek near to hers to simulate a kiss, just in case they were being watched. She noticed that he smelt of work and clean sweat and woody aftershave. 'Where's the wee 'un?' he asked as Stevie closed the door.

'He'll be scoffing a big burger now. It's Catherine's daughter's birthday so he's at her party.'

'Ah, I see. Have you eaten?'

'Er, no, I've only just stopped working.'

'Come on, what is it that ye dae?'

'I'll put the kettle on,' she said.

He dropped his bag near the hall table where Stevie had put down her post – a postcard from an old schoolfriend and her unopened wage slip from *Midnight Moon*. The motif on a big brown envelope caught his eye. A large moon with a clock face sat in it.

'You get post from *Midnight Moon*?' he said with an amused twist to his lip. 'What is this then?' He pretended to open it.

'Give me that, please!' said Stevie, quickly abandoning the kettle, but Adam put it well out of her reach, high above his head. Well, as high as the beams would allow.

'I'm serious, Adam, let me have it.' Stevie jumped up. She didn't want him to know what she did. He had made her feel sad enough, in the pathetic sense of the word, about her job. She wanted that envelope back now, but it was impossible. Adam danced around and Stevie leapt up like a Red Indian around a totem pole. It caused a very odd picture in the window, which Matthew, staring obsessively through *his* window, saw.

Despite his money troubles, despite his hiccup with Jo, despite worrying why he seemed to see Colin Seed hovering around whenever he looked up these days, Matthew still had a huge chunk of worry space saved up for Stevie. He knew MacLean was using her, probably to tempt Jo back by driving her crazy with jealousy. He knew one day soon the charm (whatever that could be) would stop and the violence would begin. Surely no woman, not even Jo, would want to see Stevie as scared and beaten as she had been. Whilst this thought was on his mind, he saw Adam MacLean and Stevie involved in some kind of tussle by the window, although hardly a fair one with her at Bonsai and him at Californian Redwood height.

Jo had just about been ready to forgive him and had come up for a snuggle when Matthew almost threw her out of the way and thrust open the outside door.

'Hey, look,' said Adam, dropping his arm, 'your man's on his way over here and he means business. Start laughin'. NOO!'

'Laughing? What do you mean, "laughing"?'

'As if we're having a good time.'

'I'm not that good an actress!'

'C'moan, nooo!'

Stevie shrugged, but complied anyway. 'Okay.' She managed a pathetically lame laugh.

'Och, try and dae better than that.'

'I can't just laugh like that.'

'Stevieareyouatiglsh?'

'Am I a what?' said Stevie.

'Quick!' said Adam.

'Quick wha . . . arrrgghh!' In a flash Stevie suddenly found herself being slammed onto the floor. Then for some bizarre reason Adam ripped his shirt open like the Hulk and sat astride her.

'What the hell . . .!'

'Sorry!' he said in advance as his hands made claws and descended.

Matthew didn't bother to knock before trying to open the cottage door, but it was locked and he banged hard on it. Stevie was screaming, which made him bang more. Although the more he listened, the less sure he was that those screams were ones of pain. She was laughing maniacally and actually sounded more like she was being tickled than assaulted. In between various requests for him to stop whatever he was doing, she was shrieking out Adam's name and that, for a reason he was not prepared to admit to himself, made him even angrier.

'Stevie, let me in!' He threw his shoulder into the door, but it was massive and oak and he couldn't have broken it down if he was Rambo with a cannon.

Suddenly, Stevie arrived at the door looking very tousled. She was so red-faced, he could have been forgiven for thinking that she had just been mainlining beetroot. Her hair was mussed up, she was straightening her clothes and he got the distinct impression that she had just been rolling around on the floor. There in the background, Adam MacLean appeared to be getting up from the same floor with his shirt ripped open and looking too fucking pleased with himself for Matthew's liking. Plus he was none-too-subtly adjusting his trousers.

'I heard you screaming, Stevie, are you okay?'

'I'm . . . er . . . fine,' Stevie said breathlessly.

'MacLean wasn't hurting you then?'

'Er . . . no, quite the opposite actually.'

Too much detail, thought Matthew with an inner wince. 'Oh, right – sorry to have bothered you,' he said stiffly. He turned to go, then, when he was at a safe distance, spun around with his finger projecting towards Adam like Harry Potter's wand.

'You hurt her, MacLean, and I'll . . . I'll kill you!' he spat. 'And leave her money alone as well!'

Adam didn't react, other than with a surprised Roger-Moore lift of his eyebrows. He stood there trying not to look amused, watching as Matthew stabbed at him a few more times before retreating quickly across the road whilst his luck was still in. Finch was being awfully protective towards this violent firebrand he supposedly couldn't wait to get away from. *Hmmm*.

Stevie was astounded. She hadn't seen Matthew act that passionately since – well, ever. Whatever she might think of MacLean, he certainly knew his *basic psychology* very well. That didn't stop her taking her hatred of him to new heights, though. *How dare he do that to her! Who did he think he was?*

'Wow,' said Adam when Stevie had shut the door. 'There's a turn up. Sorry, by the way. I saw that trick once on a John Wayne film. It worked then as well.'

'You . . .' struggled Stevie, not able to find a word insulting enough.

'Tell me why *Midnight Moon* are writing to you.'

'Go to hell,' said Stevie, snatching her letter and charging into the study where she sat and wondered if her heart would ever stop thumping.

Sheepishly, Matthew trudged back across the lane, thinking, I must have caught them at it! How could Stevie sleep with someone who beat up women? Was she so desperate to try to make him jealous that she would compromise her own safety and that of her child? If so, was it working? He honestly didn't know which leading emotion had sent him flying across the road to her defence.

Jo was waiting for him with a slow handclap.

'How gallant,' she said. 'Shame you didn't do that for me when I needed rescuing from him.'

'She didn't need rescuing,' said Matthew bitterly. 'I thought she was screaming because he was beating her up when actually they were about to have sex.'

'Sex?' said Jo.

'You know, that thing we used to have.'

'Fuck you!' said Jo, and starting raining slaps on him.

'Jo, what's happening to us?' said Matthew, wincing at her language, catching her hands and holding them still. He needed to focus on his problems with Jo, but he was having real difficulty getting the image of Stevie and MacLean having sex out of his mind. They must have been doing it on the kitchen floor. She'd never wanted sex like that when she'd been with him. Nor had he ever heard her make those sorts of noises before. He hadn't really associated her with that kind of passionate activity.

'How could he? With *her*?' said Jo.

'Why are you so bothered about *him*?' Matthew asked.

'Why are you so bothered about *her*?' Jo countered.

She pulled her hands away from him and started pacing up and down the room like a caged tiger. 'We need to move. I don't want to stay here watching Adam and that bitch living out their lives in front of us.'

'Why are you so horrible to her, Jo?'

But Jo wasn't listening; she was lost in a world filled only with herself.

'. . . I mean, is that why he said, "Okay, off you go then"? Is that why he didn't try to stop me? Not even a kiss or a hug goodbye. He even carried my bloody suitcases to the car for me. Why was that, eh? Because he was carrying on behind my back with that short, fat cow. If you think about it, it's the only answer. The bitch, the treacherous fucking bitch!'

'Did Adam let you go that easily?' said Matthew. 'I thought you said he—'

'How soon can you realize your investments, Matthew? Let's buy a house away from here, please. Leeds. One of the nice ones in the country that we saw in the *Yorkshire Post*.'

Now is the time. She needs to be told.

'About my investments,' said Matthew quietly, trying to moisten his nervous dry lips with his nervous dry tongue. 'Sit down, Jo, a minute, will you, please.'

'Okay, Matthew, I know what you said, you're broke at

the moment. We've had too many expensive meals out recently. But if we moved, we wouldn't feel the need to go out and get away from *that house* so much.'

He gently shushed her.

'Jo . . .'

Then he began.

Chapter 43

The next morning, Adam awoke to a flurry of whispering outside his new temporary bedroom door.

'Can I go in and see him?' said a small boy's not so quiet voice.

'No, you'll see him later.'

'Please, Mummy!'

'No. Now come on and don't make any noise or you'll wake him up.'

'But I *want* to wake him up, Mummy!'

'Come on, Danny, that's not very fair waking him up early, now is it? Superheroes really need their sleep, you should know that.'

'Aw, okay.'

Adam smiled. He reckoned they were counting down the days now until Dannyman, his fellow Superhero, would be back living across the road. A thought which made his smile fade surprisingly quickly.

Matthew awoke feeling totally exhausted and already started ticking off the hours until he could catch up on some sleep. He hadn't had as much sex as that in one night

since the Fresher's Ball at University, but that had been a far
less complicated experience.

Jo had taken yesterday's news that he was not in fact a
half-millionaire in the making pretty well, considering.
Although he hadn't quite told her the *whole* truth, but tem-
pered it slightly for the sake of his own pride. The story
given being that his investments had taken a substantial
crash and the only way he could recover the losses was to
leave them where they were for at least five years. He told
her he had a meeting with the bank to discuss the best plan
of action as far as his 'investments' were concerned, and was
sneaking out from work later on the pretext of going to the
dentist. Who knows, he might even find out that all was
not quite as bad as he had painted it. His story would give
him five years' breathing space to sort himself out. He
might even win the Lottery (properly this time) in that
space of time. At least it was finally out in the open to her
that he was broke *now* and that there couldn't possibly be a
big wedding in the near future, or more than one meal out
per week, if he was expected to foot all the bills. He
sneaked that in to see if she might consider actually helping
him out here by contributing. She hadn't offered.

Contrary to what he thought might happen, Jo had not
shouted or screamed or thrown anything heavy in the
direction of his cranium. She had just nodded her head
resignedly and forced out a smile and said, 'Well, that's that
then.'

Then, when they had gone to a bed in which he
expected not only the cold shoulder, but a cold back, cold
legs and cold everything else, she had surprised him by

instigating sex. Quite energetic, almost brutal sex actually. She had wanted him to bite her all over in her passionate throes. At one point, he felt like going to the window and checking to see if the moon was full, because she was like an animal – insatiable and wild. Matthew wasn't really the type to mix up pain with pleasure, though, and he fulfilled her requests quite half-heartedly. He had managed to give her a sucky love-bite on her chest, which he regretted the next morning because she wore her blouses quite open, and it was showing there as an ugly, painful-looking bruise. When he mentioned this, she had laughed and kissed him lightly on the nose and told him not to worry, and if he was lucky, they might try it again later on. Matthew didn't want to be that lucky. The whole experience hadn't sat well with him at all. He was all for passion – sex with Jo had been great and exciting in the beginning – but recently, he had found himself missing the gentle intimacy and more considerate, warm love-making which he had enjoyed with Stevie, before he got greedy. He had an uneasy feeling about this turn in their sex-life.

Adam had a day off, and as Stevie hadn't come back after dropping Danny off at school, he presumed she had gone into town. He had just grilled up half a farmyard full of bacon and stuck it in between two half-loaves of bread when the phone rang.

'Hellooo,' he said.

'Hello,' said a cut-glass voice on the other end. 'Is Bea there?'

'Sorry, hen, wrang number.'

'I can't have, she's on short dial. Is Stevie there? Stevie Honeywell?'

'Stevie's oot . . . *out* at the moment. Can I help you at all?'

'And you are?' purred the voice.

'Adam MacLean.'

'Ah, *you're* Damme MacQueen.'

Poor awd thing is deaf, thought Adam and spoke more slowly. 'No. A-dam Mac-Lean.'

'Yes, I heard you, darling.' The voice cut like glass too. 'I'm Crystal Rock, Stevie's publisher at *Midnight Moon*.'

Ah, thought Adam. *Interesting*.

'Sorry,' he bluffed. 'I apologize. Of course she has told me so much aboot you.'

Crystal gave a little tinkly laugh. She was half in love with Adam already.

'And I am getting to know all about *you*, Mr MacLean, or should I say Mr MacQueen.'

'All good things, I hope,' he sparkled back.

'Well, if the hero of *Highland Fling* is based on you, I think we can expect to have a bit of a bestseller on our hands.'

What was that name she'd asked for at first? B something or other? Adam reached over and picked up a nearby *Midnight Moon* by Betty Proctor and said craftily, 'Do you think it will be better than *Forever in Dreams*?'

'Oh, good God, I hope so. Betty Proctor isn't a patch on Beatrice Pollen. She only lasted two books. Bea, sorry, Stevie, has a very great following. Can you ask her to give me a ring and tell her, in the interim, that I *love* Damme

MacQueen, *I love* Evie Sweetwell and I want the rest of the chapters of *Highland Fling* finished ASAP. I'll simply die if he doesn't kiss her soon.'

'I will do that indeed.'

'And tell Miss Honeywell that she is a very dark horse and I expect a full update when she calls. She'll know what that means.' Crystal gave a very salacious giggle and finished with a 'ciao' that was as rich as a tiramisu. Adam put the phone down slowly. Well, well, well! No wonder she wouldn't tell him what she did after all the scorn he had, inadvertently, poured on her stories. So that's why there were Beatrice Pollen books all over the place. He worked his way along the shelf until he came to a book written by Ms Pollen, then he got himself a coffee from the nice full percolator that belonged to Beatrice, aka Stevie, settled down with book and breakfast in the sunroom, and began to read.

Matthew rang Jo to see if she wanted to go out for lunch but once again, she declined. Then their paths crossed when he was going out for 'his dentist's appointment'. She scurried away from him, which confused him, because he thought they were friends again now, what with all that sex and promise of more. She looked quite worried about something. Maybe it was delayed shock after what he had told her last night. He would buy her a present on the way back from the bank, he decided.

'Flaming heck!' said Robert Gilroy, Matthew's account handler. He looked about twelve and made Matthew feel the same age with comments like, 'What a blooming mess!'

No doubt he would send out for lashings of ginger beer in a minute.

Matthew nodded regretfully.

'Is this the full picture or is there more? People do tend to hide stuff and it's hardly wise if you want help.'

'That's it,' said Matthew. 'Honestly.'

Robert Gilroy tapped away on his laptop, and then twisted it round for Matthew to see.

'That's how much interest you're paying per month at the moment on all your debt.'

'Bloody hell and a half,' gulped Matthew.

'The thing is, we've given you one consolidated loan already and what did you pay off?'

'Er . . .' said Matthew, feeling that he was going to be asked to bend over in a moment and have a cane applied to his rear end.

'Enough said, I think,' said Robert Gilroy. 'For a person who earns this much money per annum, you should have a good amount of disposable income. I'm having trouble believing how you actually manage to eat.'

'I need help,' admitted Matthew, closer to tears than he had been in years. 'I'm a spendaholic.'

'Do you spend to make yourself feel better? Spend to win and influence people?'

'Yes.'

'Have you considered counselling in tandem with this?'

'I can't afford any,' said Matthew despairingly.

'It's free if you go through your doctor.'

'I may need to,' said Matthew. 'But so far as the actual money goes, can you help?'

'Well, yep,' said Robert Gilroy, and watched as Matthew's tense shoulders dropped with relief. 'You'll be tied to this debt for at least five years but it will give you breathing space to have some quality of life. The debt will be cheaper if you secure it against your home, obviously. That wouldn't be a problem – you have plenty of equity in the house, I see. How solid is your job?'

'Rock solid,' said Matthew with absolute surety. He was good at his job, knew what he was doing and the company was financially stable and growing healthily so there were no worries about securing the loan against his house.

'Right, now get out your plastic,' said Robert Gilroy.

'What – now?'

'Yep.'

'All of it?' Matthew started to cold sweat.

'On our own card account we can give you zero per cent interest for fourteen months. You will be able to transfer sixty per cent of your debt over to it, but when the card itself arrives, I suggest you cut it up, although I haven't said that. Okay, let's have the cards.'

Matthew felt like a child that had been asked to turn out his pockets and have all his sweets confiscated. For his own good though, before they rotted all his teeth.

Robert Gilroy handed him a pair of scissors.

'I've got a present to buy. For my girlfriend,' Matthew whimpered as the scissors scraped his emergency Goldfish.

'Give her a massage,' said Robert Gilroy. 'She'll only moan that you've made her fat if you buy chocolates.'

'I was thinking of a gold necklace.'

Robert Gilroy raised his eyebrows. 'She'll leave you anyway if you continue to wake up screaming and sweating in the middle of the night because you're so debt-ridden. If your heart doesn't give out first. Cut, please.'

Matthew sliced. So severe was the pain, he had to look down because he thought he had cut his finger off.

Chapter 44

When Stevie came home with four big bags of shopping, it was to find Adam MacLean in the sunroom, nearing the middle of a book. He had tidied around and vacuumed up. Something else she couldn't remember Matthew doing much of.

'Hello,' he greeted her.

'Hello,' she said a trifle awkwardly. She still hadn't quite got over the embarrassment of their little staged scrabble on the floor. She had kept having burning flashbacks since. Then she realized what he was reading: *Winter of Content* by herself in disguise as Beatrice Pollen. It was one of her more passionate pieces, in which an imaginary Grand Duke of Russia falls for a servant girl. She tried to ignore the fact that he was reading it. At least he didn't know she'd written it, for then, she suspected, her life wouldn't be worth living.

'I had a day off today. Didn't bring any books to read with me so I thought I'd have a go at this,' he explained.

'Oh right,' said Stevie. She refused to give him any ammunition to shoot her with and acted disinterested.

'I can see now why people buy them. There's actually quite a nice story go'n on here.'

'Yes,' she said, but not trusting him. There was a sting around the corner, she could almost smell it. He put it down, saving the page he was on with a comb from his pocket.

'Here, let me give you a hand,' he said.

'I'm all right.'

He ignored her and started to take things out of bags.

'No not that one!' she screamed as he put some tampons down on the table.

'Christ, woman, I do know women menstruate. It's of no great surprise to me!' He moved his attentions to a carrier that looked full of bulky veg to save her further blushes, though. 'By the way, you had a call from someone called Crystal. Wanted you to phone her back,' he dropped casually.

'What did she say?' asked Stevie. Trying to sound as casual in return.

'Nothing really. Funny, she kept getting my name wrong and calling me Damme MacQueen.'

Bugger!

'Oh . . . er . . . she's like that. Bit old and doddery. Thanks for taking the message.'

He grinned behind her back. 'I thought I might take you and Danny out for a pizza, if you like.'

'There's really no need.'

'I want to. I fancy a pizza and didn't want to eat out alone.'

'Thank you for the offer,' she said, not looking directly at him, 'but I don't want my son getting too excited about you being here and becoming attached to you. He's already far keener to see you than I ever expected. I don't want him getting hurt.'

'Okay, I understand,' said Adam and he did, but he could not quite manage to mask the note of disappointment in his voice. He liked the little boy. Danny reminded him of himself at that age, quiet and intense with a head full of stories about outsmarting life's baddies. Not that his mum had been anything like Stevie, and that, he considered, was a great shame.

As a courtesy to Stevie, Adam made himself scarce after saying a quick hello to Danny when he came in from school. He went off for a long run, making sure he wasn't back before Danny went to bed at half-past seven. He returned warm and sweaty to find Stevie outside deadheading a few of the roses that trailed up the front walls of the cottage, twisted up with the sweet perfumed honeysuckle.

'Hi,' he said, going into the cottage. 'Can I get you a cold drink?'

'I'm okay, thanks,' she said, and carried on snipping. He wondered if she was wishing each one was his head. He had gone a bit far the other day, chucking her on the floor and tickling her. Although Matty Boy's reaction had proved the end justified the means. He had seen the spark of jealousy flaring in his eyes, the anger that Adam was messing with something he still considered his. Matthew actually looked as if he might hit him at one point. In saying that, he was still living with Joanna, so they weren't quite home and dry yet.

He heard Stevie yelp and the secateurs drop to the ground and rushed out to see what the matter was.

'I think I've just been stung,' she said, trying to shake off her glove. Sure enough, in the crook of her arm was a still-throbbing sting.

'Here.' He pulled out her arm, then pincered out the sting, lowered his lips and started to suck.

'Ow!'

'Wheesht, woman, I'm trying to help you.'

He sucked and spat, sucked and spat.

'Christ, can't they get a fucking room,' said Jo, who had just gone to the sink for a glass of water and seen them in passing. She couldn't bear to stand and watch, but she couldn't move away from the window either. The sight of Adam with *her* was driving her mad. He was actually kissing her up the arm in full view of the street. They looked bloody ridiculous. She tore herself away and jumped onto Matthew's lap on the sofa, knocking away the newspaper he was engrossed in.

'Make love to me now,' she said. *Take away the picture I have in my head.*

'Er . . . okay,' said Matthew, as Jo unleashed her breasts, but in the end, it was only her he satisfied. There was a picture in his own head that just kept getting in the way.

Stevie watched Adam's lips work on the soft skin on the inside of her arm and suddenly felt a greater sting inside her than the now-dead creature had given her. She gently pulled her arm away.

'I think that might have done it,' she said stiffly, to overcompensate for the swirly, heady feelings that were taking over her brain. Obviously the effects of insect poison. 'Thank you.'

'Poor wee thing,' said Adam.

'Sorry, wasp,' said Stevie.

'It's a bee,' Adam corrected her. 'Wasps just keep on stinging, but alas, when a bee does it, it gives its all.'

Stevie felt ridiculously and inexplicably tearful.

'I didn't even feel him on my arm or I would have knocked him away.'

'*Her*,' said Adam. 'The drones don't have stings. They're only made to mate. It's the women that dae aw the damage.'

'Bee expert are you now?' said Stevie, the snap in her voice masking the wobble in her legs.

'My granda' used to keep bees. We lived on honey pieces – bread and honey – when we were wee. He knew everything there was to know aboot bees.'

'Is there that much to know?' said Stevie.

'You'd be surprised. I could wax lyrical, or should that be "beeswax" lyrical on the subject – they're marvellous wee creatures. For instance, did you know honeybees dance to tell aw the others where the nectar and pollen is? It's called a waggle dance. And that bumble bees come oot earliest in the year because they're basically wearing fur coats. And did you know that the bee is the only insect that produces food eaten by man? Unless you're partial to ant spittle, that is.'

Stevie smiled. *Bees with fur coats on, bees dancing*. Danny would have been fascinated by all that.

'I'll go in and get a plaster,' she said, suddenly uncomfortable in the silence that hung warm and heady between them, thick and sweet as the honey in their conversation. She retreated inside.

Adam looked across at Matthew's house. The light had just gone on upstairs and Jo was holding the curtains. She looked down at him, glared, and tugged them shut. *Yes, it was the women that did aw the damage.*

Chapter 45

Jo had a headache the next day and phoned in sick. Although she put it a little more dramatically than that, Matthew noticed as he eavesdropped over the upstairs balcony. She seemed to sob a little and say she couldn't get in and would explain later. Matthew volunteered to stay off and keep her company but she said she just wanted to sleep it off. For once, he didn't try to change her mind and went out to the car alone. The sight of Adam MacLean's fancy car across the lane greeted him once again, and though he wasn't a violent man, he wanted to rush across to it and smash into it with a sledgehammer.

Later at work, Adam was trying to catch up on some paperwork in his office but his head was all over the place. He thought of little Danny's face lighting up every time he saw him. He thought of his own heart warming up every time he saw little Danny. Then he thought of little Danny's mother and he didn't know what the hell happened to him when he saw her. She was quite the most infuriating woman he had ever met, the antithesis to everything that had ever attracted him in a woman. She was nothing like Jo or Diane, or the others before them, in their tall, slender, cold, dark-haired moulds.

There was a confident knock on his door, and he yelled out his customary, 'Come awn in.'

It wasn't a member of staff wanting help or keys or a word. It was a woman looking tall and slender, cold and beautiful in a powder-blue suit with long, swishy dark hair and eyes the colour of molasses.

'Hello, Adam,' said the smiling red lips of the last person in the world he expected to see.

Stevie pulled into the gym car park next to a red Golf. Jo had a red Golf, although it was hardly likely to be her car, thank goodness. At least in the gym Stevie was spared the sight of her destructive beauty, daring her to confront Jo with what she had done. Stevie had once purposefully confronted Linda and come off worst, and vowed she would never again sacrifice her dignity like that, but if she bumped accidentally into Jo MacLean she couldn't guarantee that her primal instincts wouldn't take over, leading her to launch herself at her rival and punch her treacherous, lying face in. She wanted to hurt her more for what she had done to her son's life than her own. It was just as well it wasn't Jo's car, after all.

She transferred the burst of energy that her sudden fury had triggered off in her by managing to do a fifteen-minute run on the treadmill, her best yet. She had grown to like coming to the gym. The physical exercise of running cleared her head – even if it was on a rubber belt indoors and not in the fresh air and the sunshine. Having such a sedentary job, she needed to get her heart pumping a bit more, although it had been on an emotional treadmill that had made it pump quite enough recently. At least it would all be over soon. One way or another.

Matthew had always been smiling in the old days when they had been together. Now every time Stevie saw him, he looked totally miserable. Crazy, really, when he had everything he set out to get. Jo didn't look much happier, either. She was always scowling, which was warped because Stevie had nothing she wanted. Jo had Matthew and his house and, with a snap of her fingers, she could have had Adam and his big house back. She couldn't imagine that Jo was jealous of her figure and short legs, so if she wasn't happy with the lot she had created for herself, then she could rot in hell as far as Stevie was concerned. Some people just wanted what they couldn't have, until they got it – only to find they didn't want it after all.

She had a quick shower and went back to her car to find that the red Golf had gone, and that someone had scraped their key viciously along her driver's side door.

When Matthew got home, Jo was still in bed. She looked really ill actually, pale and puffy-eyed, from a lot of crying.

'You need to take tomorrow off work too,' he said, soothing her brow.

'No, I need to go to work tomorrow more than any-thing,' she said, shrinking away from his hand. 'Please, Matthew, just leave me alone.'

And so he did.

*

'Guess what? Mum got stinged last night,' said Danny, flinging himself at Adam as he came in through the door.

'Yes, I know, I was there,' he said, attempting a smile, but he felt so tired, so drained.

'Come on, Danny, let Adam get in through the door,' said Stevie, pulling him gently away.

'Honey is bees' poo.'

'Danny!'

'That's what Curtis Ryder says. And milk is cows' wee. Mrs Apple Crumble made him sit on the naughty chair today for trumping in storytime.'

'Mrs *Abercrombie* did the right thing then, didn't she?'

Despite his far from jolly spirits, Adam let loose a lion's-lungsworth of laughter. It felt so good to laugh, he needed to laugh and it felt even better to be home with a family, even though it wasn't his home or his family. Nevertheless, he was grateful for the welcoming presence of a child and the warm no-nonsense of a woman.

'I don't know where they get these ideas from,' said Stevie crossly.

'Well, that Curtis Ryder has things a little wrong there,' said Adam. '*Bees* make honey for food, and they have been doing so for millions and millions of years. They collect *pollen* as food for their young.'

'Wow!' said Danny.

'Chicken nuggets!' Stevie alerted her son to the table. Was it her imagination, or had Adam MacLean given special emphasis to certain words just then? She had only seen the man for five minutes today and already she wanted to slap him.

'So, any mair news from *Midnight Moon*?' he casually asked later, whilst checking the television page.

'No, why would there be?'

'I have no idea why there would *beee*.'

Stevie put down her sewing. Danny's collars were getting ruined but there would be hell on if she threw this pyjama top away. It was one she had converted from an ordinary blue top to Dannyman super-pyjamas.

'Why are you looking at me as if you want me to *buzz awf*?' asked Adam with an angelic smile.

'You know, don't you?'

'Know what?' He looked so much the picture of innocence he should have been hung in the National Gallery. Or was it 'hanged'? Either sounded good to Stevie.

'Okay, I write *Midnight Moon* trashy, crappy romance books for a living. Satisfied?'

He jumped back in mock surprise. 'Naw!'

'I presume Crystal said far more than you admitted.'

'Perhaps. I seem to recall an extra minor detail or two.'

'Yes, I can imagine. Anyway, you may not like them, Mr MacLean, but thousands of other people do!' What was it about the man that got under her skin so much? He was the human equivalent of ringworm.

'I'm sure they do.'

Commonsense told her to walk away and go to her office. His mocking was attracting to him the anger that was swirling inside her for Jo; for her scratched car; for

Matthew's pathetic unhappy face; and most of all for Adam Bloody MacLean because she couldn't stop thinking about his lips on her arm. All afternoon her imagination had been taking those lips and putting them on other places on her body, and she didn't know why but she couldn't seem to stop herself. This wasn't in 'the plan'. But she did not walk away from his baiting. She not only took it, but she stuck her teeth into it too.

'In fact, I don't know why I didn't tell you before. It's not as if I should be ashamed. There's a skill involved, unlike managing a place where people pay an obscene amount of money just to lift up heavy objects and sweat!'

Oh, she wants to fight, does she? he thought, crossing his arms and preparing for battle.

'So, is that all I do then? And there was me thinking I work quite hard for my money.' He knew the next bit would infuriate her, but he didn't care. He was enjoying the verbal parry. It was making him forget all about the visitor who had weighed down his head for most of the day. 'Well, at least I don't sit on my bum all day.'

'Me sitting on my bum all day has put money on the table to feed my child. Yes, I'm a *Midnight Moon* writer and I'm proud of it!' Stevie jutted out her chin and nodded her head by way of an exclamation mark.

'I'm sure sad people all over the world appreciate you.'

This, unfortunately, didn't come out quite as his gentle teasing had intended, adding a pint of petrol to her already blazing temper.

'Yes, sad people with a brain who can do joined-up lettering! You patronizing Scottish git.'

She had a silly smattering of freckles on her nose. He had the sudden desire to kiss them. That would shut her up.

'I was trying to give you a compliment actually.'

'Stick your compliment up "yer ers", Mr MacLean,' said Stevie. 'I don't need compliments from a man like you.'

'And what sort of a man am I, *Ms Honeywell*? I see we're back on formal terms again.'

'The sort of man that I can't wait to see the back of on Sunday! I'm going to work. Good night,' and off she went in the direction of the office, chuntering expletives, to write about Damme MacQueen being thrown off a cliff.

Adam smiled. The angrier she got, the funnier she was, but as soon as Stevie left him, his thoughts started to drift back to the afternoon and a life that felt a million light years away from this crazy set-up. A life he had the chance to go back to. A life with a beautiful house and a beautiful woman in it. The life he had fought to win back. The life he surprisingly found he had won back.

So what was it that was stopping him?

Chapter 46

Unless a miracle happened in the next twenty-four hours, Adam's prophecy that all would be settled by Sunday was not going to come true. Matthew and Jo were very much still together, although a sneaky few spying looks in the mornings had revealed that they weren't half as hand-holdy or snoggy as they used to be, and there was even less smiling going on than at Princess Diana's funeral.

Adam had started gathering up his stuff and sorting out his laundry. His undies were drying on the line – they were white and Calvin Klein. Matthew was more of a briefs bloke – black and designer label also, but they paled into sexual second place as soon as she saw those white boxers. Matthew's bum had been a bit skinny for Stevie's tastes; Adam's was quite chunky. Not that she'd looked at it much. *Well* . . .

They hadn't seen a lot of each other in the last few days. He hadn't been in the house much, and when he had, Stevie had found herself avoiding him, shutting herself away in her office to work. Damme MacQueen was a good man – misjudged, kind, and wonderful. He didn't beat up women and he was safe to love. Evie was going to be a lucky lady.

Adam had deliberately been coming home after Danny had gone to bed, for which Stevie was grateful. It was going to be bad enough having to uproot her son again to find yet another place to live, without finding out he'd got attached to 'Well Life Man' too. It all felt terribly scary and unsettling, and she was cross at herself for believing Adam MacLean could really get them reunited with their rightful partners. He might not have been Mystic Meg, but he had her hopes up so high, the only way was down and they were coming down fast. It was something else to blame the man for.

'Can I do anything to help?' he asked, as she stomped around the kitchen, making a big noise as she transferred the crockery out of the dishwasher into the various cupboards.

'No!' she said. Then softer, 'No thanks.'

'Why the brass band?' he asked as the pans crashed together as she put them away.

'Because I want to.' Yes, she sounded petulant and she expected him to make some sarcastic comment. He didn't disappoint.

'Do you want to throw a few of your toys aroon as well while you're at it?'

'No, thank you.'

'Watch that bottom lip afore you trip o'er it!'

'Not listening, sorry.'

'I'll get you a teddy that you can throw oot your cot and make yersel' feel better.'

'Very funny. Ha ha!'

'Ah, so y'are listening! Maybe you need burping. Want me to pat your back a wee bit?'

She cast him a look that tried to kill him. She would like to have screamed at him to bugger off, but Danny was on his bicycle in the garden so she couldn't. She was finding that the pressure of keeping her feelings in was making her blow steam out of her earholes, so she rough-handled the crockery instead and dropped one of the nice plates which crashed to the floor, spattering the pieces everywhere.

'Och, now you'll have to pay for that oot your pocket-money!'

That's it!

She turned on him. 'Everything's a big joke to you, isn't it?'

'No, it isnae. But pretending you're at a Greek wedding isn't going to bring Matty Boy back to you any quicker. And there's no use snapping at me – this isnae my fault.'

'Isn't it?' Stevie laughed, a hard unjolly sound. 'This situation is *all* because of you, Adam MacLean. *All!*'

'*Okay, stop there,*' said the sensible part of her brain, looking around for the brake, whilst in the meantime, her mouth carried on in fifth gear.

'I've lost my home and my man, and my little boy has lost his chance of a family. *You* might have thrown your relationship away, but I didn't. Make no mistake – this all happened *Because. Of. You!*' She barged past him to get the cutlery, not noticing that the highly amused and gentle teasing smile had dropped like a hot rock from Adam's lips and he moved quickly to block her way.

'Whoa, whoa! Now you ho'd on a wee minute, lady. I need you to rewind this conversation. What was that bit about throwing my relationship away?'

There was something in his manner that made Stevie realize she had gone too far and was on dangerous territory, but there was no taking it back.

'Nothing, I meant nothing.' She moved to skirt him and he moved with her and put his hands on her arms to pull her back in front of him. The startled little yelp she gave made him drop his hold immediately.

'Sorry, did I hurt you?'

'No,' she said, because he hadn't, but he saw in her eyes a flashing thought that he might. That fear. He knew that look so well. He had seen it in his mammy's and his sisters' eyes so many times.

'What's going on, Stevie? What's happened? What did you mean?'

Stevie wouldn't meet his eyes.

'Please, Stevie!' He was desperate now to find out what she meant. She knew something about him that he needed to know. That look she had given him scared him. 'What am I supposed to have done in my relationship that all this was my fault? Please – what did you mean? What do you know? What have you heard? You have to tell me now.'

He wasn't going to let up on this, she knew. She slumped down on the kitchen table. She wasn't sure what was true or not any more, but at least she wasn't about to add to the mess by lying herself.

'It's what Jo told us about you.'

'Jo?' He paled. 'You spoke to Jo? When?'

'Lots of times.'

'What do you mean?'

Stevie sighed. It was like trying to get an octopus back in

a bag. She wouldn't be able to do it. It would be better to let it all out and stop struggling against it.

'Matthew and Jo got friendly at work,' Stevie began.

'Aye, I know. You two weren't getting on.'

'What?'

'That's what Jo told me. That you two were going through a rough patch.' He didn't see the need to tell her that apparently she was also dirty and lazy and a terrible mother. She would spontaneously combust.

'Jo said what?' Stevie's mouth dropped so far open, it was in danger of crushing her foot. 'God, this just gets better and better. We were fine! The reason he befriended her is because you . . . you . . . made her unhappy!'

'In what way?' Now it was Adam's turn to look shocked.

'She never stopped crying! I felt so sorry for her.'

'You met her?' He was breathless.

'She rang for Matthew one day, too scared to go home to you. I told her to come around to the house.'

'Scared – of *me*? What on earth for?'

'She was terrified. Shaking when she got here.'

'But she never said she met you!'

'Adam, we became friends, we went shopping together – I made her tea whilst she read to Danny. I even let her see my wedding dress. She was on our guest list!'

'Friends? She said Matthew loathed you!'

'She said you took all her money!'

'She said he'd called off the marriage but you were carrying on with the arrangements regardless!'

'She said you put her through hell with the names you called her!'

'She said you used to get drunk and throw things at Matthew!'

'She said you used to smack her around!'

The words hung in the air like a discordant bell. Of all the lies Adam MacLean was hearing, he found this one hard to stomach most of all. Not after all he had seen as a child, the way his daddy laced into his mammy and he had to stand there and witness it all with his arms around his crying sisters, fearful in case his mammy died but scared to move in case he got hurt too. He never quite lost the guilt of thinking of his own needs, even though he was only a wee boy.

'Stevie, I've never laid a hand on a woman in my life,' he said. A shock of tears sprang involuntarily to his eyes and he wiped them away, embarrassed. 'The reason I got together with Jo in the first place was to rescue her from some crazy guy that she was living with. He'd kicked her in the leg and she was limping. I found her crying outside the gym where I worked before this one.'

Stevie gulped. 'Top of her left thigh?'

'Aye,' he said.

'She said you did that.'

'Me!' He spun around, his voice booming, his bulk filling half the room, but he still didn't look in the least bit harmful. 'I cannae hit anyone. Look at the size o' me. I'd kill anyone I hit!'

'So you've not been in Barlinnie?'

'Barlinnie?' Adam laughed through the tears. 'Whit the hell for?'

'GBH.'

'Grievous Bod . . .? Stevie, they wouldnae give me a job at Well Life sweeping flairs if I'd mair than three points on my driving licence! I've never been in a jail in my life. I've no' even hed so much as a parking ticket!' He dropped to the sofa. 'I can't believe aw this,' he said, rubbing his head with his huge hands, though it brought him no comfort. He had trusted Jo with all the horrors of his early life and she had used it against him. He really had been a fool. Would he ever learn?

Stevie had the overwhelming desire to go to him and touch him, hold him. She knew he had been hurt by her revelations. Never had she seen even the slightest intimation that Adam was the man that Jo had painted him to be, though she knew she had wanted to see him like that, because then she could blame him for what had happened and not her darling Matthew. Eddie had been right all along when he asked, what sort of a possessive psycho was it that let his wife go for away for a week to a health spa. They'd both been had. And Matthew was still being had. *Should she tell him?* What difference would it make, though? Hadn't Catherine tried to tell her what a bastard Mick Rook was? And had she believed her? No, nor would she have done, not even if Mick had had *I am a bastard, stay away stickers* plastered indelibly over every part of his anatomy.

'I'm sorry, Adam, I don't know what to believe any more.'

'Stevie, I'm no wife-batterer, I can tell you that. Is this true? Is this really what she said, because I don't know what to believe any more either.'

Stevie nodded slowly.

'Ah well, that explains a few things,' said Adam with weary resignation. 'I wondered why Matty Boy was wagging his finger at me, telling me no' to hurt you, and no' tae spend all your money.' His brain zapped to thoughts of mutual friends who no longer called, and a fresh wave of hurt engulfed him. 'I can't believe people think I'm that sort of guy. Catherine and Eddie – they know all this?'

Stevie gave another nod.

He looked cut down, felled like a big tree that wouldn't ever get up again.

'Well, if you think there is the slightest danger to you and your child from me, maybe it would be better if I just got out of your life totally tomorrow. We'll forget our plan and you get Matthew back your way. I don't think it will be long, for the record.'

'Okay,' said Stevie with a croaky voice. She didn't want him to go, but she needed space. She needed to get away from thoughts of Adam MacLean's lips on her arm and the feel of her hand inside his. 'I think that might be for the best.'

Chapter 47

Adam lay on the treatment table and groaned in pain. He had thought a Sunday-morning Kahuna session at the gym might help to ease the tension in his back and neck and shoulders, if not take away the knot in his head. He never expected that the tiny South African masseuse Simone could be capable of such brutality.

'My God, is it supposed to hurt that much?' he gasped as the points of her elbows pierced his kidneys. He could hardly breathe. She should have had *SS* embroidered on her tunic, not *WL*.

'You have a lot of crunchy bits, Adam,' said Simone. 'I need to shift 'em'. Boy, you're tense!'

It was the sort of massage Stevie would have liked to perform on him, he thought. One that hurt lots. Then thoughts of Stevie rubbing oil in his back ran on ahead of him, her small hands kneading his muscles, her fingers tripping up and down his spine. Then he would reciprocate and dribble the warm scented oil onto her body and smooth it over her soft curves, his thumbs circling her skin and making her groan. A mutinous body part stirred and he groaned inwardly. *Och naw, that wasnae supposed to happen at all!* Then he knew why he had said 'no' when Joanna MacLean had turned up at the gym and asked then pleaded, then begged to come home.

As Stevie was preparing the last meal she would share with Adam MacLean in this beautiful house, she saw Matthew through the window walking back home with an armful of Sunday newspapers. He looked like an old man with the cares of the world on his shoulders. Her heart lurched in his direction, in love or pity or both, she couldn't tell. How was it that she could write about feelings so incisively for her characters, but when it came to her own she was such a mess? Her emotions were like a big ball of wool that had been snagged and ripped and tangled by a very vicious cat.

Danny was colouring at the table. Stevie pulled his Dannyman collar out of his mouth.

'You'll suck all the dye out of your shirt and end up being blue like an alien, would you like that?'

'Wow, yeah!' he said, which hadn't been the answer she had expected.

'I give up. Suck your collar then, Danny, and don't come crying to me when you go blue,' she said impatiently.

She turned her attention to the Yorkshire pudding mix. The flour rose up in a big cumulous cloud as the beaters hit it, blew it up her nose and made her sneeze. Adam, newly arrived in the doorway, hid the little smile that came because he was suddenly catapulted back to the first time he had seen her. It surprised him because he thought it would be a long time until he smiled again. His back was in pain from the Kahuna, his head was in pain from thinking of Jo's treachery. But it was his heart that pained him most of all.

'Have you seen a big bunch of keys, Stevie? I've put them down somewhere.'

'Oh, I thought I saw them upstairs. Or did I? Yes, I'm sure I did. Now where was it?'

She put the bowl down and went upstairs to look for them. He followed her and she did a sideways walk up in case he was taking a critical look at her bum. Not that he'd be looking at her bum when he liked a Jo MacLean kind of bum i.e. non-existent.

'Yes, here they are,' she said, spotting them. 'I thought I'd seen them. There on the windowsill.' She reached over and handed them to him. His fingers brushed against hers and it was unbearable for both of them.

'Thanks,' he said. He looked down into her lovely blue eyes and was shamed that she had thought him the sort of man he despised. His 'plan' had been stupid. It had confused their lives even more, and he would be left with a worse loss than when he started.

Stevie raised her head to his face and saw him as he really was and how she had found him, not as Jo had led her to believe he was. You only had to look into his soft gentle eyes to know he didn't have the capacity to hurt anything. And how had she missed how generous his mouth was? An unattainable mouth, because it still belonged to Jo MacLean.

Her thoughts stopped there because her senses were alerted to a noise that was hardly indiscernible to the ear, but that a mother's heart would pick up. It was coming from the kitchen and Stevie's feet flew downstairs in response to it.

Danny wasn't playing any more. He was on the floor, shaking as if in a fit and in great distress, and his lips were paling to blue.

'Adam!' she screamed. 'Adam, help me!'

Adam bounced down the stairs.

'He's hardly breathing!' said Stevie, bent over her son. She pulled her hand back to slap him on the back. Adam caught her arm before it impacted.

'No, Stevie. Get an ambulance!'

'Yes,' she said. She picked up the phone and as if she was in a bad dream, it slipped out of her hand. She grabbed it up and could hardly see the numbers, she was crying so hard.

'Stevie, there's a button missing on his collar – was there one here?'

'Yes, oh God yes, there was. Hello . . . ambulance, please.' She sobbed as the phone connected with the Emergency Services and she hurriedly gave them her details. This wasn't how it was supposed to be. She was Danny's mother; she should be in control, saving his life, not standing there – a big stupid jelly and hardly able to speak.

Adam scooped his finger in Danny's mouth.

'There's something in there. I think he's swallowed his button and it's blocking his airway. I can't get to it.'

Adam got to his feet and pulled the limp little boy up, wrapping his arms around the child from the back. He braced himself and thrust his fist under Danny's ribcage. And again. It looked so brutal, so abusive. Then something flew out of the little boy's mouth and Danny gasped and started making sicky, retching noises and then he started crying. It was the most beautiful sound Stevie had ever heard.

Disorientated, Danny looked around for Stevie, reached out for her and Stevie pulled him into her arms and rocked him. She didn't know how long for, she didn't feel part of this world any more. She was numb and cocooned in some safe bubble of time that let her savour the feeling of her son's breathing, of his life. They sat like that until the ambulance sirened up the lane and Adam met it at the door and explained to the paramedics what had happened.

'We'd better take you in, just as a precaution,' said one of the paramedics, giving Danny a quick once-over. 'Hey, young fella, how would you like to have a ride in the back of an ambulance?'

Danny nodded slowly, but he didn't say his customary, 'Cool,' which was telling. Adam lifted him away so Stevie could get up, and he cuddled up to the big Scot and wouldn't let him go. So Adam came too, in the back of the ambulance to the hospital.

Stevie sat in a cosy waiting room with Adam whilst Danny was in the consulting room with the doctor. She was remembering those awful first days of his life when her arms felt so empty. Her Little Fighter. She never thought she would feel that pain or that relief again. Being a parent gave you highs and lows that were almost an assault on the heart.

She wasn't sobbing as such, but her eyes were piping out tears. Adam watched them rolling down her face, one after the other, as if coming from an endless supply within. She looked so little, so tiny and more fragile than he could ever have imagined her.

'He was a premature baby,' she said at last. 'I didn't think he'd pull through – I was warned he might not. To have nearly lost your child once is terrible, to go through this twice . . .'

'Shhh,' said Adam, because even though he felt shaken himself, he couldn't imagine what Stevie must be feeling like.

'I told him if he didn't stop sucking his collar he'd turn blue and he did,' she wept.

'Stevie, stop tormenting yourself.'

'If you hadn't been there, he'd have died. If—'

'Stevie, if I hadn't been there, you'd have saved his life somehow, don't ask me how, but I know that without a shadow of a doubt. Now stop thinking about "if", there's no point. Danny is safe. "If" didn't happen.'

'You saved his life, Adam, and I was useless, crap. A totally crap mother.'

All her insecurities came to the fore. Not being able to keep her son's father, not being able to carry her baby full-term, not being able to keep her son's would-be stepfather, not giving Danny a settled home, not getting him to eat potatoes or bread, not being able to stop him chewing his collars, not being able to save his life . . . So many times she had wished to collapse against a big, strong man who would take control and sort everything out for her. Now here she was doing exactly that and it wasn't Welsh Jonny or Mick or Matthew, it was Adam MacLean, of all people. This truly was Fate's biggest joke on her yet.

'You're a great mother, trust me on this,' said Adam.

'You put food on his table, clothes on his back and love in his heart.'

'You've been reading my books.'

'Awa', I wouldnae read that pap.' He nudged her and she laughed, although the tears didn't stop. Each one brought out another at its end, like a magician's constant stream of sleeve scarves. Adam put his arm around her and squeezed her. She was all squashy and soft and warm and there was flour in her hair. He wanted to pull her onto his knee and sink his face into her neck.

The door opened and a smiley nurse came in.

'Hi there, Danny's mum?' Then she threw an extra 'Heeeey' at Adam, like a female version of The Fonz. 'Your little boy is fine,' she said. 'Scratched his throat a bit, that's all, but no lasting harm done. Do you want to come and get him?'

'Go on,' said Adam. 'I'll wait here for you.'

Stevie smiled at him and followed the nurse quickly out.

'So you're Adam's lady, are you?' said the nurse.

'No, we're just' – *mortal enemies* – 'neighbours.'

'Adam's one of our favourites,' she leaned in and winked. 'He raised over three thousand pounds for us when he cut all his hair off. He helps us a lot. And, of course, he's our Father Christmas. The kids love him!'

A ginger Father Christmas with a scar? thought Stevie, and as if she had heard her, the nurse said, 'He tells the kids that he scraped his face on Rudolf's antler.' She actually sighed, as if she was talking about Ronan Keating.

Then Adam's number one fan opened up a door and gestured for Stevie to go in.

Danny was sitting on a bed and a beautiful female Indian doctor was talking to him.

'Is he okay, Doctor?' said Stevie, hugging her baby.

'He's fine. Little scratching to the throat, so I'll give you a prescription for an antibiotic just in case, and we also recommend an intensive course of ice-cream,' said the doctor, trying to coax a smile from her patient, and getting a very little one in return.

'No more sucking collars,' said the nurse with a gently wagging finger.

'Okay, I won't,' said Danny. 'Can I go home now?'

'Yes, I think so,' said the doctor.

'Do I need to keep him off school?' asked Stevie, taking the prescription.

'I don't think there's a need,' said the doctor, smiling. 'See how he is in the morning.'

Stevie wrapped up her son in her arms and carried him out. He smelt and felt so precious, but if she caught him sucking collars again, she would glue his mouth up.

Adam met them in the entrance hall. Danny reached out, gave him a big Superhero hug, and moved over into his arms. The wee boy smelt of his mother's perfume. He was so like her, with his honey-coloured hair and his big blue eyes, that Adam found himself gulping back something that made his eyes distinctly watery. His hold on the boy was tight and strong as they got a taxi home to Humbleby.

'I'll make you a cup of tea, huh?' Adam said when they got inside the house. 'Then I'll get aff.'

'Will you go back home?' said Stevie. Her throat felt

worse than Danny's must have. Dry and sore. As if she had been gargling with razor blades.

'Aye,' he said, obviously not relishing the prospect.

'Stay,' said Stevie. 'Please.'

'Aye,' said Adam.

Then he went to put the kettle on.

Chapter 48

Unaware of the drama that had happened across the lane the previous day, Matthew walked into work on Monday morning and had the weirdest feeling he was being watched. Eyes seemed to linger on him longer than was necessary. He had the ridiculous notion that he was the subject of gossip.

Jo had driven her own car in very early that morning; his suggestion that he accompany her had been met with a weary sigh. It appeared that he couldn't win at the moment: if he paid her attention, he was crowding her, if he didn't he was ignoring her. He had tried to talk to her about it in bed at the weekend but she had looked at him as if he were nuts.

'That is *so* your imagination!' she had bawled at him, like a good-looking fishwife, then she demanded rough sex. This time he hadn't been able to raise as much as a smile and he had refused to bite and manhandle her, with the result that she hadn't spoken to him after Saturday morning.

He had gone into town on the Sunday, to buy her a 'sorry for whatever I did' present, something gold and expensive, but bit back the urge at the shop doorway. This was harder than giving up cigarettes years ago, but he had managed to muster up the willpower to do it eventually, so at least there was some hope of a cure. He bought her a sweet little card instead. It still lay unopened on the kitchen table where she had tossed it down.

Matthew settled himself at his desk, pondered over the dilemma of what to do for the best and then bit the bullet. He decided Jo would be less annoyed if he tried an active approach rather than a passive one, so he took a deep breath and dialled her extension.

'Jo MacLean,' she answered briskly.

'Hi, it's me. Fancy lunch?'

'Sorry, no,' she said, as if he was a sex-crazed stalker who had just asked her for a gangbang with the Board. She slammed the phone down on him and he stared at it in disbelief. What have I done wrong now? he thought, shaking his head.

Life had been so much easier and less complicated with Stevie, he found himself thinking, as he headed out of the building in the direction of Pauline's Pasties at half past twelve, again with the feeling that he was under some giant microscope hidden in the ceiling.

'Have I done the right thing, sending Danny to school?' said Stevie, shaking her head in self-disgust that she was waving through the class window to the son who nearly died yesterday.

'Okay, let me ask you this,' said Catherine. 'How was he when he got home from the hospital yesterday?'

'Bit quiet. Apart from that, fine. Considering.'

'Was he upset in the night?'

'No, he slept like a log. I didn't, though. I kept checking to see if he was still breathing.'

'And did the doctor say, "Keep him at home"?'

'No.'

'And what happened when you said, "Danny, you're going to school"?'

'I didn't. I said I was keeping him off for a couple of days but he wanted to go. They're having that Punch and Judy show in assembly this morning, aren't they? I've told Mrs Abercrombie to ring me if there was any problem at all.'

'There you go then. He *wanted* to go and he was *fine to go*. He'll be better at school bragging to his mates that he went off in an ambulance yesterday than sitting at home with a miserable-looking mother nattering over him.'

'If Adam hadn't been there, I just don't know what would have happened.'

Catherine grabbed her hands. 'Adam *was* there. Danny *is* well. There's no point in going along the "if" road. You're talking to the woman who didn't strap her three-week-old baby properly up in the car seat once and dropped him down two stairs, remember?'

'Yes – and I also remember the state you were in afterwards.'

'Precisely. I was half-insane with all the "ifs".'

'I feel half-insane as it is. I asked Adam to stay on even though I'm scared stiff that Danny will get attached.'

Catherine stared right into her friend's sad, blue eyes. 'Are you sure you're not frightened that it's *you* who will get attached?'

'Me?' said Stevie.

'Yes, you. I watched you at the party and I thought, They aren't acting.'

'Of course we were acting, Cath. Besides, the guy likes tall, good-looking women who weigh less than eight stone. How could I follow Jo MacLean? Talk sense, will you.'

'Ah yes, the lying, cheating Ms MacLean – what a catch *she* is. The more I hear about that woman, the more I think she might turn up in the *Guinness Book of Records* for being the most treacherous bitch in the world. I've always thought there was more to her than meets the eye. Clever though. But then good liars usually are – and you, of all people, should know that.'

'I know,' said Stevie. 'I know.'

They walked on a little further to where Catherine had parked her car.

'I made some discreet enquiries to Will, by the way,' Catherine said, 'like: "Could you get a job as a manager in a topclass gym if you had a criminal record?"'

'Oh, very subtle,' said Stevie with a gentle laugh. 'And?'

'Not a chance. They do a full police check.' Catherine looked hard at her mixed-up bunny of a friend. Next to Stevie's, her life was more or less flat-lined but she wouldn't swap her lot for Stevie's present roller-coaster ride. The girl deserved a break.

'So what now, hon?' she went on gently.

'I don't know.'

'Would you still have Matthew back? After all that's happened?'

'Of course I would,' said Stevie, without thinking. She

didn't want to allow herself room to think. Otherwise, what the hell had been the point of the last eight weeks?

'Hiya, wee man!' said Adam, coming in from work, giving Danny a big cuddle as he rushed at him. He was wearing new pyjamas with no buttons or collars to be seen, he noted, and his Dannyman emblem was stitched on the front.

'Hey – nice jim-jams. Like the style!' said Adam, twirling him around.

'He'll be in that style until he's forty-five, if I've got anything to do with it,' said Stevie. 'Anyway, come on, bedtime, little man.' She gave Adam a tentative smile. 'He wanted to stay up and just say "hi". I hope that was okay?'

'Of course,' said Adam. 'Why wouldn't it be?'

'Because I've encouraged you to stay away from him, and then suddenly I'm throwing him at you. I didn't want to add to any confusion for you.'

He looked at her. What was that conversation he'd had with Danny once about the most important quality of a Superhero? He reckoned Danny's mum had just what it took to be one of the best.

'Nice smell,' he said, pulling his eyes away and to the kitchen.

'I made you a steak pie. As a thank you for . . . you know what. I'll just . . .'

Words failing her, she edged backwards and took Danny upstairs for their bedtime business. Then, after discreetly checking her make-up and squirting on an extra spray of perfume, she went back downstairs to find Adam looking across the lane at Matthew's house, lost in his thoughts. Her

heart started beating a little faster in distress. After all Jo
MacLean had done to him, it was obvious that he still
wanted her, but then the heart was a wild card that didn't
play to a rulebook. It had made her half-mad for Mick,
who treated her so cruelly, it had made her agree to a
ridiculous plan to get cheating Matthew back, and now it
had turned its deranged attentions to Adam MacLean, who
was still madly in love with another woman. How could
she judge him? There was no bigger fool on this earth
than her own heart.

She carried the pie to the table, which had been set just
for one.

'You no' going to join me?' he said.

'I'm not hungry, really. I have to get some work done.
Can I get you a drink? Wine? Whisky?' She had bought a
bottle of both in.

'No, I'll just get a wee glass of water. Cannae stand
whisky!'

Stevie looked at him in open-mouthed shock. 'But
you're Scottish.'

His eyes twinkled. 'You noticed?'

'And you had a trolley full of it that day when I met you
in the supermarket.'

'That was for the hospital tombola. Jings! Did you think
it was aw for me?'

'Well, yes . . . sorry.' Stevie smoothed her hair back from
her face in a gesture of embarrassment. The 'B' file in her
head was full of so much conflicting evidence about the
man that it blew up there and then in shame. 'I got you so
wrong on all fronts, didn't I?'

'Wasnae your fault,' he said, wisely not mentioning that he had believed Jo's stories that Stevie was a complete harpy, a car-crash of a mother and a mega-slattern-fiancée.

She carried the pie in to him, smiled bashfully and then doubled back quickly into the study, although she wanted to sit with him, wanted to be near him. But she couldn't. She wasn't slim or tall or pretty enough for him to cast *that* sort of glance in her direction.

Adam sighed deeply as the study door closed behind her because he really wanted just to sit with her, wanted her to be near him. He shifted his attention to the thick-crusted pie she had set in front of him. She'd even made a pastry thistle on the top of it for him. He hadn't really eaten properly since Jo had come to see him. Strangely enough though, his thoughts had not been for her tonight whilst he stood at the window and looked across at the house opposite. They had all been for Finch, who hadn't a clue yet that the awesome hurricane which had swung into his life, would rip out his innards when it left – and that would be soon. He almost felt sorry for him. His stomach suddenly gave a big growl as the smell of the thick onion gravy drifted up his nostrils, but his heart gave a louder, hungrier growl for what that fool Finch had thrown away. Sadly, the thing that would have satisfied it was not on the menu.

Chapter 49

Matthew went into work alone again the next day, leaving Jo behind to pack for a two-day conference she had suddenly announced she was going on. A very short time ago, he couldn't bear to be out of her sight for even a few minutes, but now he was glad she was going. He would appreciate the space from her and her white-knuckle-ride moods. They were barely talking at home, they hardly spoke at work, and he knew she was avoiding contact with him there. The only place they interchanged was in bed, and even that was becoming tiresome. Her sexual demands were becoming stranger and rougher, the sulks greater when he denied her. He had come to hate the sight of that mouth gathered into a spoilt-child moue that he once considered so sexy.

He tried not to let himself believe that he had made a fatal error exchanging what he had with Stevie for this, but the evidence was piling up by the binful and he could no longer ignore the stink it made. He had been an idiot. Take away the sex and the temporary joy of spending money from his relationship with Jo and there was nothing left. Theirs was a simple arrangement: he gave out and she

took. He realized he was exhausted emotionally and physically as well as financially.

He had a lunch meeting at noon in the boardroom,
which was, at least, something to look forward to. There
would be a few big execs present and as such, the in-house
catering would be top-notch. They always rolled out the
posh sandwich fillings when people like Bill Phillips and Jim
Leighton made an appearance. It promised to be quite a
jolly affair, with a few other faces present that he hadn't seen
much of recently. Matthew badly needed the lift of spirits
such good company would give him. He passed the morning quietly, with his head down, biding his time until then.

At twelve, he walked into the boardroom and instantly
felt the air temperature drop, as if someone had switched on
a fan. There was nothing he could actually put his finger
on. People spoke to him and greeted him, but with a hint
of coolness, an awkward reservation of which he was all too
aware. Maybe he was just worn down with all this business
at home; maybe he needed to get some anti-paranoia pills.
Or Maybe he needed to be bitten by a werewolf and
become one, because that's what Jo seemed to want in bed.
He felt worse than ever when he came out of the meeting,
which had only served to depress him more than he was
already. Then, if that wasn't enough, he got a call from
Personnel at two-thirty to ask if he could bob down to see
Colin Seed for a few minutes.

Colin Seed was slightly different from his usual dull, brown
self when he let Matthew into his office. He was sporting
a trendy tie with fish on it and his hair looked slightly

darker, as if he had been experimenting with some 'Just for Men' but had got it ever so slightly wrong.

'Please sit down,' he said politely enough. Matthew sat and waited for Colin to begin, not able to imagine what this was about. He didn't have to wait long to find out.

'It's come to my attention that you are making quite a lot of personal phone calls.'

Oh, that old chestnut! Matthew breathed out two lungfuls of relief. *God, Seedy really was desperate for his backside!*

'Colin, I've made a couple, and they were local and important.'

'. . . And you've been lying about your whereabouts.'

'My what? My where—'

'Even though you are a Departmental Manager, Matthew, this company has always prided itself on equal rights for all. If you had discovered that one of your staff was at a personal meeting at the bank after filling in a request form for time off for a dental appointment, would you or would you not take action?'

'Well . . .' Matthew couldn't think of anything, except that the only person who knew about that was Jo.

'Quite frankly, Matthew, your work attitude stinks. I can't count the number of times you've been late in recently.'

This wasn't happening.

'The worst, I'm afraid, is yet to come,' Colin said, his voice tightening like a tourniquet. 'Your blatant harassment of Miss MacLean will not be tolerated by this company.'

'My what?' He rose.

'Sit down!' barked Colin. 'I myself have been witness to

your phone calls to her, obsessively keeping tabs on her, deluging her with unwanted gifts, seen first-hand the disgusting violence you've subjected her to . . .'

'Hang on, what's this got to do with work? We live together, Colin, we're lovers! You've got no right to interfere . . .'

'Miss MacLean asked me for help.'

'Whaaat?'

'I think your inability to realize that your relationship has ended has greatly affected your function in this company and made your position untenable. We are a big family here, we protect our people, we don't want men like you working here and threatening the safety of our females. So it is with great regret, especially after such an unblemished career, I have to announce that we shall have to let you go.'

Matthew laughed derisively. He was in a bad dream, brought about by the stress of performing sexual gymnastics fourteen times a night.

'What do you mean, I can't accept my relationship's ended? This is nuts! It hasn't ended – it's still going strong! *We* are still going strong! We're planning our bloody wedding, for God's sake!'

Colin shook his head as if Matthew had just proved how delusional he was and so there was no point continuing this conversation.

'You'll be paid until the end of the month and obviously your holiday entitlement will be converted into salary.'

'You have to be kidding.' Matthew felt sick, lightheaded. This was surreal. 'I'm being sacked? For living with my girlfriend?'

'No, Matthew, for gross misconduct,' said Colin Seed with loud disgust. 'At Miss MacLean's request, though frankly I think it's a hideously overgenerous one, I will not record on your personnel record what a disgusting, violent little bully you are if you go quietly and discreetly. The poor girl is a wreck. She can't breathe without your permission. You're lucky she isn't pressing police charges. Now get out, and if you aren't out of this building in ten minutes, I'll get Security to throw you out.'

Security threat or no, the first thing Matthew did when he got back to his office was ring Jo's mobile. It clicked straight onto voicemail. He grabbed his coat and blindly stuffed things into his briefcase because a *Countdown*-type clock was ticking in his ears. So he hadn't been imagining things; people really *had* been looking at him strangely. Worse than that, even, with sex-beast specs on. He felt like crying from the injustice of it. He didn't look up; he didn't want to see the stares of people who had it all wrong. But then, not meeting their eyes made him look guilty. He didn't know what to do for the best and he couldn't bear it. It was like being trapped in a nightmare. There was no oxygen in the building. He left quickly and quietly, and almost fainted when the fresh outside air rushed into his lungs. He would sort this; he would clear his name. He needed to see Jo – she would back him up against that twisted, sex-starved old woman Colin Seed. She would make everything all right.

Jo MacLean heard the mobile ring and she clicked 'ignore'. It was Matthew. She relished the thought of the panic he must be in now, but she felt no sympathy. Not once had he convinced her he was the Golden Goose but a second time, with that ridiculous paltry lottery win. What he had coming to him would serve him right, because if she had known the truth about his financial state, she would never have left Adam.

Out of all the men she'd had, she really had regretted letting Adam go the most. He'd been lovely – kind, generous and so very gentle. She hadn't even minded that much about the revolting ponytail and long straggly beard he had been growing to shave off for charity, and that spoke volumes. She wished now that she had stayed and married him – well, for a while anyway. He had been bitten hard before and was nervous about taking that step, but she would have won him over to the idea, had she not been distracted by Matthew and his hot-air talk about his so-called investments.

She had started to notice weeks ago that Colin Seed was a far more frequent visitor to the department than usual. Matthew had hit the nail on the head thinking Jo was the attraction. It had been so easy to hook him: a few tears by his Bentley in the executive car park and he was putty in her hands. He was the contingency plan she put into place, just in case things soured with Matthew. Jo MacLean always liked to have a contingency plan. She made sure she was in total control of her own destiny.

Then she had seen Adam with Stevie and it had driven her half-crazy. It surprised her, because she didn't think herself capable of feelings that deep. She wanted him back immediately, and it never occurred to her that the space she had left in his life would not still be open to her. She had gone to see him at the gym, wearing one of the suits he had bought for her, her hair down as he liked it best, but he had turned her down. He said he didn't love her any more.

Now Jo's suitcases were in her car ready to take to Colin's house – Colin's monstrously huge eight-bedroomed house in the most elegant part of Leeds suburbia – and even better, she had persuaded him to take the position in New York.

Adoration, love-gifts, a new life in the Big Apple and pots of real money to look forward to – this time Jo MacLean, the ultimate bird of passage, thought she really had cracked it.

Matthew drove carefully home because his hands were shaking too much to speed. He felt as if he was in *The Blair Witch Project* – a big foresty mess that he couldn't get out of, and things could only get worse. He pulled up noisily outside his house, plunged the key into the lock then crashed through the rooms, calling out Jo's name in despair. She was not there, and nor were any of her things. His house looked shabby and dusty and full of ugly unwanted bits. It wasn't unlike his life.

Jo rang Adam from the car, just before she turned into Colin's drive. She told him she had left Matthew and had nowhere to go. She found herself sobbing real tears, and when she told him that she was sorry for everything and loved him, truly loved him, she meant it.

He told her she had no idea what love was and he put the phone down.

Chapter 50

By her own admission, this was ridiculous. Stevie had all the same feelings as a seventeen year old on her first date as she waited for Adam to come home from work that night. She had been so full of nervous energy back then, waiting for David Idziaszczyk to knock on her door and take her to Rebecca's nightclub, that she had been sick on her shoes in the hallway and had a mad scramble to wipe up and spray her legs with her mum's Youth Dew. She dipped into the memory of her first love and smiled. On the day she finally learned to spell his name, he'd dumped her. She thought her life had ended and there were many dramatic wailings to be had. The heartbreaks didn't get any easier with age but neither did the love-bugs, now tickling the walls of her tummy, get any less active.

Danny was staying the night at Catherine's because there was a teachers' 'inset' day at school tomorrow, whatever they were. Latin for 'a rest from the little buggers' probably. Cath was always offering to babysit at the moment, for her own mischievous reasons, and tonight, well, Stevie was not prepared to look a gift horse in the mouth.

She checked the large coffee cake cooking in the oven.

She was quite proud that she had managed to make it without blowing up the lovely cottage kitchen. The vegetables were all ready in their pans, the fillet steaks in the fridge waiting to be cooked, the wine breathing on the work surface. Why she was going to all this trouble was anyone's guess. Adam MacLean wouldn't look in her direction in a million years, she knew that, but some little romantic (and stupid) part of her wanted to run with the feeling that he might. Just for a few days. Just until her head could get around the fact that soon they would go their separate ways and probably only see each other in passing in the gym. Then one day she would see him roaring past her in a sports car with a gorgeous, tall, slim woman next to him, her long, dark hair streaming behind and Stevie would be a distant memory, an amusing after-dinner tale at best. *I once knew a woman who wrote for* Midnight Moon. *Now, what was her name again . . .?* And Stevie would still be alone, still writing out fictional lives full of the hope and love that she wanted so much for herself.

She was just rolling the edges of the big cake in battered-up Flake when he came in, dropped his bag by the door and smiled as the cocktail of nice domestic aromas hit him at full pelt. He carried a couple of bottles of wine in his hand. He just wanted to savour the last few days of being with her, he knew that was all he had left. He should have told Stevie that Jo had gone, but he feared that would accelerate her journey back to *his* arms. He should leave now and not prolong the heartache, but he just wanted to be with her, a little longer, an hourglass-worth of time with someone who had the same voluminous capacity to love as he did. Someone warm and generous, imperfect, irritating, annoying, frustrating, bloody lovely.

'Hi,' she said. 'I got some steaks, if you want one. Nothing special.'

She had baked. This was special. Well, to him. No one, except his Granny Walker, had ever made him a cake before.

'I got some wine, if you fancy a glass.'

'Yes, I do, thanks. There's a bottle open already over there.'

'Ho'd on a wee minute until I get oot o' this clobba.'

He said he liked his steak well done, not still moo-ing and struggling on the end of his fork, as she had once thought he might. She slapped them in the pan and as they sizzled in the hot olive oil, she smiled to herself, thinking about him upstairs, changing out of his work 'clobba'.

He poured two glasses of the open red, when he at last came down in a T-shirt and jeans. She tried hard not to look at his muscular arms, the definition of his chest under the snow-white material, his fantastic chunk of a bum and big crushing thighs shaping the denim.

'Where's the wean?'

'He's at Catherine's. They're having a cinema night. *The Incredibles* again, I think, for the forty-billionth time.'

'Och, that's a shame. I was going to have a kick aboot wi' him in the garden.'

Fond of him as Matthew had been, he had never once said 'that's a shame' when Danny wasn't around, Stevie suddenly realized. Then again, she had realized quite a lot recently. Mostly how pale her real relationship with Matthew had been, even when placed at the side of this imaginary one with Adam.

'Can I help?' he asked.

'Yes, you can pass me the brandy and those peppercorns, unless you want your steak plain.'

'Aye, plain for me, please. I want to taste that meat, it looks braw . . . good.'

'I understand you now, you don't need to translate.'

He smiled. The wine swirled in his head already. He wanted to get horribly plastered and rip all her clothes off, but for now, he got on with slicing some tomatoes.

'Bea Pollen!' he chuckled, when they were sitting down on the sofa, mellowing after a lovely meal and gentle banter. They had both suggested having a sobering raspberry-truffle-flavoured coffee afterwards. He, before he really did rip her clothes off, and she before she leapt on him and made a complete twat of herself. They had both kicked off their shoes and their feet were inches apart on the big long footstool. She couldn't imagine ever borrowing his socks. He had the biggest feet she had ever seen. She tried hard not to think what that might mean, scale-wise.

'Whatever possessed you to call yourself Bea Pollen?' he asked suddenly.

'It's *Beatrice* Pollen, actually. It was my granny's name. Crystal didn't like me to use the name Stevie, said it sounded too much like a man. Men don't sell well, you see, and my granny always wanted to see her name on a book. So . . .'

'Oh, I see. Is Honeywell your married name then?'

'No,' said Stevie. 'I went back to my maiden name after Mick was killed.'

'What happened? Only if you want to talk aboot it,' said

Adam, twisting his position so he was sideways on to her, his arm dangerously close to her head.

'He was in a car crash. On the way to the airport.'

'Och no. Business trip?'

'No, it was most definitely pleasure,' she said with a mirthless little laugh.

Adam looked at her in a quizzical way that prodded her to go on.

'If you must know, he was running off with another woman. She was killed outright too. Apparently they didn't suffer, which I'm glad for, if you know what I mean. Whatever they did, they didn't deserve to suffer.'

'Oh God no! I'm sorry. Did you know about her?'

'I found out about a month before. I'd had my suspicions but he denied it. Then one day, he just stopped hiding her away. He would ring her in front of me, come in stinking of her. It was a nightmare time. Sometimes he was away all night, sometimes he got into bed beside me but he wouldn't let me touch him. I didn't know where I was. I was out of my skull with pain.'

'I'm no' surprised,' said Adam, who had long since stopped being shocked by the cruelty of people to each other.

'I followed him to her house once, confronted her, asked her . . . begged her to stop seeing him.' Stevie fell headfirst into the memory of that day, how she had waited outside in the car for over an hour tormenting herself with images of what they were doing together until she saw Mick leave and drive away. She had breathed deep, crossed the road and knocked hard upon the shabby peeling council-house door, determined to chase her rival away once and for all. Linda had looked through the side window to see who was at the door before brazenly appearing in a cheap and tacky negligée, the smell of sex and cigarettes and Mick hanging around her like a heavy fusty cloud.

'I pleaded, I cried, I threatened all sorts. Totally lost every bit of dignity I had,' Stevie went on. 'She just laughed and shut the door in my face, made me feel *this* big. I think I went a bit mad really.' Stevie cringed, but the wine had loosened her tongue and it felt easy to talk about it, even if she would probably recall this in the morning and want to die. 'I did everything to get him to come back, except leaving him alone to get it out of his system. I thought if I dogged him he'd give in, you see, but it got me absolutely nowhere. The only thing I had left to try was letting him get on with it and see if he came back, but I ran out of time for that one. On the day I got my pregnancy confirmed, I came back home to find him packing. He said he was leaving me to go and live in Tenerife with Linda. The car crashed on the way to the airport.'

'Oh my!' Adam's hand reached forwards and brushed her fringe back from her eyes in an instinctive and sympathetic gesture. She let him do it without slapping his hand away, which amazed him.

'Mick had remortgaged the house to raise the money to go – got Linda to fake my signature, I presume. I was in big financial trouble when it all came to light and Linda's family were going crazy. They made a huge scene at the funeral . . . it was an awful time.' Stevie gulped. 'His mum had a head-stone done, but that was destroyed and his flowers kept getting kicked over.' She recalled Mick's mother ringing up in tears, expecting Stevie to go and clear up the mess with her, shouting at her to forgive him in death, not understanding why that could be so difficult for her, considering this was all Stevie's fault.

'*If you had been more of a wife, he wouldn't have left you and he'd still be alive.*'

'I was really sick, carrying Danny at the time, and found it hard to go out to work. But I had to, there were so many debts. Mick had cancelled all the insurances, you see, and I didn't know.' Stevie managed a little smile. 'Then *Midnight Moon* came up trumps for me and gave me a chance to find my feet.'

'Do you think it would have made a difference if Mick had known about Danny?' Adam asked gently.

'He did know,' said Stevie, poking an escapee tear back inside. 'I told him, showed him the test I'd done in case he thought I was trying to trick him. He told me to get shut and send him the bill. Six hours later, he was dead.'

Adam winced. 'Do Mick's family ever see Danny then?'

'I rang when I gave birth and left a message on their answering machine telling them how ill Danny was, and that if they wanted to see him, they ought to come straight away, just in case he didn't make it. I sent them some Polaroids, but they just sent everything back with a note to say they'd pray for him.'

'Some godly faith, turning your back on a wee baby!' said Adam. Stevie shrugged. It was just one more rejection in her book.

'They blamed me for not being a strong enough wife to

keep Mick. If he hadn't been running away from me, you see, he wouldn't have had the accident, that was their reckoning.'

'What nonsense,' said Adam, shaking his head in outrage. 'How on earth could you have been to blame?'

'People need to have someone to focus their anger on, Adam. It's easier blaming outsiders than the ones you love.' Stevie's voice faded, realizing exactly what she was saying. She saw Adam shift a little uncomfortably too. Yes, it was all too easy.

'It must have been hard for you alone, with a wee baby,' he said, moving swiftly on.

'We got through,' she smiled. Looking back, she didn't know quite how, but they had.

'Ye're no' close to your own family?'

'Not really. Catherine and Eddie are my family. I'd have been lost if it hadn't been for them. That's why I feel such a failure for Danny. I wanted him to have the family life I never had. I thought we'd found it with Matthew.'

'So why Matthew? Why did you fall for Matthew?' he asked quietly.

'My ex-husband Mick was wild, live-for-the-moment, intoxicating, a one-man charm offensive. Matthew was considerate, affectionate, faithful . . .' She gave a little laugh at that last quality. 'I think I fell for what Matthew wasn't, rather than what he was, if that makes any sense. Mick exhausted me, burnt me out, stamped all over my heart, then along came steady, nice Matthew. Chalk and cheese, or so I thought.'

'They weren't really all that different though, were they?'

said Adam with his objective eye. 'From where I'm stand-ing, they were both takers in life.'

'Probably,' said Stevie, nodding. 'Anyway, I wasn't special enough for either of them in the end. I thought more of them than they did of me, if that doesn't sound like roman-tic claptrap.'

'Naw, it doesn't at all,' said Adam, thinking of Diane, of Jo, of his mother. He knew what it was like only too well to be on the begging end of love and the insanity it produced.

'So come on, why Jo? Stevie asked him. 'Why would you want someone as gorgeous and flawless as her?'

He laughed and flicked her hair, and she turned to him with her sweet, funny, smiling face and deep blue eyes. It was as if he was looking at it for the first time. It wasn't the perfect, magazine-cover face of someone like Jo; there were fine lines around her eyes to show how much she had cried and laughed and loved and lived, but Stevie Honeywell's was making his heart do flick-flacks in a way that no one else had ever made it do.

'Jo, eh? Because, if *this* doesn't sound like romantic clap-trap, Jo promised me the sort of love I've been looking for all my life. Some people just have to ability to mould them-selves to what you want. Jo was one of them.

'I was just recovering from a nasty divorce. My wife, Diane, had run off with her boss. You know the type: thirty years older than her, Satsuma tan, married of course, owned the company. If that wasn't enough, she then tried to get half of everything I had, too. I went a bit mad masel'. Actually, I shouldnae really be telling you this after what you thought of me.'

'Oh, go on,' she said, poking his arm with her finger.

'I got a solicitor's letter saying she was entitled to half of everything. So rather than sell the stuff, I started to halve it with a chainsaw.'

'Half of everything? I'll give you half!' he had roared, when she finally confessed that all those late nights hadn't been down to 'finishing a project' after all. He'd started to divide their furniture all right. He'd got as far as slicing two dining-room chairs down the middle then realized he was scaring himself more than he was Diane.

'No!' said Stevie, horrified but sympathetic.

'Yes. I regret my outburst now. Only because she ran off with my wee cat, though – och he was great, I loved him a load. She took him and then she gave him away, can you believe? She just didnae want me to have him. Diane was so cold, and then along came Jo with her "vulnerability" and her soft words, just when I needed them most.' As he was telling this to Stevie, Adam realized just how much of a gift Jo had when it came to manipulating men. She had played to his insecurities; that initial warmth she had used to reel him in had chilled by a few degrees every day to keep him interested, to keep him on the begging end of her attention. 'The rest, as they say, is history.'

'Crap at picking partners, aren't we?' said Stevie. 'I once went out with a policeman who was knocking off grannies behind my back.'

'I can beat that. My first proper girlfriend said she wouldn't sleep with me unless I covered my hair up with a shower cap.'

'I can understand that, though.'

'Och, you cheeky wee . . .'

He leapt on her playfully and she shrieked with laughter, and suddenly the words and sounds dropped away because there was no more need for them, and his hands were cradling her face, and his lips started an achingly slow descent to hers as if he was scared she would push him away, but she didn't. Her heart was pumping some weird chemical around her system that was making her drunk with smiley feelings. The air around them was still as if it too was holding its breath. Adam's lips brushed Stevie's teasingly and she thought she was going to explode if they didn't come into land, like *now*.

Then someone knocked on the bloody door, and kept knocking.

Chapter 51

'Matthew, whatever's the matter?' asked Stevie, forced to answer the door before he bashed it down. He looked terrible: bleached and distressed, and his hair was stuck up like Ken Dodd's.

'Can I have a quiet word, Stevie?' He looked past Stevie to Adam, who melted into the background, leaving them to it.

'What is it?'

'Can you come across the road, please?'

Stevie looked horrified at him. 'Over there? No, I can't. Why?'

'Jo and I are finished.'

'What?' Stevie's head started swimming with shock.

She looked behind her. Adam wasn't there, but she knew he must have heard what Matthew had just said. She wanted to go and find him, and see what that piece of information had done to him. Then again she didn't. *Jo was free. It was obvious what it would mean to him.*

'Please, Stevie!'

Despite the frustration in her heart and her body, she couldn't say no. She couldn't have deserted anyone in that state. Except Jo, maybe. She could make an exception in her case.

She slipped on her shoes, took another look behind her and followed Matthew across the road.

'I don't want to go in there,' she said, as he opened up the door.

'Please. There's no way she'll be coming here again,' he said, and disappeared inside. Cautiously, she went in behind him, feeling a prickle at the back of her neck as if Adam was watching her.

It felt odd to be in the house. It was as if she had never lived there, but remembered it from old photos. It was horribly untidy and there was a film of dust everywhere that gave the room a dull, dead appearance. She half-expected to see Miss Haversham covered in cobwebs sitting in the wing chair with a big spidery wedding cake.

'Stevie, I'm sorry, I just don't have anywhere else to turn.' He was walking up and down in front of her, over-dosed with nervous energy.

'Matthew, sit down, please. Start from the beginning.'

'I don't know where the beginning of this mess is. I've been sacked. Jo's left me. I came home today and all her stuff had gone. I don't know what to do.'

Stevie gulped. Jo had left him. Would she try to come back to Adam then? Would she walk straight back into that soft, forgiving part of his heart that was forever reserved for her? Stevie felt panicky and wanted to go back to the cottage. She stood up to go, but then Matthew started to make strange groaning noises and she knew she couldn't leave him.

'Why have you been sacked, Matthew?'

'For harassing Jo. Yes, don't look at me like that. I know what you're going to say.'

'I don't understand.'

'I think Jo has been spreading stories at work that I've been hitting her.'

'You hitting her?' Anyone who knew Matthew would-n't believe that, surely. Then again, people judged on hearsay – wasn't she herself testament to that?

'It gets worse. I'm also, apparently, a sexual predator.'

'Why would she say things like that?'

'I think she got the idea that I had more money than I actually have.' He looked shifty at that point. 'When she found out I was broke, things changed. She started . . . *Oh God! That's why!*'

Matthew slapped his forehead as the realization of what all that rough sex was about hit him like a bullet to the brain. *The bruises! That was why she wanted him to bite her. How thick was he not to have seen it?*

'What, Matthew?'

'She started asking me for . . .' *What a knob I am!*

'For what?'

Matthew blanched. This really wasn't the sort of thing Stevie should hear. But he was desperate, and to get the right sort of help, he needed to tell her everything. Just as if she was a sort of heart bank manager in the mould of Robert.

'Rough sex. She wanted me to hurt her.'

Stevie shifted a little uncomfortably. It felt weird, listen-ing to details of his intimacies with someone else. She couldn't tell if it hurt; her feelings were too mixed-up to pick out any pure emotions.

'And did you?'

'No, of course not! Although . . .'

'What?' she encouraged eventually, after no details were forthcoming.

'I gave her a love bite, here' – he indicated the place on his own chest – 'it looked pretty nasty. But it wasn't a real bite. And we both got a few bruises from banging into walls and falling off the bed and things. I'm not into that pain stuff, as you know.'

'But why tell all those lies? Why didn't she just leave you?' asked Stevie, steering the conversation away from the history of their own sex-life.

'I don't know.'

Unless she had a new lover. Wasn't that what she had done to Adam? Invent cuts and bruises to get the new sucker onside? thought Stevie, in full-on Miss Marple mode.

'What are you thinking?' said Matthew. He was half-talking, half-hiccuping like Danny did when he was upset.

'Have you tried ringing her?'

'She's not answering.'

'No, she wouldn't,' Stevie said, sourly.

'I've just secured my house against my job. I'll lose everything.'

'Why have you done that?'

Matthew sighed and prepared to sacrifice a big chunk of pride.

'I've got no money, Stevie. No, actually, I've got minus no money. I'm up to my neck in debt.'

And so you took Jo on holiday. With my son's holiday money, Stevie thought, but she didn't say it aloud. However much he might have deserved it, she couldn't kick Matt when he was down. And he was about as down as you could get, by the look of things.

'Please stay with me for a bit longer,' he said, as she looked eagerly across the road and saw a light switch off. 'Just ten minutes. Stevie, I've been so stupid. I'm not even sure she was telling the truth about Adam now. Maybe he didn't hit her or do all those things she said he did.'

'I'm quite positive she lied,' said Stevie. 'He's a good man.'

'Can I make you a coffee?' he said, noticing the wistfulness in her voice and therefore changing the subject. He did not want to know how good Adam MacLean was, because Matthew didn't feel like a very good man himself.

'Just a quick one then,' said Stevie, who didn't want one, but couldn't bear to see someone so lost. Matthew had a long sleepless lonely night in front of him; ten more minutes in his company wouldn't kill her.

'You can help me, Stevie. I hate to ask but you are the only one who could.'

'In what way?' she asked cautiously, in case he wanted her to be some intermediary between him and Bitchface.

'Can you tell them at work that I'm not violent?' he snuffled. 'I'll never work again if they think I'm a sexual predator. I can't stand it that people are thinking that about me.'

And because Stevie had once been accused of apple

scrumping at school and couldn't bear to see injustice, she said that she would.

When she went back to the cottage, only one light was on and Adam had gone to bed. She knocked gently on his door, but he was obviously asleep and didn't answer.

His plan had worked, after all. Jo was free. There was nothing stopping him going to her.

Stevie didn't think she could bear it.

Adam was awake, tracing the sounds of her footsteps up the stairs, her soft knock on his bedroom door, and he wanted so much to say, 'I'm here, come into my room. Come into my bed,' but he didn't answer. So it looked as if his plan had worked, after all. Matthew was free and with one click of *his* fingers, he had managed to get her over the road again. She had leapt out of Adam's arms to go to him. The sand in his hourglass had run out. Matthew was free. There was nothing stopping her going back to him.

Adam didn't think he could bear it.

Chapter 52

Adam had left for the day by the time she had got up the next morning. He must have crept out, Stevie reasoned, because she hadn't heard a thing. In a panic she tore into his bedroom and threw open his wardrobe, but his clothes were still there and she almost wanted to sob with relief. Then she rang Catherine and asked if Danny had been okay. Catherine told her that he had trotted off to school with the others as happy as Larry, and she was going to pick him up as well because Eddie had promised he could go over to the allotment with Boot and Chico, the two dogs, and dig his mum out some veg. Stevie was to come for him after tea at six, and if she even tried to take him away earlier she would be in big trouble with everyone. Then Stevie told her she was the best friend in the world, and Catherine said she knew and demanded chocolates every day of her life, and every single detail of Adam MacLean's willy, if she ever got them. Stevie laughed aloud for the benefit of her friend, but inside she felt hollow, because she knew she never would.

She wrote a text to Adam, asking him if he was okay and could she ring him. Then she deleted it before sending. It was only fair to give him time to come to terms with Jo being available. Of course, Jo would hurt him again, but he loved her and she was his for the taking; Stevie knew that from all the jealous looks Jo had cast her at the barbecue. Adam needed space; all men did. According to *Men are from Mars*, anyway.

She went over to Matthew's house at nine-thirty as she said she would. The sunlight didn't do him or the house any favours. He hadn't slept, that was obvious. Or shaved, or showered.

'Who do I need to ask for?' said Stevie, picking up the phone.

'Colin Seed. He's Head of Personnel. He's been giving me the evil eye. Obviously hates my guts.'

'What's he like?' said Stevie.

'Rich, mid-forties, looks seventy, fat, 1982 trousers, eyebrows that vultures could nest in, jowly, drives a Bentley, lives in a big house. He'll be the next CEO in a year, if they don't ship him over to New York now that his mother's carked it,' said Matthew bitterly.

'Rich, did you say?'

'Loaded.'

'And this evil eye – can I make a guess that it's happened quite recently?' said Stevie, her brain downloading info faster than high-speed Broadband.

'Yes. Do you think that's relevant?'

'I think it may be,' said Stevie, and picked up the phone.

An hour and a half later, Stevie had just got out of Matthew's car and was walking across the forecourt to the entrance of 'Doyle International Foods' by the Leeds canal. It was a hip, buzzing, colourful place, full of vitality and people who looked happy enough to be working there. She booked herself in at Reception, under the name Ms B. Pollen, her business with the Head of Personnel being research for her latest book. She had told Colin's secretary on the phone that she only wanted five minutes of his time, and the secretary, who was an avid *Midnight Moon* fan, had pushed her in a free eleven o'clock slot, on the proviso that she would autograph her copy of *Golden Bride*.

The secretary collected her from Reception and was twitteringly delighted to meet her in the flesh. After Stevie had autographed the well-thumbed book, she was shown through to Colin Seed's huge corner office, overlooking the canal. It was a very neat, modest office; the office of a man who obviously liked straight lines and things ordered and above board. Minutes later, when Colin Seed walked in, Stevie caught an imaginary whiff of mothballs. It was a shame really, because he wasn't a bad-looking man at all. The love of a good, caring woman could easily have transformed him.

'Ms Pollen,' said Colin, with a strong handshake but a surprisingly warm smile too that knocked a good fifteen years off his age. He gestured to Stevie to sit down. 'How can I help you? I'm very intrigued.' He did not say that his recently deceased mum used to read *Midnight Moon* books, and that the last one she had read was by Beatrice Pollen. That alone had won her court with him today.

'Mr Seed,' began Stevie, tremulously because Colin had a strong persona and she felt way out of her depth here. 'I confess, I'm here under false pretences. Yes, I *am* Beatrice Pollen, but I'm not here about any research. Please forgive my duplicity. I'm here about,' Stevie gulped, 'Matthew Finch.'

Stevie watched Colin Seed's welcoming smile elope with the warmth in his eyes, and his Adam's apple jump up and down like a fairground test-your-strength machine. However, he surprised her by saying, 'Go on.'

'I'm Matthew's ex-partner. I understand he's been sacked for harassing an ex-friend of mine,' the name stuck in her craw, 'Joanna MacLean.'

'Amongst other things, yes, that is correct,' Colin answered, stiffening before her eyes.

'I'm here on my own volition, after I heard the news. Matthew is not a sexual predator. Jo MacLean, however, is an incredibly devious wom—'

'Thank you, Ms Pollen, but I really do not think this is a matter for discussion with an outside body.' Colin rose, preparing to show Stevie out, but Stevie stood her ground, or rather sat it, and continued to speak. She felt sure now that Colin Seed was personally, as well as professionally involved with Jo MacLean.

'Please hear me out, Mr Seed, then I will go quietly, but there is too much at stake here for me to leave before I have said what I came here to say. I happen to know Jo MacLean's ex-partner very well too, a lovely, respectable, gentle man – a Mr Adam MacLean – the local Father Christmas for the hospital. He first met her in a car park, crying that she was in a violent relationship . . .'

'Ms Pollen . . .'

'. . . and though not "rich" rich, he's comfortably well off. Then Matthew, Head of Concessions, high-flyer here caught her eye and she was led, I think, to believe that he was quite rich. Surprise, surprise, when did he first start talking to her? In the car park here, crying that she was in a violent relationship and needed to get away. Funnily enough, that relationship started to sour round about the time that she discovered he made church mice look like members of the Getty family. That, for your information, was very recently.'

Colin looked as if he was going to interrupt again, but stayed silent.

'Then suddenly, Matthew is accused of being violent and predatory, and loses his job. Now, I was very hurt when he left me, so much so that I could have let him rot in this mess, but I can't stand back and watch someone's life be destroyed by malicious lies. Matthew Finch might be guilty of many things, but I'd stake my life on it that sexual violence wouldn't *ever* be one of them.'

Colin Seed was processing the information. He was using his professionally trained brain to study body language and voice inflections, sifting for lies and truths.

'One more thing, Mr Seed,' said Stevie with an air of innocence. 'I'd deduce from Jo MacLean's modus operandi that she has probably found a new partner. A sitting target with a nice house and plenty of money. Someone who happens to meet a crying Jo MacLean in a car park with a heart full of sob stories about her violent ex. She'll probably show them a supposed boot mark on her left thigh that Matthew did. In the same way that she showed it to

Matthew and told him Adam did it, and in the same way she showed it to Adam and attributed it to the violence of the ex before that.'

Stevie had only guessed that Jo would have done that to Colin, but from his small cough, she knew she had guessed right. Colin seemed to pale before her very eyes. She felt quite guilty that she was the one to bear the news that would probably break his heart.

'I understand you've had a recent loss,' said Stevie tentatively.

'Ms Poll . . . I don't see . . .'

'Sometimes when we're in pain, we'll snatch at anything that promises to stop it. Hope makes us see what we want to see.'

'I really must end . . .'

'All I'm saying is that if something appears too good to be true, it's probably because it is.'

Colin Seed gulped. That was one of his mother's sayings and as such, it resonated loudly within him.

'I won't take up any more of your time, Mr Seed. I thank you for agreeing to meet me. Please think about what I've said,' and with a gentle, caring smile, Stevie added, 'And good luck.'

There was a nerve ticking in Colin's neck, Stevie noticed. He nodded goodbye as if his throat was constricted and held his hand out towards her. Stevie shook that hand, warmly with both of hers, and then she left and closed the door quietly behind her.

As she walked out of the building via the revolving door, Jo MacLean came in from the opposite side. As if in slow motion, they turned to stare at each other. For once, Jo's eyes had none of that victorious haughtiness in them. Stevie's cocksure presence in her workplace unsettled her greatly. She hadn't bargained on Matthew finding a champion after her claims, because no one wanted to stick up for a sex beast. Least of all a disgruntled ex!

Stevie fought down the impulse to double-back, grab the bitch by the hair and proclaim it to the busy atrium of people just what a life-wrecker Miss Gorgeous Body really was, but instead, she held onto her dignity, turned her head away and walked out into the fresh air of the day. Let someone else clear up the rest of this mess now; she was done with it.

Outside, sitting in his car, Matthew watched Jo MacLean strut towards the offices like an arrogant peacock. He almost didn't recognize her, for there was little resemblance to the soft and fragile woman he had met that day in the car park. She looked cold and proud and hard. He didn't even think her very beautiful any more; she was a stranger to him. Then, seconds later, he saw the familiar unchanging form of Stevie emerge from the building and he automatically smiled. The sunlight had lodged in her hair and she looked like an angel coming towards the car. That's what Stevie was, an angel. A lovely, sweet, golden-hearted angel.

He drove home, unable to stop beaming gratefully over at Stevie and saying that he couldn't thank her enough. Stevie nodded, but didn't say much. She just wanted Matthew to stick his foot down and for her to be home. With Adam.

*

When she got to Humbleby Cottage, Adam was gone, and so were his clothes. There was a note on the table that said *Dear Stevie, We both need some time to think. I will be in touch. Love to Danny, goodbye – Adam.*

Her eyes bloomed with tears, as once again she thought, How final goodbye sounds.

Chapter 53

Of course, Adam had lied. He didn't need any time. He knew what he wanted but he had to get out of the way and not complicate things for Stevie. She had waited so patiently for Matthew to come back to her and now she had him. So how could he upset all that for her by declaring his feelings now?

He pushed the door open to his house – only a house, never his *home*. It was so chilled and without heart, warmth, laughter or little boy's mess. There was no Mr Greengrass Head on the windowsill, no comfy clutter of pens or books with clocks-and-moons motifs on the covers. There were no clouds of flour billowing from the kitchen and no monster pans of chilli on the hob. He had never liked this house, but now he hated it. It was big and bare and echoey, and the memories stored within its walls were cold and hollow. He would ring the estate agent that afternoon and get it on the market. Then he would award himself some time off work so he didn't bump into Stevie.

Stevie.

Adam MacLean dropped himself on the cold leather sofa and thought of the softness of her face as he held it,

remembered how she had gulped as he stared into her eyes
and how his heart had trembled when her lips had touched
his. He had never loved anyone in this way before, with a
depth that made cheap parodies of all the other times he
thought he had been in love. Stevie deserved to be happy,
and he so much wanted her to be happy – with him or
without him. And it looked as if it was going to be without him.

At that thought, big fierce boxer-faced Adam MacLean's
head fell forwards into his hands. He didn't stop the tears
when they came.

Chapter 54

Jo sat in her bedroom in the Queens Hotel staring into her compact mirror as she applied a slick smear of lipstick. Was that a line appearing under her eye? she wondered. It was becoming more and more urgent to hook a rich fish who would be able to finance her fight against the ravages of time. Beauty was a talent on a timer.

Suddenly Jo lauched the compact across the room, smashing it against the wall. She didn't even think of clearing it up. Any mess outside the boundary of Jo's clothes was of no consequence. She was interested in nothing but the fulfilment of her own needs.

'Damn you, Stevie Fucking Honeywell,' she snarled. Had it not been for that short, fat cow she would be in Colin's lovely oak-panelled house now, being petted and fussed over, and not in the cheapest room in a glory-faded hotel paid for by pawned jewellery. Or better still, she would be with Adam. He wasn't as rich as Colin, by far, and no one was more surprised than her to realize that it didn't seem to matter. Jo MacLean's mantra had always been, 'Happiness doesn't bring you money.'

There was a two-day Porsche business convention going

in the hotel, and a wealth of suits spilled into the large reception area, the wine garden, the bars and restaurant. Jo slipped on a plain black dress that emphasized her long, slim body, the cut of it adding the illusion of curves. She had never failed to 'pull' in that dress.

But before she explored the potential downstairs, there was one final thing she needed to do. She couldn't just leave it there with Adam and Stevie. If she couldn't have what she wanted, then why the fuck should they?

Jo MacLean picked up her pen.

Chapter 55

On the last day at work before his self-imposed break, Adam's hand stilled on the envelope in the middle of the pile of post in his office at Well Life. There was no stamp on it, so it had obviously been hand-delivered for maximum effect. He knew the beautiful precise writing with the artistic loops well. He should have thrown it out, but curiosity got the better of him. It was Jo at her manipulative best.

Dearest Adam, whatever you think about receiving this from me, grant me one final kindness and read it to the end, I beg you.

They were iron words, cushioned in a velvet glove of girly curls. *I'm so sorry I hurt you . . . I will always care for you . . . I have to say this . . .* He didn't want to read it, but the masochistic part of him couldn't rip his eyes away from the hypnotic soft swirls of ink.

She put it oh so beautifully, how he could never be right for Stevie because he would never conform to her dull, vain type . . . *and you deserve to find someone who will love you for the strong, selfless, unique, big personality that you are.* She said that playing happy families with Stevie and Danny was a mere illusion, because Stevie's own horrid experiences with step-parents would never allow him to be really accepted unless he were perfect. She was saying this to be kind, of course. *Darling Adam, you were the best thing that ever happened to me and I shall always regret my stupid mistake at falling for the lies of another. I still love you and if you ever change your mind, I will drop everything and come to you. Be happy, you wonderful man. Jo x.*

He read the letter through to the end and the words continued to sting him long after he had ripped it up and thrown it into the bin. Adam MacLean might have known his *basic psychology* well, but Jo MacLean was a past master.

Stevie found the letter on the welcome mat. It had been hand-delivered and bore her name in extravagant script on the front. There was a friendly little smiling face drawn in the final 'e' to lend it affection. Stevie didn't want to open it, but its very presence gave her no choice.

Dearest Stevie, I know you will never forgive me but please allow me this one act of genuine friendship and read this letter to the end . . .

The words were exquisitely put, needles embedded in cotton wool. She knew this, but still she read on. *Adam is using you . . . he never stopped loving me . . . He invited me to the gym to talk about a reconciliation . . . He told me evil things you had said about me . . . I so regret believing him and scratching your car in temper . . .*

Stevie gasped. She remembered the day well. Why else would Jo have been at the gym, if not to talk to Adam?

Be careful of little Danny's heart . . . as you know only too well, dear friend, step-families are doomed to fail. Jo told her how Adam's 'type' would always be tall, beautiful, thin, dark-haired women, and how Stevie needed to find some-one to love her for the *wonderful curvy sunshiney woman* that she was. *You deserve so much more than any of us. You were the best friend I ever had and I shall always think of you with a smile. I so much regret that you will never be able to do the same for me. Be happy, darling Stevie. Kindest regards and love – Jo x.*

Stevie ripped the letter up, but the words left a poison deep in her heart and there was no one on hand to suck it out for her.

Chapter 56

Catherine snuggled up to Eddie's big body under the thin cotton sheet. There was a light breeze ruffling the curtain, blowing cool and gentle onto their skin. They only needed a cheesecake and it would have been heaven.

'Can't believe after all these years you're still that good in bed,' said Catherine.

'Is that a compliment or not?' laughed Eddie, slapping her on the backside.

Catherine sighed. If she could, she would have split her bliss and given half to Stevie. She was functioning day to day but Catherine wasn't fooled. Her friend was an automaton, an empty shell bravely guarding the remnants of a heart that was smashed to pieces.

As if reading her thoughts, Eddie asked her, 'How's Stevie getting on?'

'You know Stevie,' said Catherine. 'She's stuck a smile on for the outside world and says she's fine, but I can tell she's not good. Not good at all.'

'I reckon Matt will try and get back with her.'

'Probably,' said Catherine. She didn't voice it, but that's what she was afraid of. Stevie and Adam MacLean might have been the world's unlikeliest couple but there was something sparking between them that she doubted they even knew was there. She didn't want Matt to slip weakly back into her best friend's life. She wanted that big, strong Gaelic man to confess his undying love and live happily ever after with Stevie and Danny in that beautiful cottage.

'I wish there was something I could do,' she said absently.

'You keep out of it,' said Eddie with as stern a voice as he could muster.

'I'm not the keeping-out-of-it type.'

'Force yourself,' said Eddie.

'I wish Stevie could find what we've got,' said Catherine with a heavy sigh. 'Well, maybe not all seven kids.'

'Talking of kids, I saw Rip Van Winkle today,' said Eddie. 'I said "By heck, James, it's Saturday afternoon, what are you doing up?" And by the way, we've only got six.'

'Aye, well, remember the night of Pam's wedding, when you got all frisky dancing your big meaty legs off to that Birds and Bees dance and then came home and gave me what-for . . .'

'Yes, I most certainly do,' said Eddie with a big beam. 'I wasn't bad, was I, if I say so myself.'

'Well, you left a bit of you in here.'

Eddie sat up in bed. 'You're never!'

'I flaming am!'

He threw his arms around his wife and squashed her to bits.

'Bloody fantastic,' he said with a grin that stretched so far across his face, his lips nearly joined around the back of his head. He took her hand and kissed the back of it tenderly. 'Mrs Flanagan, I love you. You're chuffing magic.'

'Well, if magic has got anything to do with it, let's send some of it on,' said Catherine, and laid her own kiss on top of Eddie's, then blew it in the direction of Stevie's house. Surely not even Eddie could rebuke her for interfering in Stevie's life on that plain.

Chapter 57

A week had passed when the loud knock landed on Stevie's door and her heart started racing as she rushed to open it. It dropped like a stone though to find Matthew standing there; nevertheless, she formed a small, welcoming smile, which was roughly a quarter the size of his own.

'I've got some great news!' he said, angling for an invite.

And Stevie being Stevie, she said, 'Come in.'

'Is er . . .?'

'No,' said Stevie, anticipating what he was going to ask. 'Adam doesn't live here any more.'

Matthew's smile suddenly got a bit wider.

'Coffee?' said Stevie, because it would have been rude not to.

'Yes, please,' he said, because it would give him an excuse to stay a little longer. 'Lovely cottage,' he commented, looking around. Not only lovely but also shining and polished and clean, and there was that indefinable something in it that turned a house into a home. His house didn't have it any more. It hadn't had it since Stevie left.

'Yes, it is lovely,' she said quietly. She would be sorry to say goodbye to it too, so sorry. So many times she had picked up the phone to ring Adam on the pretext of asking him when she needed to get out of the cottage, only to put it down again in case Jo picked it up. He would be a fool to have gone back to her, but Jo MacLean was like a flame to men and she attracted the sorts of hearts that could not stop themselves burning their fragile moth-wings many times against her. Adam must have taken her back; why else would he have left and not been in touch?

'Sorry I've not been across before, but it's been a mad week,' said Matthew.

'Oh yes?' said Stevie, barely realizing how many days had passed. She had locked herself away in her office when Danny wasn't around, occupying all thought-space with Damme and Evie, because she did not want to think of her own empty life.

'I've been offered my old job back!' said Matthew.

'Good, I'm pleased,' said Stevie.

'But . . .' He left a dramatic pause. 'I'm not taking it.'

'Why ever not?'

'Because I've decided I'm going to have a fresh start. I'm selling the house and clearing some of my debts with the equity, and then I'm moving to London. I've got interviews lined up and I've found a flat, sharing with some other people. It's cheap and cheerful but it will do nicely until I get back on my feet. I've made too many mistakes here and I want to get away. And by way of an unofficial apology, Doyles are giving me three months' paid leave and they've wangled me a tax-free bonus. I hear it was old Seedy who came through for me in the end, can you believe?'

'Yes, I can believe it,' said Stevie. He had looked a decent man. One who must be hurting terribly at the moment too.

'He's going to live in New York apparently.'

'Good. A fresh start for him too. And . . . Jo?' asked Stevie, although she still had difficulty saying the name.

'*Got flattened by a stray meteorite, died an agonizing slow death*.'

Okay, so she imagined that.

'No one knows. She didn't turn in for work the day after you went into the office and hasn't been back since.'

Adam hadn't been seen either. He hadn't been working at the gym. They were obviously together. Maybe they had gone off on holiday – after all, isn't that what couples did to escape the trail of devastated hearts they left behind – run off to the sun? Not that it mattered really, for the words of Jo's letter had stung her hard and deep. Even with no Jo MacLean on the scene, Adam's heart wasn't going to be fulfilled by a short, lumpy woman and someone else's kid.

'Apparently Colin looked rough for a couple of days after your meeting,' said Matthew. 'Someone said he was caught crying in his off—' A five-ton penny dropped. 'Hey, you don't think Jo and Colin . . . do you?'

'I'm almost sure of it, Matthew.' Stevie had been instrumental in that avenue of escape being closed to Jo, which would almost definitely have driven her back to Adam as a safe haven. She shooed that thought away and turned her attentions back to Matthew. 'So how come you know what happened at work?'

'Well, people started ringing me again – once the truth filtered out that I wasn't a psycho-woman batterer. I think they felt a bit guilty about believing the stories and tried to over-compensate. Anyway, I got some presents and good luck cards in the post and I'm meeting my department for a night out before I move.'

'I'm glad for you, Matthew, I really am. I hope you enjoy London.'

'Unless you . . . er . . .' Matthew stumbled. Stevie looked up into his eyes. They were soft, brown, warm and open, and he was looking nervously at her like the first time he had dared to ask her out.

'Unless of course you didn't want me to g-go and . . .' he stuttered on.

Stevie gulped. This was the moment she had been waiting for. Adam's plan had come through for her too, it seemed. So why wasn't she hearing brass bands playing in her heart? There was nothing but the faint piercing sound of retreating bagpipes.

That week she had finally faced up to the fact that her love for Matthew had started to die as soon as Adam showed her the holiday confirmation; its roots had been wrenched out with the break of trust. She knew she had clung on blindly to the fantasy that it was still a plant alive and growing because a buried but determined part of her wanted to win Matthew back from Jo, to make up for the fact that she had lost Mick to Linda. She wanted so much to see him as the strong, reliable bloke her heart was waiting for. But he wasn't that man. Someone else was.

'No, I don't suppose . . . you would, would you? C-consider – you . . . me – again?'

'No, Matthew.' She answered him in a kind voice

because there had been too many hearts broken, too many emotional casualties.

'I was a thick twat,' he said with genuine frustration. 'My grass was lovely and green and I went looking for better stuff and ended up with Astroturf.'

She hoped his next job wasn't going to be writing romantic fiction, because he just might give her a run for her money with lines like that.

Matthew looked at her, her spun-gold hair, her lovely blue eyes, warmth and nice-person radiating out from her in waves, and once again he could not believe he had let her go. Ironically, her strength in saying, 'No' to him made him want her even more, but her eyes were only looking back at him as if he was ordinary. They weren't registering that he was special any more. They looked at Adam MacLean quite differently, he had noticed. Jim Bowen's voice welled up in his head with the Bull's-eye tune playing in a minor key: *Look at what you could have won.*

'It's him, isn't it – Adam? You really fell for him then?'

'Yes, Matthew, hook, line and sinker.'

'I thought you were just joking at first, you know. You'll laugh but I thought it was all a sort of plan to get us jealous.' He laughed at how stupid that seemed now. As if! 'So what happened?'

'I don't know,' she shrugged. 'I presume Adam and Jo are together somewhere, planning a new start. I haven't seen or heard from him since . . . well, since . . .'

'Since I came round that night, by any chance?' Matthew said, his shoulders scrunching up with shame and embarrassment. Stevie didn't answer; she couldn't. There was a big lump in her throat, and there was no Adam around to perform a Heimlich manoeuvre on her to shift it.

'I'm sorry,' he said apologetically. 'I seem to have developed rather a habit of wrecking your life.'

For once she didn't say her customary kind, 'No, don't be silly,' to let him off the hook. Matthew knew, by that, just how deeply he had hurt her. The sooner he got to London the better. Maybe there he would finally grow up.

'When the house is sold, I'll give you some money from it to cover Danny's holiday and of course the wedding costs. I'm sorry, Stevie. I've been a total bastard. I look at myself and I don't like what I've become. I used to think I was a good bloke. I don't want to be this Matthew. I want to get right away from him.'

'When do you leave?' she asked.

'Next week – got to pack up the stuff I need and get rid of the rest. Might even do a car boot sale.'

'You can earn quite a bit on those.'

'Hey, remember when we did that one, that freezing Sunday morning?'

'Yes, I remember,' she said, smiling a little at an old faded memory, of a time when they were happy. A lifetime ago. Those two people didn't exist any more though.

Matthew was viewing the same memory, although his mind glasses had deeper rose-shaded lenses at the moment: snapshots of them eating burgers at eight o'clock in the morning just to keep warm; the old woman bartering them down from thirty to twenty pence for a leather wallet; the man in the Shredded Wheat wig they'd tried so hard not to giggle at. Stevie had been so sweet, so much fun. He hoped there would be another Stevie in London to meet.

'Thanks, Stevie, you're a diamond and I owe you big time,' he said, and he threw his arms around her and hugged her for the last time. She wasn't as pliant as he remembered. She didn't melt against him and envelop him in her affection. But then, she wasn't his any more.

'Goodbye, Matthew, and good luck,' she said, and kissed his cheek, and though she smiled, the light seemed to have gone from her eyes. He wished, at least, he could put that back there for her.

That afternoon, Adam MacLean was watching something mindless on the television about doing up gardens hosted by a woman with jolly features and wayward breasts, as he imagined Stevie's would be in that garb. He'd always gone for women with scraps of meat on their bones, like his mother, but Stevie had a bottom he wanted to bite lumps out of. She was so soft and curvy and warm, but Jo's words in the letter had haunted him. Stevie would want more for herself and her son than a 'unique' (i.e. ugly) man who made noise wherever he went.

He knew he would have to speak to her soon about the arrangements for the cottage, but he was scared he would turn the corner and see her back in Matthew's house, and find Humbleby Cottage lying as empty as his heart felt. He would have to face it, but not now. Just a few more days until he found the strength to look her in the eye, wish her all the luck and happiness in the world, let her go for ever.

He looked around at the cold, characterless room and

decided that he really needed to clean up. The house hadn't been vacuumed in days, nor had the dishwasher been switched on. Then again, there had been no plates to wash because he hadn't been eating. He had managed to drag himself to the shower, but not over to the shaving mirror. He looked half-wild with his auburn stubble and flat, tired eyes. He caught sight of his reflection in the smoky glass of the display cabinet and decided he wouldn't have liked to meet himself up a dark alley.

He ignored the first 'bing bong' of the doorbell, as he wasn't in the mood for visitors. After the fifth bing bong, he thought he had better address the irritation and get rid of it by telling them that, no, he didn't want to convert to their religion, thanks, he was quite happy being a Satanist. No, he didn't want to sponsor them, vote for them, buy their windows, look at their brochure or convert his energy supplies. He had no energy to convert.

The fuzzy shape that he saw through the glass was a man's, and when he opened the door, it was to a rather pale-looking Matthew.

'Hi,' his unexpected visitor said with a big gulp and a hand held up in a 'how'-like greeting. 'I realize you might want to murder me, but before you do, can I please tell you something?'

Chapter 58

Stevie dropped Danny off at school then picked up some empty boxes from the Happy Shopper en route to home. As she opened the cottage door, silence greeted her and the quiet was uncomfortably deafening in a way that Adam's noise could never be. She missed his big, booming voice more each day. She missed seeing his cavernous sports bag by the door. She missed his boxers on the washing line. She missed the heavy tread of his large feet on the stairs, the way he crashed through doors and blasted out 'Flowers of Scotland' at three billion decibels in the shower. She missed everything about the man. And Danny's insistent question-ing didn't help. *Where's Adam? When is he coming back? Will he be back tonight?* He hadn't asked half as many questions over Matthew or Mick combined. It seemed that her little boy was hurting as much as she was.

Her mind had taken her to some horrible places that week – to Majorca, spying on Jo, in her white size-10 bikini and blissfully stretched out at the side of Adam in the sun. She wished she could wish she had never laid eyes on the man, but then she might never have discovered she had the capacity to love to that tremendous depth. This had been no love on the sidelines that made compromises, this had been a fall into an abyss out of which she had never wanted to crawl.

She hoped Matthew would find contentment down south, although she knew deep down that he would. She hoped Colin Seed would enjoy his new life in New York and find someone he could love and look after who would drag him into Burtons occasionally. And most of all she hoped Jo would realize what she had nearly lost and take better care of Adam's beautiful big heart. Stevie found out that true love made it possible to let someone go to be happy with another.

She started to put books into one of the boxes until her eyes clouded over so much that she couldn't see what she was doing. She'd gone and fallen for Humbleby too, and having to leave it would half-kill her. It sounded stupid, but the cottage felt 'sad' that she would be going soon, as if it had been lonely in its enforced long emptiness and had rather enjoyed having a funny little boy, an incurable romantic and a rather loud Gaelic giant enjoying its warmth and protection.

She was going mad, obviously, thinking about old houses having feelings. What next? Imagining the dishwasher sobbing as it scrubbed the pots clean? She needed to get out. Somewhere in the presence of other human beings doing something that would bat these ridiculous notions of emotional inanimate objects out of her head. Filling up her water bottle, she grabbed her gym card and car keys and headed out to Well Life.

★

Stevie looked at the calorie counter. Apparently, she had burnt up 350 of them in the last hour and she still wasn't tired, but then her body didn't feel connected to her head. Her legs were pounding but her brain wasn't giving out any messages for them to stop. It was too busy blotting everything out. It wasn't connected to her ears either so it didn't hear the track 'Loneliness' playing once again and it wasn't connected to her eyes so she didn't see the screens showing MTV and *Morning Coffee* in front of her. Nor did she see Adam MacLean walking up the side of the StairMasters either.

Not until she saw a big, hairy arm put a small jeweller's box on the water-bottle shelf and heard that big thunderous voice of his saying, 'Ah hear you've fallen for me hook, line and sinker, woman,' was she even remotely aware of his presence. And in shock, she lost her footing, cracked her head on the control panel and did the sort of backwards flip that would have knocked the Romanian gymnasts off the Gold Medal spot in the Olympics.

Chapter 59

'So once again I make a complete prat of myself in front of everyone because of you,' she said in his office as he applied a bag of ice to the fast-growing egg-shaped lump. 'Ow, ow, ow!'

'Wheesht, woman.'

'And if vibrating me off the machine with your voice wasn't enough fun for you, you give me an empty box as well!'

'Course it's empty. I just wanted to see what your reaction would be.'

'You are a sadist. I was right all along.'

'Not at all. Choosing a ring is an important matter. I'd only have got something with too many diamonds on it.'

'Is there such a thing?'

He smiled a little and had a good look at the lump. 'I think this might hatch at any minute.'

'Anyway, what did you mean by you've heard that I've fallen for you hook, line and sinker? Which mentally deranged nutter could possibly have told you that?'

'Stop moving your head, woman! Matthew came to see

me earlier. Very brave in the circumstances. Said I was an idiot if I'd let you go.'

'Matthew?'

'Aye. He said you were the most wonderful woman he'd ever known.'

'Yes, well, I couldn't have been that wonderful if he dropped me like a hot brick, now could I?'

'He also said that he'd asked you to go back to him but you were in love with me. And you were under the impression that I was back with Jo.'

'Did he now?' She cleared her throat in preparation for the next question, 'And are you?' It came out all shaky.

'Oh aye, that's why I'm giving ring boxes to you.'

'Empty ring boxes though.'

'I explained the reason for that. You have tae wear the thing for ever, so it's no' fair fo' me to force ma tastes on youse, is it noo?'

'I suppose,' said Stevie. Her heart was thumping so loud she thought it might even deafen Adam. 'But you still haven't answered the question.'

'Stevie.' Adam looked her squarely in the eyes so she could read the truth in them for herself. 'I don't know if I ever was in love with Jo. I was besotted, but I don't even know if there is a real Jo MacLean. I think she just borrows personalities aff a peg and wears them like a suit. The trouble with that is that none of them ever quite fit properly. I certainly didn't know her – I realized that at Will's barbecue.' He didn't say he could trace that moment back to when she shoved little Danny away and he saw the hurt in the wee boy's eyes. He knew then she wasn't the woman she had presented herself to be. She wasn't the woman he had waited for all his life.

'So how come you left me a note saying we both needed space?'

'Because even though I knew I wanted you more than anything, I needed to give you some time to find out what you felt for Matthew once he was free. I mean, I'm no' exactly your archetypal romantic hero, am I noo? You like handsome men who whisper and I'm a big, ugly, noisy bugger.'

'I don't want Matthew. I'm from Venus. I'm not like you Mars lot, that sod off into caves and play with elastic bands or whatever it is.'

'No, you're not like anyone I've ever met, Stevie Pollen Bumble Bee Nectar or whatever your name is.'

She blurted out a big pocket of laughter that pulled out a few bonus tears with it.

'Stop crying, woman,' he said gruffly. 'Okay, I admit it. I saw how quickly you jumped when Matty Boy called and I judged you on that. I thought you'd gone back to him. After all, it's what we planned for all along.'

'He was suffering, Adam. Jo stuffed him too. I couldn't have walked away and see him branded a violent sex pest.'

'Aye, well, I know that noo.' He took the ice-pack away and bowed his head. 'But, stupid man that I am, I thought I'd lost you just when I was on the brink of getting you. And Danny, of course. Ba' Christ, I've missed the wee laddie.'

'You stupid, stupid man,' said Stevie, for Danny and herself.

'Hang on a wee minute – you loved Matt, you didnae even like me!'

'Oh, Adam MacLean, you've got a nerve, considering how marvellous you thought I was in the beginning!'

Adam laughed, remembering the flour and the cocoa and that snotty 'I hate you' look on her face and her friend with the mad pink hair. How very deceiving those first impressions had been. On both sides too, for at the same time, Stevie was thinking of the wild, red man pushing a holiday reservation up her nose in Matthew's front room. Who would have ever thought she could have loved him to the same degree that she hated him then?

'And all the time I was thinking that now Jo was available, you'd be straight off back to her.'

'Naw,' he smiled. 'How could she compete with you?'

'Yeah right,' said Stevie.

Adam looked at her sweet, disbelieving face and realized she would never know how lovely she was, which was a shame. He wanted to tell her how very deeply he had fallen for her, how she seemed to have flooded every chamber of his heart as only the right person could. But there was time, lots of it to come. For now, a kiss would suffice. He put down the ice pack, took her face in his great hands and carried on where he'd left off that night of the fillet steaks and her home-made cake and the raspberry-truffle coffees and the interrupting knock on the door.

Her lips were sweeter than honey.

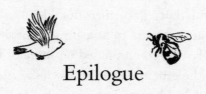

Epilogue

They married at the beginning of the next summer – a day full of balmy May sunshine. There were Scottish pipers and the bonny bride carried an armful of wild wooded bluebells and heather instead of a formal pink rose bouquet. Adam took his vows in the tartan-trimmed church with a heart that was truly satisfied and content. There was no feeling that a part of him was pleading to an inaccessible part of his lady; he knew she was all his. For Stevie it was better than any ending she could have written. Like her alter ego Evie Sweetwell, she had found her Damme MacQueen. And he was even better in the flesh than he was on the page.

Matthew sent the happy couple a silver-plated bluebirds of happiness – he paid for it in cash – and a building society cheque for three thousand pounds, made out to Mrs Stevie MacLean. It was the first time she had seen her new name in print and it made her insides as runny as the waters of the Clyde.

They had a Ceilidh at the reception and a Scottish band, and wore kilts and danced jigs and reels such as *Blue Bonnets* and *The Birds and the Bees* well into the night. Things went awry as the champagne flowed, and some of the dancers ended up with different partners from the ones they started out with. But that seems to have turned out all right.

The newlyweds compromised on some of the Scottish traditions – the groom didn't drink whisky and wore very nice Calvin Klein boxers under his kilt. He did, however, eat a Sassenach alive for breakfast the next morning. And by all accounts, she rather enjoyed it too. They honeymooned for five days in an old castle by a beautiful loch, then they picked up Danny from Catherine's and whisked him away to EuroDisney for a week.

Highland Fling became the best-selling *Midnight Moon* ever. The critics panned it as romantic claptrap, of course, but the readers loved it so much that a film was made with a gorgeously rough American actor who could actually manage quite a good Scots accent. Apparently, the top girls of Hollywood clawed each other to death for the part of Evie. The enormous cheque for the film rights arrived with Stevie exactly eighteen months after Adam MacLean first kissed her.

Adam discovered the increasing turn-on of women with soft curves, freckly noses and absolutely no ability whatsoever to control flour. Stevie was to wonder how she had ever lived without large crushing Highland thighs, red stubble and thunderous, unintelligible endearments.

Adam bought Humbleby Cottage for himself and his bride, his wee adopted laddie and their auburn-haired newborn daughter, Rìona, and they all still live happily there today with a huge sloppy dog, a mad ginger kitten and an enormous black rabbit called McBatman.

Life, for the MacLean clan, is *braw*.

Acknowledgements

A very sweet part about writing a book is being able to say a very public thank you to a swarm of wonderful people.

To the totally fabulous guys at the agency – Darley Anderson, Julia Churchill, Emma White, Ella Andrews, Madeleine Buston and Zoe King. And at Hive HQ – Simon and Schuster – to Queen Suzanne Baboneau, Libby Vernon, Nigel Stoneman, Joe Pickering, Amanda Shipp, Caroline Turner, and the lovely Grainne Reidy who always make me feel so welcome when I fly down there and, of course, to my gallant chaperone Paul Evans. And to the ultimate Worker, Joan Deitch, for combing out all the crappy bits from my manuscript.

To the nectar in my life – my friends: Alec Sillifant for allowing me to refer to his smashing children's story 'The Useless Troll' (published by Meadowside Children's Books) and the best male mate in the world Paul Sear. To Ged and Kaely Backland, Cath Marklew, Maggie Birkin, Sue Welfare, Debra Mitchell, Sue Mahomet, Rachel Hobson, Tracy Harwood, Judy Sedgewick, the enviably artistic Chris Sedgewick, the gorgeous and superbly talented Lucie Whitehouse and my S.U.N. sisters – Karen Baker, Helen Clapham and Pam Oliver – all friends in the greatest sense of the word.

To Sara Atkinson at haworthcatrescue.org who is an absolute honey!

To the decidedly 'uncrusty' Dr Peter O'Dwyer and my solicitor David Gordon and the Attey gang – Bev Stacey and Mary Smith who have got me through a B of a year with kindness, support, expert expertise and very strong coffee.

To the smashing Steph Johnson and Steph Daley at the *Barnsley Chronicle*, the delightful Jo Davison at the *Sheffield Star* and the magnificent Jayne Dowle at the *Yorkshire Post* for all the nice things they've said about my book, my hair and my house!

To our man in the Highlands – Iain MacLennan at www.Scottishquality.com for his Mcexcellent Gaelic Translation services.

To Miss Kate Taylor at Barnsley Sixth Form College who made me see Jane Austen as she was meant to be seen and turned English into my favourite subject.

To my beautiful 'pupae' – Terence and George for not telling me to 'buzz aff' when I ask them if I've told them recently that I'm a novelist.

To my very special parents Jenny and Terry Hubbard for babysitting, making me huge Sunday dinners then listening to me drone on about my weight.

And last but by no means least – to the inspirational clan of Glasgow both past and present – all those wonderful warm, big-hearted, generous, funny, crazy aunts, uncles, cousins and friends who coloured my childhood days with bright tartan and flavoured my memories with square sausage, steak pie and Jocks' Loaf.

Tapadh leibh – you're the Bee's Knees, every single one of you.